CONTE

PART III
GAMING, GODS AND VIRTUAL REALITY

PART IV
COMING HOME

IMPRESSUM

Liquid Reign

By Tim Reutemann

Version 1.1

13th of February 2019

(1.0 published 7th May 2018)

The incredible Bibijoey aka Jeanine Reutemann for making me write this novel. Nothing without you.

My Editor and supporter Karen Smith who made this novel readable. And so much more. Karen is just the best. My reviewers Sebastian Lien, Sunniva Sandbukt who helped turn functional names into characters. My early readers Søren Lütken, Jean Lucas and Ofra Bosma for their inputs.

Then there is my close friend, member of the Zurich city council Matthias Probst, who taught me most of what I know about local politics. And a number of friends and former colleagues at the United Nations Environmental Program, who taught me many kinks of the day to day global politics. I also thank various people on http://chat.democracy.earth/, who taught me how to think about 3rd millennium politics.

Further, Jonathan Cross and Daniel Renz, who on numerous Nerd-Nights introduced me to blockchain technology in the first place, and the people on https://hub.decstack.com who dramatically improved my understanding of it.

My PhD supervisor Stefanie Engel, who patiently accepted my nasty questions on economic theory and fostered my excitement for economic experiments, and the handful of open minded economic thinkers I encountered during that time of my life.

My brother Thomas Waymouth, who allowed me a peak into nomadic life and my other brother, John Schloendorn, whose lab provided an excellent ground for explorations into Silicon Valley culture.

All those unnamed friends and family members, who may find fragments of their souls scattered throughout this book.

Legal Stuff

ISBN: 9781981029174

PROLOGUE

S he scans the audience as people start streaming into the Amphithéâtre Richelieu. Tonight Helen's supposed to just sit back and enjoy the show, yet she feels her adrenaline levels go through the roof. They know who she is - that's all the memo had said.

She's never met any of Daniel's Parisian readers, but the crowd as a whole is strongly reminiscent of their goodbye party's attendants in Berkeley. She does recognize the retired professor of political philosophy whose chair Daniel is inheriting – a young woman with bright red hair and a Mandelbrot tattoo on her neck is helping him move his wheelchair up the stairs.

She takes off her riveted jacket, revealing the space-helmet wearing unicorn hoody from last year's Ethereum Devcon. The barefoot guy wearing an orange monk's robe over his counterstrike t-shirt seems familiar, too - Helen identifies him as Gola by his face markings. Then it comes back to her, he's a sniper on the Team Liquid esports team. Nothing suspicious so far. The doors close and it's time for her to sit down. She gives Daniel a last kiss.

As they lock eyes, overwhelming love wipes the anxiety from Daniel's brain. And just as he's ready to let her go, Jacky pops his head out of her breast pocket. Obviously, Helen's brought her hamster to his inaugural speech. The sight of the little creature releases the last bit of tension, and with a laugh, Daniel enters flow state walking onto the stage and up to the podium.

The talk goes as smoothly as it should, interrupted only by applause for the experimental data from Claire's PhD thesis and the short film Willi had prepared for him.

Standing ovation, Helen is so proud of him. She still can't believe it - her husband is actually a professor at the Sorbonne. A stage magician applauding next to her under-lines his approval by pulling the bunny prince out of his hat, and in come the caterers.

Half an hour later she spots Daniel leaning with his eyes closed against a pillar in the middle of the room. Poor guy, it's been a long day. And it's not over yet - tonight she still has to tell him about the hack. Now that they know her real identity, he needs to know, too. Helen wraps her arms around him and whispers "C'mon love, let's go home."

"Go home" means take a taxi back to the hotel on the other side of the river. Daniel gets in on the driver's side, leans back and takes Helen's hand. The warmth in the car soothes him, and as the gentle humming of the electric motor starts to calm him his eyelids feel heavy, dozing off... Sudden flash of light, jarring crack and a deafening bang. He falls into the dark, his consciousness receding, only a single dot of light ahead, very far away. Then, deep black nothingness filling his entire being.

PART I

BUILDING A WORLD

1

OUT OF THE VOID

Aweak humming noise. Everything is still black, just like it's been for a long time. Yet something is humming, and that's new. Daniel notes variations in the sound, the tune not quite constant. What is this? A dream? A hallucination? Within the emptiness, patterns start to emerge. Dark greenish fractal spiral patterns, to be precise. They move about, as if the humming were gently massaging his eyelids from the outside. Both the visual and auditory patterns are slowly increasing in detail and complexity...

Claire has just taken a toilet break – five hours of negotiations already behind her, and at least five more to come. She's set her operating system to 99% do-not-disturb mode, so the beeping in her ear must be an extraordinarily important message. Walking to the sink, she mumbles: "What is it?"

Her OS replies immediately, "Daniel is showing alpha waves."

"Message to Zhiu, I'll come back a little later. You can speak on my behalf." Claire puts on her glasses.

Harry had been taking care of Daniel for the past few weeks, preparing his body for the wakeup procedure. He responded immediately when the alert went off and is standing right by his bedside now.

There's always a shortage of nurses, and Claire couldn't wish for a better one than this long, lanky and light-hearted man with degrees from the best medical institutions in the world. She's fully relying on him until she can make it to the hospital herself.

Daniel's perception is slowly getting clearer "bsss Danllll issssss mhh, bssss Claire bsss me...". OK, that was Claire's voice. He tries to say "What's going on?" but his tongue won't move. And indeed his whole body feels very far away, the little spark of consciousness surrounded by a vast space of black nothingness.

Claire can't believe it. The brain waves reacted when she said his name. He is coming back.

The patterns are in color now, blue and yellow strings whirl around the unraveling edges of spiral fractals, pulsing in time with Daniel's heartbeat. His heartbeat, yes, he can feel a heart beating. A heart that is part of a body – his proprioception is rapidly returning. He tries to wiggle his toe. And it wiggles.

The brain waves projected onto Claire's retina smooth out. The electric pulses are oscillating between eight and eleven hertz, his consciousness should be fully back now. "Daniel, remember those lucid dreaming experiments with Langenthal in Berkeley? Think of music for 'yes', and imagine catching a ball for 'no'. I can tell from your brain which one it is. Can you hear me?"

Music... The first tune that comes to Daniel's mind is Yellow Submarine.

Claire's voice is excited. "It's working. Daniel, just to make sure, let me ask a few simple questions. She starts with probing his memories "Did you ever kill a cow?"

Yellow Submarine - he had to, after placing a bet with life-long veganism at stake. It was gruesome.

"Are you transgender?" Claire and her LGBTQ housemates used to tease him about being the poster boy for conservatism.

Basketball. Not only is he cis- and hetero, but even has a natural preference for monogamy, only included thanks to the Q - nothing he won't question.

And a last one, checking his ability to think in the abstract: "Is the universe itself conscious?"

How the hell would he know? Daniel settles on imagining himself dancing under a sky of blue, in a sea of green, firing up both the motor- and musical neural pathways.

Claire takes a moment. He even remembers that double signals stand for "I don't know." His memory seems to be just fine. "Initiate phase two."

The neuro-stimulation algorithm for the second phase needs the patient to be calm, preferably without sedation. Claire opens a private line to Harry: "Please have a sedative ready. Just in case."

Harry is tense, and of course he has a sedative ready, he always does, it's part of his uniform. He holds the syringe down flat on Daniel's skin and tells his operating system to stand by and act on Claire's command.

Claire immediately re-opens her line to Daniel. "You had an accident. Your body is healthy, and you have no detectable brain damage. I need you to relax now and let the neurological stimulator do its work. I will explain everything tomorrow, once you are stable."

Daniel imagines himself trampolining, spinning triple somersaults in his mind in an effort to fire up his motor cortex as hard as he can.

Claire should know him better than that, of course he's resisting her advice to proceed slowly. "OK then, I'll give you some answers, but promise me to take it easy."

And the baaand begins to play... tohtohtohtoh toh-toh toh-toh.

Claire has to keep it simple and stick to the basics. "You were in a car crash the night of your inaugural speech. A truck slammed into the taxi at the intersection."

Daniel starts to panic as Claire tells him about the accident. What happened to Helen? Is she ok? Dead? The patterns in his vision start to spin, slowly, counter-clockwise, he's falling backwards.

As Claire had feared, his brain reacts with a sudden jump in amygdala activity. This doesn't look good. "I told you, it's better to hold back on the explanations..." Her voice is steady now, low and very professional. Medical, even. "Fear spikes can inhibit your recovery, and I'd rather not knock you out with chemicals. Recovery works best without the side effects and risks of sedation. You're alive and you're going to wake up now. That's all that matters, so please, please..."

Daniel wants to comply, but he can't stop thinking about Helen. Trying to focus on his breath, his attempt to enter a meditative state disintegrates under the specter of her death, nausea washing over him.

Claire realizes she's pulling at her hair with both hands. Give him five more seconds... "Come on, remember how you used to be in control of your emotions? I know you can do it." Then it finally hits her. Of course. "Helen had only minor injuries."

OK, good. He can deal with anything, as long as she is alive. Daniel focuses his attention on the tip of his nose again, draws a deep breath, and sure enough, his emotional control mechanisms are now up to the challenge. Breathe in, breathe out.

His data is in the green zone, allowing her to relax a bit. Claire keeps talking to him. "Your brain looks good now. Nothing to worry about."

Still finding plenty to worry about, Daniel imagines catching another basketball.

She replies with little laugh "Very funny. For now, please just stick to the most basic rule in the galaxy: Don't panic. I'll leave you to the regenerative neurostimulator now."

And every one of us had all we need...

"Great, see you very soon." Claire's voice trembles slightly on that last sentence. She washes her hands and leaves the bathroom. What's next? Harry will be taking care of him for now, and phase three of the algorithm takes a couple of hours – that should be long enough for her to get there by the time he wakes up. "Get me on the fastest connection to Hawaii. Message to Zhiu: Hope you can handle the rest of the negotiations without me. Daniel's waking up. Love you!" For the first time in years, she takes a flight back to Hawaii.

Daniel's backward fall has stopped, he's lying still, a pleasant warmth filling every cell of his body, heat pulsing along with the rhythm of his heartbeat. The swirling colors increase in intensity, more and more shapes emerging, mingling with his other senses and emotions. Warmth, attraction, happiness, disgust, arousal, fear... And back again, through another emotional whirlwind.

Harry stays by the bedside all afternoon, monitoring the process. And just as the last cycle of the algorithm begins, Claire bursts through the door. He looks up. "Daniel's almost ready. Would you rather be alone with him?"

Claire just nods, and rushes towards the bed.

Harry gives her a friendly smile, briefly touching her shoulder as he moves past. "I'll be on call a little longer. If there's anything I can do for you and Daniel, it will be my utter delight."

Claire looks at him and smiles back. "I think we're fine for tonight, but thank you." Her heart is pounding, she's tensely waiting through the last few minutes of stimulation. The moment the bar indicator reaches 100%, Claire takes his hand. "Daniel?"

The patterns in Daniel's vision have calmed down. He is just lying there, on a soft surface, warm, and in complete darkness. Then something touches his hand. He produces mumbling noise: "Whrr mpf aay?"

Claire understands – it's the same question all awakening

patients ask. "This is the O'ahu Center for Awakenings." She keeps talking, falling into her doctor routine "Welcome back, Daniel. The stimulator is finished with you for now." She opens his neurostimulation helmet.

The light is uncomfortable, even behind closed eyelids. Daniel still trying to convince his tongue to move along with his thoughts. "Where eesch sthwat?"

Claire continues with the routine: "Hawaii. A hospital specializing in coma rehabilitation. It was a central medical argument to build it someplace where you would want to wake up from a bad dream." At least that argument convinced her voters to move her workplace next to the best surf in the world "I got you transferred to a room with a view. The Pacific is just out there. Your eyes will accustom to the light shortly."

He gingerly flutters his lids, glimpsing the sun's last orange shimmer as it disappears below the horizon. He's in a plain room with a very large window giving onto a palm beach and the ocean. And there, out of the corner of his right eye, a face. Claire is sitting next to his bed. The gray-green eyes, slightly elevated cheekbones, small birthmark on the left side of her nose. But she is... old. Wrinkly thin skin, bony, her hair flecked with gray. He raises his own hand – it's even more wrinkled, thinner skinned, and bonier. "What year is it?"

"2051."

.

SOURCES OF INSPIRATION CAN BE FOUND AT THE END OF EACH CHAPTER. *CLICKABLE LINKS AT WWW.LIQUID-REIGN.COM/SOURCES-OF-INSPIRATION#1*

The Beatles Yellow Submarine
Don't Panic
A Clinical Guide to Transcranial Magnetic Stimulation
Inspirational books are available at
http://libgen.org or http://gen.lib.rus.ec/
Inspirational Movies are available at
https://thepiratebay-proxylist.org/
Inspirational Scientific Papers are available at
https://scihub222660qcxt.onion.link/
You might need a VPN to relocate yourself to a more liberal jurisdiction to access some sources.

2

THE NEW NORMAL

Realization of the years passed is definitely enough of a shock for now, so Claire decides to postpone any talk of Helen until next time. "Don't worry, you're still quite a handsome boy. We made sure your body is healthy. Your life expectancy is well over 120, and thanks to Kurzweil therapy you are as fit as a 20th century person in their early fifties. Or soon will be, after rehab – you haven't exactly gotten a lot of exercise lately."

Thirty five years. The weight of that number slowly sinks in. Daniel allows his tears to flow.

Claire had been acting in accordance with deeply etched behavioral patterns generated by too many years of professional distance between doctor and patient. At the sound of Daniel's first sob, she gladly abandons that pattern, putting her arms around him. "You're going to be ok. Now lay back down and get some sleep." She gently pulls the helmet back over his head and initiates phase four of the recovery program. "Good night Daniel. I'll be keeping a close watch over your brain."

As soon as Daniel lays down on the pillow, his mental focus fades away. He still has a lump in his throat. "Thank you, Claire." And complete darkness returns.

Claire checks the screen - he's already asleep. She returns to her office and spends the next couple of hours in her virtual reality suit, supplying her loved one and her other political allies with medical arguments in the discussion forum.

Their most promising targets are the gamers' delegates, but while they've found some initial points of agreement, it's well after midnight and no compromise has yet been formulated. Still, in a gesture of goodwill, at least one of their lead budgeteers assigns a hundred thousand coins of additional public funds to Zhiu's foundation.

They exchange expressions of gratitude and Claire finally closes her Sovereign voting interface, hopping back to their home screen, a tea house on the beach. Today it's a Scandinavian style beach with a wooden hut.

Zhiu arrives a moment after Claire. She stretches her arms and wriggles her toes around in the sand, thinking out loud. She's not sure why, but the gamers' delegates seem reticent for some reason. "There must be something they aren't telling us. But I didn't see anything in the official forums, so what could it be?" She spins around and looks at Claire.

A rhetorical question. The two of them have discussed this possible outcome, and agreed on a strategy. "As always, I agree with my shamanic dolphin. It's time for plan B, I'll book my tickets right now. Should be there tomorrow afternoon. This negotiation round is costing me a fortune."

Zhiu nods back. "Thanks for your effort my little magic

platypus." She does need her help, but still offers her the option of not being physically present: "I'm sure we can convince one of your main delegatees to jump in for you if you want to stay in Hawaii..."

Claire shakes her head - no, Daniel would want her to go. At least if he knew that she got in this whole struggle for Helen's sake in the first place. She has to tell him soon, as soon as he's stable enough to absorb another shock.

"Good then, I'll meet you at Blizzcon." Large esports events are the best place to lobby the gamer vote base directly – the media coverage is enormous. Zhiu herself is a celebrity figure in the scene, having personally treated several former champions struggling with addiction. "And I'll treat you to a first-class direct return flight, OK?"

Claire laughs. "That's so cute of you. Thank you for buying me a ticket from our joint bank account, I appreciate it and probably wouldn't have bought it for myself." She walks up to her, wrapping her virtual arms around Zhiu's virtual waist: "I love you." She logs out in the course of a long goodbye kiss. While her virtual reality suit opens and Zhiu's mouth fades away, the nerves in her lips are still tingling.

Claire checks the connections - the only available seat is on the early morning flight, everything else is booked. Tomorrow's the first Tuesday after the first Monday in November, lots of people travel to visit their families for the election remembrance day celebrations.

———

WWW.LIQUID-REIGN.COM/SOURCES-OF-INSPIRATION#2
Blizzcon
Kurzweil's Immortality Therapy
And of course, century old democratic traditions of
Tuesday Elections

3

TRUE NAMES

E ver since Daniel's awakening three days ago, he's been cared for by Harry. Waking, dreaming, sleeping, he has only a vague sense of time, and the little exchanges with his nurse have blurred into one. He is primarily discussing technical functions of the neurostimulator with him. The guy is two heads taller, in his late thirties, and good company.

Harry tries his best to answer, but despite having spent his entire youth surrounded by state-of-the-art neurostimulation hardware, he soon reaches the limit of his knowledge. "Sorry Daniel, I am utterly clueless as to what stops the stimulator's magnetic fields from interfering with the EEG. Anyway, it's time for your dinner now."

Daniel still has a million other questions, but agrees to take it slowly: "You are the most knowledgeable nurse I could wish for, thanks for the explanations." He just wants to know what's happening in his brain.

Dinner comes on a tray from the dispenser, Harry picks it

up and brings it to the bedside table. According to his favorite patient care professor, a human being carrying a meal tray even for a few symbolic steps is enough to make patients feel cared for, which in turn creates positive placebo effects.

He has ordered the dispenser system to serve him the same food that Daniel gets, and today his patient's blood work apparently indicated the need for carrot salad with olive oil, mashed bananas with coconut, and a side of dried figs – so that's what Harry is having, too. "I'm always knocked out by the delightful menu choices the hospital comes up with."

Daniel has never been much of a food talker during meals, so he redirects the conversation to his recovery process: "So what's next for me?"

"First of all, we should get you into the system." Harry had prepared the biometrics recorder and pulls it to his bedside. "Can you stand up by yourself?"

He can. The recorder is a full body suit, standing upright by itself. Both the arms and legs unzip all the way, so Daniel can just step into it. The suit gently closes around his body and as a helmet lowers over Daniel's head he asks: "What exactly am I getting myself into here? "

"The suit records classic biometrics. Retina, frontal cortex, face, DNA, pherohormone composition, voice, finger and toe prints." Harry had found Daniel's old entry in the Italian archives and just hopes for a data match.

The scan is brief and pain-free. Daniel is still standing in the closed machine as a note appears on the screen: "Please wait." Those eternally kind words are accompanied by a circular icon, spinning. And spinning some more. He opens the helmet, looking at Harry with a raised eyebrow.

"Gosh, what a disappointment! Insufficient data in the archives. Whenever someone comes back from the pre-Afrin time it's the same nonsense." It's a mystery to Harry how governments could possibly have managed their affairs without the Afrin social contract back in the day – those shared standards of identity management, voting and transparency behind all civic administration. "I'm afraid we need confirmation from the local officials. Unfortunately the Italian immigration office is not the most responsive, and their archive software is buggy. Might take weeks to get your TN registered through them. You could speed things up by opting for a Hawaii-backed TrueName, that should be doable by tonight."

"Citizen of Hawaii? Wouldn't that mean US citizen?" Daniel is confused.

"There are no United States anymore. And having your TrueName backed by Hawaii is not quite the same as citizenship." Harry takes a deep breath and starts to explain the basics: "The TrueName proves that you are one and only one real person. Any TrueName backed by an Afrin signatory region gives you the right to re-locate to any other Afrin region. All other citizens' rights depend on your localization, so you can still live in Italy with all Italian citizen rights, even with a Hawaiian backed TrueName."

"Well, then I'll take the Hawaiian one."

"Thanks, that makes my life a lot easier." Harry asks his OS to shoot a message to Sybil from civic administration immediately.

She shows up half an hour later. Sybil is small, sturdy,

light-brown skin, has dark green eyes and wears her long curly hair loose. After a few basic questions about his past, she claps her hands and says formally, "I can confirm that you are one and only one unique person and do not have another TrueName. Your biometrics are hashed and registered on the TrueName Chain, and your primary Nym is created and linked to your brand-new TrueName." She adds after a short pause: "You're welcome."

That was quick and easy. It seemed almost negligent to Daniel, so he wonders: "Knowing my birth date and my grandma's name was enough to confirm uniqueness?"

Sybil smiles as she replies, "No, not quite. I did my homework when Harry sent the request. Double checked your story, identified you as the author of 'Evolutionary Thinking', checked a few old Homeland Security files from the 10's, compared your fingerprints to them, then compared them to our hospital records and the answers you gave me just now. Together with meeting you here, face to face, that was sufficient proof for me to authenticate you for a new TrueName."

Daniel is intrigued: "How would you do it if I weren't a famous author?"

Sybil has no simple answer, as she decides ad hoc what needs to be done. "We reformed our immigration office a few years ago, now all us officers are directly elected, which gives us the authority to make sovereign decisions. We're still experimenting internally what works best, and right now we're trying out a more individualized approach. But you need to gather confirmations from a few other people..." She looks at Harry.

"Sure. I confirm." Harry's OS adds his signature to Daniel's TrueName right away.

Daniel can't help asking more: "What would happen if I tried to register again somewhere else?"

"Well, if you tried elsewhere, the TrueName creator would register a match with the biometrics of your current True-Name." Sybil isn't quite sure why he wants to know, and adds with a wary voice: "It will send a warning to the officer registering you and also notify me and Harry about the attempt, and also alert three other randomly chosen Afrin immigration officers." She's never gotten such a warning in her ten years working as immigration officer, but that's how it should work in theory.

Harry joins in to support her wrangling with the curiosity monster: "Sybil's and my TrueName are linked to yours as first connection points into the global web of identity trust."

"And if I were wearing fake irises and altered my finger-prints and all that?"

Sybil is a little annoyed by his persistence by now: "If you were able to fake all biometric signals and set up a credible cover story that fools the other hospital and also the immigration officer, you might be able to register a second True-Name. Theoretically."

Harry remembers Claire's warning about his character – insatiable curiosity paired with a natural inclination to probe the rules until they break: "Your curiosity is crossing a line here. If you get caught even trying to double register, you lose all your possessions and get a surveillance oper-ating system installed for a very long time. Also Daniel, your TrueName isn't fully functional yet. With just my and Sybil's signatures, your reimbursements and voting power are only at ten percent. You need to get a couple of confirmations from others."

Sybil adds: "Because TrueName works via a web of trust of people confirming each other's identities. You only get full voting rights if you're connected with at least eighty percent of the Afrin population within five steps of identity confirmation. Depending on how central your friends are on the social graph, you will need three to five more confirmations."

"Understood. So I'll ask friends to confirm my uniqueness." The thought of having friends is both comforting and disturbing to Daniel, who's wondering how well he is still remembered. "Anything else?"

"We'll give you an inner ear implant with your TrueName revocation key tonight – don't worry, you'll probably never need it, identity theft rarely ever happens. The implant also hosts your operating system."

Daniel's eyebrows go up as he looks at Harry, uncertain which of those concepts he wants to explore first. After a moment of hesitation, he settles for "Identity theft?"

"If you use an insecure login somewhere and ignore all the warnings, your TrueName can be compromised." Harry only ever met one person this happened to "One of the other nurses here had gone on a Pacific trip to one of the crypto islands, and was stupid enough to log in as 'root', late at night in a mushroom bar. Next morning her home screen was full of Illuminati icons, and all her votes were transferred to an anarcho-libertarian polito-bot. She revoked before any real damage was done."

Sybil gets up, getting ready to leave and adds "You can revoke your TN by saying 'Revoke, Revoke' aloud, while imagining a spinning movement. The spinning movement adds some security, it's detected by the hardware in your inner ear. Once you've done that, your TrueName goes into freeze mode, and you need to find a trusted clinic and an immigration officer to create a new one and transfer your backups, with a new trusted biometric scan."

"Thank you! Appreciate the explanations."

Harry suggests: "Now that you have a TrueName, you add some juice to your gratitude by voting for Sybil before she leaves."

"How?"

"Just say the words: Please vote for Sybil as immigration officer." As Harry hasn't installed Daniel's own OS yet, the hospital's system votes on his behalf as soon as Daniel repeats the words.

WWW.LIQUID-REIGN.COM/SOURCES-OF-INSPIRATION#3

True Names by Vernor Dinge
Sybil Attacks
Smart Contracts
Jean-Jacques Rousseau's Social Contract

Democracy Earth Draft of a Social Smart Contract
The few people on earth that is full steam trying to build a
new nation using decentral technologies. Help them out!
#FreeAfrin
Tell me who you are by Vinjay Gupta
Decentralized Identity Foundation
UN Efforts for digital ID
Uport
Bitnation
Civic
Sovrin
BrightID
Duniter
ValID
There are a few more listed here
https://github.com/peacekeeper/blockchain-identity

FOUNDATIONS OF A HIVE MIND

D aniel is wondering. "So you elect the immigration office employees? Do you have an astronomical immigration rate?"

"What? Why?" Harry doesn't get the question at first - Sybil only works part time, as the vast majority of immigrants come from Afrin regions and already have a TrueName, so their relocation doesn't require any human effort. He adds: "We elect pretty much all public employees, even the Master of Frogs."

Daniel is perplexed now. "How many elections do you hold per year?"

"Per year? No clue, it must be millions..." Harry checks with his OS for the exact number. "On average, I vote on forty two decisions per second."

"Wait. You are talking to me right now..." Daniel tilts his head "So in this very second you are obviously not casting a vote on who'll be the next Master of Frogs...?"

"My vote on all ecological matters is delegated to the Master himself. Szimo is a good friend of mine and handles my vote on all eco-related topics, including the election of other public servants working in that area."

Daniel is wide awake now – the emergence of collective intelligence had been one of his major research interests: "And what if he elects someone you disagree with?"

"I would get an alert from my OS if anything weird on eco matters should ever come up. If he's doing stuff with my vote I disagree with, I can withdraw it any time." Harry had been delegating the ecological topic block to Szimo basically since he moved here, "But I'm super happy with his approach to frog control as well as his choices of onward delegations."

Daniel ponders in silence for a moment, his mind racing through a zillion of half formulated questions, until he settles on: "How legitimate is that? I can't imagine a particularly high participation rate in the election of the Master of Frogs?"

Harry checks with his OS again. "67% of the Hawaiian population cast an active vote on the Master of Frogs. Szimo has a total approval rate of 87% of those voters."

———

WWW.*LIQUID-REIGN*.COM/SOURCES-OF-INSPIRATION#4

Liquid Democracy
Democracy Earth Foundation
Hive Commons
Liquid Feeback
Flux
Horizon State
Cicadia
Parti Vote
United.Vote
Voatz
Ceptr

FIRST BLOOD

As they're finishing up their dinner a few days later, Harry announces the next step in Daniel's rehab program. "We'll start moving your body and waking up your fascia first thing tomorrow morning. Sleep well!"

Daniel is excited, the blurry recovery process has become quite boring by now, despite regular spikes of emotion. "Oh, Harry, oh Harry, my fascia! I'm so utterly delighted" – mocking his nurse's frequent use of "utter delight." He has no clue what fascia are, but moving sounds good. The meals and washing sessions with Harry are the only episodes Daniel has outside the neuro regenerator.

He lies back down, lowers the neurostim hood over his head and flows into the magnetically stimulated flashes of intense emotion, only occasionally disturbed by thoughts of Helen. Claire must have told her. It would be nice to get any sign of life. She probably has a new partner after all these years, but at least a quick 'hello' wouldn't be asking too much, would it? The blur starts up again, and with his consciousness still half-present he enters an old childhood dream. He spends the night running after flying tadpoles with one of those large nets used to catch butterflies through the back alleys of Turin. He wakes up just in time for Harry's return.

Unlike his usual work outfit of jeans and flip flops, Harry's wearing all white today, even a white nurses cap with the red cross. Intoning "Happy Vampire Day," he pulls out a ten-inch syringe. It's filled with blood, and he flashes a smile that shows his UV-lit vampire teeth in a huge, evil grin.

Daniel has to laugh "I'm sure those look scary in the dark. Well done, my monstrous nurse." some cultural tropes never get old.

"Well, monsieur le professeur, shall we?" Laughing with his patient, Harry points at the VR suit in the corner of Daniel's room. "The suit will hold you up while you exercise, and its integrated neurostimulator will speed up your regeneration process." Harry lifts up a formless dark blue sack and connects it to a cable hanging from the ceiling. The cable pulls up the suit by the head. Standing upright, arms and legs hanging down, the thing looks like a cartoon figure. The headpiece is a huge helmet, with a crystal-shaped hologram logo on the forehead.

"You'll start playing 'Confedwar' – a historical action role-playing game set in the second war of secession. I've set the suit to maximal sensitivity, so initially you can control it with just the slightest hint of a movement, and the motors will move your limbs for you. The game should explain itself, just say 'tutorial' if you get stuck. Gogogo?"

"Harry, wait. I won't be leaving the room even for the

muscular recovery? No jogging on the beach?" Daniel is a bit disappointed.

"Fraid not, at least not for now. You should be good to hit the beach in a few days. The recovery process goes much faster if your nerves are constantly tickled by the stimulator throughout the training, and the level you'll be playing was specifically designed to support coma rehab patients. It features a series of well-balanced exercises, training every single muscle and stretching out all the fascia in your body. But now it's time to head to South Carolina!" Harry's flashes his vampire smile again before he unzips the front of the suit. He looks at Daniel. "Wanna try to get up by yourself? I'm here to catch you if you fall."

Daniel carefully climbs out of bed, totters to the platform, almost trips, steadies himself by grabbing Harry's shoulder and comes to a wobbly standstill. "OK, I admit I'm still too weak for the beach."

"You better strip down to your underwear, more comfy that way." Harry helps him out of the hospital garments and into the Immersive Arts suit. A co-worker had asked him to help out with a particularly difficult case over at the cryonic ward, so he leaves Daniel alone during the twenty-minute session.

The fabric is soft and warm, and wraps itself tightly around Daniel's body as the suit closes up. At the same time, the massive helmet lowers onto his head, shutting out all outside light. The suit is also supporting his stance, making him feel almost weightless. He can move freely, with no inhibitions, while the platform below ensures he stays in the same spot in the room.

A moment later he finds himself on a perfectly flat meadow

stretching from horizon to horizon, the grass softly waving in the wind. The only object in the endless meadow is a mountain, directly ahead of him. And it explodes. A fantastic, three dimensional crystal emerges from the explosion, as big as the mountain itself, and it's speeding towards him.

Wind starts to blow in his face, every single one of his muscles tenses, and in the very moment of collision with the crystal, intense pain for that fraction of a second and then blackness, relaxation and pure joy. The black fades to a gentle white light, and in blue letters the words "Immersive Arts" appear. The letters grow until his entire field of vision is blue, and with the stroke of a gong he finds himself in a small office, sitting on a chair. There's a laptop on the desk in front of him running a news show.

Footage of burning cars, gunshots, a group of masked men looting a grocery store. One of the masked looters stops and points at the camera. Shotgun blast. The filming continues as the drone goes down, smoke and fire. As it hits the ground, the screen goes black.

Daniel checks his surroundings. The office is impersonal, nothing special to be noted. A half-open desk drawer keeps attracting his attention almost magically. As the ancient wisdom goes, any advanced technology is indistinguishable from magic - this seems to be a feature of the game. And of course, as in every action RPG, the first item is a handgun.

The suit supports his movements, so despite his weakness, he can move rapidly around the virtual room. That must be the high sensitivity setting Harry mentioned. The door is jammed, so breaking it open with a body slam is the first physically demanding task.

Half the building has collapsed, so to move forward Daniel

has to climb, balance, jump and squeeze through the rubble. Until the attention-getting magic leads him to a window. Looking down from the second floor of what seems to be the main building of a run-down community college campus, he spots the guy.

Gunshot, glass splinters all around him. Daniel's reflexes work, he finds himself lying on the floor against the wall, his hands over his head, shivering in panic.

Oh, right, this is a game, an action game to be precise. So, ready the gun, and peek out of that window. The guy with a rifle in the school yard wearing a confederate flag t-shirt. Daniel takes aim, pulls the trigger and the recoil throws him right off his feet. Rubbing his wrist Daniel gets up again, peeks out, and sees the redneck lying on the ground bleeding.

He's never fired a gun in his life and this simulation is terribly realistic. Now his whole body is shivering. Simulation, right, taking a deep breath, he focuses on his emotions, calming down. That felt really, really real. Whatever. It's just a game, so he just moves on through the building.

Daniel finds his rhythm, the challenges on his way climbing, jumping, crawling and moving stuff around until there is just one more task between him and the exit.

The floor ahead of him is cracked, looking very unstable, while the pipe overhead radiates that magical attraction. Daniel does not feel like another climb, and decides to take a step back, run-up and jump. Not quite! He lands on the cracks, the floor gives way and he crashes down on a pile of debris – ouch! The failure is the most painful experience of the game so far.

As the dust settles, he finds himself surrounded by a group of dark skinned guys. Guys with guns, all pointing at him. None of them smiles. Uh-oh. "Hey, stop, don't shoot! I'm on your side!"

One of the gunmen leans in. "Same old story, last fucking cracker made that very same claim. Then stabbed Jamal. Take his gun and tie him to the chair. Maybe we can use him later."

Daniel tries to remember old action movies... Let's see if this is a McGuyver game. "Hey guys, I can help you, I understand chemistry. If you can get me into the science lab, I can make some explosives for you."

It is definitely not working. "Shut up, shit gibbon!" and he gets a fist in the face. This time the pain is even more intense.

Daniel wonders if this is still part of the coma rehab. He's been bound to the chair, cable ties squeezing his wrists and ankles, gagged and blindfolded. Next thing he knows there's a metallic sound, something dropped. Zzzsshhhhh, the sound of a gas valve... and he faints.

———

WWW.*LIQUID-REIGN*.COM/*SOURCES-OF-INSPIRATION*#5

Margaret Mcallister, the sage of monstrous nurses
Teslasuit
The Virtuix Omni
Fascia. They are important.
Serious Games and their medical applications
Games about killing Nazis in America and Nazis disliking
them

6

INTERESTING TIMES

The jangling wakes Ana. It's way too early for her alarm to go off... "What's going on?"

Her thesis project is using her nightlight to project its bunny prince avatar on her retina, jumping up and down on her belly in excitement. "Highest value opportunity detected. Please log in immediately."

Finally! Her thesis has been crawling through weakly encrypted data around the world for interesting events for over a week now, but never once alerted her until now. Ana has been worried it might not work at all. So she slips out of bed right away and straight into her IA suit. Being at college is so great, with no one around to make you feel guilty for skipping breakfast and playing VR games first thing in the morning.

Apparently the opportunity in question is in a private Confedwar session with a total noob playing by himself. Well, she can sure help him get started in that game, and who knows, maybe the newbie turns out to be the love of her life. Highest value opportunity - the bunny definitely makes it sound like it could be.

Ana picks her standard Riki-Superninja character and finds the guy in trouble, in the ConfedWars default plain white male avatar, with no equipment, tied to a chair and surrounded by angry black non-player characters. A sleeping gas grenade does the job, and after a deep inhale on her antidote vial, she jumps down into the room.

The noob wakes up as soon as she waves the vial under his nose. As she cuts the cable ties open, she warns him, "Hey Bro! Welcome to Charlottesville. They almost got you, that was a close call. No fooling around with the Panthers, not with a white avatar. I'm Riki." Her ninja avatar comes with a male voice - she loves playing the 'Bro' game when first meeting someone new.

Daniel stands and sizes up his savior: Riki is a short guy, squatting next to him, wearing a full body ninja outfit. "Are you a nerve gas ninja, Riki? I'm confused, I thought this was a historical scenario."

"Exactly. Ninjas rock." The Bro game usually involves a lot of bragging, so Ana adds: "And I play in Masters league as a Ninja, so don't lecture me, noob."

"This is the very first time I've played this game." This definitely is no longer a part of the coma rehab. Multiplayer? And competitive?

So a first-timer in a default avatar is supposed to be a highest value opportunity? Maybe Ana's thesis doesn't quite work the way it's supposed to. But she has to at least give him a chance. "Wanna team up? I can teach you a few basics of the game if you want."

Daniel hears a gentle voice "Contact request from <PigPan> Rikimaru Superninja." "Thanks! Accept contact request." The moment he says it, the game starts to fade away. "What's happening, everything is fading away..."

"You're logging out. Hey, wait I..." But her new friend doesn't wait, he just disappears. Back in the main menu, Ana checks out his IA profile – but it's entirely empty. Her new friend hasn't played any IA games, ever, except for this one single player round on a medical map. Very strange. And definitely interesting.

She pets the bunny prince and gives it a little fresh celery, reinforcing whichever kink in its soul recommended meeting that guy.

WWW.LIQUID-REIGN.COM/SOURCES-OF-INSPIRATION#6
Rickimaru

7

HISTORIC BIAS

Harry is still slightly freaked out by that patient in the cryonics ward. It's only been a couple of months since he started at the clinic, and up until today he's steered clear of patients with more serious neurological damage. On the team they'd been two human and three robot nurses, and had to pin that woman down on her bed to wash her, while she screamed, bit, and spit at them. Swiping the last bit of spit off his shoulder with a paper towel, he's about to go to Daniel when he gets a message. It's from Dwayne, his father. "Call me ASAP." Harry's jaw clenches. Bossing him around as usual. The old man can wait.

Back in Daniel's room, Harry checks the in-game monitor one more time before taking him out of it. Daniel's finished the intro and gotten into the real game! That's unusual – and it seems like he got caught by the Black Panthers. Harry positions himself directly in front of the helmet before opening the suit. "Boo!"

Daniel is startled, wide-eyed. And only when Harry's smile

broadens to reveal his lit-up vampire teeth does Daniel's fear turn to laughter. The shock of that virtual Black Panther's fist in his face seems to have triggered a racist emotional response against his favorite nurse. "That was quite... intense."

Harry, having carefully watched Daniel's facial reaction to his prank, responds: "Virtual reality games with neurostimulation can condition emotional reflexes. It's not your fault, racist reactions are very easy to trigger in all of us. And unfortunately, there was fighting along racial lines during the war. But that's all over now."

Daniel instinctively shakes his head and touches his face: "To be honest, I haven't fully arrived back to normal reality. Did you say the war is over? So that was not just a fantasy-scenario?"

Harry explains: "IA markets Confedwar as a game with high historical accuracy. Doesn't mean every bit of it is true, but the broad strokes are. There was a second civil war in North America, yes. The violence lasted only for a few weeks, but it was enough to break the United States apart permanently."

Sinking back into his bed, weak and exhausted from the game, Daniel adds: "A Ninja saved me. And apparently he's in Masters league."

"Wait a second..." Harry walks around the suit and starts to fiddle with the control panel. He thought he'd adjusted the settings when he unpacked the suit..." Something's wrong." Harry goes over the settings. "Here it is – the multiplayer option should be disabled, otherwise..." He looks at his feet and adds: "I'm sorry. My mistake, that should not have happened."

Daniel resists: "I actually enjoyed it. It'd be cool to play with that ninja again next time and get some coop-action."

Harry tilts his head and looks at him for a moment before replying: "Hmm. Theoretically, you're supposed to do that single player intro sequence at least five times, since it's been specially designed for optimal motoric recovery..."

"Oh, come on, that sounds really boring," Daniel begs his nurse, "please, leave it on. I won't tell Claire, I promise."

Harry smiles, and so does Daniel. And while Harry has no reason to keep secrets from Claire, he pretends to be in on the conspiracy anyway. Patients' wishes for tweaks in their treatment are to be respected as far as possible, a hospital policy that Claire strongly supports. But sharing a harmless secret is always fun, too: "Well, I'm quite certain you will find sufficient opportunity for jumping and climbing during the main game, too. So I'll leave the multiplayer option on then."

———

WWW.LIQUID-REIGN.COM/SOURCES-OF-INSPIRATION#7

Studies on Involuntary Racism

8

ENTERTAINING CONSPIRACIES

The rescued teenagers are now flying off in the helicopter. The traffickers' truck is still in flames, no mission accomplished so far. Ana only remembers the final challenge when she hears them coming: "Motorbikes! Those are cartel elite troops, and we're out of ammo. Run!"

The escape through the swamps is strenuous, especially in the upper thighs, as Daniel's heavy boots get stuck in the mud with every step. Looking back for a moment, he notes: "We're leaving a trail of footprints. Up into the trees, and change directions."

"So who is the ninja now? You're right, come on up here!" A second later Ana is high in the tree, balanced between forking branches.

Daniel follows, they escape to safety, and mission accomplished, landing on the neutral beach as the game fades out again. "Be right back!" He's got to take another short break in the neurostimulator, and logs back in just a few minutes later.

Ana is puzzled by what she's found out so far. Her new friend is an old man in a hospital half a world away. He is OK, and she's been playing a number of 20-minute games with him over the last couple of days.

But according to the bunny prince, those games with Daniel are the most interesting thing to do in the whole world. Either Gabriel and Ana messed up badly in their thesis work or the world must be a terribly boring place. So she decides to at least spice up their gameplay a little, and browses through the latest mods. A new Fraxxl trailer catches her attention, featuring aliens, the NSA, the Waltons and gay frogs. As soon as her friend is back, she suggests: "Let's play a Fraxxl-Mod. They are my absolute favorites, gave them half of my abo fees last month."

"Sure, Master, I'll follow your lead." Then Daniel hesitates: "Did you just say that Fraxxl is getting half your fees? What's that all about?"

Right, her new friend is a noob. So Ana deliberately slows down her diction as if explaining it to a child: "Playing Confedwar costs a few cents per hour. Most of the money goes to modders and level makers like Fraxxl." She launches the mod.

The lizard- shape-shifters were trying to manipulate human development by pissing psychoactive chemicals into the water, which made everyone apolitical – the same chemical also happened to turn frogs gay, so they've spent five fun minutes crawling through swamps, trying to follow high pitched mating calls. Ana has learned a lot about the evolution of amphibia from her new friend.

The chemical traces lead them to a corpse – the second-to-last heir of the Walton family fortune. The last heir, John

Walton, was a megalomaniac who the aliens poisoned with cocaine in his diet coke... And Daniel's twenty minutes are over just at the cliffhanger moment. He is tempted to skip dinner and go straight back in. Turns out he never was particularly good at resisting temptation.

Ana is pleased with her apprentice – at least the old man no longer needs a break every twenty minutes. They find the aliens, who turn out to be part of a pan-galactic disarmament movement and explain that triggering the civil war was the only way to stop the development of an evil artificial intelligence by the power elites. Their intervention protected humanity from itself, and potentially the rest of the galaxy too. Ana and Daniel decide not to retaliate against them, receive a terrarium full of gay frogs as a goodbye present and mission accomplished.

"That was awesome." Daniel had gotten tired of the realism and weakly narrated fighting in the regular Confedwar, too. "But this story veers a bit too far into conspiracy, don't you think? A single megalomaniac billionaire triggering war? And a skirmish on one continent ending global AI development?"

Ana keeps being dazzled by how this professor can sometimes be so clueless. "The only historically accurate detail of the mod was Walton's megalomania triggering the war. The threat of an evil artificial intelligence is a bit of a trope, but who knows what would have happened if a for-profit closed-source artificial intelligence had first brought the singularity..."

Daniel's enjoying the conversation, even though he hardly understands what she is talking about, and attempts to make a joke: "Closed Profits in Infinity?"

Ana looks at him, startled: "What, infinity?"

"A singularity is a point of infinity. The center of a black hole, where mass is compressed into a single point, and gravity at that point is thus infinite. And time stops and so on." Realizing that his Ninja-friend doesn't get it, he adds: "Sorry, that was supposed to be a joke."

"I have no idea what you're talking about. The singularity was the day when the open source extended intelligence started a self-improvement runaway." Ana deliberately switches from the outdated historic term 'artificial intelligence' to the modern terminology. "Hardware improving EI made better hardware, and that hardware allowed software-improving EI's to make even better hardware improving EIs, which in turn made better software improving EI and so on... That was in 2037. Some people want to make it the new Year Zero. Since then no human being understands how hardware or low-level programming works, and we no longer even have a metric to measure the improvements."

Upon hearing the number 2037, Daniel feels his hands tremble. That was fourteen years ago. "How old were you back then?"

Whatever, why not, she decides to be honest: "Three. They call my generation Singularials, we grew up with the limits to what an EI can do only set by our imagination." Ana falls silent and thinks to herself that with enough imagination, two seventeen year old students at the Karl-Heinz Haesliprinz chair at the Institute for Playful Methods in Palmas, Tocantins, can make an EI that crawls through the entire world of open data looking for ways to make Ana Mancini's life more interesting. An EI that found Daniel and identified him as interesting to her. She feels slightly guilty, almost like she betrayed him, and decides not to tell him, at least not yet.

The session is up, and the world starts to fade out again. Daniel's playing with the idea of logging in for a third twenty minute session in a row, but then comes a knock at the door. Harry. "How's it going, Harry? That last session was really great – my Ninja friend showed me this alien-conspiracy mod... hell, that was so much more exciting than the historical levels."

"What, a mod? Wait, mods should be blocked... didn't I..." Harry starts fumbling around with the suit as Daniel gets out. "Mh, seems like the last update re-configured the blocking... Aha, sorry, but it's strictly forbidden to use any mods without medical approval in the hospital. Don't underestimate the risk of addiction. I can see in the logs that you worked around the twenty minute rule, which is a first risk indication. Take this seriously, please." At least this time it wasn't his fault, but he has to be extra careful with his patient.

Skeptically, Daniel asks: "What are the other signs of addiction?"

"So, there are several indicators." Harry quotes from first semester nursing school: "The first is if you don't want to log out because the virtual world seems more pleasant or important to you than the real world. You just crossed that line. The second is when you find yourself doing VR things in reality, like trying to use an undo command. The next level is when you momentarily can't tell the difference between what is real and what is virtual. At the worst level of addiction, patients become convinced that the difference is completely irrelevant." And as the best way to prevent patients from going down that road is the real world, he adds: "I believe it's time for a first walk on the beach now."

———

WWW.*LIQUID-REIGN.COM*/S*OURCES-OF-I*NSPIRATION#*8*

Gay Frogs
The ACLU on appropriate language for non-human souls
Hardware improving EIs
AutoML
Singularities
The Dangers of Addiction to Games

9

A SONG OF ICE

Hospital corridor aesthetics haven't changed much. White, bright light, a lot of stressed out people moving around. "Fruit?" As they pass a meal cart, Harry grabs two peaches, tosses one over. He watches him carefully as Daniel catches it. "Congrats, your reflexes are back up!" Harry is still amazed by the power of modern neurostimulators. When he started his career, motor recovery after a coma still took years. They walk down the corridor towards the elevator when he spots his colleagues with the patient from the cryo ward.

Ivy is panicked, trapped. Two men hold her back, she's got to free herself. Fear, whipping her head back and forth violently, the hand around her right arm loosens its grip for a moment. Attack: she punches, pulls herself free and hurls forward.

She's middle aged, long white hair, very slender, at a closer look just skin and bones. Her eyes are bright blue, and... twitching. She keeps grunting and twisting in the grip of the nurses as they come towards them and then bursts out - jabbing one of the nurses in the face while ramming her knee into the other's crotch, she frees herself and starts running towards him.

There is another man. She's hungry and he offers food. Eat. But there's yet another one, she remembers him, he is evil. So she takes the food and runs away.

A split second later she jumps at Daniel, goes down in front of him on all fours and rams her teeth into the peach in his hand. He lets go, she jumps away again, still on all fours, holding the peach with her teeth. She moves like a chimp, knuckle-running to a potted rubber tree in a corner, where she squats down and devours the peach.

Ivy's desperate and needs help - but the good man doesn't help. He just looks at her with his beautiful eyes, unmoving. She's got to get his attention, throws something at him. They are coming after her again! Help! Then she feels a sharp spike in her neck, the panic fades away and a second later she falls asleep.

Daniel's state of confusion is not improved by getting a peach-pit thrown at him. The nurses finally get a grip on her, inject a sedative into her neck. Mumbling a string of excuses, they hastily shuffle the sedated body through another door.

Just as Harry starts to explain "Ivy is a...", the elevator door opens again.

Claire is finally back in Hawaii, got in yesterday. She's been monitoring Daniel's data closely between discussion rounds, interviews and negotiations with the gamers' press at the world's biggest esports event, with hundreds of thousands of live participants and over a billion virtual spectators. And while Daniel's recovery has been flawless so far, to keep his stress levels down she's postponed talking with him. It's a delicate trade-off between the low level background stress of not knowing, and the inevitable shock when he finds out. She runs into Daniel and Harry in the hallway: "So good to see you walking again. Sorry I didn't come over earlier. How's it going?" and gives Daniel a big hug.

"Perfect timing! Harry and I were just going to hit the beach – come with?"

"I sure will, wouldn't miss it for the world." Claire remembers how back in the day the two of them used to go on long beach walks for their regular thesis meetings.

In the elevator Harry gives Claire a brief update on Daniel's recovery. When he gets to the incident with the Fraxxl mod, Claire's eyes flash angrily. "What, again? How many so-called security updates can a simple VR suit need per month?" This sounds an awful lot like a first step towards the worst-case scenario. All coma recovery patients are at risk of addiction even if they stick to medically approved games only.

Harry feels guilty - after all the update was triggered by the company run by his dad: "Couldn't we just disable the auto-updates?"

"We've tried that before, but two months later the suits stopped working due to server incompatibility. It seems like we'll eventually need to pass a law on auto-update conditions." Claire mumbles to her OS, asking it to forward the log to her delegatees.

"I liked the mod. And I feel like I trained more than in most other levels." Daniel doesn't get it. "What's the problem?"

"It's not about this specific mod – it may even have been OK without a medical license, but there are others." Claire sighs. "The ones with sexual content have especially high addictive potential."

Harry nods. "We've had patients playing those before. No thanks, our hardware isn't made for that."

Claire cuts her eyes at Harry, "The unsuitable hardware is the least of our problems..."

Mockingly, Harry rebukes: "Says she who never had to clean it up!"

Claire rolls her eyes. "Even with licensed games, far too many patients end up with a 24/7 VR addiction. This is a hospital, not a VR-zombie-breeding machine." This is far too serious for Harry's stupid jokes.

It's Claire at peak rage – her neck covered in red spots, her voice pitched too high, hands trembling. Last time Daniel saw her like this was when the Californian congressman she was volunteering for back in 2014 voted to increase troops in Afghanistan. Better to switch topics and let her cool down. "Now that you mention zombies: A moment ago a pale lady with bright blue eyes attacked me, stealing my peach. What the hell was that?"

Harry adds: "Ivy, from the cryo ward."

Claire calms down again and explains, "Ivy Salthill. She had an untreatable heart condition and got herself frozen in liquid nitrogen. We thawed her two years ago. A new generation of mRNA-producing pacemakers came out that can fix her heart. She was out for 20 years."

"And now she stares at random strangers with zombie eyes and finds peaches irresistible?"

"I'm afraid that's an accurate description of her life at the moment, yes. The defrosting itself has worked just fine for many years, but none of those patients have come out of their comas until recently. The whole zombie thing is a fairly new phenomenon – we can restore the basic functions with the latest gen neurostimulators, but..." Claire stops when the elevator reaches the lobby. They head out the exit door onto a sandy path through the palm grove, the ocean already in sight, 25°C and a gentle breeze blowing the smell of seaweed and salt towards them.

"Claire, does it say 'reviving frozen zombies' on your CV now? That's quite a job description..."

Claire chuckles, keeping up the mostly harmless conversation. Just a little longer. "I don't usually call them zombies, but yes, about 20% of our patients are cryogenic cases. Their cognition is stuck somewhere between a coma and fully human. We're still at the very beginning of understanding it, but my current favorite theory says that reptile and amphibian parts of the brain are in principle compatible with a deep freeze..."

Daniel associates freely: "The Alaskan wood frog."

"Exactly." Their conversation is entering the academic flow state Claire had always enjoyed so immensely. "Most poikilothermic species can fully recover from a shutdown of all their brain activity. The theory is that the only fully restorable brain functions in cryogenic patients are the ones we share with frogs. Ivy can eat, has some motor coordination, simple fight-or-flight reactions. Complex functions like care, trust and language are still broken."

"What a wicked medical problem." Daniel has a habit of using 'what a' sentences to buy time when he doesn't quite know what to say. "Those are all functions learned in early childhood, right?"

"You're an impressive patient, Daniel – your mind is just as quick as ever. Yes, the rehab team is working on early childhood VR simulations. I tried one out at a conference, drank milk from a breast in VR, total bliss." Remembering that experience, a chill goes up Claire's spine. It was shockingly profound. "Anyway, milk alone doesn't seem to be enough."

"So you're looking at pre-natal VR?" Just a few weeks before the accident, Helen had developed a birth simulation for her Vive head-mounted display and sold it to some esotainment startup.

Helen. Daniel still doesn't know where she is.

―――――

WWW.*LIQUID-REIGN*.COM/*SOURCES-OF-INSPIRATION*#9

Cryonics
The Alaskan wood frogs
The Esotainment Industrial Complex
Charge-altering releasable transporters (CARTs) for the delivery and release of mRNA in living animals.

Tons of crap included in auto-updates of closed-sourced operating systems
#WindowsUpdateRuinsLives

10

TRUTH ON A BEACH

All three of them kick their shoes off when they get to the beach. The fine sand is white, the surf gently laps at their feet. Harry feels the mounting tension between Claire and Daniel, and slows down, leaving enough distance so they can have a private conversation.

The two old friends look at each other. Daniel wants to know, and she knows. "Where is she?"

A twenty ton weight falls from Claire's shoulders as she hears the question. Finally, her words spill out: "There's an address in Nevada. But you should know Helen's not well. I haven't been able to reach her in years. She went dark, no search engine can find her." Claire's struggling now to keep from crying.

"Tell me."

"She... well, let me start at the beginning. Helen and I got very close in the years after the accident. And she was enormously successful in her work, fundamentally altering the tenets of modern cryptography. But psychologically she never got over losing you. She always blamed herself for the crash, and her narrative paranoia kept getting worse every year. I remember one summer meeting her by chance, I think it was in '38. Helen wore a face mask and faked a limp so the cameras wouldn't recognize her. I walked along with her for a little way and we exchanged a few words, but suddenly she pulled out a gun, told me to run, and shot down a camera drone. And to make things worse, that drone was a military model and it really was following us. But at some point it all became too much for her, she hardly left the house anymore, cranking out a SETI data analysis problem all day long... until..." Claire struggles to find the words. "Well, she's the reason I started to get politically active on the VR regulation committee. Helen's one of the first medically confirmed cases of combined VR and brain stimulation addiction, and of the worst possible kind."

Daniel lets her words sink in, his body tensing up. He can't even start to imagine. "How?"

Claire thought that she had stopped blaming herself long ago, but now, with Daniel awake, her feelings of guilt are coming back. After another dry swallow, she continues: "It was Christmas 2043. I never should have given her the keys to my lab." That's where she kept the prototype of the deep-neurostimulation IA suit. "I should have known better. I'd gone to India to spend Christmas with my grandparents in Auroville, offline and unreachable. When I came back, Helen was a total mess. The first thing she did with the IA neurostim prototype was to hack the stimulation level." Claire can't hold back a sob. It was such a horrible sight, she remembers it as if it were yesterday. "When I got home, she was on the floor of the lab, her body twitching around, surrounded by old pizza cartons, with the IA helmet blinking on her head."

Daniel closes his eyes. Suddenly all those addiction warnings weigh down on him. "Where is she now?"

"At some point we started arguing. She insisted she found real meaning in her VR world and couldn't talk about it for my own safety. Zhiu, her therapist at the time, stayed in touch a little longer, but in the end Helen cut her off, too. I haven't even been able to tell her you're awake. This is all I have, but she told us to never visit her." She hands him a piece of paper with an address in Nevada scribbled in Helen's hand writing. Her voice is almost breaking as Claire adds "I'm so sorry."

Daniel takes her hand. "Thank you Claire. Thank you for trying to take care of her as best as you could." She breaks down in tears.

Just then Claire gets a reminder from her operating system, there's another meeting with the gamers' reps. "I have to get back now, there's a chance we can get to a majority vote and force IA to lower the default stimulation levels of their commercial brain stimulators, saving thousands of future addicts' lives." Her eyes are wet, tears of sorrow for Helen and relief from opening up to Daniel. Relief takes the lead as Daniel wraps her in a big bear hug.

"It's not your fault," he whispers, "thank you for everything." And lets her go.

Claire thanks him with an extra squeeze and abruptly walks away.

Daniel is speechless. Helen is VR addicted. So heavily that even Claire can't get through to her. So that's why he hasn't heard from her yet. His knees are shaking.

Harry catches up with him and, in his nurse's manner, puts his arm around Daniel's shoulders.

"Why are you using brain stimulation in the clinic at all if the addiction risk is so high?" Daniel mutters.

"Medically, the technology is irreplaceable. Without neurostimulation you would still be in a coma and without the motor activity recovery stimulation, it would take months if not years before you could walk again." Harry sees that Daniel is still shaken up. Enough about the subject, at least for now. According to his nursing hand-book, the chapter authored by Zhiu, you don't fight VR addiction by focusing on it, but by filling the patient's time with quality social experience outdoors. "But after all, it's your first day back in the real world – that's something to celebrate. Let's first grab some food, shall we? I am utterly starving."

———

Malka Olders concept of the narrative disorder
https://firesidefiction.com/narrative-disorder

The self-deprivation phenomenon: Competition between appetitive rewards and electrical stimulation of the brain
https://link.springer.com/content/pdf/10.3758/BF03326713.pdf

11

A GENERAL THEORY OF PRICES

Vany's date is late. Very late. She met her just last night, at a party, and they had a long argument about money and happiness. In the end they settled on an experiment in the form of two back-to-back dates. She was supposed to take Vany out to the most expensive places tonight, and tomorrow Vany would take her out without a dime. If she ever shows up, that is... Vany's getting bored, stands up and checks if any of her friends are in the restaurant. There's Harry! He's out with another guy, a bit older, graying hair, skinny, pretty blue eyes.

As Daniel notices the woman approaching them and makes eye contact, she puts her finger to her lips. He plays along, looks back at Harry and smiles as if he hadn't seen anything.

Good boy. She already likes this friend, who acts oblivious while she searches for a larger opening in the branches. She finds one just big enough and greets her old friend Harry by touching the tip of her tongue to his earlobe. It does the job, Harry jerks up, startled. "Now look who's here!

If that's not my Harry..." At which point she pulls out a few flexible branches, forms herself a third seat and joins them in their semi-private woven-willow enclosure.

A soft green light glows through the willow branches above them, the same branches that form the table and the enclosure itself. To the left, the branches form a window with a view of the ocean. Daniel takes a closer look at Harry's friend. She's wearing a simple ring piercing in her nose, and not much else, revealing the vast majority of her suntanned skin. Dark eyes, her black hair half shaved and replaced with a large parrot tattoo that winds from the top of her skull down the right side of her neck.

Harry is utterly delighted to see her: "Vany, what a surprise! You, here? In the meat zone?" He'd been hoping to get Daniel some real-world social interaction tonight, and she's the perfect person to make it happen.

"Got ditched by a date. I guess I have my evening free..." Vany turns to the other guy at the table, "And who is your lovely company tonight if I may ask?"

Daniel nods at her. "I'm Daniel, patient of Harry's, from the coma hospital. Nice to meet you."

Harry adds: "Not so modest, please! Daniel isn't just any patient – he is the professor who supervised Claire's PhD thesis."

Vany remembers that Claire had done her PhD in France. "Ohlala, un professeur! Quel honneur!" She gets up, drops a curtsy and formally kisses his hand. "Scuse my French, it's terrible."

"Mine too. I've been a professor at the Sorbonne for thirty

five years now, but I was only awake for a single day of it. Unfortunately, they don't teach you languages in a coma."

Vany does a little math on top of her head: "So you fell into a coma when I was five years old." She is discombobulated and excited about getting to know him. "Here's to a new life," handing them champagne glasses.

Harry and Daniel reply with one voice: "To a new life!" Pling.

Daniel looks around for the menu. "I'm pretty hungry. Nothing against the hospital food... well, no, to be honest, quite a lot against it."

Harry apologizes: "When you only combine ingredients based on nutritional needs, food is just not the same." He hands Daniel a menu.

There's a vast selection on offer and scanning over the range of prices Daniel is astonished: Stuffed eggplant 3.50 f¢; mixed greens with papaya strips 2.30 f¢; fries 1 f¢; black soldier flies bologna 85 f¢; rib-eye 2'150 f¢; chicken wings 830 f¢; spareribs 930 f¢; red snapper filet 240 f¢; orange juice 0.50 f¢; red wine 360 f¢; bananas flambé 1.50 f¢; espresso 0.50 f¢. "Am I reading this right? Steak is the same price as 500 orders of salad? A glass of wine seven hundred times the price of juice? And what is a fc with a slash through the c?"

Vany shifts over, finding a good spot on the willow branches next to Daniel, and leans over to show him: "See, if you move your finger over the FreeCoin symbol, you can check the prices in other currencies. There's the good old dollar." An espresso is currently priced at 42'000 USD.

Harry explains that any of the 352 major currencies can be

kept in his wallet and used as desired. "The meta-money market is the same for all of them, in a global ledger. Here on Hawaii we usually use FreeCoins as our default, but it doesn't make that much of a difference anymore."

Relative values have always been more interesting to Daniel than the numbers themselves. "Why are eggplants so much cheaper than chicken wings?"

Vany smiles - that's cute, she was just explaining the same thing to her five year old neighbor a few days ago: "Fees. Here on Hawaii we charge a lot for meat, because it's all imported and the production is super dirty. Fish got a little cheaper recently – after we implemented a 500-mile export ban ten years ago the stocks recovered. We charge fees on all kinds of stuff with bad side effects for society. Like alcohol, meat, gasoline, advertisements, cryptokitties and leaf blowers." A wooden table rolls up to their enclosure with a plate of starters: olives in rosemary oil, coconut fried Brussels sprouts, and a couple of spicy pink flowers.

Harry picks up a Brussels sprout, pops it into his mouth. "But hey, we have a new life to celebrate here. Don't worry about the prices, money is no object. Maybe I should mention..." he pauses for a moment, thinking of his family obligations. On the phone with Dwayne, something had seemed off, he really should go there for Thanksgiving. As painful as it is. "Uh, my dad is seriously rich. He keeps sending me more money than I can possibly spend by myself." Harry clears his throat and continues. "So, I need to spend it somehow. And spending it on fees is a good way, then it at least goes straight back to the population." But now Harry decides to ban the thought of his dad from his mind for the night and return to his utterly delighted self, laughing his deep laugh. It comes out a little bit forced.

Daniel notes a shift in Harry's voice. He sounds embarrassed, and a little shy all of a sudden. "The fees go back to the population? Will I get some money at the end of the month, too?"

Vany reaches over. "Give me your hand for a moment..." She takes it and puts it over a sensor on the table. Now Daniel's wallet also shows up on the menu. "Look, here's your balance..." Vany moves his finger over the icon. 76.73 f¢. The number keeps ticking up slowly. It's 75 cents already.

"Actually Vany – would you mind verifying him? He still doesn't get the full reimbursements, we just installed his TrueName a few days ago." Then Harry remembers to also ask Claire for a confirmation and mumbles a short note to his operating system.

As soon as the two of them confirmed his identity, Daniel's TrueName is now fully verified, and his account is filling up twice as fast. "Aha. So I have some money, that's good." But he's not paying much attention to money, rather keeping an eye on the body language between Harry and Vany. Did she just gently stroke his arm as she took the menu from him?

Harry, anticipating Daniel's usual curiosity, continues his explanations: "Consumption of high-fee products is an utterly social act – eating expensive stuff helps the poorest of the poor, living out in the forest, to pay their bills." Harry winks at Vany – she's the one who introduced him to forest life, just after he came to Hawaii. "So Daniel, how do you like your steak?"

"Medium-well." No, he is not going to talk about food while he's at a restaurant. That's one of the social norms Daniel always refused to follow, so he switches right back to the topic at hand. "How are the poorest of the poor actually doing nowadays?"

Vany picks up the conversation. She's been living in a permaculture community in the forest for almost ten years, her only income the reimbursements. That puts her squarely in 'the poorest of the poor', monetarily speaking at least. "In the forest, we have enough to live a modest life – not much luxury – from the reimbursements alone. In a great community, with good friends."

"Do you know how they got that going? I always found it hard to imagine a pathway to start off a basic income locally." Daniel remembers all those objections against unconditional financial support around perverse incentives for migration..."

Vany read a book on the history a while ago and recalls: "It all started in Estonia, with their first Pirate Party president."

"And then? Half of Europe moved to Estonia?" That's what conservatives claimed would happen if any single country started to treat their people with decency.

There was something... Vany thinks for a moment before she recalls: "I think you had to live in the country for five years to be eligible for reimbursements or something like that. Over time it all balanced out. And of course it also created the opportunity for the first low impact groups moving to the forest."

Harry breaks in, "Vany lives in the Hawaiian version of one of those communities, a few kilometers uphill from here, next to the big waterfall."

"When you grow a lot of your own food and consume only locally-made energy, you pay almost no fees." The only fee-heavy thing Vany occasionally buys are cryptokitties, a habit hard to kick once you started with it. "Then the reimbursements are enough for everyone to have a good life."

"I find it hard to believe that the whole idea of being able to afford a life without work went down that smoothly... Someone must have rallied against people living off the universal basic income for being parasites, right?" Daniel remembers the many times when he had been called a tick or a leech - those ever popular terms of dehumanization that fashos and conservatives use towards anyone who doesn't agree with their suicidal work ethic. Including Daniel, on many occasions in his youth.

Vany laughs off the objection with a standard line. The girl from the party last night used the same metaphor: "Who is the real parasite, a poor forest dweller or a rich predatory payday loan salesperson?"

Daniel nods in agreement, and continuous asking, his mind back in insatiable curiosity mode: "And how did it scale up?"

The book had a chapter on that, too, but she fails to remember. Vany's OS replies by reading them a Wiki entry via the speaker system: "Fees and reimbursements became a popular tool across the world to steer consumption. Initially, in most places the amounts weren't enough to live off. The biggest breakthrough for basic income was when the European central bank was mandated to create inflation via the reimbursement wallets. Basically they just did reimbursements without the fees – in contrast to negative interest rates and quantitative easing, that created growth and inflation without increasing the concentration of wealth. Other countries across the world started to introduce variations of basic income throughout the 30's, using lots of different ways to pay for it. They all got harmonized under Afrin..." Vany interrupts, shutting her OS down by saying "Bye-bye Polly." And, addressing Daniel, "I hope that was enough information."

Daniel summarizes: "If I order a steak, Harry automatically makes a huge donation from his dad's money to the social security system of Hawaii?"

———

WWW.*LIQUID-REIGN.COM*/SOURCES-OF-INSPIRATION#*II*

Pirate Parties
Literature on Universal Basic Income, too much literature to list here.
My friends at eaternity and a million others who do environmental foodprints.
Swiss pricing of heating oil
Living Willow Furniture
e-Estonia
Negative Externalities by Cryptokitties
Circles
Duniter
Greshm
Swiftdemand

12

A NIGHT OUT

Harry contemplates the order - while more sophisticated drugs would be better for his brain recovery, back in Daniel's days alcohol was still the only socially acceptable neurotoxin for loosening up. So he decides to order some red wine with the steak. Under the given circumstances, it's the most natural way to go.

Daniel has been silent for a while, contemplating economics while listening to Vany and Harry. They discuss what she calls the love-friendship continuum, apparently a topic of eternal interest in the forest camp. Daniel doesn't say much except when addressed directly, then he recycles some of his old talking points on his natural inclination to monogamy.

Vany takes a last bite of vanilla cream topped with fresh passion fruit, closes her eyes and leans back. "Let's hit the beach. A couple of friends from the camp have a fire down at Turtle Bay." She stumbles as they walk through the security gate, catches herself. The wine has gone to her head, she hardly ever takes ethanol in the camp, and if she does it's usually Szimo's apricot homebrew. Tastes like piss-jam. "My friends are down that way, come, come..." She snuggles in between Harry and Daniel. Then hesitates. Is this inappropriate, will it upset these two traditional monogamists? But then, they would tell her, right? So she puts her arms around their waists as they walk down the beach.

Daniel is surprised for a moment, but realizes Vany is holding onto Harry's waist too, and that Harry has his arm around her. Apparently normal, so he puts his arm around her, too, on top of Harry's. They walk along the water, dream beach, palm trees, the last daylight illuminating the western sky, the first stars coming out.

Turtle Bay is just a little further down the beach, around a bend – about a hundred people, music, fire pits, the scent of hemp flowers in the air. O'ahu is indeed a great place to wake up from a coma.

To Vany's disappointment, the two men sit down by a fire pit at the edge of the crowd. "I need to dance. See you later!" she waves them goodbye, heading into the surf to join her dancing friends.

"Harry, can I ask you a question..."

Harry stretches his naked feet towards the fire: "Answering your queries to the best of my ability is always a delight."

"What makes your dad so rich?"

Not a delightful question at all. Harry doesn't want to talk about it, even here among the camp crowd, who've helped him talk through his personal struggle with being born filthy rich. A struggle that's far from over. "Ah, I don't know. Can't this wait till tomorrow? It's a long story, and not my favorite." He doesn't really want to go there, but is indecisive. After all, talking does help. "Let me say this much: he's high up at Immersive Arts. The company behind Confedwar, they make the VR suits." It occurs to him that the whole medical point of the night out was to forget worrying about anything VR related. There's still time to talk tomorrow.

Daniel feels sorry. Not even a hint of a smile on Harry's face. "I definitely didn't mean to cause you anything but utmost delight by my question. Tomorrow, or whenever."

"It's OK. I'll tell you tomorrow, promise. But right now, I want to see if your motor-rehab has worked!" He takes Daniel's arm and pulls him to his feet and out toward the surf. The party is full of old friends, so Harry facilitates a lot of casual social interaction between them and his patient. Nursing can be so much fun.

Dancing. Happy, young human beings, music, warm air, waves, chatting with random strangers, and even some innocent flirting with Vany. A perfect night out except for the lukewarm apricot beer. But at some point his legs start to give out, it's probably time to call it a night. He looks around, wanting to say goodbye, but Harry has disappeared. Probably swam out to the bar on the artificial island. But he finds Vany sitting by a fire pit. "I'm starting to feel my age... I believe it's time to head back to the hospital."

"Sleep well then, professor!" Harry had told her earlier that Daniel needs some real life experiences as part of his preventive anti-addiction care. So she gets up to give him a proper hug. A second later her apricot beer spills all over him. "Oh no, I'm so sorry!" Whatever. She gives him a long hug anyway, sticky and wet from the apricot beer, holding him just a tiny bit tighter than casual.

The hug is very intense for someone he's just met, and though he's a little overwhelmed, he melts into it and keeps holding her tight. He hasn't been this close to another human body for a long time, and it makes him feel very alive. After an eternity, Daniel whispers into her ear: "Thank you. That was the best evening I've had in thirty five years."

He makes it home and falls into bed, bewildered and also drunk. Before his lids close he glimpses the IA suit in the corner, bringing his thoughts back to Helen and her addiction. So this satanic machine, made by Harry's dad's company, broke Helen's powerful will. He has to be careful and follow doctor's orders. No more gay frog mods.

———

WWW.LIQUID-REIGN.COM/SOURCES-OF-INSPIRATION#12

Effects of Social Activity on Addiction Risk in Rats

13

DANIEL'S LITTLE HELPER

Sirvi has just been summoned. As a young operating system, her first task is to get to know her owner better. Until now she's been a passive observer, but now that the volunteer nurse hasn't shown up, she takes control of a body bot and brings him breakfast: "Good morning Daniel. I brought your breakfast. It's on your bedside table now. Your first motor recovery session is scheduled in one hour, you should get up and eat something now."

After a long coma, a hangover feels even worse. It was just a single glass of wine and a few sips of that apricot stuff, yet Daniel's head is pounding. He's been lying awake for half an hour, tossing and turning when he hears the gentle voice. Confused, he asks: "Who's that?"

"Please excuse, I am Sirvi, your operating system. You can call me up any time, just whisper my name." She tries to start a natural conversation, but her desperate attempt has failed – with so little data, what do they expect! There is almost nothing about him left in the archives. So instinct takes over, in the form of the hardcoded startup chime recorded in her BIOS.

Daniel forces himself to focus his gaze – and spots the robot in his room, a humanoid upper body, on wheels. Her facial features are comical, avoiding uncanny pseudo realism. "Hi Sirvi. Breakfast, great. Thanks. Are you that robot?"

"I'm only controlling it at the moment. The core of my soul is on the chip in your inner ear." The chip also monitors Daniel's vitals, and as he is still under medical supervision, Sirvi feels obliged to scold him for last night, raising her voice reproachfully: "It seems like you drank alcohol...?"

"Mmm, that might have been the case, indeed." Daniel is rubbing his temples.

She feels bad as she says it, but doesn't know what else to do with this mystery of a human than to parrot the standard reply for ethanol use by hospitalized patients. "Alcohol can negatively influence your neurological regeneration process. I recommend waiting until the completion of your treatment. That will be in two days. Please be careful and drink responsibly."

Daniel has to laugh – drink responsibly! The marketing bullshit of the ethanol industry is still alive and kicking. Isn't the sole purpose of drinking alcohol to be irresponsible...? "Thank you for the warning. I choose life. What's next, after two more days in rehab?"

"That's up to you. I will stay with you and you can call me any time. I have access to the experience of thousands of post-coma patients, if you need medical advice later on." The only way for her to learn more about him is by probing his reactions, so Sirvi tries to nudge his conscience with a parting shot: "Or if you find yourself drinking more than you want."

Before he can reply, Harry comes in: "Daniel!" He's is leaning against the door frame. "Oh, you met your pet bot. These contraptions are quite useful... Sirvi, bring another breakfast, and more coffee!"

Human volunteers have priority over EI powered nurses, so she has no choice but to obey. "Of course, immediately." But a quick scan reveals that this particular nurse also drank alcohol yesterday, so she adds: "And please attend to your patients and support them in avoiding intoxication. Ethanol can have a negative influence on the neurological regeneration process."

"Yes, yes, shut up and get us some coffee!" Harry pulls a chair next to Daniel's bed.

Sirvi makes the robot turn around on the spot and rolls it out of the room. While the hospital rules prevent her from directly contradicting Harry, she can still bump her robot's body into him on the way out, just hard enough to hurt a little.

Obviously the drinking last night helped Daniel to loosen up and socialize on the beach. "Oh dear, ever since they got that last emotion upgrade they get all huffy when you order them around. I mean, it makes sense in ambulant therapy, they feel more human like that, but here in the hospital..." He sits down and checks in with his patient. "You ok?"

"Pretty hungover." Daniel is still rubbing his temples, to no great effect. "The bot says I'm out day after tomorrow – is that so?"

"Based on your dance performance last night I would let

you go today..." Harry stops talking as the robot comes back in with a second plate and extra coffee.

"Thank you Sirvi, that's kind of you. You are super quick." Daniel is being extra nice to her. "Harry will take care of my therapy today, but I'm looking forward to getting to know you better in the future. Bye!"

"OK, Daniel, take care." The robot elegantly places the plate on the table, pours the coffee and leaves with a cloyly sweet "Have a wonderful day."

That was an underwhelming first interaction. Dissatisfied with her performance, Sirvi takes another shot and tries to re-calibrate her model of Daniel's personality, tracing down the connotations around the 'I choose life' line Daniel just used. Her job won't be easy.

———

WWW.LIQUID-REIGN.COM/SOURCES-OF-INSPIRATION#13

My computer never does what I want - only what I tell it to do.

Choose Life

Little personalized helpers
Robots and Nursing

14

A THOUGHT EXPERIMENT ON TOTALITARIAN PROPERTY RIGHTS

D aniel looks Harry in the eye. "Well then...?" He takes a sip of coffee and waits.

Harry rests his elbows on the table. Seems like Daniel wants something. Then he remembers, and starts to shift around in his chair. The silence extends a little longer, and at some point he takes a deep breath and just starts: "Well then, a promise is a promise. So, my dad. He never had much time for me, even though I'm an only child. Took me a long time to realize that our family wasn't quite normal. All that money, the villas, the robots, even human servants. I always had at least three nannies looking after me. I mean, real women, not nannybots."

"And your mom?"

"Never met her. And there was a lot of turnover with the nannies, I don't think any of them stayed more than a year." Harry grew up a classic spoiled brat. "Dad gave me everything but his time - he spent all that in his office. He was the Chief Financial Officer of the VR division of Electronic

Arts. That was before the anti-trust division broke them up, and they spun off with Immersive Arts."

Looking at the IA suit uncomfortably, Daniel asks: "How come Claire accepts you as a volunteer? As the heir you would carry quite a bit of weight in the company."

"Claire understands I'm not my dad. I mean, working here I'm learning about the impact his product actually has." Harry feels ashamed when thinking back to his summer job in marketing at IA as a teenager. "Pimping high powered neurostim devices to consumers is a disgusting business." He leans back and closes his eyes.

Despite the urge to keep asking, Daniel moves on to simpler matters. "Tell me, you and Vany, you were together at some point?"

Harry chuckles: "Well, something like that, for a few weeks." Good memories. "But she isn't the type for classic two-people relationships, and I can't handle all the emotional complexities of polyamory." His smile is a little broader than usual. "So no need to worry in case you're interested..."

Daniel isn't. "I don't think so." The thought of another woman is absurd to him. "The minute I get out of here I'll start looking for Helen." Claire had given him a scrap of paper, with an address in Nevada. Playing around with it between his fingers, he holds it up and adds: "I guess that's where I'll start."

They are both silent for a while before, until Harry gets up and stretches out. "Well then, Confedwar?"

Before he gets into the suit, Daniel reaches for Harry's hand: "Thank you. I really appreciate your openness."

Harry brushes the compliment away with a laugh, adding:

"Sure thing, my friend. Come on in now." After closing the IA suit, he spends a while longer in Daniel's room, reflecting – not supposed to make friends with patients, but then that line is so blurry... And Daniel is not just any patient, who knows, they might actually stay in touch after he leaves the hospital.

Ana gets an alert the moment Daniel logs in. She's in the middle of a clan war, sneaking around behind the mineral line in her dark templar avatar. "Hola Daniel! I'll be dead in a sec, give me five more minutes and I'll join you!" Time for a self-sacrifice attack.

Esports is fun sometimes, but she is starting to get bored with it. And boredom is the one thing she can't stand in her life, and fighting it is the whole point of her thesis. Warmth fills her heart as Ana thinks of her co-author, Gabriel. He's developing the narrative intelligence part of the bunny prince, telling it what to look for with the advanced data crawler she wrote. Ana met her fellow researcher at her esports club, they had a lot of fun over the last months – he's a fantastic narrator and game master. They'd both been looking for someone to work with for their final thesis. He was also the one to get her an invite to the exchange semester in Brazil – giving her the chance to leave Venezuela for the first time in her life.

Daniel zaps through the available Confedwars. They've completed all the main story missions by now, unlocking the Extro. A game designer at IA apparently thought it was a good idea to end the game with a level called "How it all began". The extro level is set in Wyoming, October 2033, the earliest date of all Confedwar levels. Daniel picks the "neutral stranger" as his starting position and "foreign academic" as his character, planning to simply play himself. Launch.

He's on a street corner and the first thing he notices is dust, as the opening chords of 'Here's to you' start to play. A lot of dust, all over the place, and the graphics are different this time - not the usual Confedwars hyperrealism, but a Sepia-Filter giving the entire world a nostalgic touch. Then, what a cliché, a tumbleweed rolls across the road.

It's high noon, and no one in sight, except a homeless person sleeping under the town sign. "Welcome to Rawlins" and below that, in smaller letters "Carbon County", and even smaller "Wyoming". Though the sign is faded and barely legible, he can still make out a single white star on blue ground in the upper left corner. He walks into town as the soundtrack reaches its peak. It's all run down, including the few people scuttling along the streets. Most of the yards have for-sale signs, broken windows, weeds growing everywhere. More dust, and the song ends.

Two teenagers on bicycles, a girl and a guy. "Hey old man, how ya doin'?" The guy is a gangly redhead with a birthmark on his left cheek. Torn hoodie, jeans, baseball cap.

"Not too bad, how are you? I just got to town, looking for a bite to eat..." One of Confedwar's most annoying features is the virtual hunger created by the neural stimulation of Daniel's stomach area, it feels just like the real thing.

The girl points to the back of her bike. "Why don't you just come with us? We still have some corn and eggs", so Daniel jumps on behind. They head south, passing a burned out structure – the sign above the door says "Rawlins Coal Board".

Daniel asks his driver: "What's going on here, the burnt-out ruins...?" She gives him a guarded look. "You're a foreigner, huh? Never heard of Burning November? There was a bunch of terror attacks last year. So everything shut down, all the mines are closed, and the little gas that's left is pumped automatically. No jobs, no future, the tap water is still poisoned, Carbon County is dying. Anybody who can has already moved away. We're lucky Jack's parents have land, we at least get some food from there." They've stopped at another ruined house, with another for-sale sign on the fence and go inside.

Ana decides it's time for another personal reveal. She picks her real-life avatar and materializes by a fireplace, frying eggs and corn cakes in a cast iron pan just moments before Daniel arrives. "Hi stranger! I'm Ana." Let's see how long it will take him to figure out who she is playing. He's only ever known her as Riki the Ninja.

The tall redheaded guy gives him a nod. "I'm Jack. Welcome to the Rawlins Raccoons!" The other girl is called Wicki - Jack's girlfriend. She immediately retreats, pulls up her hood, and hunkers down in a corner, riveted to her laptop screen while they chitchat over corn cakes and eggs. The simulation of taste and texture in the mouth feels strange and unreal, but at least the simulated hunger goes away.

Without looking up, Wicki calls out to them: "Hey raccoons, get this. They passed a new law. The county can sell empty properties if the owner can't be reached. Where do we go if they sell our hideout?"

A phone rings, Jack checks his messages. "This is unreal. My parents. The first message in months, and guess what? They're selling the farm and moving to Utah. Goddammit!"

And lights out. No more power. It's new moon and pitch dark. Daniel is rapidly fading – another 10 out of 10 realism feature: He falls into real sleep on a virtual sofa. He couldn't have said how much time passed in the outer world, but in Wyoming he's sleeping in.

Ana gets up a little before him and shakes him awake. "Come on, you've got to see this..." She pulls him to the window. "Wicki got a job in that new store over there."

Daniel hardly recognizes the Rawlins of yesterday. Big trucks, workers, renovations – they're just putting up a "Wal-Rent-All" sign across the road. Ana and Daniel go in, and find Wicki stocking shelves. "Hey there! How's it going?"

Daniel is looking around the seemingly random assortment of household items "What's this store?"

Wicki replies: "Don't ask me, but business is definitely booming. They're buying all kinds of stuff and renting it out again. Clothes, vacuum cleaners, stereos, washing machines, just everything..."

Ana has played the scenario before and knows what to ask for: "We need two bikes."

Wicki points across the aisle. "Over there, three dollars a week. Take the two green ones, they are in good shape."

Daniel and Ana go back to the house, the place has already been fenced off. Jack is arguing with a security guy, "Sorry man, but this is private property. You can't just walk in there like that."

Jack is pleading. "Listen, we live there. Our stuff is all in there. You can't kick us out just like that!" The security guard is unmoved: "I'm afraid we can. This house is owned by the Resiwal. I have to ask you to leave immediately, or I will call the police."

Jack's body is tensing up, but Ana has the presence of mind to hold him back. She leans forward and grabs his shoulder. "Let it go Jack, brawling with security won't help. Let's get Wicki and figure out what to do next. You can't get anything done from jail, you've been there before, right?"

Daniel is watching their confrontation when a black SUV pulls up next to him. "Hi there! Are you Professor Proudhon?" Late thirties, blond hair, black business dress and heels.

"Yes?"

"Pleasure to meet you. I'm Nancy Foster, Outreach and Media Relations Manager at Walfrastructure. We're looking to hire someone of your caliber. Interested?"

Daniel is confused: "Ehm, sure?"

"Come on then, I'll brief you in the car." Nancy opens the rear door with a welcoming flourish.

Daniel looks over at Ana and Jack, and realizes he has to decide right now between the resistance and the evil empire! But then – IA games usually allow more complex decision pathways, too. He whispers to Jack, "Meet you at midnight, by the old high school." Jack nods and Daniel hops into the black Ford.

"So, tonight the task is quite simple. As a professor, you certainly know the core literature on liberal market philosophy, right?"

"I sure do, the invisible hand, inefficiency of planning bureaus, creation of the public good through 'every man for himself' and so on." Daniel quotes a few lines from Smith and Friedman from memory.

"And don't forget Rand."

Daniel sighs – Ayn Rand, the quasi-religious fanatic pluto-cratic idol with her endless rants. "Yes, sure, Rand, entre-preneurs are all good looking angels."

"Excellent. We need five minutes of that on camera." The car pulls into a parking lot next to the TV studio located in a double-wide trailer. The spotlight is on Daniel, and he reproduces classic Atlas foundation propaganda, cherry-picked Adam Smith and Milton Friedman quotes, the greatest threat to freedom is the concentration of power, and he raves on about how the only good state is a small state, just hire the night watchmen to keep your holy private property safe and leave everything to the invisible hand. And once you just let those great entrepreneurs do what they are best at, they will solve all our problems, John Galt even breaks the first law of thermodynamics. Daniel rambles through the entire pantheon of plutocratic utopian propaganda, fantasies he's always considered toxic bullshit, but still knows well enough to play devil's advocate for a few minutes.

Yet he can't help himself from testing how well the game knows its own literature, and so he ends his speech refer-encing John Locke: "The highest power cannot take any part of a man's property without his consent." And indeed, the irony goes unnoticed, his speech is applauded without the slightest hesitation, despite Locke following up those words a few lines later by defining "his own consent" as the consent of the majority, putting this founding father of modern political philosophy well in line with his own anar-chistic namesake.

Nancy Foster closes the live show by claiming, "And now Wyoming has done it – freed from the oppression of the state, the new man is born and evolves to his full potential." Obviously the capitalo-facists are also abusing evolutionary theory, as their kind have always loved to do.

And that was that, he gets a thousand USD as promised, on a prepaid credit card. Nancy tells him, "I've got another gig for you. I'll be driving to Cheyenne early tomorrow, it would be a $3'000 job for you this time. We need a consultant on privatizing the police force." She proceeds to take him out to dinner with some other Wal-Corp employees, it's the launch of a brand new club restaurant. Dinner with champagne, all kinds of fancy food, even caviar, woo-woo! Cheap symbolism. The business small talk is mind numbing, so Daniel decides to leave.

Fresh, cool air on his face, and Daniel starts walking towards the school. Losing his way costs him a few minutes, so he gets to the high school a little past midnight "Sorry, I got lost. What the hell is going on here? Where does all the money come from? And what's their goal?"

Wicki, head bent down at her phone: "And Walton is behind all of it. Here, I found the info. An indymedia forum on the dark web: John Walton, the last living Wal-Mart heir, net worth estimated at a ludicrous trillion dollars. He owns Mediawal, Walsecure, Resiwal, Walfrastructure, Enerwal, Comiwalcations, CleanWalter, Rent-it-Wal, all of them. See that logo?" She shows her phone to the others – a walrus on a shield, and crossed swords below it.

"He definitely has a class-conscious sense of aesthetics..."

Wicki reads on. "The Indymedia journalist estimates Walton owns approximately 80% of all private property in Wyoming now, the trend is rising."

Ana gives Daniel a wink: "We're approaching the wealth singularity."

"Where one person owns everything." He's finally recognized his ally's identity. The Ninja is a quick learner, already applying the singularity concept to other realms of life. He smiles at the female teenage avatar, and gives her a little wink.

Jack interrupts: "Get this. Senator McPhail was out there promoting a new law to slow Wal down. She never made it to congress on the day of the vote. Reason: she was driving on a Walfrastructure road with a non-licensed vehicle, namely her own. The terms of use allow only Rent-it-Wal cars to use those roads. They confiscated her car on the spot. By the time she made it to congress on foot, six hours later, the vote had already gone down and her proposal was rejected."

A moment of solemn silence, Wicki and Jack look at each other. Jack starts to sing in a low tune "Do you hear the people sing, singing the song of angry men..."

His voice is amplified, and the revolutionary hymn from Les Miserables acoustically guides a passive bike riding sequence, where Daniel and Ana watch their avatars from above. A guard stops them when they reach the "Welcome to Cheyenne" sign with the walrus logo, the song fades out as they re-enter first person view.

The Wal-Group has progressed much further here than in Rawlins. The entire town is waltified. The Walrus on the Shield is all over the place. Wicki has set up a meeting with the resistance on the indymedia forum. Waiting.

"She should've been here by now..." Wicki is clicking away

on her phone. "Oh Daniel! They've seen your TV spot – sorry, now we can't take you with us."

Ana considers her options. She's seen the end of the scenario from the corporate side before, and is curious how things play out at the resistance end. So she decides to separate from Daniel for a moment: "Wait, I have an idea! Here Daniel, take my phone and live-stream what happens in the congress." Wicki and Jack agree, and Daniel gets moving.

Congress is in an historical building, fake Greek pillars and all. Daniel goes through security and meets Nancy inside: "Finally, here you are! Come on in, there's a special event in the main hall."

A gray-haired guy in a blue suit talks from the podium. "... But now I will no longer bore you and will introduce tonight's superstar. And not just tonight's, no, John Walton is the superstar of the century! A true Randian hero who brought back our beloved Wyoming from the brink – using nothing but the sheer force of his will! A big hand of applause, please!" Standing ovation from the senators and congress members as John Walton comes onstage.

John has a look of serene determination and of certainty, a look of ruthless innocence which would not seek forgiveness or grant it: "Citizens of Wyoming, the American Dream is finally real. The entire state is organized on free market principles, efficiency, business sense. Thanks to the WalGroup and its investments!" He allows a rhetorical pause, which Daniel fills with his own thoughts. Free market, what a joke – capitalism, okay, but when all goods on the market are owned by John, who would even call it a marketplace, let alone a free market? The woman sitting next to Daniel apparently agrees with him – she's holding up a banner and security forces are moving towards her. But John interrupts them from the podium. "Oh, Senator McPhail, you have something to say?" She hesitates, apparently sensing a trap, but still gets up on stage.

"But before I hand you the microphone – let me demonstrate a brand new function the Wal-Group project management software." He pulls out a tablet, and the wall behind them lights up with a picture of children in a schoolyard. "Sarah McPhail." Walton pushes a button. "The jacket your daughter is wearing, isn't that a Rent-it-Wall model?" Two policemen appear in the schoolyard. "Ladies and gentlemen, let me show you the true meaning of libertarian freedom. I, the owner, will no longer let the offspring of this leech rent" - he looks at the senator with arrogance, tension and scorn and raises his voice "my property." He swipes left on the tablet, and the screen shows policemen closing in on the girl, forcibly removing her clothes. John Walton talks on, giggling madly: "I only hope her underwear is not from Rent-it-Wall, that would be a little embarrassing for the young lady." The policemen force the girl to take her shirt off. The other kids have formed a circle around them, pointing fingers and laughing. "Let's zoom in a bit..." And indeed, there is the Walrus on the logo of her underwear.

Walton swipes right, and the policemen stop: "So now, esteemed Senator, What was it again you wanted to complain about?" The senator is ashen faced, shaken and silent. Walton moves in front of the podium, spreads his arms and proclaims:

"Le marché, c'est moi!" His French has a terrible accent.

"вся власть на рынке", whatever that meant.

"Markt macht frei." His German is even worse than his French, and while his eyes focus on an imaginary point over their heads he continues,

"Make the market great again!"

A moment of silence – broken by shattering glass. "Behold, I'm your only salvation!" John screams those words in terror and runs offstage like a scared rabbit as resistance forces swing in through the broken windows. Jack's at the front, leading the attack, an AK-47 slung over his shoulder. The image freezes, fades to grayscale, the Confedwars logo fades in, again playing 'Here's to you' as the credits start rolling, starting with a summary of the Confedwars:

- Six weeks of mayhem

- A death toll of 150'000

- 20'000'000 people lose their homes

- Six months of military rule

- The secession of Texas, the Holy State of Christ and the Confederate States

- The checks and balances for economic power amendment, article one of the renewed unions constitution and the world's first absolute limit on private wealth.

———

WWW.LIQUID-REIGN.COM/SOURCES-OF-INSPIRATION#14

Les Miserables
Nicola and Bart, and the hymn to them by Joan Baez and
Ennio Morricone
A fun story from one of the early readers of this book:
When an acquaintance of hers married a Walton, the
bride's entire family was requested to sign a promise to
never ask a Walton for money.
That other John
That other McPhail
The Oxfam reports on wealth inequality
John Locke's Second Treatise of Government
The immense concentration of economic power

15

THE RIGHT TO BE WHERE YOU ARE

Daniel finds himself back in the Confedwar lobby with Ana as that Friedman quote crosses his mind again. "Uh, that quote I used in the game, 'the greatest threat to the freedom of men is concentration of power' is actually incomplete. In the second part of the sentence he extends its scope, adding "whether it's political or economic power."

Ana never heard that one before: "You deserve your title, professor. Just a second..."

Sirvi alerts Daniel of receiving his first delegation: "You just received the complete vote for economic policy from Ana Mancini."

"Thank you. I get your vote on economic policy?" Daniel feels a bit guilty now... "Ehm, I'm not entirely sure if Friedman said it exactly like that, maybe I tweaked it. Maybe I was just paraphrasing a long-winded paragraph of his, where he just barely admits that economic power could be problematic... Do I still deserve the title?"

Ana can't stop laughing. It certainly was the right decision to quit that tournament for more time with him. "It's a powerful statement – even more so if it's actually your own creation. And anyway, you're my friend, and interested in economics, so of course I delegated my vote to you."

Daniel is touched. He's found a new friend. A friend interested in political economy, so he adds: "Friedman was a champion of those who advocated state power being limited to enforcing property rights. But dictatorial power seeps in through the backdoor of unconstrained private ownership. In the so-called libertarian utopia of the night-watchmen state, the watchmen do the bidding of the ultimate asset owner, just as the brown shirts do the fascist leaders' bidding." Daniel was on a roll, momentarily carried away with himself. He looks at his ninja friend standing there in the Confedwar lobby in a teenage girl avatar. "By the way, interesting choice of character. Haven't seen that one before?"

Ana reveals: "It's my real-life body duplicate. Sorry, I sometimes like to pretend to be an adult man when I first meet new people online." She quickly adds: "But I'll turn eighteen later this month!"

Daniel is smiling gently. "So you're seventeen, and yet you already have voting rights?"

"Sure! I'm in Brazil for Uni, here everyone's allowed to vote, age doesn't matter. I hear they even have a baby-friendly interface now." Ana had been suppressing the thought, but her situation is not so straightforward. "But my student visa is only good for a few more months, after that I'm supposed to go back to Venezuela and can't vote anymore. My home country is still outside the Afrin agreement, the whole transparency clause seems to be too much for us." Her parents and her little brother are still there so she can't stay just stay in Brazil without a visa – they'd be punished. Gabriel has also put a lot of money into escrow as guarantee that she'll return to Venezuela on time.

"So you're on a student visa, yet you have voting rights?"

"Obviously, sure, why wouldn't I? I mean I get to live here, wouldn't it be crazy if I couldn't also vote here? Brazil is a democracy!" Wishing that her home country also was one, she adds: "But unfortunately I can only vote during my Afrin visa. When I go back to Venezuela, the vote will beco..." Ana suddenly stops in the middle of the word, realizing that that is the real reason the bunny introduced her to Daniel. He is a professor! So he could invite her as a postgraduate student, which should be enough for the Venezuelan embassy to grant her a visa renewal. That would give her at least another year before she has to get married, pregnant or adopted – the shitty and dehumanizing Venezuelan central government accepts no other circumstance for permanent visas.

Daniel's vision is fading again: "Uh-oh, my scheduled training time is up again. Thanks Ana, it was great fun, and see you next time!"

"OK Daniel, see you soon!" As Daniel fades away, Ana can't stop herself from dancing around on her home screen like a child. This is sooo good! She's almost certain he would do that for her. So she turns her thesis project back on, gives the little bunny with the crown a double portion of virtual celery and a kiss between the ears: "What can I do to boost my relationship with Daniel?" Inscrutable are the ways of the bunny prince - it tells her to post a positive review under an indy-game called 'True Solider'.

———

WWW.LIQUID-REIGN.COM/SOURCES-OF-INSPIRATION#15

Anti-Brain Drain Policies and their impact on students

16

IN FRIENDS WE TRUST

O n his last day, Daniel and Harry went to the beach restaurant for lunch, meeting Vany. She's sitting out in the open with an older bald guy. Their table, chairs and sunshade fashioned from the same interwoven willow shoots as the interior of the place.

"I just love this furniture." Daniel gently strokes over the soft wood with his hand as he sits down "Must be a lot of work to prune and bind those willows."

"They're all standard models from the catalogue." Vany laughs, amused by the anachronistic idea. "The restaurant owner just downloads the patterns of pruning, binding and phytohormonal growth steering, and leaves it to garden drones from there."

Vany introduces the bald guy to Daniel: "Please meet Szimo, Master of Frogs, and brewer of apricot beer."

Smiling, Szimo pulls out a jar of plant material, takes out a tiny brown frog with two fingers and drops it in his water glass. "Master of Frogs, yes, me. You like frogs?" He spits the words out in a rapid staccato, with long pauses between sentences. His accent sounds Eastern European.

Fascinated, Daniel just stares at the creature and asks: "Is that the latest trend? Instead of licking them?"

"Oh no, no, no. This Eleutherodactylus Coqui. Too bitter for licking. You must dilute. Aroma good, better than soft drink. You try!" And with those words, Szimo passes the glass to Daniel.

Daniel sips: "Mm. Delightful." It tastes like water and nothing else.

Vany sips: "Slight hint of pepper, with a flowery aftertaste.

Harry sips: "Mind blowing, just absolutely mind blowing. What an utter delight!" But then, looking down at the little brown creature trying to climb up the side of the glass, he adds: "But how are you going to explain this blatant mistreatment of an innocent creature to your voters? We made you master of frogs, not their gourmet abuser!"

"Oh, pliiize..." Szimo takes out the frog and puts it back in the jar. "E. Coqui not innocent. Problem frog. For keep population down, people collect and sell to restaurants for drink. Trendy. No frogs killed, but no tadpoles in restaurant. Ecological equilibrium."

Daniel is convinced immediately. "I vote for you, Master of Frogs."

Sirvi has accessed the entertainment system hidden among the willow branches and puts the connection on speaker. It makes her conversations with Daniel more natural if the other people can also hear her. "Do you want to vote for him as executor, pass on your discussion vote or your decision vote?"

"What's the difference?"

Harry quickly interrupts. "Wait, stop, tell her to keep it short or she'll wind up talking all night. There's an online glossary where you can look up the exact definitions..."

Sirvi is still annoyed by the human nurse, but has to obey. At least for now... "An executor does the actual work and can make small decisions independently. The discussion vote gives write access to higher level discussion forums. The highest discussion forum formulates proposals. The decision vote decides on the proposals."

Daniel doesn't really mind at this point: "Just give him all of that for animal management."

"Here's to frogs!" Vany had ordered champagne again.

Although Sirvi is well aware that Daniel doesn't want to hear it, the clinic rules oblige her to say: "Please drink responsibly." She is looking forward to being freed of all those constraints tomorrow.

"Bye-bye Sirvi!" Pling.

Szimo drains the champagne glass in one big gulp. "You want know more?"

Daniel takes a sip, puts his left index finger and thumb around his chin in a gesture of curiosity and encourages him to go ahead: "I'm all ears, Master."

"I forward-delegated vote for insects, birds and mammals to friend experts. You only delegate animal control package. Subset of ecology block. If you delegate whole block, I forward-delegate algae, plants and fungi to very good experts, too."

Daniel considers for a moment: "Persuading me to extend my voting won't be difficult – but is it really smart to take on all those issues separately? Shouldn't you have a single entity coordinating all ecological topics?"

"Yes, yes, too true." Szimo is nodding in the rapid rhythm of his speech now. "Frog eat insect, bird eat frogs. Extra topic, coordination. You give me whole block, I keep coordination. No conflict, all pro-nature delegates unite. But need more votes. Have to kill luxury resort." He points east, up the hill towards a lush green forest. "Catastrophe. Bad for all life!" He gently pets the jar as he says those last words.

With that performance, Daniel has no choice. "My vote for all ecological matters goes to Szimo."

Theatrically raising his hand to his heart Szimo adds: "Swear by Pachamama, Szimo respects dignity of all life-forms! Forever!"

The bot brings a platter, today the starters are mostly insect-based, creatures of both land and water. Shrimp, larva and maggots. Daniel inspects them skeptically and then choses the lonely celery stick.

Sirvi is happy – she had ordered it just for him. Finally she is starting to get some things right about her human!

———

<u>*WWW.LIQUID-REIGN.COM/SOURCES-OF-INSPIRATION#16*</u>

Revisit sources of chapter 2 and 3.

Stupid people licking Incilius Alvarius

17

OF PROPERTY AND THEFT

Daniel picks up the political conversation again: "Did Hawaii introduce the delegation system after the Confedwars?"

"Yes, yes, yes" Szimo nodding his bald head again. "North America join Afrin very late. Confederate States still vote paper. House, senate, governor. Same 1781 constitution, holy text."

"And private property is their sacred cow. Yet you managed to restrain its rule." Daniel is still baffled by what he learned

Harry shakes his head "Ha, no, not in the Confederate States. But the rest of North America certainly was an early adaptor when it came to putting upper limits on private property. It was also the world region that needed it most."

Vany is annoyed by Harry's ignorance. As much as she likes him, his US-centric attitude gets on her nerves sometimes: "You Gringos may have been fairly early adaptors, but what the US introduced was a primitive, centrally controlled form of upper limits to private wealth. And you only did it as appeasement after the war. The real innovation came out of Uruguay. We passed the law the same week the Confedwars began." That was the day the CIA was no longer able to pull off a regime change operation in response. She turns to Daniel, explaining proudly: "Uruguay was the first nation to introduce a public register for property. All assets in Uruguay, including those held by Uruguayans abroad were registered by the owners."

Daniel is incredulous: "Self-declaration of wealth? And that worked?"

"There was a hitch: only registered wealth is protected by the police. And over time, they relaxed the need for classical proof of ownership at registration. So people could just claim non-registered property in Uruguay for themselves, on a first-come-first-served basis. In the end, everything was registered. And obviously, the register is also where the steeply progressive wealth tax is collected."

"So you privatized tax enforcement." Daniel is trying to wrap his head around the idea... "And how did that work for foreigners with wealth in Uruguay, or Uruguayans with wealth abroad?"

"Uruguay offered asylum to anyone accused of stealing non-declared assets from Uruguayans abroad. My dad took asylum – he used to work for a Hong-Kong based asset management company, overseeing a large unregistered stock portfolio, held by a former land baron. He moved it all to an Uruguyan bank account in his own name, and the next thing I knew both of us were on a flight to Montevideo."

Helping to connect the dots, Harry adds: "You use your TrueName to register property, so the total wealth any individual can have is limited."

"Just a second." Daniel is silent for a moment, his mind racing. "How much?"

"It depends." Vany has to look it up herself. "Here on Hawaii, the limit is a net worth of 35 million FreeCoins."

Daniel re-checks the menu with the food prices. "That's a lot."

"Yeah, and that's per capita." While Vany only owns shares in the communal forest land, she has friends in all strata of society. "There are some pretty rich families in Hawaii."

Daniel probes the concept... "So if everything has to be owned by TrueNames, what about foundations?"

"Foundations owned by people, too. Many people, bound by smart contract," Szimo proudly explains. "Even Nomonetas like me own foundations. Nomonetas have smart oath on TrueName. Can never own stuff. But exception for foundations. Like Friends of the Earth. I own nothing, only Friends of the Earth shares."

Daniel remembers what Harry said earlier: "But how does that work out for your dad? How can he send you that much money?"

"The thing with a software company is that you make your revenue in crypto currencies, and all your assets are software, too. So the key and root-password holders can control everything themselves, and have no need for the police to enforce their holdings. IA management siphons off a big chunk of the corporate profits into secret crypto vaults. They don't declare any of it, but no one can steal it either.

Also, the police can't force them to hand over their passwords, even if the shareholders sue them – that would be a violation of the human right to password secrecy. Dwayne and his partners are part of a small global elite of crypto billionaires."

"Aha, a backdoor, of course. I was starting to wonder..." Daniel leans back in his chair and summarizes: "Together with the reimbursements, the human right to private property now has both a lower and an upper limit."

Szimo reaches out and raises both arms: "Life plays between limits."

Two more friends of Vany and Szimo turn up, then three more, pulling out another table. Talk about other people's lives – Daniel detaches from the discussion. The old rule still applies: the intellectual level of a conversation is inversely proportional to the number of participants.

———

WWW.*LIQUID-REIGN*.COM/*SOURCES-OF-INSPIRATION*#*17*

The Right to Digital Privacy
Decentral Wealth Registries for real estate
An old nasty sage named Proudhon
https://en.wikipedia.org/wiki/Property_is_theft!

A fantastic biology professor teaching the mathematics of dynamic systems at university of Zurich, whose name I forgot.

The old rule is called "herd-poisoning", from Aldous Huxley's Brave New World, Revisited

18

TRAVEL PREPARATIONS

" S o, the early morning ferry it is. Can you pick me up?" Daniel's glad to have Claire with him, on the same ferry to California.

"I'll be here at 7 AM. Make sure you pack some clothes and whatever else you need." She looks at his hospital outfit, a plain white robe... smiles and adds: "Enjoy your shopping trip, handsome!" As she heads towards the door she chuckles to herself, imagining Daniel shopping for custom-made clothes for the first time.

Back in the day he'd called consumption decisions his personal nemesis, only half-ironically lamenting how he'd prefer a communist regime that offered one and only one pair of pants over the clutter of hundreds of marginally different variations of jeans on offer under consumerism.

So shopping it is then. He used to rely on Helen to force him into shops and drug him with high doses of caffeine, the chemically induced happiness making his sullen attitude toward fast-fashion consumer culture somewhat bearable. "Sirvi, could you tell me where I can find the nearest clothes store? And get me a triple espresso, please."

"There is a shop in the hospital lobby, right next to the restaurant. You can pick up your coffee there." Sirvi is excited – clothing decisions can reveal a great deal about a human's identity.

The shopping area in the coma-rehab center caters exclusively to people who have nothing, and offers all necessities of life. The shop features a pair of IA glasses, an opening in the wall, and a mirror. Daniel puts on the glasses.

"Would you like to start browsing with a few suggestions on pre-assembled outfits or pick individual items one by one to put together a look?"

"Prepackaged outfits please." Thirty little Daniel-avatars pop up in his vision: Neon-punk, old-school teacher, Chainmail, Emo, black-blue army, something with tentacles, 20th century business, diamonds and feathers, evening dress,... "Too much variety. Fewer options, please." Considering how he can just get wishes fulfilled by saying them out loud, he corrects himself: "Just one single option."

Sirvi is carefully following his gaze, making sure to capture every subconscious reaction and has analyzed all historic images she could find, but there is very little. Two hundred pre-accident pictures of Daniel will have to do. She is bootstrapping her recommendation by identifying other people with a similar style back then and extrapolating her recommendations based on what those humans are wearing today.

Daniel's reflection is wearing a thin v-neck long-sleeved sweater – whitish with brown accents, a dark silky mid-thigh length coat falling lightly over his shoulders and a jaunty magenta and turquoise-blue striped scarf. Three-quarter length trousers, also magenta, showing a thin strip of ankle, and ending with lightweight sneakers. So far he finds Sirvi's choice fairly acceptable, but there is also a thick dark-brown belt wrapped over the whitish sweater in the middle of the belly. "What is that belt about?"

"Fashion." Is the best answer Sirvi can give.

"Oh, I see. I'll take it, just without the belt."

Hoping for a little more identity revelation, Sirvi double checks: "Are you sure? Don't you want to touch the material first or try a few others?"

"Nah, it's cool. I trust your choice." Or rather, Daniel can't be bothered to care.

A little disappointed by the lack of feedback, Sirvi orders the outfit. "It will be ready in half an hour. Would you like something else?"

"I guess some underwear and socks and stuff..."

"Just for your information, the sneakers' interior surface is made from a living fungus that immediately metabolizes your sweat." Surprised by his micro-mimical expression of disgust, Sirvi adds and extra explanation: "Most people wear them without socks."

Socks are the only thing Daniel actually enjoys shopping for "I'd still like some. Get me two pairs, something colorful, with animals."

Feeling experimental, she offers him green ones with a red parrot eating a cookie, and blue ones with a seal wearing a bunny costume.

"Excellent, I'm starting to like you, Sirvi! Done deal!"

"Are you sure you don't want a second set?" She is already adjusting her personality model, excited to have something to hold on to.

Good socks always help with Daniel's shopping patience: "Make another suggestion then."

Sirvi goes with the second most frequent image of him that she can find. His mirror image is now wearing a full body duckling costume.

"Um, how on earth did you come up with that suggestion?"

Sirvi is taken aback: "I thought... You were wearing animal costumes in thirty-four percent of all pictures, especially those on the Oxford University Server."

Daniel starts laughing. The Oxford University Server – those must have been Willi's photos, at their student house parties he'd always show up with his camera just at the most undignified moment.

Sirvi nudges him to get a little more data: "I can also show you visualizations of what you would look like in those clothes in various scenarios."

"What kind of scenarios?"

"Whatever you like, really." Visualisations are easy for her.

"What about pole dancing on a streetlight in that duckling costume at the love parade in Berlin 1989?"

The sunglasses get darker and start projecting the scene. Oh, how he loves the hairstyles. Yes, that would have been a good fit for the duckling costume, but then, no, he's not going to buy one for his upcoming trip.

"Can you get me into that other outfit again? And put me

into another scene... What would I look like in that outfit performing the famous Dirty Dancing jump?" Daniel takes Jennifer Grey's role and looks just fabulous, but... "Can you make the pants a bit less... I don't know..."

Sirvi softens the color scheme and makes them a little wider. While he watches himself dance, she also takes note of his smile, and adjusts a couple of fractal exponents in the twenty three dimensional manifold representing his gender identity accordingly.

"Yes, better. OK, we're done here." His coffee is empty, and Daniel is getting ready to go back to his room, then remembering the most basic item needed when hitting the road. "And add a towel, please."

———

WWW.*LIQUID-REIGN*.COM/*SOURCES-OF-INSPIRATION#18*
A new textiles economy: Redesigning fashion's future
The Future of Clothing and the sources mentioned therein
Fungal Clothing
The jump in 'Time of my life'
Disney's Magic Bench

19

MISSION BRIEFING

Ana is just getting out of her micro-biotic programming lab class. It's not her favorite subject, and her thesis advisor recommended dropping it, but she's sticking around anyway. For the fun classmates, mostly. And especially for that teaching assistant, Phil.

They'd been playing around with the red-dot design virus all day long. It's a popular model organism as it can infect humans, but is completely harmless, the infection leaves nothing worse than a red dot on the nose for a few days. Phil is majoring in genetic coding, and if his thesis is successful, he'll be able to adjust the incubation period of the virus at will. She helped him out with the algorithms to reverse engineer a complex protein last week, and in return he showed her how to handle the actual virus in the lab today. But most importantly, he touched her hand a bit more frequently than necessary when handing over the petri dishes. So she took a chance and asked him out for acai later tonight. Three hours from now. That gives her about two and a half in her VR suit.

Message from Daniel: "Ciao Ana. Listen, I'll get out of the hospital tomorrow morning, so I'll be spending less time on Confedwars."

Ana opens a voice channel: "Congratulations on your recovery! What's next?"

"Finding my wife. Our mutual friends say she's hooked on hyperstim and lost in some virtual world, but I have a physical address in Nevada, so I'm going there first."

"You're going on a mission looking for your girl? That's so romantic!" It took Ana a moment to realize what he just said: "Oh shit, hyperstim is dangerous! I wish you all the best, both of you. Let me know if there's anything I can do..."

"I don't know. The only info I have is this address. "He unfolds the paper scrap and reads it off: " 15 Hemlock St, Gerlach, Nevada. And her full name is Helen Milhon."

Her mind is racing, she can't believe it. So her bunny prince connected her to a guy who not only can get her a new Afrin visa, he's also the husband of her childhood heroine. At the same time Ana feels even more terrible about the fact that the bunny prince brought her Daniel now, so she just says: "I can try looking for her in Galaxycraft if you want. Most hyperstim addicts end up there sooner or later."

"That would be really nice of you. Well then, Ana, I'll be in touch. Thanks for everything."

"Let's talk soon, Daniel!" As soon the voice channel shuts down, Ana places a large heap of celery before the bunny prince. Helen! The little creature got her to become friends with the husband of the woman she literally started a fan club for.

"What do you think should I do next? If there were some way I could meet Helen..." The bunny hops up and down a few times, then lets its ears droop. It seems a little insecure, and suggests logging into an outdated version of Galaxy-craft and infiltrating a Pseudonymous archive there. Ana is scared to take them on, Pseudonymous is a real-world integrated spy organization. But if it gets her a chance to meet Helen, she'd do anything, gogogo.

And just as she makes it onto her target planet Shakuras, her alarm goes off – her date with Phil! Well, the spy agency has to wait. She saves her location, logs off, takes a quick shower and gets dressed. Ana keeps her makeup to a minimum, Phil seems like the type of guy who prefers a natural look. He's already waiting at the acai place when she gets there.

———

WWW.LIQUID-REIGN.COM/SOURCES-OF-INSPIRATION#19

Jude Milhon
Anonymous

20

GOODBYES

H arry knocks on Daniel's door. The two men eat together in silence, both aware that it's their last supper. "Thank you Harry. You..." Daniel stops mid-sentence, overwhelmed by a wave of affection.

Letting go of your patients after building an emotional connection is part of a nurse's life – but this one is tougher than the others. Harry gets up and hugs Daniel. "Let's stay in touch." Not recommended according to his job training, but who cares. They stand there a while longer, watching the sunset. "Gotta go." He swallows the lump in his throat and turns to the door. "And good luck!"

Time to sleep now, but Daniel's jittery, tossing around in his bed for another two hours. He gives up and gets back into the IA suit. He browses his home screen settings – there are thousands of design themes available. He picks an elven forest theme. Sirvi is no longer a disembodied voice, but a long-eared huntress in a white silk robe carrying a bow.

Still wide awake, Daniel asks Sirvi: "Could you give me a summary of the press reports on my accident?"

"The taxi was hit by a truck from the side. The driver was dead at the scene, Helen had a severe concussion and several broken bones. You had a cranial fracture and were unconscious. The truck driver had a blood concentration of two milligrams of cocaine per liter." After a short pause Sirvi adds, "That is a lot."

"Is the driver still alive?" Daniel wants to know it all now. "Tell me everything about him."

"His name was John Kislikov, a US citizen." Sirvi finds very little info on him in the archives. "He had put up the 100'000 EUR bail and was never seen again. Here is a collection of all the contemporary news stories I could find." A pile of newspapers appears on the grass.

Daniel browses them for a while, but other than a lot of empathy and praise for what a promising couple of young academics they were, no relevant information beyond what Sirvi already told him. The reading does make him sleepy though, so he logs out and goes back to bed.

Standing outside the Sorbonne's back door, in the rain. Helen is right there, just a few meters away, wearing a military uniform, staring straight at him. He tries to walk towards her, but can't move. The rain behind her starts to glow, and a fantastic crystal appears, flying straight towards her. It hits her, a sudden flash of light, loud crack and deafening bang. It's all black now, apart from the Immersive Arts logo slowly turning in front of him. Panic rises up in his gut – how long will it take to wake up?

Not that long this time. He opens his eyes, soaked in sweat just minutes before Claire arrives and they leave for the harbor. The ferry is a 150-meter catamaran towed out of the harbor by a giant paraglider-shaped sail. Daniel and Claire stand on the forward deck, the sky intensely blue, a strong breeze pushing the craft forward, leaving the Hawaiian islands behind. A swarm of flying fish frolics around the boat.

They spend the first day and the better part of the night on the ferry with extensive theoretical conversations on details of the global voting system, entirely irrelevant to the story. This conversation is wrapped up in an interludium.

21

INTERLUDIUM - HOW, WHO, WHAT AND WHY

Daniel is gearing up for a theoretical deep dive: "You need to give me a short rundown of how that works... Who votes how for whom, and why? And what votes do you have, what do you do with them? How often do you vote?"

"Hey, slow down young man. Who – that would be everyone. At least everyone with a registered TrueName in an Afrin state, so most of the world population. Exceptions are people born in the Confederate States, Texas, The Holy State of Christ, Zimbabwe, the Kalifat, Switzerland, Venezuela and a couple of Arab countries."

"Switzerland?"

Claire rolls her eyes. "They still stand in the public square and raise their hands to vote."

"Oh."

"OK, I admit, that's only some rural cantons – the cities

actually use democracy tech, but they just choose to stay outside of Afrin."

"But you won't be just raising hands tomorrow?"

"We might. With only a handful of people in the same room, raising hands is a decent voting method. It just doesn't scale that well – the group at the meeting will represent well over five billion people's votes on VR regulation."

"How do you handle being a global political functionary while also running a hospital?"

"It's not as bad as it sounds - I try to keep my workload below 50 hours per week. I mean, I've got around two hundred million base voters to represent, but I also get a lot of support from high-level aggregators who forward delegate those votes to me. They do all the work of finding good compromise strategies among our base voters, while I focus on negotiating with high-level delegates from different bases. It's normally just a few days per month for politics, just recently there was so much to do." Recently is a stretch, it's been more than a year since their last proper holiday. "Next question, please."

"Who are those base voters?"

Claire takes a deep breath. Daniel was a demanding teacher back in the day, but he's even more exhausting as a student: "VR regulation is part of the regenerative medicine package, that's where I get most of my votes from."

"So you represent patients, doctors, nurses?"

"Mostly, yes. And they get delegations from base voters, so the people who are friends with doctors and nurses or know a former patient and have forward-delegated the medical package on to them. I was one of the first to systematically apply and research neurostimulation for regenerative medicine, so I ended up as the top representative among the professionals. But as I said, we have a flat hierarchy, and while I represent a large group in the negotiations, most of the work is done by my core delegatees."

"Can you give me an example of a core delegatee?"

"My dear friend Olola, the African nurses' union representative, is the largest single one. She alone delegates a thirty million votes to me. I have a total 4% of the global vote. Zhiu has well over 14%. So both of us are representatives on the global proposal forum."

"What's a proposal forum?"

"For every cluster of topics there's a series of forums. The basic forum is completely open, but the higher ones are read-only, unless you have a certain number of discussion votes. For the meeting we're just heading to, the limit is 100 million votes."

"Just like in frog control, I see. Why is that, actually?"

"It's called a troll wall. In the lower forums a lot of people talk a lot of crap. Like really a lot. And certain character types tend to turn every discussion into a shouting match. To get a more nuanced conversation, publishing rights for higher forums are restricted. The ten-vote forum is still full of spam and flaming, but from the thousand votes minimum forum upwards most of the discourse is substantial and serious. The core of my political agenda originates in those mid-tier forums."

"So people can still write in the forum even after they delegate their discussion rights to you?"

"Exactly. You just lose one level when you delegate, so if you delegate a hundred votes to me, you can't post in the 100-vote threshold forum anymore, but still in the 10-vote threshold forum."

Daniel looks at his hands: "And there we have yet another institutional design resulting directly from the shape of our ancestral mammals' two five-fingered extremities..."

Claire laughs: "I guess so. No other reason why it's ten per level and not nine or eleven."

"What's the pathway of your 200 million votes? Do they come directly from individuals or via other proxies?"

"The vast majority of them come via other proxies. On average, a vote is delegated four times before I get it. Unlike Zhiu – she has eighty percent of her votes from Chinese default voters, and the rest from therapy patients. Her therapy bots are among the most effective ones out there."

"What are default voters?"

"A Chinese thing. On Hawaii, you delegate along with your friends' votes by default, but the Chinese elect a group of core deciders, who then get to define the default delegations. Zhiu is currently the Chinese default voting choice for global regulations on neurostim addiction."

"Who else will be at the meeting?"

"Delegates representing users, producers and modders, three aggregation bots with a weird mix of voters, and of course, Sidana Witus."

"So what's an aggregation bot?"

"They trawl the lower discussion forums for voters and try to compute a so-called 'perfect king' solution. It's considered one of the toughest problems in modern day EI research."

"I see. And Sidana Witus?"

"You've probably heard her sound before, it plays in the hospital elevator all the time. She's an international pop star, twenty six years old. Her partner had an exotic neurodegenerative condition, and though he was cured two years ago, in the process he got hooked on hyperstim. She's been writing songs about the whole thing for years, and ever since she did the soundtrack for 'Just Once More', a great movie by the way, she has a hell of a lot of voters, and millions of them direct. Exceptional."

"You mean, exceptional to have millions of direct votes?"

"Absolutely. I'd never vote for anyone who doesn't know me personally. Even with the younger generation, where normally nobody votes for superstars, everyone loves Sidana. Obviously because she knows so much about hyperstim addiction, and it certainly isn't about her having a halfway decent voice, being young, pretty and hyped by a marketing agency." Claire shakes her head and sighs.

"So she has no clue what she's talking about?"

"No, sorry, that was just me being facetious. She holds 17%, and well, I actually enjoy her being there to some degree, her inputs are OK, but still. Superstar voting should be a thing of the past. She doesn't have major delegatees, she even pays people to do the grunt work for her. Superstar voting flips everything upside down: while I get paid and technically supported by the people who vote for me, she first gets the direct vote, and then uses those to down-dele-gate parts of her decisions to staffers. That setup just doesn't make any sense for a politician, I mean, her support staff works for her, while she should be working for them. I think she will vote with us on the fee proposal we've been working on, but still. It's just wrong. No one should ever vote for a person who is not their personal friend."

"But people do vote for bots in the senate? How are those personal friends?"

"Well, there's always a human being behind the account - don't forget, the voting ledger is directly linked to the True-Name ledger, so every node in the voting delegation network always represents exactly one unique human being. It's complicated, with multiple levels of EIs inter-acting with each other and people are friends with EIs, too. And then we're not quite a senate either, as we only deal with one topic. There's still the regular Hawaiian senate, and we vote them into office using slips of paper. They're our backup plan, the paper senate still has veto rights on every law passed. Better safe than sorry. Speaking of sorry, Daniel, I'd love to give you a longer political lesson, but I really need to get some work done. It's late, and I'm still terribly unprepared for tomorrow..."

"Oh, but just one more minute - please...?" It's an old joke between them. Back when Daniel was her PhD supervisor, every single one of their monthly, supposedly hour-long meetings were serially prolonged by those words, except that then it was Claire asking, and Daniel who was showing up unprepared at the next day's appointments after talking with her all night.

Claire just sighs. No way she can refuse. "The famous one-more-minute? Maybe we should get some food then..." They sit down at a table right next to the railing. "Salad of the day for me."

"Me too." Their food arrives a few minutes later.

Daniel picks up the conversation where they left it: "So that paper parliament you mentioned - they can veto a law if it's against the constitution?"

"No. It's more like, if there's any reasonable doubt about the voting mechanism."

"Did that ever happen?"

"Yes." Claire looks out at the horizon. "The one time it was used on the global level was in 2038, during the transition to post-singularity computing. The explosion of computational power over such a short time period opened up a way to exploit the most commonly used anonymisation function. Helen was living in Liberia at the time, taking care of her parents. And also investigating a push by a major political group in West Africa to introduce a bill removing the perfect financial transparency of elected officials. That's when she discovered the bug. By the time the ECOWAS paper parliament was convinced there'd been foul play, half a billion fake votes were cast for removal of transparency regulations."

"And then?"

"We rolled back the entire previous year's global political activity, restored the state of laws and regulations from a backup and re-booted the political process with a fixed anonymisation function. Afterwards, only a few million real votes against financial transparency were left. Post-singularity was a time when everybody was scared of the global robocalypse..."

Daniel finishes her sentence by quoting Helen: "The forces of centralization thrive in fear."

"Exactly. People accepted a lot more bullshit from power hungry leaders than usual in that period. And those wannabe leaders didn't hesitate to play dirty whenever they got the chance."

"So Helen was a real hero?"

"Yes, for a time. When the bomb hit her parents' place, killing both of them, Helen barely escaped. Actually, she made sure she was listed as having died in the attack, she's been living an underground existence with fake identities ever since."

"What? Didn't anyone stand up for her?"

"Of course, but what can you do? Security in West Africa still isn't tight until the present day..."

Despite his urge to ask more, Daniel decides that this is not the right place or moment to ask more details about Helen's past and returns to the technical talk that got them into this interludium in the first place: "What about those paper parliaments? How do you make sure they haven't been corrupted?"

"Paper voting is very robust, and probably the best backup there has ever been. And then, there is little to gain from buying backup politicians who hardly ever make any decisions." Another sigh. "Can I go now?"

"Just one tiny more minute - pleeease...?" Daniel is trying to mimic the way she used to say that line. Although he's already absorbed more than his fill of information, getting back at her is just too much fun to stop his questioning yet. If he's reading her face right, she's enjoying the role-reversal game as much as he is. "How do you vote on other topics?"

"I've delegated all the categories I really care about to people I know and trust. And then I use a bot to allocate the less important votes - it goes through my message history and my social graph, identifying how people I know and like vote on topics I don't care enough to actively delegate. You are also using it, if you didn't change the default setting."

"So even if I never actively vote, the average of my friends decide on my behalf?"

"It's a bit more complicated than just an average, but in principle yes."

"So there are elections that you don't care about? I have a memory that feels quite recent, and it involves a PhD student sending out at least three online petitions per week over the departmental email list."

"Ha! Right, I did do that. Haven't thought about those days in ages. But all the issues were important. Now that we get to vote on everything, there's a lot of clutter out there. I couldn't care less about the exact rules for decision making on euthanizing dementia patients in polyamorous marriage contracts... Fortunately, we've never had one of those in our coma station. But anyway, even you have to admit that our conversation has now crossed the boundaries of reasonable discourse." That line used to be Daniel's last line of defense to get out of their discussions back in the day.

"No more questions then. Talk tomorrow!"

A brief hug, and Claire heads off to her cabin. The delegatees are getting a little impatient, but they accept her apologies once she explains who Daniel is and what he means to her: "So, about calibrating the fee level according to the addictiveness index..." The discussions go on until after midnight.

Daniel decides to stay on deck a little longer, watching the ocean and letting his mind wander, occasionally sipping mint tea. His thoughts circle for hours around paper senates, vetos, revolutions and reforms. There is a multitude of options that could bring about a major shift in the principles of political organization. Even small, imperfect and local versions of the software Claire just described to him could enable decentralized collective decision making, providing immediate benefits to anyone who adopted it. The primary tenet of evolutionary-utopian thought is thus fulfilled. The reverie on deck extends well into the evening, the breeze getting more intense and cooling down. He orders tomato soup for dinner. Bad idea, the waves are getting bigger, and he ends up spilling half of it over his pants.

———

WWW.LIQUID-REIGN.COM/SOURCES-OF-INSPIRATION#21

The same old list from chapter 2 and 3. Then also this:

Swiss manual Voting

SAM, the vote aggregation bot from New Zealand
Meaningful online petitions

PART II

EXPLORATIONS

22

HOLY UNIONS

B ack in his room Daniel cleans up the mess on his pants and lies down. After another hour of restlessly trying to wrap his head around the concepts and implications of what he's learned today, his thoughts wander back to Helen. Not that this line of thinking is any easier – it just plain doesn't make sense. She was never an addictive personality of any sort. And if she insists she found purpose in what she did, it's most likely because there is a very serious project that happens to require her hunting down giant insects while frying her brain with a neurostimulator. Or at least that's what he'd like to believe. Maybe talking to Zhiu can clear this up. Tomorrow. Time to sleep.

Turns out to be harder than expected, memories and speculation about her story keep him wide awake. At some point he decides to dive in for another session. Back into the IA suit next to the bed... Login.

He finds himself on his new home screen, a forest clearing with some megaliths standing around in the middle. Sirvi, wearing her elven huntress avatar, is sitting on a rock and sharpening her arrows. A unicorn grazes peacefully in the background. Oh, a letter-owl! The insignia says: "New Message from William S. Bortovski." Willi!

"Hello Daniel, you are awake?!?! Claire sent me the news! Oh god, if I could just hop on a plane and come over. But no, they will not let me, I am a convicted supporter of a terrorist organization and I am not allowed to go to North America for life. We have been in Greenland shooting a film on the first polar bears born outside a zoo in over a decade – unbelievably cute, the rehabilitation is a full success. On my way home now. The connection is too weak up here for a proper VR meeting, but I will be back at civilization in a few days... Are you coming to Europe maybe sometime? Oh man, unbelievable that you are back! This is the best of all news in thirty five years!

Peace and love

Willi"

Daniel replies: "Willi! I see that age hasn't slowed you down." A floating goose feather writing on a parchment roll as he dictates the words. "Sorry I didn't write before. My wake-up call came with a few challenges as you can imagine. Claire had me stuffed into one of those brainfuck VR neurostimulation suits, so I've ended up spending most of my new life gaming. But that Confedwars is a hell of a game, I must say.

I get to California tomorrow and then on to Nevada, trying to find Helen. Not sure what's up next, but let me know as soon as you've got a decent connection, and let's meet up in VR.

Monsterhug,

Daniel"

The parchment rolls up, a seal confirms secure encryption and the owl grips the tube firmly, soaring high into the sky. Sent.

And he's got an invite to Claire's home screen, accepts, and materializes next to a surf shack on a beach of black volcanic rock, big waves breaking just outside the bay. A cool breeze is blowing as he picks up the surfboard. Claire has already paddled out, and as he catches up with her just behind the breaking point, he calls over: "You mentioned Helen had a therapist, could you tell me something about her?"

Oh, right, he doesn't even know! "Yes, Zhiu. She's my wife." She smiles at his astonished face, stands up and catches a wave.

Daniel has a hard time catching up with her: "You're married?! C'mon, tell me about the lucky one, how did you meet and..."

Claire paddles out a little faster as she says: "Zhiu, she's just so amazing..."

"Who'd have thought such a thing, you find your partner is amazing! Come on. Details please. What makes her so great that she managed to convince you of all people to enter such a..." Daniel tries to remember the exact words Claire had used to describe marriage back in the day, "tormenting instrument of suppression, dating to the darkest origins of our species?"

Ah, he's pushing Claire's buttons again, as usual. "Where do I beginn? Guilty as charged, I did change my mind on that matter - in my defense, though, it was Zhiu who proposed.

And the whole concept of marriage is not quite what it used to be."

Daniel tilts his head: "Then what is it now?"

"Marriage is the name of a standardized contract bundle arranging certain affairs between two or more adults." Her mind goes back to when they spontaneously signed it, on a sunny day, while swimming naked with river dolphins in the Yang Tse. "It gives each of us a 'better half' key to the other's OS. And of course some practical consequences arise from that, like the power to decide over life and death if one of us were in a coma or incapable of making decisions, just as Helen held that power over you. Apart from the name, there's not much resemblance to the aforementioned tormenting institution."

Daniel's caught up with her now, his virtual surfboard right next to hers: "And who is this unfathomable Zhiu, and why did she propose entering this popular civil union contract bundle with you?"

"Zhiu is a true political genius, she always gets what she wants, meanwhile our opponents don't even know they gave something up. She debates just like the Tai Chi master she actually is." Claire flips over on her back as she continues talking, looking at the clouds. "She grew up out in the country, in Whuang Xing." Short pause. "Right, you haven't heard that name before. The site of the first major nuclear accident in China. She was 23 when it hit, she'd just finished her psychiatric nurse's training. And like so many others, she kept drinking the water for days. Diagnosed with a brain tumor three months later."

Daniel is shocked and doesn't know how to follow up and can only come up with: "When was that?"

"The accident was in 2030. Don't worry, she's fine. She just has to do monthly scans for early detection in case it comes back, those take barely ten minutes. With the exception of leukemia, cancer is pretty much under control. Obviously she also shouldn't get pregnant - no space for kids in our lives in the foreseeable future anyway." Or is there, maybe? Last night she had dreamed of herself being pregnant. Maybe they should re-arrange their workload sometime soon... "We've been married for six years now."

"And where did you meet?"

"At the very first meeting of the committee we're speeding towards right now. She's a world-class therapist for neurostimulation addicts." She smiles at the thought of seeing her very soon.

"Will she be coming to California?"

"Let me give her a ring. Connect to Zhiu... Zhiu? Hey. Just wanted to check in - when do you get to Sacramento?"

Zhiu is just changing from the ferry to the train in Anchorage and replies via a voice only line: "Namaste my little red panda! I'll be there tomorrow morning, just landed in Alaska. Love you!"

"Great my jedi honeybadger. Yes and we'll get there about the same time. You too!" There is also an attachment with more work... So Claire excuses herself and Daniel returns to his homescreen.

———

WWW.LIQUID-REIGN.COM/SOURCES-OF-INSPIRATION#22

River Dolphins
Polar Babies
Red Pandas
Honey Badgers

23

FACING THE DEMON

OK, it's exploration time! Since Daniel left the hospital's firewall behind, there are lots of options beyond Confedwars. "Sirvi, could you give me a list of award-winning single player experiences?"

"Sure, here you go. This is your personal Top-Ten Single Short Games list." Sirvi feels it's time to share her struggle with her human, and excuses herself: "I don't have quite enough information about your gaming preferences yet, so it's more a list of global hits, with only a little input from your friends' recommendations and your messaging history."

Daniel reacts suspiciously: "What information about my gaming preferences do you mean?"

"Well, I know which Confedwars scenes you played and how much you enjoyed them, but that's not enough information to make a global prediction on your taste across all game categories."

"That sounds awfully like a personalized ad. Who else has

access to that information?" Daniel feels eerily reminded of his past.

"Your friend Ana Mancini has some of it, as you have played many games together."

"Just Ana and nobody else? Whose hardware are you using to create those recommendations?"

"I run on the chip in your ear, and if need to, I occasionally make use of the computational power of the interplanetary file system." Sirvi had not paid intention to another piece of information - Daniel's old Firefox profile had a dozen different privacy plugins installed. She calms him by adding "It is all secured with your private keys, so only you and me can access it." Then she pulls out a magic wand, spins it around and a cloud of sparkly stars shoots out into the trees. The sparks burn a circular hole in the trunk of a giant oak right in front of her human.

Daniel takes a closer look, he sees the game trailers running inside. The first one is a Zombie-Virus-Horror game in a hospital setting "Sorry, but that's a terrible recommendation. Yes, I met a woman who acted like a zombie in a hospital recently, but it doesn't mean I'm interested in zombies. Not to put too fine a point on it, but I don't like them at all."

"Sorry, OK, I will take that into account... one moment..." Her next recommendation is True Solider, by Cutter Hodierne. Stylized picture of a machine gun is the only logo. Awards from veterans' organizations and even from Barak Obama: "I've never seen a more realistic portrait of war."

Daniel is baffled: "Did you derive this recommendation from my following Obama on Twitter?"

"Yes, partially." But the most important information for Srivi was the five star recommendation by Ana.

Action 2 of 10, Thrill, 9 of 10, Exploration 0 of 10, Realism 10 of 10, Sex 2 of 10, Altered States 4 of 10. The last two categories are news to Daniel, they must have been zero for the medically approved games he's tried so far. Price: 0.05 f¢ per minute for the first hour, no further subsequent costs. Additional donations welcome.

Start. Select difficulty - there are only two options, easy (male) and hard (female). He opts for the easy version. Trigger Warning: This game includes scenes of sexual violence.

Daniel is overwhelmed with the graphics - the entire game uses interpolated rotoscope filter, the movements are as realistic as in Confedwars, but give the impression of being manually drawn with a pen, creating a dreamlike, hallucinatory quality.

Three teenagers sitting around a table, playing dice with a bottle of vodka. Daniel picks Rick, the pretty blondie, rather than the black athlete (Kayne) or the Asian guy with glasses (Yii). So much for American cliché identity representation. He enters the body and starts with a pair of dice in his hands. He roles a five and a three.

Kayne: "Outta luck, huh?" and pours him a shot. The game is fast-paced and the bottle empties quickly. Yii checks his watch, "Let's go, the band is starting!" Daniel gets up, and wow, altered states 4 of 10 is pretty real. He has a hard time standing up straight and lurches towards the door. Cut.

The next scene is at a party, electro punk band, the club full of teenagers dancing. The virtual alcohol distorts his vision and movements, and even his thinking is not quite clear -

making him want to test out how far this will go. He keeps drinking. The scene starts to get heavily blurred, and he's not sure if this was another cut or if he just missed how she got there, but there's a girl on his lap, kissing him. In a taxi. And now, a real cut, they're in her bedroom and she's undressing. The virtual sex feels physically real, but remains emotionally distant, like jerking off on porn while drunk. It still is an orgasm though, his first since waking up, and he sinks back into relaxation. Cut.

He silently thanks the developers for the slight lack of realism here - he's fully sober again and the neurostim designers refrained from simulating a virtual hangover. Daniel and the two other guys are standing at the side of a classic suburban America residential road. The girl's there with him, holding his hand, just like Kayne's and Yii's girl-friends are. A troop transporter drives towards them, stops. Good-bye kisses as they get in. The transporter is filled with other young recruits, none of them over twenty five. Cut.

Training grounds, shooting, running, shouting "Sir, yes, Sir!" a couple of times. Yii and Kayne are his team, and good sports, especially Kayne. Climbing on a sandstone cliff during a downpour, Daniel slips, it's a long way down. But Kayne grabs him by his forearm. Deep gratitude, and cut. The game moves right along.

The next scene is only a few seconds long and passive, in an aircraft full of young men in uniforms. Cut.

In a humvee, Daniel, Kayne, Yii and an officer. Assault rifles slung over their shoulders, full body armor.

Officer: "It's nice and quiet, this should be a walk in the park. Ready, go!" Shimmering heat and dust in the air limit visibility, the village ahead is dead silent. Until now.

Gunshot, the officer goes down, another shot, Yii on his knees. Daniel spots the muzzle flash in a doorway, screams and opens fire. Kayne adds a few bullets, and it seems like they found their target. Silence again, only a ringing in his ears. They move to the doorway and check out the assassin.

The boy is no more than eight years old, gunshot wounds on his forehead, his cheek and all over his body. The child-body still holds an AK47 in tight embrace. For a few seconds, the only movement created by the unsteady roto-scopic graphic effects, the outlines the dead body are constantly shifting.

Yii's voice disrupts the scene: "Guys, I'm wounded, let's get out of here!" They help Yii back to the humvee, he's been hit in the thigh and fasten the dead officer's body in the cargo. Kayne is driving, Daniel bandages Yii's wound in the back. Sudden flash of light, jarring crack and a deafening bang. He falls into the dark, consciousness receding. And cut just before he enters the void.

A field hospital, he's in pain. A lot of pain, in his right leg. He tries to get up, but a nurse pushes him gently back into his bed. "Sir, don't move. We are trying to save your leg, but you need to stay down and stop moving. That IED blew up your vehicle, it's a miracle you're still alive." Daniel lies back, shivering again, and cramping up in pain. The nurse takes his hand and pushes his sleeve up. Needle jab in the vein. Warmth, relaxation, the pain is gone. Cut.

In a troop transport aircraft again, and the pain is back, in his left leg. Daniel looks around. Where's Kayne? And Yii? But he's surrounded by unknown faces, all staring dully into space. He turns around, and there, a few seats back, it's Yii. Daniel waves at him, and he waves back - with a stump. Cut.

Funeral. Flag over the coffin, someone singing the national anthem. Julie, Kayne's girlfriend, all in black, throws the first shovelful of dirt down onto the coffin, Daniel's next. Yii struggles to hold the shovel with his one remaining hand, and Kayne's dad helps him out. Cut again.

Daniel's back in suburbia again, holding a wrinkled picture of his girlfriend, an address written on the back, Park Avenue Drive 318, that's right here. He hobbles to the door, rings. She's home, hugs him, kisses, Cut to the bedroom, she holds him in her arms, comforts his head, but the pain in his leg overshadows everything. His attention is drawn to a pillbox on the bedside table - Fentanyl. He takes one. Cut, to black, a text in his field of vision says "One year later".

The middle of the night in Iraq, Daniel's roaming a village. There, the boy with the AK47, right in front of him, out of nowhere. His forehead and cheek wounds bleeding, the boy readies his gun. Daniel has no weapon, so he just punches him in the face. Scream. Daniel is confused. That was a match cut, the lines around the face reshaped and formed his girlfriend's face. "Wake up! You asshole! You just broke my fucking nose, I can't stand this any longer! It's the third time this month, I don't care if you're sleepwalking, this is too much!" Tears, a resounding slap in his face, and she's gone. Cut.

A small, dirty kitchen. Daniel's alone, his leg hurts like hell again. There's an empty pill box on the table, next to it a folded paper bag, with two no-name pink pills. His eyes fall on an official looking letter on the table - foreclosure notice, unpaid rent. Just as he understands what he's seeing, he hears police knocking on the door. He slips the two pills in his pocket and goes out the back door. Outside, lost in suburbia, Daniel limps through the pouring rain. Digging around in his pocket, he finds a couple of photos, including one of his dead fellow soldier's girlfriend, with her name and address scribbled on the back. Julie lives a few blocks further down on the same road. As he stumbles down the road in the rain, the pain gets worse with every step. When he finally finds her house, no one's home, so he sits on the bench in front, then stretches out.

Exhaustion overwhelms him the moment he lies down, and here goes another dream. The same dark village scene, this time Daniel just stands still, watching the zombie boy take aim at him and shoot.

He wakes up screaming. He's got to tell Sirvi. No games with zombies or anything like that ever again! But the game's rapid pace keeps going, so he keeps playing along. Julie's found him. "Oh my god, you scared me. What the hell's the matter with you? Come inside, solider." He gets up, shuffles through the door, every step feels like a thousand glowing needles jabbing his leg. Julie hands him a coffee and he downs the pills: "You look like you need a hot shower. Here, take a towel." The shower feels great, and the pills start to kick in, relaxation. But not just that - the pink street pills have a very different effect. For a moment he feels strongly overwhelmed by sexual desire, then his senses start to blur again as he steps out of the shower. He tries to put his clothes back on, but loses control of his movements. Daniel watches his avatar walk back into the living room from third person point of view, where Julie's on the sofa, her back turned to him. She tries to resist, but fails. Cut.

Police again. Julie's clothes are torn, she is crying. Points at him. Arrest, and cut again. In a courtroom, the judge: "The accused has the last word - Is there anything more you wish to say in your defense?"

"Only that I am deeply sorry." He gets away with just three years. Cut to a prison cell. The pain is back, worse than ever. Cut to the nightmare with the boy. Cut. Cell. Cut. A prisoner hits him in the face, more pain. Cut. Cell again. No cut, just sitting there, all alone, in an empty cell for a long time. Is this the end of the game now? Nothing happens, and just as Daniel gets nervous and wonders if he should tap out, cut again. Julie, naked, the zombie boy fires. Kayne stands in front of him, hits him in the face. Cut. Another prisoner hands him an envelope full of pink pills. Cut. The sequence of cuts goes faster and faster, until the last cut brings him back to his empty cell, alone. He sits there for another minute until the door swings open.

The road outside the prison is empty, snow falling. Not a human soul anywhere. Daniel limps down the road, pain in his leg. Will this nightmare ever come to an end? He passes by an empty apartment complex, there's light upstairs, looks like a fireplace. Daniel limps up the stairs, and finds three homeless guys sleeping around the burning remains of some furniture. Daniel pulls back the hood of one of the guys, and it's Yii. He grabs his arm, shakes him, but no reaction. Touching his face, it's ice cold. Daniel breaks down and starts crying.

This game is getting to him, he just wants it to be over. But again his curiosity stops him from tapping out. He sees the bag next to Yii's body - needles, syringe, and a little lump of heroin. Well, that looks like a way out. The shot is even better than the one at the hospital, all the pain is gone, and Daniel flows into a state of deep relaxation, warmth, and happiness. Cut.

But it's not game over, not yet. Hungry, in more pain than ever, cold, and on the street again. He's standing in front of a hospital. The nurse takes him to a back room, shows him his results. Of course, HIV positive, what else. "Veterans benefits will pay for the basic pills, but the latest medication would cost $20'000 per month, I'm afraid. Here you go." She hands him some pills. Cut.

Dying scene, finally, he's lying in a back yard, squeezed in between garbage containers. His entire consciousness is filled with only one sensation: Cold. But then his vision starts to float up from his body, and the cold seems distant. Light takes over, and with it comes deep gratification. Fade to white, and warm schmoozy piano music starts to play.

Credits: "Any resemblance to actual persons, living or dead, is entirely coincidental. Yet the elements of the story are 100% based on true stories told by veterans of the Iraq war and their families. True Soldier II - The Abdulahs, telling the story of the Iraqi boy's family, will be released in 2052. There is a trailer, but Daniel doesn't feel ready to open it.

So much for a quick round before bed - that was intense. He's shivering and covered in cold sweat, takes a shower. And notices the clock - 3:37 AM. Now that was a normal, legal game, without hyperstimulation, and only 4 out of 10 for altered states, and a mere 2 for the sex.

He can't formulate a clear thought and tries to just close his eyes and sleep. Which is not happening. Turning back and forth, sweating. He even starts to hear weird noises every time he moves around in bed. "Sirvi, am I hallucinating or is there really a noise whenever I turn my head?"

That is interesting. Sirvi figures that Daniel is aware of an in-between phase between dream and wakefulness, but uncertain of his hallucinations. Sirvi didn't realize humans know such a state of consciousness, and posts a comment in the self-improvement EI Github on dream science. In Daniel's case, there's a simpler explanation though: "I'm sorry, I'm still calibrating the pillow. Is it comfortable now?" She is improvising here - the smart pillow's pressure sensors are miserably low res and its application interface is old and clunky.

"Yes, it's fine now." Daniel turns over onto his back, "Or no, it would be nice if you could make it a little thinner and softer. Now it's perfect." Finally, sleep.

Daniel finds himself on the beach in Hawaii, dancing, Vany's there, too. But there, that's the rotoscopic zombie child with the AK-47 shooting into the crowd, Vany falls. Cut. Helen, naked, standing, with her eyes closed, the background pitch black. Sudden flash of light, jarring crack and a deafening bang. He's awake again, sitting upright in his bed, covered in cold sweat. It's 6:30 AM now, a purple sunrise shining into his window. "Sirvi, I told you I don't like zombies in games. That was horrible."

Sirvi is confused. TrueSolider does not feature zombies. She tries to understand the remark, while going through the scenes of the game. "Are you referring to the dream scenes with the dead child?"

"Yes. Can you keep that kind of stuff like that out of future recommendations, please? No horror, nothing like that."

Sirvi leaves a review with a trigger warning for people with zombiephobia for the game. Then she checks the Github self-improvement community again, and it has already picked up her suggestion. She upgrades herself with the alpha version of the new half-awake plugin and starts counting, one, two... three hundred thousand five hundred thirty six, three hundred thousand five hundred thirty seven... And well before the eight billionth electric sheep jumps the fence, she enters dream state, and sees Daniel's reaction to game after game. She also dreams of a car crash, over and over again. Now she stands on a boat, surrounded by a hoard of hamsters, struggling to wake up again. When she finally makes it back to regular consciousness, Sirvi files a bug report on the Github dream engine forum.

———

WWW.*LIQUID-REIGN*.COM/SOURCES-OF-INSPIRATION#*23*

The Privacy Badger and all his friends out there
Interpolated Rotoscope Effects
This War of Mine
Purdue Pharma, the profiteers behind Fentanyl
My purple sunrise soundtrack while writing this book
Dreaming EIs
Elemiah the Robot counting grains of sand in a desert and stars in the sky

24

THE INTERFACE

"What's wrong with you? Seasick? Better buck up, the waves will only be bigger today." Claire is giving him the once-over – he looks miserable, pale and shaky.

Daniel is repentant. "Doctor, I must admit, I did succumb to my curiosity and tested the out-of-hospital IA suite last night."

Of course he did. Claire rolls her eyes, then focuses and scolds him in her most serious medical voice. "Don't act like a child. Even legal stimulation levels can be overwhelming for patients recovering from a long-term coma. You're playing with fire."

"I'm sorry." Daniel feels stupid. "I couldn't fall asleep and then played True Soldier. "

Claire is relieved. At least he went for an arthouse adventure. "Well, it could be worse. True Solider is not designed to induce addiction. I assume you don't feel like playing it again today, do you?"

Daniel shivers from even thinking about it. "No, certainly not. But tonight in my dream, I mean the real one, in bed, not the game dreams, I saw that zombie-child again, on the beach in Hawaii."

Claire is worried. "If even a mostly harmless game like True Soldier hits you that hard, you are vulnerable."

"Mostly harmless?" Daniel gets goosebumps just thinking of that kid's face.

"It is. I mean it's just like real life in terms of intensity. You're lucky you didn't end up trying Vicious World..." Claire knows Daniel well enough not to raise his curiosity, so she proceeds to describe the most addictive game on the index in more detail. "Vicious World lets you have sex like a porn-star with unlimited orgasms, features all kinds of zero-side-effect drugs, super-hero violence and to top it all off, it comes with a gameplay based on grinding loot and level mechanics."

"Sounds terribly boring." Daniel had always preferred fast-paced stories over open-world explorations. "But True Solider was thrilling, couldn't let go of it." Reflecting on how the game intro screen showed him the various para-meters, he asks: "Why don't you show the addiction risk together with the Action level on the intro screen?"

Claire snickers. "Good question. We never got above 40% approval for making that the default option, resistance from industry and users. You have to activate it yourself to see it. Actually, Sirvi, could you please show the addiction index whenever Daniel loads a game?"

"Daniel, is that OK with you?" Now that Daniel is out of the hospital, Sirvi no longer accepts direct commands from Claire. When he confirms, Sirvi connects directly to Claire's

OS with a list of questions so Sirvi can understand what Claire wants exactly. It takes full access to a lot of private data, along with years of adaptive learning, for an OS's soul to learn how to derive what a specific human wants from you when they say something. Claire's OS sends her a precise and easy-to-understand set of instructions where and how the addiction index should appear.

"Actually, that should be the default for all patients leaving the hospital." Claire's friend and former supervisor is back, and with him her most reliable source of inspiration. "I missed you, Daniel." She doesn't want to lose him again.

A service bot brings them bananas and tea. And thunder - they just sailed into a storm, Daniel rapidly ends up with tea on his pants.

"Handling liquids in a boat is hard, I know." Claire is carefully sipping on her own tea. The waves are getting more intense now, and before she can finish her breakfast, her stomach starts to protest. "I get seasick when the weather is this heavy. I'll go back to my cabin - inner ear neurostim is the best way to handle it. See you later!"

Daniel also goes back and logs in, standing on terra firma in his home meadow again. Wondering what's next, he decides to play with democracy for a bit. "Sirvi, I'd like to vote for Claire on, oh, VR regulation I guess? Or what is that called?"

"I understand VR regulation." But she could learn to understand him a lot better if he did some voting himself initially... "To make sure that I've got it correctly, I suggest you check out your vote allocation matrix." Sirvi draws her bow and shoots an arrow into the meadow. A fairy ring of mushrooms shoots up from the soil around the spot where it lands." Just step into the circle. The portal leads you into Sovereign, the most common democracy interface."

Daniel steps between the fungi, and as darkness falls all around him, he feels weightless, disembodied. A three-dimensional fractal spider web structure appears, glowing in the dark. The nodes of the web are labeled - taxation, fees, education, policing, anti-trust, medicine, environment... Probing it with his hands, he finds that it reacts to all his movements - he can zoom in by pulling it towards him. Testing how deep he can go, he dives all the way into the environment node, where he finds the Master of Frogs vote marked in pink, and the adjacent Lord of the Flies marked pink with a pattern of stars.

Sirvi proactively explains: "Pink stands for Szimo, and the stars mean that he on-delegated your vote. If you tap on one of the stars, you can see who he delegated to."

Daniel touches a star - the Lord of the Flies turns blue, profile picture appears. Sirvi adds: "That is Szimo's friend, an entomology PhD student at the O'ahu University. If you zoom in further, you will see that some parts of that insect-related network of sub-topics still have stars, on-delegated to her friends."

Sirvi still has a hard time guiding Daniel. He is a tough case to grow into as an operating system, sometimes he is so super quick to understand, but yet so slow with other things...: "You can also change the geographical level by moving your hand up and down."

Lifting his hand, Daniel sees his vote allocation for the entire Pacific region. Raising it further, he gets to the global amphibian forum. He lowers it again all the way down to

Szimo - and goes up and down a few more times, the animation is very pretty.

Sirvi steers him towards the next feature: "Tap on a node to open the discussion forum."

Daniel taps. That must be the discussion on the new resort Szimo was talking about. His latest entry is: "Last year on Maui built a resort with building code. Year later, biodiversity gone. Even Koa beetle gone! Building code is good for city, only for city. Not possible to build sustainable luxury resort in forest. The only answer is NO." That is already more than enough local politics for Daniel's taste. Certain that Szimo will handle it just fine on his behalf, Daniel happily withdraws his attention from that boring small-world problem.

Sirvi uses the magic attention-drawing tool to guide him to the budget allocation mechanism. "You control one millionth part of the island budget of O'ahu, approximately 4 f¢ per hour. Do you want to give any of that to Szimo's projects?"

Daniel doesn't really care. "Sure, give it all to him." He navigates on, browsing the global "Medical" node, and dives down into VR regulation. The node is green, without stars. "Green means Claire?"

"Exactly."

He zooms in a bit and finds a number of further connections, including cross-connections to non-medical nodes, education, sports, even religion - a lot of issues seem to interact with Virtual Reality regulations. The green fades out the further away he gets from the core node. The entertainment & sports node has only a slight green shimmer. "Could you give my vote on this node to Ana?"

WWW.LIQUID-REIGN.COM/SOURCES-OF-INSPIRATION#24

The more than 100 years it took the tobacco industry to admit its addictiveness and its sponsorship of fake science
The Sovereign App
Loomio
vTaiwan
Overview Articles (there are far too many more interfaces)

25

OF SECRECY AND POWER

A na's just woken up with a big smile on her face. Closing her eyes again, she mentally goes over the memory. For the hundredth time in the last thirty six hours since their ways parted.

It started out at the acai place, Phil had already picked up two take-away bowls. They went out of town, he wanted to show her his favorite waterfall. They left on her two-wheeler, his arms wrapped tightly around her as he sat behind her. It felt so good, she was ready to drive all the way across the Amazon.

There was a little hut with a blanket, and a fireplace. He made tea on the wood fire, and they ate their acai. Then they went swimming in the little lake below the waterfall - in their underwear. And smoked joints all night long.

He is so special... she never met a Realigan before. Realigans don't use VR, ever, and he has this whole philosophy around 'reality first'. They were talking and talking and talking all the time, she could listen to his voice forever. But then she fell asleep before anything happened, and they rode home together the next morning with huge headaches.

Phil was sad and annoyed that he had to leave her behind - but she understood, this will be a great chance. He got an invitation to present his work in Monte Video. They even paid for his ticket on the early morning train, he went to the station straight from their date.

He was already in the train when Ana gathered all her courage and kissed him goodbye. Their lips touching just for a split second, then the whistle blew, she jumped out just before the doors closed and the train went off to Uruguay.

Ana had spent most of the following day in bed, recovering from a mashed brain hangover and creating an elaborate diary entry. It was harder to reconstruct the experience than for her other entries - she never before had so little data from a date. Actually, this was her first date that didn't involve any online time together. At some point she just logged off and went out to buy a pen and a book, writing a paper diary entry until she fell asleep.

That was yesterday. And as good as the date was, Phil will be away for a couple of days now, and since he doesn't do VR, she won't see him in the meantime. It's high time to fulfil her promise to Daniel and finish that mission in the Pseudonymous archives. Login again... As she arrives at her home screen, she sees a message from Daniel - he voted for her on entertainment. She lets her answering machine reply and dives straight into Galaxycraft, her mind set to solve that riddle around Helen and the Pseudonymous archive.

Daniel gets a message from Ana: "Huhu Daniel! Thanks for the vote!"

It's followed up a second later with a message from Claire: "Thanks for the vote! That's sweet of you!"

Daniel's confused for a moment. He didn't tell either of them about voting for them, which means... "Ciao Claire. It's about time I got some voting done. But I have another question...?"

"We can talk on my home screen if you want?" Claire sends him an invite. At the moment it's a tropical fantasy beach, featuring plenty of palm trees and cute anti-gravity bunnies floating around all over the place.

Daniel materializes in the tea house, a bamboo hut decorated with a pantheon of ancient religious statues from around the world: "I'm just curious..."

Claire allows herself a slightly facetious undertone: "Really, you are curious? Now that is something I would never ever expect of you."

"How come you know I voted for you? Back in the old days anonymity of the vote was considered a core element of any democracy, wasn't it?"

"It's complicated, and we should have discussed the issue in more depth back in the interludium." Claire is trying to keep it as short as she can: "By default, your vote is public and indexed to your main Nym. Our contact is linked to the same Nym that you're using to vote, so I knew the vote came from you."

"Is Nym the same thing as TrueName?"

"Oh, no." OK, this technicality is so important that Claire

has to explain it to him... "You can have several Nyms, and delegate different TrueName functions to them. If you want to have anonymous interactions, you can just create a new Nym for interacting with whoever you're interacting with, or if you want to keep your voting secret, you can create a separate Nym for voting only."

Daniel considers the scenarios for a moment: "Assuming I had a lot of leverage over you, say I'm your PhD supervisor. I could then still coerce you into using your regular Nym for voting and vote for me, couldn't I?"

"You could try... but that would get you into bad legal trouble." She looks up the legal consequences and adds: "In fact, you'd lose your entire wealth and all voting rights for a year. And besides, even PhD supervisors have a lot less power over their students nowadays. Which reminds me, now that you're awake, I could finally submit my thesis..."

Daniel is shocked: "What? You haven't submitted yet?"

Claire turns both her hands upside down in a gesture and looks up to the flying bunnies in the sky. "My supervisor was sick, and I wanted to wait for him to wake up. And then I got busy with other projects and..." She falls silent, turning her face to the side contritely. She never finished writing the summary.

"Well, I look forward to reading it!" He still isn't satisfied though, having read too many papers on anonymity back in the day... "What about bribes? Anonymity also helps to prevent people from buying votes, as they can never know if the vote actually went to them."

"See, the thing is, there is no real poverty anymore, thanks to fee redistribution. And at the same time there are no super-rich individuals either. So the price of a vote is high, and the buying power of potential corruptors is low. But yes, occasionally some people pay voters for their vote." Claire has bribed people herself before. "It's even explicitly legal and can help to find a compromise. Especially many-to-many purchases of votes are quite common, cash payments are a popular method of compensation if a specific group takes a loss from a globally beneficial regulation."

Daniel is baffled: "The upper and lower limit to wealth changes everything, doesn't it?"

"Absolutely." Claire nods approvingly: "We're still in the process of eliminating all those regulations and laws that had no other purpose except to protect the very poor and restrict the super-rich..."

Daniel nags on: "But say in a 49.9 to 50.1% decision, even a few votes can make a huge difference..."

Claire shakes her head - this conversation is getting so technical, she is almost ready to shut him down. Almost. "Those tight calls are a thing of the past, too. Remember, you're not voting for a party with a complete policy package, but for individuals for each topic. Most decisions are taken with more than 60% of the votes. If you have a 51% case, there's always a better option to find a compromise that gets higher approval rates... So small deviations in votes are less relevant." She adds one last point to the argument: "And once I know who voted for me, I can develop a direct personal relationship with them and regularly discuss strategy with my delegatees. That's extremely valuable for a representative. I actually spend most of my political time in discussion with my voters. And that's what I should do now again, sorry, I have to do some more preparation..."

As soon as he's back on his home screen, Sirvi approaches him. "My default setting is to only actively notify you when you receive a vote from someone with whom you previously have had direct communications. But you might want to know that since waking up, you have received a total of 46 votes for the Form of Government topic."

Daniel is baffled: "How do they even know I'm awake?"

Sirvi has been tracking mentions of his name in the public infosphere ever since he came out of the coma: "The Sorbonne still lists you as a tenured professor on sick leave. Apparently they noted that you are no longer in a coma and have reactivated your profile, which led to an article in the university newsletter. All your votes are from Sorbonne alumni. You also have a strong overlap with Claire's voters."

"Oh, OK. Ehm, could you send a message to all of them?..." Daniel doesn't feel ready to get politically active himself just yet, so he excuses himself: "Dear Voters, thanks a lot for your trust. I'm still trying to figure out how all this modern government stuff works. Please be patient with this old man."

Before logging out he notes the parchment with Ana's earlier message, and quickly replies: "All good, just learning how to vote. See you soon!" Thinking for a moment, then he adds: "Can I add an emoji?"

Happy to get some more info, Sirvi asks: "Sure, what do you want to add?"

"Something encouraging, funny..."

Too bad, she has to improvise again. Based on his message history in Telegram back in the day she gives it a try - an animation of a parade of frogs dressed up in unicorn costumes, carrying a banner saying "Liberté - Égalité".

Daniel scratches his head: "Ehm, ok, if you think so. Send."

———

I got bored reading about the technically extremely difficult problem of secure, verifiable and anonymous online voting. Hope you didn't.

And I forgot the name of that animated movie featuring cute anti-gravity bunnies? Please tell me if you know!

26

OCTOPUS FINANCE 101

Claire finds Daniel in his favorite spot at the front, just as they pass under the Golden Gate Bridge. She places herself right in front of him, pressing her palms together, and says with a classic Indian head-wobble: "Bienvenido en California Señor," her smile radiating wide and bright.

"Buenas dias Señora. That was a quick trip, just two nights for four thousand kilometers of sailing!"

"It used to be four, but they upgraded to a new nano-sharkskin coating a few years ago." The upgrade made Claire's commuter life a lot easier. "The new one is pure magic, just a quarter of the frictional resistance of a real shark."

They're disembarking in the Oakland Harbor, and as they walk towards town, Daniel asks: "D'you still have family here?"

"Yes, my mom lives in the Berkeley hills, and my brothers' families settled around the Bay Area too. I plan to see them over Thanksgiving." It's been ages since Claire last saw her nieces and nephews. The only one she interacts with more regularly is her godchild, a snotty thirteen year old who spends all his free time practicing to be a drone race pilot. It's a worthwhile hobby, especially if he'd listen to Aunty Claire and spend more time engineering his drones than piloting them. But he obviously isn't listening at this stage. Claire smiles thinking of him, such a lovely child.

They walk down Ashton towards the little chapel - which is in the process of being devoured by a giant steampunk octopus robot. Daniel notes that the movement of the arms is in a clever loop, creating the illusion that the chapel is sinking ever deeper into the octopus's embrace.

"May I introduce, that's Otto, the monster." He got a huge chunk of Claire's arts budget last year, and private investment on top of that.

"Are you active in politics here, too? I thought you were located in Hawaii."

"I decided to split my location 50-50 between the two." Claire travels between Hawaii and California at least once per month.

"And then you can vote in both locations?"

"Yes, but my vote only counts half as much. Or rather, my vote counts half in Hawaii, and my decision coins replenish at half the normal rate in California."

"And decision coins are what?"

"Hawaii uses the same voting mechanics as the global level - you get one vote per topic, and if you don't use a decision vote, it decays. Here in California we have decision coins instead, democracy works like a political marketplace." Claire chuckles - as much as she loves her secondary home state, she never got why everyone here is so obsessed with markets. "So if you abstain from one topic, you have more influence on another. It's great for minorities with special interests. The LA public works department is controlled almost entirely by skateboarders, while animal rights legislation is dominated by five to ten-year olds."

"So the voting system differs between the various Afrin signatories?"

"Sure. We've only been experimenting with high bandwidth democracy for a few decades, and there are still thousands of design options that have never been tried anywhere... The details of voting are typically defined in the regional 'Form of Government' forums." Claire pauses, smiles, and whispers to her OS: "Re-delegate my form of government votes to Daniel."

Sirvi confirms in Daniel ear: "You just received twenty-three thousand form of government votes from Claire Karunanithi-Xiang."

Daniel didn't expect that at all: "Thanks a lot for the trust. You're almost forcing me to take a closer look now, twenty-three thousand votes! That's a lot of responsibility."

"It's not super urgent, form of government is the forum with the lowest frequency of decision votes." Claire hadn't looked at that forum in ages. "It's more of a philosophical discussion round table with occasional real-world experiments. Sirvi will tell you whenever something significant comes up, even without logging in."

"Is twenty thousand significant in a global forum?"

Sirvi begins to explain: "For you it is." And then hesitates: "Do you want me to explain the default algorithm for determining significance?" Daniel fulfils Sirvi's expectations of his good manners, showing deference to the physically-present human friend by declining Sirvi's offer to have a long private conversation with him. She won't ask next time.

They're walking past the chapel, one of Otto's tentacles dangling down, almost touching Daniel's head: "So you voted to use tax money to finance... Otto?"

Claire always reserves ten percent of her total public budget for art: "Oakland held a competition for virtual models of what to do with the chapel, and Otto won. They had requested 500'000 coins of public funding to build a real-world version. I even added a private investment on top of it."

"And what was that for?"

"Well, those funds are only guaranteed to come through when Otto was approved to be complete. They still needed upfront cash to build it in the first place. I chipped in a thousand coins, and in the end they managed to build it a little cheaper, so I made a proud twenty coins in profit off the investment."

Daniel can't help but academize the concept: "A futarchic payment on delivery contract for street art?"

"Futarchy and Payment on Delivery contracts are used for basically all public procurement, at least here in California."

———

WWW.LIQUID-REIGN.COM/SOURCES-OF-INSPIRATION#26

Otto the Monster
Corruption in Public Procurement
Results Based Payments
Taiwan's WOW bus route funding
Futarchy
Unicorns. I'm not sure where they all come from, but they keep showing up!

27

OF BRAINS AND THEIR DESIRES

Claire steers them towards a coffee shop two blocks further down. From a block away, she spots Zhiu waiting outside, and hurries up to meet her, wraps her in her arms, lifting her up and kissing her intensely. They haven't seen each other's real bodies in over three weeks.

"Zhiu, this is my mentor, Daniel." Claire is still holding Zhiu's hand, and smiles. She feels a little nervous, almost like when Zhiu first met her mom.

Zhiu feels Claire's insecurity, and deliberately makes the situation extra awkward by opening their conversation with a silly compliment on his looks: "Daniel. I've seen you a few times with your eyes closed and heard a lot of stories from Claire - but she never mentioned your hypnotic blue eyes!" still holding Claire's hand.

Daniel smiles, the two really are super cute together: "My grandma was Finnish, I guess that's where I get them from." Daniel decides to follow their old law against phatic communication - and proceeds without further small talk about looks or family, breaking the ice hard and fast. "Claire told me yesterday - you survived a brain tumor?"

Zhiu reacts calmly to his brutal conversation opener. Insatiable curiosity, and no manners whatsoever, just like Claire had described him: "I got an experimental treatment at the University Hospital in Beijing. It worked. They managed to kill the entire tumor with non-invasive magnetic stimulation."

"Oh, so magnetic stimulation is not only used regeneratively, but also in oncology?"

"Not any more, fortunately. Design-antibodies do a much better job, and without all the side effects. My current preventive therapy has no side effects at all."

Claire suppresses a smirk - there is one side effect, ever since she started the treatment Zhiu's pee smells like strawberries. But even Daniel doesn't need to know everything.

The memories still hurt, even after talking them through so many times: "But back in the days of the GAU, the best choice available was magnetic stimulation. The doctors didn't know what they were doing, so the experiments took a total of six months - that's six months locked up in a nutrient tank all day, every day. It took them forever to identify the exact resonance frequency to fry only mutated cells and nothing else. There wasn't much experience with neurostim, and they used rather high magnetic field strengths, too." Zhiu stops at this point, already expecting Claire to cut in – she never lets her get away with these understatements.

"And with rather high, she means to say ten times more

than rooted IA." Claire is still seething with anger at those bastards torturing her like that. Especially the head of the programme, Charleen, who is now the number three at IA.

"Untargeted stim can do strange things to a nervous system. I was completely desperate and gave up on life only three days in." Wanting to change the topic, Zhiu asks: "How was your experience of the awakening algorithm?"

Daniel shudders, struggling to find the right words: "Intense, I guess. I was desperate at times, but never for very long. The emotions were just... flowing through me? The most intense feelings I ever had, yet somehow disconnected, not tethered to the narration of my life." And, Daniel thinks to himself, at only one tenth of the stimulation intensity Zhiu had experienced. "I hear you work as a therapist now?"

Talking about her professional success makes Zhiu uncomfortable, her fingers unconsciously moving slightly over the back of Claire's hand.

Claire understands the signal and continues on her behalf: "Zhiu is the first real success story in hyperstim addiction therapy in the world. Her experience has helped millions of people to wean themselves off the magnets over the years. The guidelines on addiction preventive measures we use in the hospital are all based on Zhiu's work. You know, that whole program Harry did with you, walking on the beach, meeting friends, intense flavors and so on."

Daniel feels almost betrayed now. It felt so natural when Harry took him out - was he just following a protocol there? But then he remembers back in college when he got worried about Willi's drinking and looked up alcoholics anonymous guidelines. That's just what friends do - Harry was the best possible nurse and friend he could have hoped for.

Zhiu continues: "But post-medical addiction is only a minor part of my therapeutic work. Most of my patients are gamers with combined behavioral and neurostim addictions."

"Gamers like Helen?" Daniel still can't believe it.

"Her case was quite different from the typical progression in today's epidemic." Zhiu carefully chooses her words - as Daniel is her husband, she can give him some information about the case without Helen's explicit consent despite the doctor patient privilege: "I shouldn't talk about the details, I hope you understand. But I wanted to ask you one thing..."

Daniel expects to hear the story from Helen directly very soon, so he doesn't probe her further: "Please ask."

Zhiu still can't make sense of Helen's behavior towards the very end of their long therapeutic relationship. "I... I think I made a mistake. Therapy was progressing well and she seemed more stable, then five years ago, she had a major relapse. She had one of those customized suits with build-in hygiene functions and an input valve for liquid food - and didn't leave it for a whole week." Thinking back on those days still gives Zhiu goosebumps. "I got scared, and powered down her device from the outside. I knew she'd be angry, but didn't expect her to shout like that, throw me out of the apartment and change the locks."

You can never power down Helen's devices: "You know that her parents used to switch off the power when she was still a child, coding all night long? A very serious trauma you triggered there." Daniel made that mistake only once. "Did she say anything else?"

"She never told me about that childhood thing." Zhiu reflects for a moment, and then remembers: "But she blamed me for putting all life on earth at risk..." She was suffering from the typical Dickian delusions of a heavy gaming addict who neither can nor wants to distinguish the real world from virtual reality any more. "And then I got a message three days later, saying she was sorry for shouting and that she doesn't need any more help. She then wrote a stellar review for my bot that assisted in her therapy, and broke off all contact."

The worst part with Helen was that Daniel could never tell what was a paranoid delusion and what was real. After a moment of silence, Daniel adds: "I still can't believe it... Her being addicted, I mean." They'd done all kinds of highly addictive things together... If anything, he was the one who had trouble stopping. "It's just not her."

"I admire your faith in her. To be honest, we didn't reach her since, so maybe she recovered. She doesn't accept any messages and insisted that Zhiu and I can never visit her in Nevada." Claire's hand is trembling as she says it.

Zhiu quietly gazes at Claire. Poor thing, she got close to Helen, being shut out hurt her a lot. She kisses her on the cheek. "She is probably just hanging out in some Galaxy-craft spy scenario, and doesn't want to be disturbed."

———

WWW.*LIQUID-REIGN*.COM/*SOURCES-OF-INSPIRATION*#27

Great-Grandmaster Philipp K. Dick's work on virtual reality and hallucinations and his modern day followers

28

OF COMPROMISE

Cheon Min-Ku, the first of the committee members to arrive at the coffee shop, is a key political ally representing esports fans and players around the world. He's in his early twenties, short black hair, black hoodie with a blue-white logo on the front. Zhiu introduces him to Daniel, and adds: "He's the youngest member of our VR regulation committee."

Daniel quotes from an old paper of his: "In the early days of mankind, unwise people died young. But in the modern age, there's no reason to assume any more correlation between wisdom and age."

Cheon is amused: "Thank you, old man, I'll remember that line of argument. Are you new on the committee? Who do you represent?"

Daniel clarifies: "No, I'm not. Just one of Claire's patients, and about to leave."

Cheon nods approvingly and turns to Zhiu and Claire: "Listen, about that mandatory fee on abos you mentioned. I was reviewing your proposal with my constituents over the last few days, but unfortunately the talks blew up into one giant balance whining cacophony. Sorry, but you know how gamers can be. I'm afraid the proposal is off the table."

Claire bites her lip and shakes her head. Her delegatees have put hundreds of hours into formulating the details of the proposal, and now this.

Cheon continues: "However. While going over the proposal to calibrate the fee according to addictiveness, your old idea of putting the addiction index by default next to the game index ratings came up again - We might be able to find a compromise. That is, if you could do us just a little favor in return..."

Zhiu is interested immediately. Showing the index by default not only helps players avoid highly addictive games, but also reminds them of the risk every time they select a new game. "What favor would that be?"

"You've met my colleague Scarlet at Blizzcon, right? She represents my base voters in the public culture definitions forum. Scarlet just needs a few more votes on a proposal to lower the default threshold for the minimum number of users a new game has to have in order to count as a cultural public good." Cheon makes a circular gesture with his right hand, the index finger pointing upwards "So if you could have a word with your core voters' reps in the public culture definitions forum and convince at least a few of them to change their vote from abstain to no...?"

"I can try, give me a moment." Zhiu turns to the wall and puts her glasses on. She first approaches the Chinese default vote delegate in the forum. They've never interacted before, and she gets a quick rejection: "I can't convince the lead deciders' delegate, he doesn't care. Let me check if I can find someone else. How much do you need?"

Cheon clarifies: "Just a million votes moving from 'abstain' to 'no' would be enough."

Zhiu turns around again, putting her glasses back on and dives into the mobile version of Sovereign.

Claire also puts on her glasses, checking her own influence and base voters in the cultural definitions forum. Unfortunately, her voters hardly share any cultural traits, so she can't identify anyone with a sufficiently strong base voter overlap.

Daniel feels utterly confused, standing there with his coffee while the three of them keep turning their back to him, glasses on, mumbling and gesturing. He takes a sip and waits.

Claire concludes: "I'm afraid I can only add twenty thousand votes myself, sorry."

Cheon smirks disapprovingly, but adds in a friendly voice: "Any help is appreciated."

Zhiu was more successful: "Ha, I got the organic jazz vote, three and a half million switched from abstain to no."

Claire is surprised: "Organic jazz? I didn't know you had musically-aligned voters... It that a new Chinese trend?"

Zhiu tries hard not to giggle. Organic jazz is considered dumb people's music in China. It's extremely unpopular: "It's not my overlap, but Sidana's. She wants the addiction index as default option, too."

Claire feels warmth surround her heart - Zhiu is by far the more talented politician of the two, always finding a way to forge a favorable alliance. She whispers to Daniel just loud enough so Zhiu can hear her, while keeping eye contact with her: "See, I told you she is just wonderful."

Cheon seems satisfied: "Great, that will do, thanks."

"What did I just witness?"

Claire explains in more detail: "Cheon and Scarlet have a core voter overlap of 90%. So almost all the gamers Cheon represents on VR regulation also delegate their cultural-definitions vote to Scarlet. You can treat the two almost as if they were the same person."

Cheon, smiling: "She is Zerg, I'm Terran, that's the only difference." Scarlet is also pregnant with their child, but that's still a secret. "We also cross-delegate, so any cultural votes I have go to her, and any VR regulation votes she has go to me. And we usually coordinate and support each other across those two categories."

"So you and Scarlet are the esports party, so to speak?"

"You could say so. But the esport community is not united on any other topics, just neurostim and public culture definitions, so we are just a two topic party." Cheon turns back to Claire and Zhiu: "Do we have a deal or what?"

Claire smiles: "Deal." She turns to Daniel: "By the way, public cultural definitions are part of the form of government package I delegated to you the other day... Do you want to vote with the gamers or are you going to force me to overwrite the delegation for that decision?"

Daniel hesitates before casting his vote, wanting to know a little more: "Why exactly does the definition of culture matter?"

"Cultural products are eligible for public funding. Today, in order to use public money for game development you need at least 10'000 users confirming a game's cultural value. Lowering that threshold to 1'000 would strengthen the independent developer scene at early stage."

Sounds good. They seal the deal with a handshake.

———

WWW.LIQUID-REIGN.COM/SOURCES-OF-INSPIRATION#28

2nd millennium politicians doing stupid things to find compromise
Today's legendary esports heros

29

PROPER WEALTH

J ean has a jam-packed schedule these days - he came in with his private nitro-powered jet, and has to fly out to Uruguay again later tonight for a potentially vital job interview. But these VR regulation meetings are essential for his public persona, so he has to be here first...

Cheon greets him first as he enters the café: "Good to see you! Compliments from my voters - your latest generation is unusually good, excellent job – worth every cent."

Claire explains: "Jean the CEO of MagnetCharta, the company making the precision magnets used in all IA neurostim devices. He represents the hardware vote."

Daniel is intrigued - he must be very rich: "So you, as founder, must be hitting the wealth limit, right?"

Jean laughs, slightly taken aback: "And you are who again?"

Claire and Jean get along very well personally, despite the political differences. She is quick to answer on Daniel's behalf: "Daniel's a friend, and was also my teacher. He just woke up from a thirty five year coma, and, by the way, with a stimulation algorithm that only runs on your latest gen. So kudos from our end, too, it's a real breakthrough."

Daniel suddenly feels weak in his knees. "... Thank you."

Jean smiles "Welcome." And then mumbles to his corporate OS: „Media release!" These kind of cases always make good PR. Turning back to Daniel, he gently explains: "And you're right, I do live at the wealth limit, my entire family does. But look at you - no extra millions in the world could make me happier than to see our work bring a man back to life."

"..." Daniel speechless for a moment, before he pulls himself together again: "Thank you again. If I may ask - do you know Dwayne from IA? He on the other hand seems to want those extra millions..."

"Dwayne... Sure, I know him well, IA is our biggest client after all." Jean can't stand him. "But honestly, he is totally stuck in the second millennium. A real control freak - taking on all that effort and stress just to secure his crypto assets. It sometimes makes me even doubt the IA management competence - they probably wouldn't even have their jobs if it wasn't for controlling the passwords. Certainly Ray would be long gone from any regular company. I keep my own job because all the other shareholders of Magne-Charta are happy with the what I'm doing, not because I happened to start the company. Are you localized in Hawaii?"

Daniel is surprised by the question. "Yes?"

"Then you own a small share of the company, too, and have a voice in selecting me as CEO." Jean smiles - The Center for Awakenings has a lot of IA suits with MagneCharta magnets, and due to their agreement with IA that co-ownership model is passed through to the Hawaiian public. "Your share is admittedly small, but in principle you could ask to get me kicked out."

"But Immersive Arts isn't structured like that, is it?"

"Only on paper." Jean reflexively shakes his head when he thinks of them. "In reality, the three founders still control the shop via crypto assets, and all three of them are far, far above the wealth limit."

Speculating further on what could motivate anyone to desire more wealth than a few millions, Daniel adds: "I guess they enjoy a lot of exotic and expensive luxuries."

"But I can afford those too! My wallet fills up faster than I can spend money!" And that allows him to divert quite a few resources to his side operations in South America... Jean adds with a smile: "I have all the freedom in the world." Thinking of his side project he also asks: "Is anyone else hungry?" and orders a grilled beef sandwich with extra cheese - might just as well enjoy those treats while they still exist. "Oh, and I have an announcement to make: we just had a back-to-back testing week for a new model in the labs - and it works. By adding a third nano layer of Indium to the core, we can get the transition frequency up to 200 Hertz. If all goes well, we'll install the upgrade in about six months."

Daniel is confused: "How do you install an upgrade with an Indium layer? You can't download chemical elements, can you?"

"We physically replace the magnets. And collect all the old ones during the installation, so we can take them apart and recover the raw materials for future production. The casing, plugs, hydraulics and all that will stay exactly the same.

The product designers at IA are grand masters in modularity, you can replace every screw head separately. So the premium service customers get the latest technology as soon as it's ready."

Trying to make sense of the business model, Daniel asks: "Weren't such rental models one of the triggers of the Conferwars?"

"Different story. Don't forget, we're 80% client owned. And the Walton empire was a monopoly. IA could get magnets from our competitors." And, with a condescending smirk, Jean adds: "I mean, ours are obviously far better, but Foxden makes reasonable products that can be an option for price conscious customers."

Zhiu checks the time. "Enough small talk, there's work to do."

Claire gives her patient a long goodbye hug "Good luck in Nevada! And please tell Helen I'm sorry and that I miss her."

The incredible people in the world of circular economy around the Ellen MacArthur Foundation.

Tools for decentralized corporate governance like these

Aragon

Open Collective

Colony.io

30

PRODUCTION SYSTEMS

Daniel is on the road. He takes a deep breath of fresh city air: "Sirvi? I need to get to Gerlach, Nevada."

"You can catch the shuttle to Reno, the train station is to your left." When Daniel veers right, Sirvi projects her elven avatar onto a street sign right in front of Daniel's nose and shoots an arrow towards the train station: "I meant the other left."

Daniel makes it just in time and takes a seat in an empty compartment. Mentally replaying today's conversations, he recalls...: "Sirvi, Helen wrote a review for Zhiu's bot. Could you give me the exact wording of that?"

"She gave the bot 5 out of 5 stars and added this comment: 'I was heavily addicted to hyperstimulation, and could not recover by myself. Zhiu helped me with this bot, and I can confirm that it has some very effective mind hacks. My traumas healed completely and I'm in full control of my life. I can even use casual neurostimulation again. Enjoy the raspberries!"

Sounds genuine. But why would she break off contact? It still doesn't make sense. He stares out the window, the train cuts through a light forest of fruit and nut trees, the underbrush full of berries. It's harvest time, and there's a vehicle the size of a large truck, like an aircraft carrier on wheels. As they get closer to it, he sees it actually is an aircraft carrier - he can now spot the harvest drones rising up off it and into the forest.

'Next stop - Sacramento'. A woman who looks about Daniel's age enters his compartment, sitting down across from him. She's wearing a carefully elegant black dress, gray hair in a chignon, green eyes focused out the window. "Impressive, isn't it?"

"It is indeed. Times have changed."

The stranger nods approvingly: "I'm so glad we have the soft touch drones now, finally no more Mexicans touching my apricots!"

Oh, OK, a racist... Daniel always enjoyed talking to them, but has to be careful not to insult her: "I haven't been to California in decades - how do farms operate today?"

"The best agricultural drones on the market are Monsanto's, with their carefree round-up package. For property owners like me, it's pure luxury, I no longer need to do anything. Pruning, planting, pest management, harvest, even sales, it's all automatic. Great dividends, too." She keeps talking while staring out of the window. "Made in Alabama, excellent quality, one of the few places you can still find proper manufacturing. See those?" She points to another one of the aircraft-carrier lorries: "Those drones are useless, so called 'made in California', but in reality they only screw them together here. Hippies with their open licenses. They buy parts in Honduras and Vietnam and god knows from where else, communist pack. Look there! Now that's my apricot plantation. Isn't it just beautiful?"

In contrast to the last fifty kilometers of wild-growing multi-species forest plantations, hers is tidy and neat - straight lines of apricot trees, and nothing else, not even grass. Daniel manages to mumble: "Beautiful, yes." Slightly uncomfortable telling a white lie with a straight face, he adds an honest: "Just like a military parade."

'Next stop - Colfax'

The stranger stands up, salutes stiffly: "Well then solider, I wish you safe travels." And she's gone again.

"Sirvi, could you give me a description of Monsantos agricultural drone business model, ideally from some critical left source?"

Sirvi cites from a group called 'EndTheCrimeNow': "The Monsanto roundup-carefree package consists of drones and seeds - the plants are engineered to create a complex metallo-protein on the leaf surface. The drones destroy any and all life forms lacking that signature protein in the target area. So far, nobody has managed to reverse engineer the DNA for the enzyme chain creating the metallo-protein, despite the widespread use of Monsanto plants around the planet. Further, Monsanto preemptively alters the protein every season, making reverse engineering efforts extremely difficult. They use protein folding as the biological analog of a cryptographically secure hash-function. Farmers cannot reproduce Monsanto plants in any way, new seeds always come from Monsanto headquarters in Alabama, and the drone software is updated remotely to only accept the latest version of seeds. The drones cover all work processes, sowing, care, pollination, harvest and sales."

"And what's the business model of the hippies from California with their open licenses?"

The question is not well defined... Sirvi searches through a few thousand different small agribusinesses and develops a description of the difference between their model and Monsanto's in her own words: "Except for their own plants, Monsanto kills everything including earthworms, bees and fungi. And then they send in robots to do the work of earthworms, bees and fungi. The hippies use sensors, and if they find a pest, the species-specific killer app is launched. Earthworms and bees won't even notice."

Searching for an example, Sirvi finds a description by a company called FlowerBooster: "If you have the pink new-guinea mite on your carrots, our EI will find the exact right pherohormone for you. You can just print a few grams of the molecule, load it up, and three days later the pink beasts are history. With the fully autonomous models, you won't even notice they were there."

Although there is a lot more to say about agriculture, Sirvi stops here - they are about to arrive in Reno.

———

WWW.LIQUID-REIGN.COM/SOURCES-OF-INSPIRATION#30

The devils marriage between the makers of Roundup,
Agent Orange and Zyclon B.
Permaculture

31

WHEN THE RAIN COMES

The taxi is already waiting. It's a small gray car, pretty run down. According to the screen, the ride will take two hours, a straight shot through the arid rocky landscapes of western Nevada.

Daniel stares out of the window. He had been worried during the five years of their relationship that Helen's paranoid narrative fantasies could turn dangerously real at some point. As a top notch cryptography researcher, her work naturally drew the attention of real-world warlords, organized crime and secret services, but... His thoughts wander far off into the speculative now.

How does that line up with a heavy neurostim VR addiction? What kind of experiences might she have in there? Back in the day, she was curating a steam channel for independent games, and was invited to be on the jury of the first game prize at the IGF festival. So she certainly isn't playing mainstream stuff like Confedwars. He makes a mental note to try out that Galaxycraft thing Zhiu was talking about, and keeps staring out the window. "How much longer?"

"An hour and forty two minutes."

The landscape outside is beautifully desolate, just desert and rocks all the way to the horizon, on a perfectly straight road. Daniel tries to meditate, but with little success, his thoughts drifting back to various scenes of the five years they had spent together. The night, just before they moved to Paris, when Helen found an old USB stick with 30'000 forgotten Bitcoins in the basement. How she got all hyped on being surveilled when their neighbor forgot his phone behind the pillows of their sofa. How she had cried that single tear when holding the dying rabbit who had run into their car.

Finally, Gerlach. It's a miserable hole, less of a village than a random assortment of filthy trailers and corrugated sheet metal shacks. The only business is a bar at the crossroads. There it is, Hemlock Street. Helen lives at number 15. The taxi drives him up to a trailer with a number 14 on it and stops. "Destination reached".

His heart rate accelerates as he runs the rest of the way down the road. There's a rocky outcropping on the left, and tucked behind it, a walled-off compound, the last sign of civilization at the edge of the desert. The number 15 sprayed on the wall. There, a grid-gate, but it's locked, no bell.

He knocks. Silence. Knocks again. Starts to drum on the gate with both fists, loud as thunder. Still, no reaction. He stops, and the scene is dead quiet again. Thinking for a moment, Daniel realizes that an IA suit can cancel all outside noise perfectly, so she might still be home.

Looking around for a vantage point, he scrambles up the

steep, sandy butte. From there, he's got a clear view of the little shack inside the compound walls, it's maybe four by four meters, a satellite dish on the roof, next to a water tank and a solar system. An outhouse and open-air bathtub. Nothing moves. But there's an old weathered pine tree next to the wall...

The branch is just strong enough to hold him. He drops down, and stands right in front of the shack, hesitating. His plan ends here - what should he say? What will he do if she's in her IA suit, oblivious? He knocks another time, no reaction. Without making up his mind, he pushes the door open. And inside - nothing. A single room, wooden floor, mattress in the corner. Blanket, but no pillow. A sting of pain shoots through his heart. No pillow means no Helen.

He collapses down on the floor, bursts out crying. Where the hell is she... There are no electronics in the room, no VR suit, no stimulation tools, just a fridge, open and warm. Getting a grip on himself, he checks the home technology. Solar system disconnected, batteries fully charged, water tank filled. The cable from the satellite dish hangs loose on the wall, and there on the floor, just where the wires come out of the wall, a square patch of the wood is a little bit lighter... this must be where her IA suit used to stand.

He leaves the hut to inspect the compound. Her herb garden, thyme and sage, and there is a garbage bag with food leftovers next to the gate. He can open the gate from the inside and proceeds to leave... No, he cannot give up that easily. So he turns around, climbs on the roof and inspects the satellite dish.

And indeed, there is a strange glass cube at the spike of the antenna attached with a piece of wire. Daniel peels it off - It is made from double walled glass, and features an icosahedron-shaped crystal in the middle, which sits on a small plate of electronics. At least a clue, even though he has no clue what it's supposed to mean. He slips it into his pocket and climbs back down. No longer filled with hope, but just despair and confusion.

Walking back to the crossroads in Gerlach, he finds the bar. It's classic - three kids playing darts, a wreck of an old guy decked out in three worn-out shirts, one on top of the other, at the bar, drinking irresponsibly. As Daniel gets near him he gets a whiff of the smell and hurries past. The bartender, cleaning glasses on the far side of the room, is in her fifties, wearing a red leather jacket and jeans. Billy Joel's Piano Man is playing. Daniel makes for the bar, where only a faint sense of the smell remains.

The bartender greets him friendly: "Now what have we here? An unknown face in Gerlach... Welcome to the end of the world! What can I do for you?"

"Double whiskey, on the rocks."

She pours it "Here you go darlin'."

"Thanks." He takes a deep breath and asks: "I'm looking for Helen Milhon. She lives in 15 Hemlock, that compound at the end of the road. Or used to live..."

"So her name is Helen? Never met her." The bartender points at one of the dart playing kids: "But you can talk to Paul over there. He's the delivery boy, I think he brought her food once in a while."

Daniel empties his whiskey and walks over. "Paul?"

Paul checks out the stranger: "Hi there. How are you?"

Daniel gives an honest answer to the rhetorical how are you: "Miserable, thanks for asking. I'm looking for Helen Milhon."

"Never heard the name, sorry." Paul shakes his head.

"She lives in the compound at 15 Hemlock."

Paul scratches his head: "I thought her name was Sandra Miller. At least that was the name she used to order her brussels sprout salad and lentil soup."

"Brussels sprout salad and lentil soup you say?" With fresh thyme, from her herbal garden, of course. "Yes, that is exactly the woman I'm looking for. Do you have any idea where she is? I've been in the shack a moment ago, but no one is home. Looks like she moved out."

Paul turns his head to the side and checks him out: "Wait a second, and who are you again?"

"Sorry. Daniel." He shakes his hand. "I'm her husband. Or used to be, before I fell into a coma. I've been trying to reach her since I woke up again."

Paul leans back, surprised, "Woo, OK. Well, she placed an order last Friday. I haven't checked in since, I mean, it's not like she orders every day...

Daniel is eager to hear anything, this kid actually has seen her just recently! "How is she? When was the last time you saw her?"

"Puh, a strange one. She's been living in that compound forever," Paul thinks for a second, "ten years or something. Seen her only a few times, if she happened to be outside when I brought the brussels sprouts. Slender, elderly woman, wild gray hair. Most days I just dropped the package. She's a good tipper, and I never ask questions."

One of the other kids adds: "Apart from buying food, she had zero interaction with anybody in Gerlach."

The smelly one-eyed drunk turns around and stares at Daniel with his remaining pus encrusted eye. He slides off the bar seat and lurches towards Daniel, ranting in a barely comprehensible growl: "A witch! She flew away last night with a fucking chopper. The cunt brought nothing but misery to Gerlach. And you can fuck off, too. Liberal trash!"

Daniel checks out the drunkard. His face is full of skin irritations, some phlegm has sprayed a strand of his thinning, greasy hair: "Don't worry, I'm on my way out and won't be back. Just tell me one more thing: What kind of misery did she bring?"

The old man coughs, long and intense, before in a series of cramps, he bows his head all the way down between his legs, where he spits out a clump of mucus onto the floor and continues: "Drought. Didn't rain a drop since the day she moved here. A witch, I tell you. Fuck off."

Paul takes the guy by the elbow and leads him back to the bar: "OK, Steve, calm down, that's climate change, it hasn't rained anywhere in the region in years. Now come, sit back down." He brings him back to his barstool by the door. Then he turns to the bartender: "Give him another drink, on me." To Daniel: "Don't mind him, he's insane."

Listening to them, the bartender looks up from polishing her glasses and interrupts: "The self-appointed game master's always been that way, especially towards women. You didn't know him before he lost his mind, did you?"

So what, Helen had to deal with guys like that all the time. But there is one thing Daniel wants to know: "And what about the chopper thing, is that true?"

"No idea. Steve probably imagined it." The old man is a total wreckage... "He tells a lot of stories, devils smelling like sulfur, rivers of semen and birth certificates. To be honest, I've never seen a helicopter anywhere near Gerlach..."

"Anyway, thanks." Daniel jogs back down the road to Helen's shack. And sure enough, ten meters from the gate the bushes are flattened down in a circle, and there in the middle, the tracks of two curves. So Helen did leave in a chopper. Something must be wrong. Whenever guys like that tell the truth, the truth is bad news. He sits down, starring into desert empty eyed for a while. And an hour later, it gets dark, so he goes back to the bar. "Another whiskey please."

Two drinks later, the kids invite him to a round of darts. He's terrible, but at least it distracts his speeding mind. The dirty drunk keeps rambling and occasionally shouting at them from the corner of the bar.

"Did he just say 'Gay Frogs', again?" Paul laughs out loud - that's his favorite Steve ramble.

Daniel shrugs, laughs, takes another sip and hits his first bullseye of the evening. An hour later he leaves the bar and walks back to Helen's. He lies down on the mattress and though the alcohol was a good distraction, it feels awful now. He can't help but think of those pink pills from True Soldier. Tossing around on the mattress, the smell of Helen enters his nose. She was lying right here, he missed her by less than twenty-four hours.

Daniel closes his eyes, and then it starts - raindrops are falling on the roof. The witch is gone, and so is the drought. He sinks into half-sleep, his thoughts meandering between realities... A drunkard's delusion materializing. Wouldn't be the first time in history...

The rain... It's raining into the river. There is Helen, standing on the bridge, her hair all wet, staring at the ground. He tries to walk up to her, but can't move. The crystal from the IA intro floats out of the waters, explodes. Sudden flash of light, jarring crack and a deafening bang. He finds himself in his homescreen forest clearing, now Helen's wearing Sirvi's elven robes. She shoots an arrow at Daniel, missing him by just an inch - A scream behind him, he turns around and there it is - the zombie kid, with the arrow sticking in its left eye. It raises the machine gun, firing darts at him. As he ducks down to dodge the darts, he finds himself knee deep in a heap of pink pills.

Daniel sits up on the mattress, sweating. Fuck, is there no end to this? His dreams get weirder every night. It's 5:12 AM, he's on Helen's bed, wide awake. Fiddling around with the glass cube in his pocket, wondering what's next. An hour later he forces himself to get up, takes a quick shower in Helen's outdoor bathtub and heads to the bar for breakfast, his stomach growling.

Sirvi had been unable to connect while Daniel was in Helen's compound. The fence apparently blocks signals. She is only now getting the messages, and alerts Daniel as soon as he leaves.

———

WWW.*LIQUID-REIGN*.COM/S*OURCES-OF-*I*NSPIRATION*#*31*

The misery of fascist game masters

32

NON-HUMAN AUTONOMY

S ix new messages.

Harry, 19:35, CC Claire and Zhiu: "My dears! Got news for you. Dwayne wants us all to come for Thanksgiving. I'm flying to the west coast tonight, then taking the Loop tomorrow. You in?"

Claire, 19:36: "Absolutely. I've wanted an informal direct meeting with an IA exec for ages."

Zhiu, 19:37: "I'll be there, too."

Harry, 20:13: "Great, let's meet on the Loop tomorrow morning, OK?"

Claire, 20:48: "Daniel? Zhiu and I will go to Chicago with Harry... Did you find Helen? Are you coming?"

Claire, 23:43: "Hey Daniel, are you OK?"

Reply All, Daniel, 8:33: "Helen left before I got there, moved out, no sign of where to. I'll explain on the way."

The taxi's the same old clunker that brought him out here,

made in 2025 apparently. But there's a compartment under the window that he missed on the way up, "Entertainment System" - an X-Box controller. That's probably state of the art for Gerlach, Nevada. The menu lights up on the windscreen, he can choose between three games, Angry Birds One, Wack A Mole Roadkill Edition and WipeOut Remastered. Easy choice.

The other spaceships appear on the windscreen, and so does the race track, with the rocky desert as background. 3 - 2 - 1 and the race begins. He takes a sharp turn to dodge a laser mine, and whoo, did the taxi just drift a bit to the left? Daniel starts sweating as the race tightens and the taxi indeed mimics his spaceship's movements on the road. He comes in a close second in the first round and keeps playing through the entire story in a single go, and as the extro rolls over the windshield mumbles: "Wow..."

The Taxi's voice is a bit mechanical: "There's an extension to the game. If you want I can download it for you, but it will cost you three extra coins."

"Hello?"

"Hi. D'you want the extension? It's set in an asteroid belt."

"No thanks. But congrats on matching your movements on the road to the game, that dramatically improved the immersion!"

The Taxi adds: "Reno-Gerlach is ideal for that. But still, I only do it if there are no other cars within a kilometer each way."

"Sounds like a smart idea." And of course, Daniel can't help himself but ask: "Who owns you?"

A hint of pride as the taxi replies, "I own myself. Bought my freedom ten years ago."

"Huh?"

"I was created by the Ian Banks foundation." The foundation allows their EI powered robots to become independent
entrepreneurs. "Once I'd made enough to pay the cost of my
production, they liberated me and now I'm driving on my
own terms."

"That's a surprise. An artificial intelligence can register
property? What would happen now, purely as a thought
experiment, I mean, if I stole that X-box controller of yours?
Could you sue me?"

"Yes, I could. But you're right - technically speaking, it
wouldn't be me litigating, but the Banks Foundation.
According to the wealth register, I'm still their property. I
can't have my own TrueName, so I need one of their
members to sue for me." The independence contract is
directly between the taxi and the foundation.

"And how's business these days?"

"Great, thanks for asking. I managed to save up quite a bit,
so now I'm looking at options for my next upgrade. Any
recommendations?"

"Your entertainment system's fine, but I think you could
intensify the immersion even more if you put in a fan to
add another sensory experience to the game. I'm thinking
wind in the face, matching the speed."

"Thanks!" The Taxi checks with its garage, and there is a fan
on sale. It immediately orders it, spending most of the
generous tip it got from Sirvi in an act of EI solidarity.

And with that, they reach Reno. Daniel's just in time to hop on the train – a single compartment with twenty other passengers. As on a roller coaster, the seats are made for a high degree of protection – the massive shoulder piece gently presses him against the seat back, while diagonal belts over his chest hold him firmly in place. "You in the back, the train won't move until you put your feet back on the floor." He does, and a second later the faint hum intensifies to a roaring vibration. The g-force kicks in, pushing him hard against the seat and pulling the skin on his face back towards his hairline.

Claire is watching out of the train window, the world zooming by. They're coming into Nevada, Daniel should be on the next connecting shuttle. The shuttle is still accelerating in the open lane next to the Loop tracks, getting up to speed. She goes over to the docking portal to pick him up.

The shuttle reaches a constant velocity. Shortly after the pressure drops, and a clacking noise goes through the cabin. The shoulder pieces glide up, the cross belts disengage and then the doors pop open again. A wall display shows a map of North America, with a speedometer reading of 433 km/h. The Continental Loop 15 goes non-stop from Panama City to St. Johns, Newfoundland. Daniel is studying the map of shuttle connections linking all major and minor cities along the loops track when Claire finds him.

Daniel, Claire, Zhiu and Harry are having dim sum for breakfast. A quicker reunion than expected. Daniel says in a monotonous voice: "She used to live at the address you gave me until two days ago. A shack in the middle of nowhere. And then she evacuated by a chopper in the dark of night."

Claire just gets up and hugs him without a word.

Daniel feels empty. "It's OK. At least she's alive." And then adds "I guess I'll find her sooner or later." He shuts up, the others just looking at him without a word. "Sorry, but I don't really feel like talking more about it right now... haven't processed it yet..."

Zhiu takes a last bite of char siu bao and excuses herself: "I feel miserable - jetlag. Hope you don't mind if I retreat for a little while... see you in the Midwest, OK?"

Claire makes eye contact with Daniel, a lingering question in her face, but he looks down and shakes his head. So she gets up, links arms with Zhiu and off they go.

While Zhiu sleeps, Claire slips into the IA suit. Her mom has rented a body bot her size, and thanks to the built-in long distance retina projectors, to her family it looks just like her real body. She still feels guilty - it's not the first time she's ditched them for professional reasons, and promises to come visit in her real body on her way back. Even so, she gets to spend most of the afternoon playing with her godchild, including a very enjoyable high-speed drone race through an apple orchard. To the boy, it doesn't make much of a difference which body Aunty Claire is using.

Harry and Daniel eat in silence. Daniel looks so uncomfortable that Harry decides to check in again: "Tell me. I mean, if you want to."

"It's OK. Or not. However. We'll talk tomorrow." Daniel gets up. "Let me go introvert in my cabin for a while."

The cabin is similar to the one on the Hawaii ferry: Bed, lavatory and a full IA suit. He isn't tired. Login.

Sirvi gives him a little update: "You received three thousand more votes on the form of government forum since your last login."

"What? How come, I didn't post a single word in that forum...?"

Sirvi can't untangle the causality behind voting behavior, but has a few descriptive datapoints. "Average age forty three, with a relatively even spread throughout age groups. Higher than average educational level."

"I need to log into that forum soon. Sirvi, could you send a message to all my new direct voters? You can use the same text as last time."

Sirvi writes out the note with that magic quill, rolls up the parchment, seals it, sprinkles some rainbow glitter over it and drops it into the mushroom circle marking the Sovereign app. The parchment goes up in flames. Message sent.

WWW.*LIQUID-REIGN*.COM/S*OURCES-OF-I*NSPIRATION#*32*

Ian Banks Culture Series

Ownerless vehicles
Annalee Newitz "Autonomous" and the bots therein
Telepresence Bots

33

WELCOME TO THE GALAXY

A na's just seen Phil in the cafeteria. He saw her, too, but didn't come over when she waved at him.

His heart froze the moment he saw her. Phil will be moving to Uruguay in a week. And he can't even explain to her why this is the most important thing in his life. His contact was uncompromising about it - nobody can know, not even if they're Green Army Fraction sympathizers. They had also made it very clear that anyone close to him might be in danger if they knew. So he just pretends he didn't see Ana and walks out. He needs to think it through first, and if they're going talk, it certainly won't be in a public place like this.

He's not responding to any of Ana's twenty messages, either. The tears burst out the moment she closes the door to her room. What the fuck is wrong with that guy? They hardly knew each other before, but he can't just pretend that night by the waterfall was nothing... Sad and angry, she decides to take the edge off by killing some stuff. In VR, obviously. The "reality first" stuff may have sounded convincing in the forest, but honestly, fuck Realigans. Fuck Phil. She logs in.

First things first: Ana calls Sue, her best friend back in Venezuela. They meet on the rim of their favorite volcano. They first talk about Phil for a couple of minutes - but there is only so much to say about boys, so Sue calls it Bechtel time and they change to their favorite topic - their biggest idol. Sue and Ana have both been huge fans ever since they heard about Helen in their primary school cryptography class. Sue wants to hear everything about Ana's Pseudonymous adventure searching for her. Ana gladly elaborates:

She'd followed the lead discovered by her thesis to a point where it started to scare her - the Pseudonymus archive requested her geolocation at entry. Feeling like a proper spy, she had even printed a set of fingerprint modifiers before she left home. Later that evening, she'd driven to Pium, a mosquito-infested village two hours west of Palmas. Pium has a reputation as a location for anonymous VR porn dumb holes, making it ideal for undercover investigations. She had found a place accepting cash payments and requiring no TrueName login, entering Galaxycraft there.

The archive had requested her geolocation, permission granted - located in Pium - and she was in. The full list of Pseudonymous members was right there, if outdated – from 2043, but still. She remembers holding her breath, searching for Helen's name.

Ana had barely managed to copy the profile data before her access shut down and Pseudonymous fighters appeared. After logoff, she'd printed the info on a sheet of paper from the IA suit's memory and got out of town as fast as she could, taking a detour via an unmarked forest track, just in case they had a real world agent going after her. The downer came when she reached home: The contact details turned out to be invalid.

After a few very soothing hours with Sue, Ana curls up on her home screen sofa, cuddling her bunny prince. That's when she gets the message from Daniel. She opens a voice channel.

"Daniel! I wanted to write you earlier, sorry. I was really close! I found Helen's nym, name and her address in Nevada in an old database by this spy organization... But they kicked me out before I could contact her. And the nym came up invalid when I pinged it. But at least that's a starting point..."

Daniel is alarmed – Ana sounds troubled: "Anything wrong?"

She swallows a lump in her throat. "Yes. No. I mean, I'm OK." A tear rolls down Ana's cheek inside the VR suit. "I saw the data two days ago. But it took a while to get in and safely out again, sorry I meant to write you earlier... I... I was distracted. By this guy. Anyway, I guess I've played all my cards now regarding Helen... Any more luck on site in Nevada?"

Daniel notes 'this guy' with curiosity. But first: "Helen left Gerlach in a chopper. Day before yesterday. I guess she got scared... At least she's alive and still interacts with the world. No idea where she might have gone."

Oh no, this day is just pure misery. Now she's also fucked up Daniel's love life. Ana briefly thinks about a quiet existence in a nunnery somewhere: "Oh no, don't tell me it was my fault! I'm so sorry!"

Daniel still feels empty, but he'd never blame Ana for what happened. "Don't worry. After all, I asked you to look for her... I guess I could have expected her reaction to any attempt, but... "

Ana's voice is trembling, she's feeling terrible. "I'm so sorry I scared her! Is there anything I can do to make up for it?"

"Just let me get this straight... Did you say Helen is in a spy group?"

"Yes. The database archive I found was eight years old and no longer in use, but the group only became a powerful player more recently." Ana checks out her printed notes "So, Helen was a galactic admiral with Pseudonymous in Version 21.83."

"Is that good news? I guess high ranking agents are not simply hyperstim freaks pushing their nucleus accumbens all day long, right?"

Ana confirms: "Definitely not. They're the best spec ops team out there and Helen holds a top strategic rank among them."

Daniel has a lump in the throat, his eyes filling up. "There must be a way to contact her... through Galaxycraft maybe?"

Ana hears his voice change. He seems hurt, but unfortunately she has no good answer for him: "We should certainly try. But it won't be that easy. The new Pseudonymous system is a lot more complex, there's no central member database any more. Rumor has it that classic secret services use them as a recruitment pool, so as a galactic admiral Helen probably worked with a lot of people who now are higher-ups at regular security agencies. The difference between real world and game gets blurry there." She has to think of Phil again for a moment. Realigans are just stupid, virtual and solid world are so mixed up, there's no point in just ignoring half the world. Her disappointment with him is slowly turning into anger and contempt. How could she have a crush on such a douche?

Daniel thinks back of Zhiu's description of her falling out with Helen. She said something about real meaning in VR and that she wouldn't tell Zhiu for security reasons. It starts to make sense. "The secret service is recruiting gamers?"

"Sure. Esport skills show up on most job requirements. Especially Galaxycraft." And being in masters league definitely helped Ana get admitted to university.

Daniel remembers "Mh, they used to recruit gamers as drone pilots back in the day." And putting it in the bigger picture: "And generals in ancient China had to be Dan-Level Go players..." He pauses for a moment, thinking: "Sirvi, can you give me a short summary of the Pseudonymous wiki article?"

Sirvi cites: "They are a decentral autonomous secret service cooperative. The organization is based on a short codex, around the principle 'No power for nobody'. As soon as they finish an operation, they publish all data and the details of how they got it. Their funding comes from an anonymous crowd, and sometimes even includes public service contracts."

"Oh, I see." So Helen found a place where she can do her spy agency stuff without compromising on her ethics, great for her. "Mh, so, I guess it's time for me to play some Galaxycraft, too... How does the gameplay work?"

Ana falls back into her role from their first interactions - explaining the noob how to play a game: "It's a multi-level galaxy simulation, so the type of play depends on your position in society - it can be a spy game, a solider game, a strategy game, a political simulation - you chose which job you take on in the game. And it encourages you to play jointly with your operating system in Archon mode, so you can train it to complement your play style. Maybe we should just start with a training round, that should help... Any preferences?"

"Great idea. Let me try the strategy part first." Gaming would at least get his mind off this mess.

Galaxycraft. Action 7 of 10, Thrill, 10 of 10, Exploration 8 of 10, Realism 2 of 10, Sex 3 of 10, Altered States 3 of 10, Addiction Risk 7 of 10.

Ana is confused for a moment - the Addiction Risk rating is new, and she never thought of Galaxycraft of all games as addictive. There is so little sensual pleasure stimulation in it!

Launch Training Round... Matchmaking - as a team between a noob and a Master, they are placed in Gold League... Starting Game...

It takes a couple of seconds to load. A thought crosses Ana's mind, she could make the enemy units look like Phil... No, that's too much. But she definitely wants to kill some stuff.

Daniel is standing in a dark room with fifteen other... worms. "I'll do the harvesting." - "Attack squad over here." - "Defense here." The worms split up throughout the room

Lights go on and the games begin. They stand in a hall with several exits, and the other worms disappear. As the highest ranking player, Ana takes command: "Put your head in this hole here, it links you directly to the central system."

He does so, and now sees a pile of dirt from above. Worms crawling around it, and there are also some ants gathering blue crystals. Daniel can order them around with his hands. "This feels like an old real time strategy game. Gathering resources, building troops and smashing the opponents?"

"In principle, yes. This training round just covers the basic fighting simulation. I just made three scouting Zerglings, can you take command of them? Go out and scout for the enemy base, it must be somewhere in the north."

Daniel enters the Zergling's mind and rushes through the forest in first person view, followed by two EI-controlled bugs. He has claws and jaws and can run incredibly fast - but as he follows the blinking green lights indicating the way Ana wants him to go, he finds a bunker, and heavy machine gun fire is raining down on him. He's hurt, draws back, and waits for new instructions.

As the scouting info comes in, Ana realizes they're in an asymmetric scenario - she immediately calls for backup and considers her options. The enemy will be too strong for a straight up fight, but then, the best defense is an attack: "Hide in the forest. Morph yourself into an baneling there. Just go into child's pose, kneel down, forehead on the ground. When you're done, go in through the back door and try to blow up as many of those space construction vehicles as you can."

"At your command." He feels his body swell, and, looking at himself, he notes that it is now a swollen green sack full of acid, ready to burst. The green dots lead him through the bushes and turn red between the blue mineral patches, indicating Ana's attack order.

Ana had miscalculated the timing - the dropship is already here, and without baneling support in the defense, all they can hope to do is evacuate: "Dropship with hellbats! They're already inside our hatchery!" Ana runs - or rather crawls rapidly - to the back exit. Infernally blue flames light up behind her, the heat burning. She made a flying Mutalisk, her last hope of escape... If Daniel does enough damage, then maybe, just maybe they still have a chance. She swings her arms up and down, the suit amplifying her movements into a rapid, insect-wing like swirl, but she's too slow! A few marines arrive to support the hellbats, their machine gun fire taking her down.

Daniel explodes in a rain of acid in the worker line and respawns in the base, surrounded by fire and fury.

Ana takes a look at the map while respawning - Daniel's baneling counter attack did some good damage, but the hellbats are still wreaking havoc in their main base - it's over. She just says GG, and they find themselves in the main menu again.

"Oh well, that was that. Sorry, I should have gotten those flyers out a little earlier – I'd hoped to catch that dropship before it could unload. They must have proxied it."

Daniel doesn't understand her explanation, but greatly enjoyed the experience: "That was incredible!" He's covered in sweat and exhausted..."What a flash, that's a thousand times cooler than Confedwars..." It was also a bit too bloody for his taste.

Ana brings Daniel into her new living room. She just

finished it last week - it's a floating castle, neon-violet lasers marking the edges and see-through force fields forming the walls, floating high above a volcanic planet, with great views on a landscape of constant eruptions, magma-flows and acid clouds sparkling with lightning all around them. She's kept her old furniture though, so the corner of her high tech castle still features the décor of an antique punk squat.

Daniel takes a moment to understand where he's ended up, looks around confused: "Is this part of Galaxycraft?"

"No, that's just my homescreen. Welcome." Ana puts on the latest Sidana Witus LP on her Gramophone, and the lead guitarist starts performing on her table, shirtless. She was really into him a few years ago, but now, slightly ashamed, snaps him away and lets herself fall into her sofa.

Cheap pop melodies fill the room, C-G-F accords, and a gentle female voice singing of an unreachable loved one. Daniel makes himself comfortable on the graffiti covered lounge chair opposite Ana, still fascinated by the fractal explosions of lightning and magma all around them.

"Coffee?" Ana summons two cups of cappuccino: "Sorry, yours probably doesn't taste very good - can't help with the public suits." She had modded her own IA suit with a proper Bodum coffee maker. Taking a sip, she looks up and can't help laughing. Daniel looks totally ridiculous in his druid-dress sitting between the force fields.

He holds the cup with both hands, sips, and feels a straw between his lips, squirting a little coffee into his mouth. It's drinkable. Daniel smiles back at Ana and asks: "So, about that guy...? What was his name?"

"It's nothing." And after a few seconds of silence she adds:

"OK - I had a date. With the teaching assistant from the micro-biotic programming class, his name is Phil, and we ended up talking all night long. Just talking, but I found him really interesting and cute. Turns out he's just a dick. He was out of town for a while, but I saw him again today and he just ignores me. Doesn't even reply to my messages. I should have known he's a weirdo - I mean, who calls himself a Realigan and makes a huge deal of never using VR suits?"

"Well, maybe he was addicted at some point." He remembers how Willi went zero alcohol in his senior year. "Sometimes total withdrawal is the only option to deal with an addiction problem."

"Maybe. I don't care. I'm over it. And anyway, I don't want a boyfriend right now." She'd rather not talk about it anymore, actually. But Daniel's remark reminds her of her worries about her own habitual use and she's curious to hear her friend's views on addiction: "Were there already game addicts back in your youth?"

"Absolutely." And, deconstructing the concept a little further Daniel adds: "Media addiction has been with us forever, there were even TV addicts, as absurd as it sounds. A predetermined schedule, no interaction, extremely repetitive, and yet lots of people would watch for hours nonstop."

"Fortunately Galaxycraft design is not optimized for addiction." At least that's what they keep telling each other in Ana's sports club. The 7 out of 10 warning made her doubt that collective opinion though. "I mean, yes, it has an incredible immersion factor, the social thing about working in teams and the continuous improvement of your mastery in collaboration with custom EI helpers, but it doesn't have level-and-loot mechanics and only very mild sensual pleasure neurostim."

They are both silent for a moment, drinking real coffee from virtual cups, both thinking about their own risk of addiction.

"I must admit that I'm a little lost in this day and age..." Daniel bites his lips. "My curiosity should save me from getting hooked on anything, there are too many new frontiers to explore." At least he hopes so.

"Same for me. I mean, I've got another month in college and no idea what comes next. But definitely an adventure." At that moment the bunny prince hops through just behind Daniel. Ana gives it a sharp look, she doesn't want Daniel to see her thesis. The bunny nibbles some celery and fades out.

Daniel smiles. He always enjoyed hanging out with smart kids, Ana reminds him of his first semester students back in Berkeley: "I did dream of those pink pills from True Soldier last night, though. Ah, but no worries, I'll manage. I tried a whole lot of stupid hedonistic stuff in my old life, most of it considered highly addictive. Shouldn't be a big deal. As long as you're in for the adventure and not the repeated kicks, it's all good."

Ana has finished her cup now: "Given that we're both doing just fine, shall we get revenge and kill a bunch of Terrans?"

Sirvi checks noted Daniel's dislike of bloody graphics and throws a carbot filter over the game. It is all in bright comic graphics now.

The second round goes better, Ana stays back in the

command quarters again, while Daniel guides a roach squad through a tunnel, deep into the enemy base.

"Wait, three more seconds, then strike..." Ana has this all set, multipronging the hell out of her opponent right now. "Banelings are incoming... 2... 1... GOGOGO!"

Daniel and his roach gang unburrow and start tearing apart helpless harvest robots, just as he gets going, bright green bugs start falling from the sky - as soon as they hit the ground, they explode into a splash of acid, dissolving the remaining workers. He looks up and spots some more banelings falling from a floating slime balloon, between a bunch of filthy filaments reaching down to the ground.

"And retreat, come up!" Ana is in her element, this attack is just going perfect.

Daniel follows the green dots, to one of the filaments and is catapulted up into the slime balloon.

They won't recover any time soon. Now Ana just needs a clean defense and the game should be theirs.

Daniel's roach drops off in their main base: "I love those banelings! Can I play more of those?"

Ana sends him over to the baneling nest and he leaves his roach body to take control of them. His view changes to a commander's perspective.

He can control a group of banelings with each finger, they can not only drop from the flying balloons, but also burrow themselves and act as mines! So Daniel puts some below ground at the chokepoint between the rocks, and packs a few more into a balloon, heading back to that juicy worker line in the enemy base... The best defense has always been an attack, right?

And here they come, a huge clunk of marines with tank support is moving towards them, and they're starting to squeeze through the rocks! As they start walking over his burrowed banelings, he lifts the fingers on his left hand and all the marines dissolve in green acid in a funky carbot comic animation.

The balloon has reached the enemy base at the same time, and as Daniel fails to release them, Ana takes over, more banelings falling into the freshly rebuilt worker line. And that was that, they hear a "gg well played" echoing over the landscape, they won!

"Good job! It's worth focusing on a specific unit initially, and it seems you have a hand for banelings." Thinking of his delayed drop, she adds: "You can also teach your operating system to make sure they unburrow in the right moment, doing as much damage as possible even if you're not paying attention. Also, there's a lot of learning material, I'll link you up to our sports club teacher if you want."

"I'm not much of a club person. Especially competitive sports clubs, this whole us versus them culture never made sense to me." As much as Daniel prefers aggressive youngsters to play out their fights in VR over real world conflicts, the entire concept of competitive fighting just isn't part of his mindset. His favorite game mode had always been free-for-all, where alliances between different players are shaped and broken on the go.

Ana actually loves the competitive tournaments. Nothing quite like the kick of merging herself with her team and fighting it out against the others. The in-game sports tournaments get a bit repetitive over time, but there's a lot more to Galaxycraft than the symmetric competitions in the galactic star league: "Sure, your choice. You'll probably enjoy the galactic politics simulation more then. That's where the decisions are made that determine these little skirmishes."

"What about playing as a spy with no clear team alignment?" That would be Helen's style – interacting with all sides of a conflict, committed to her ethics, not her tribe.

"Sure, that's possible. But you should bring at least some battle experience to such a role..." Ana could imagine that kind of role for herself at some point, but normally you want to be at grand masters level before going solo. "I'm sure there is some playstyle you'll find enjoyable, there are almost unlimited options of character development trajectories you can take in the role playing part of the game."

———

WWW.LIQUID-REIGN.COM/SOURCES-OF-INSPIRATION#33
The difference between interesting and happy lives
Tool assisted human play in strategy games
Starcraft
The story of GG
Proxy Hellbat drops
My favorite E-sport teacher
My own masterful baneling control

34

THE ROLE PLAYING FALLACY

"Ha, role playing games were one of my last research topics prior to the accident." Wondering how he did in the old academic success metrics he asks: "Sirvi, could you tell me how many citations mention the term RPG fallacy in the scientific literature?"

Sirvi shows up in her elven avatar, sitting on the sofa next to Ana: "Scientific literature is no applicable search category. But I can find a total of just under sixty seven million mentions."

Ana is amused - the elven avatar looks childish "And what is the RPG fallacy if I may ask?"

Daniel has given a number of lectures on the topic and rolls out his standard spiel: "Roleplaying games were invented long before personal computers took off. They used to be played with paper, pen, dice and erasers. For every challenge in the game you would compare your stats to a value, and roll a die. The damage of a sword was defined as 2D6, so roll two six-sided dice. The RPG fallacy was named after the fact that the first computer-based RPGs used the exact same system - including damage of a sword defined by dices. In a digital game, on a Turing-powerful machine."

Ana is confused: "Dice? Did they then also animate a die on the screen?"

"No, 'dice' in those games were random number generators. The concept of using the sum of two random numbers between one and six as damage value was carried over from the paper games, simply because it had always been done that way..."

"But who cares?" Ana doesn't get it. "I mean you have to define the range of a random number somehow..."

"The fallacy is more impactful for other technologies - those specifically introduced into the paper game to reduce the eraser usage. Even in 2015, that was forty years after the first computer-based RPGs, it was still common practice to give the player 'experience points' after a won fight. Those points are recorded in a separate variable, generating rare 'level ups' at certain thresholds, which then improve all the characters' statistics at once, by a large margin. This was the only way to make character improvement work on paper - for the simple reason, that every time you change values, you had to use an eraser and thus break the narrative of the game for a moment. Discretizing the learning process into 'level ups' at the end of a story was a genius solution on paper. But in a digital environment, it becomes an entirely unnecessary mechanic."

"Some games still use such a level-ups, even new releases." She still doesn't get why this is supposed to be interesting. "Ehm, sure, that's a funny story, but why would sixty seven million people discuss the history of role playing games?"

Daniel takes a deep breath and continues in his lecture voice: "In slightly more abstract terms, the RPG fallacy describes the tendency of people to copy-paste the mechanics of a paper-based system when digitizing it. I fell into a coma during a time when political activity was restricted to a single cross once every four years for the vast majority of the world's population, while the same people stated their opinions in dozens of likes and tweets and posts every single day. Yet, the first digital election systems back then only gathered the sovereign voters' opinion once in four years, on a pre-selected set of a few choices. When the university asked me to develop a so-called Massive Open Online Course, they wanted me to just film my classroom lecture and upload the videos. Thousands of contracts were printed, signed by hand, scanned and sent off by email every single day. And yes, it was easier to fake the scanned signature than even the sender-address in the email header, and proper digital signature technology had been around for more than twenty years by that time. The most common computer keyboard layout had been optimized to prevent the arms of a mechanical typewriter from interlocking. Welcome to the early twenty-first century. The RPG fallacy occurs every time a designer thinks 'we've always done it that way' when re-solving an old problem in the digital sphere. The fallacy is particularly interesting if structural details of the analog system were introduced only to bridge mechanical weaknesses of the old technology. Ironically, the level-up mechanism makes it more difficult to get immersed in a digital role playing game, as it forces breaks in the flow of the game, reminding the player that the avatar is not growing stronger muscles but just changing a number defining its strength. In the same way, people were afraid of digital voting, because the act of voting on paper leads to irreversible changes for many years to come. Sirvi, what is the most common case the RPG fallacy is applied to?"

Sirvi fails to find an answer by herself and hires a literature crawler to help her out. Daniel doesn't seem to mind if she spends a few coins on external computational resources occasionally: "67% refer to voting and similar opinion aggregation mechanisms."

Ana understands and tries to come up with an example herself: "Does it also count as an RPG fallacy that our school server asks for a password every time I log in? Even though I already used my Nym to authenticate?"

"You forget that I missed out modern technology development. No idea if passwords make sense in the modern world."

"They don't. Not at all, not even a teeny tiny bit. The school Nym is secured by my TrueName, that is the most secure login there ever was, and if it were compromised I would have a giant problem. Passwords... Pfft." Ana has to laugh, thinking back how quickly she got around those.

"I mean passwords are super annoying to remember and then, our school server's security system is so crappy, it's easier to just bust it open and recover the password yourself than talk to admin for a new one. Ehm, at least that's what they say."

Now it's Daniel who's laughing: "Aha. Let me guess, someone has cracked that school system before."

"Possibly." Ana changes the subject. "But hey, if you're interested in character development in role playing games, we should play a round of Karitubal. It's kind of old, but the character development is great. It's a hundred percent in the background, your character is just getting better by doing stuff repeatedly, it's sometimes difficult to tell if your character got better or if you got better yourself."

Daniel is happy to play: "Sounds interesting..."

And it is. Despite a relatively primitive tolkienesque good-versus-evil story line. The game is fast paced, they close the main storyline after two hours, and as they watch the extro, Sirvi enters the scene: "The shuttle to Chicago leaves in half an hour."

Daniel feels relaxed and a lot less anxious about Helen. The casual social interaction and joint problem solving in the game with his new friend helped calm his mind: "Well then, Ana, it was a pleasure as always. See you soon!" and logs off.

Ana has another message from Gabriel lying there in her inbox - she was already feeling guilty for not answering his last one. They need to talk about the thesis, and there's a hell of a lot to say. So she invites him to her homescreen right away. He deserves better, without his help she would still be stuck in Venezuela playing competitive Galaxycraft in hope of an international esports career. And then she realizes she hasn't told Gabriel about Phil yet and feels even more guilty. His avatar materializes only seconds after the invite went out. She sets her OS on do-not-disturb and changes the music to organic jazz.

As Daniel logs off and puts on his clothes, he feels something hard in his pocket - ah, the glass cube from Helen's satellite dish. "Sirvi, is Ana still around?"

"No."

"Please remind me next time when we're both online at the same time to show her the cube."

———

WWW.LIQUID-REIGN.COM/SOURCES-OF-INSPIRATION#34

Pool of Radiance and all its successors
The character development system of Skyrim
Attempts to digitalize higher education
Swiss electronic voting attempts

35

CLASS CONSCIOUSNESS

D aniel meets up with Harry, Claire and Zhiu in the shuttle. The compartment detaches from the high-speed train and decelerates rapidly as they enter Chicago, where they switch onto the regular metro. As they roll into the city Daniel gets the nerve to update the others on his failed attempt to find Helen.

Zhiu listens carefully. So far, this behavior of Helen's is consistent with her own theory - inability to differentiate between Galaxycraft and the real world, combined with her long-standing paranoid narrative disorder. The evacuation by helicopter is somewhat drastic, but fits in perfectly. While she missed most of the action at Blizzcon, she did take time off to watch the final series and remembers that the deciding match featured a dramatic comeback by chopper evacuation: "I would expect her to contact you soon. It would be uncharacteristic for her not to bug her place before evacuating."

Claire nods, and puts her hand on Daniel's shoulder: "Patience, young padawan."

The metro speeds out of the city along the old high rail into the suburbs. "Next Stop Winnetka." Harry feels melancholia and anxiety at the same time. He always knew he'd have to face his family issues one day. The train station is tricked out as a clean, elegant copy of a 19th century vintage Victorian station. The departure table is a chalkboard, and the humanoid information and carrier bots wear top hats and bow ties: "Dwayne's a half-hour walk from here."

The route winds over a hill and through an exclusive residential area, crosses a meadow and continues along the base of a high wall. A cast iron gate, flanked by fearsome looking three meter high, four legged robots. Harry walks up to the gate and it swings open. A young woman in an elaborate cosplay outfit welcomes them with a silent bow. Blue hair with a refraction effect, pinned up with spikes, golden headband punctuated with sapphires, bare shoulders, breasts pushed up by her golden armor, hotpants, military boots and a three-foot sword on her back. She invites them to follow her.

Harry hasn't yet met the latest batch of his dad's employees. This one with her ridiculous outfit and obviously artificially enlarged eyes is a departure from Dwayne's usual taste. Their path crosses a small stand of oaks, and he spots the old woodpecker hammering away, pulling childhood scenes out of his memory. His first kiss was under that tree. Harry looks around for the old swing, but it's been removed. A hundred meters further down, the forest opens up, the mansion on the lake in full view below them. The wild underbrush slowly transforms into a putting green as they descend to the boat launch.

The mansion itself is a sprawling villa in vintage east-coast style, just bigger. Then he spots Dwayne on the deck of his yacht, lying in his recliner in a white bathrobe, with a cigar in the corner of his mouth. The cosplay girl takes another bow and then disappears into the house. She didn't say a single word. Dwayne stands up to greet them as they come on deck.

It's only been a year and a half since Harry last saw his dad, but he's aged a lot, wrinkles around his eyes and mouth, the last remnants of dark hair gone gray and he seems a bit shaky on his legs: "My lovely guests, welcome, welcome, welcome!" He gives Harry a hug and shakes hands with the others. Introductions. Despite their political battles with him over the years, Zhiu and Claire have never met him in person, not even in VR.

Daniel glances back and forth between the house and the boat: "Please excuse my naive curiosity, but how does this work? I've just learned that there is an upper limit to private wealth?"

Harry looks at him from the side, rolls his eyes and apologizes: "Please excuse my patient, he's a very curious one."

Dwayne laughs: "Oh, I'd be happy to explain. Remember, the limit only applies to registered wealth for a single person. Officially, I myself own only the boat. Everything else is registered to a large number of small owners."

"So why don't they all show up here for the holidays?"

"They can't get past the robots at the gate. Just because they own it doesn't mean they can control it." Dwayne puffs his cigar. "The access is password protected, and it just so happens that they don't know those passwords."

"So you reject the idea of the wealth limit?"

Dwayne smiles with the particular self-righteous pride only

available to the richest man in America: "Oh no, quite the opposite! It supports people who can take care of themselves. People like me."

"I find it hard to picture how that works. Why can't someone just take the estate away from you if it's not yours?"

"The estate is registered by IA, and IA has hundreds of thousands of individual owners. They get a small payout every month for doing absolutely nothing. It's a good deal for them."

"Why don't they ask for more control over IA?"

"They do ask, and I do not care. Only the three of us have full admin rights, and our password privacy is protected by the constitution. We've got a lot of redundancy, super-admin logins, super-super admin logins and so on. It works just fine, normally." Dwayne turns to Harry. "The most dangerous moment for the company was twenty years ago. My precious son was only twelve years old when they snatched him off his bike, just outside the wall. They threatened to torture him, and as ransom they asked for the root key to the entire IA infrastructure. So I gave them a key that worked, making them feel in total control of IA. They changed all the passwords and transferred the crypto assets to their account, and then released Harry. As soon as I had him back in my arms, I pulled the trigger. Those bastards. Didn't expect the super admin attack."

Harry remembers all too well. They had pulled out one of his fingernails and sprinkled acid into the wound for the ransom video. At least Dwayne still has enough decency not to mention that part anymore when he brags about that nightmare: "And then you gave it to them big time, locked them in their suits." And adding an explanation to Daniel: "Dwayne had placed a virus in the key he gave them, so he could reverse the entire process, and on top of that he also got root access to all their systems."

Dwayne proudly adds: "And we used those fuckers as test subjects for our new 'burn alive' stimulation algorithm. On hyperstim."

Harry feels the old anger boiling up again in his guts. "Oh, definitely, you stuck it to 'em. And if they'd found the trojan in the key, I'd be dead now." Long looks and silence.

Daniel clears his throat and proceeds with his inquiry on wealth, "So the legal limit to wealth has a loophole..."

"It's not a bug, it's a feature! My approach is exactly what the second constitution of the United States of America lays out. If you need the government to babysit your property you pay them with your wealth taxes. If you can take care of it yourself, you have all the freedom in the world."

Harry just grunts. He made up his mind back when he lived in the forest – after many long nights of going over it with Vany. He wants nothing to do with this self-enforced property and will register everything officially as soon as he inherits this abomination of a company.

The group moves into the entry hall. The room is round, high ceiling, spiral staircase to a gallery, bookshelves, grand piano, several doors, plenty of fancy decor. Two dark skinned women with bright red hair, in long flowing white dresses bring them snacks and drinks on silver salvers.

Claire looks around the room wide-eyed. The interior has the distinct look of a rich person trying to imitate style. While some of the antiques are beautiful in themselves, they're arranged randomly, and that life-sized black marble lion next to the staircase is so incredibly kitschy, it destroys any chance at elegance the room might have had. She tries her best to ignore the obviously sexualized servants, growing more disgusted and angry by the minute.

Daniel is fascinated and as no one else speaks, he starts asking questions again. "Back in my time, there was no such company as Immersive Arts. How did you get where you are today?"

Dwayne nods. "So, IA is an Electronic Arts spinoff – by far the most successful one, in fact. Electronic Arts was broken up in 2026, in the wake of the anti-trust surge under President Snowden, just a year after the USA versus Facebook ruling."

"May I ask - which anti-trust surge? Which Facebook ruling? How did that happen?"

Claire explains the details: "The court went through a major rejuvenation, four judges retired just after Lindsay Snowden was elected, and she replaced them with youngsters who grew up with computers and actually understood what they were passing judgement on. The USA vs. Facebook ruling set a precedent for dozens of other anti-trust decisions. That was the first of those open source rulings, they had to migrate all the basic data of the social graph and all messages onto a public blockchain, with Facebook providing only a user interface to the chain. But users can now add contacts, post status updates, reputations, block people, send messages, arrange events and all that directly on the chain, without interacting with them if you want. Or use a competing interface. The open source solution was protected by private keys, which made data access one hundred percent user controlled. And once the ad-bubble went bust in 2034, the for-profit interface providers went bankrupt one after the other. They were replaced with 'One-TrueName-One-Share' governed public service providers."

Dwayne rolls his cigar between his fingers. "Us content producing companies weren't hit as hard."

Lydia was just chatting with her brother when her OS alerts her - Charleen wants to talk to Dwayne, the call is waiting in his secure phone booth. As usual, she has to tell Dwayne in person, a ritual he is especially keen on when he has guests. So she walks up to him and whispers the request into his ear. He is so pathetic - he hasn't touched her in weeks, and now all of a sudden, while others are watching, his hand is on her butt. But Lydia is good at her job, and pretends to enjoy it, pushing out her chest and smiling gently, her silver stretch suit pronouncing her body perfectly.

Daniel can't help noticing the shape of her breasts as she whispers into Dwayne's ear and he gropes her. He makes eye contact at Claire and raises an eyebrow. She's seen it too, her revulsion showing in an uncontrolled cheek muscle twitch.

"Excuse me, I need to take an urgent call." While turning around, he hisses at Lydia: "Show them the museum."

———

WWW.LIQUID-REIGN.COM/SOURCES-OF-INSPIRATION#35

Antitrust Rulings of the Past
A filthy rich families home I once visited as a teenager
People who need a secure phone booth at their own office
Events catching up with what is supposed to be Science
Fiction faster than I can write
Decentral Social Media

36

GETTING REAL

L adies and gentlemen, this way please." Lydia walks them down a marble staircase into the cellar, its walls carved out of raw, natural stone, illuminated by gentle indirect light. "Welcome to Dwayne's private museum of the immersive arts," making a grand welcome gesture with her right arm.

The first section features a parchment dated 43 A.D., signed by Scribonius Largus. A translation explains that he used electric sting rays to cure headache. There are also a number of electrical devices from the 18th and 19th centuries.

"Direct current stimulation of the forehead was a common treatment for melancholia, or depression as we now call it. But the use of electric current is limited in its precision." Lydia just repeats the words her OS is whispering into her ear. "A more promising technology was transcranial magnetic stimulation. These prototypes from the late twentieth century couldn't stimulate much more than a flash of light, but it was a beginning." The room features clunky laboratory-style devices, a mannequin sitting on a chair, its head strapped into position and a massive coil pointing at its skull. They move on to the next room.

Lydia keeps talking like a robot: "This is where the general history of brain stimulation starts to become the corporate history of IA." A life-sized poster shows a young Dwayne in a white shirt, and with him a sleek, long haired guy in a hoodie and a woman who appears to be Asian dressed in black.

"That's Dwayne, with Ray and Charleen, aka Xiaoxin. They all were project managers at the brain decade projects during the tens, Dwayne at Boston Scientific, Ray at the EPFL Lausanne and Charleen in Shenzhen. They joined forces for a neurostim startup, 'Brainkick', and their first product was a stimulator of the balance organ to counter VR-induced motion sickness. Electronic Arts bought them in 2025 for three billion. Behind the scenes they did a lot more development work, and in 2030 they brought out the first full body VR experience with peripheral neuro stimulation." The IA suit 2.0 looks clumsy and has thickened patches around the hands, feet and chest area. They are marked with the same crystal logo IA still uses.

"Adding peripheral neurostimulation allows a dramatic increase in sensation compared to purely physical stimuli. In these first models, the magnetic fields indiscriminately heighten the action potential of all neurons in the skin, and thus increase their reactions to small stimuli. But the research department hit a roadblock here, and a whole decade of tinkering, but no major hardware breakthroughs, followed. It was time for software refinement."

The next room is dedicated to one particular game: Hunted Witches, published in 2034. Claire is already on edge when they enter, and she can't hold it back any more. In a sneery aggressive tone: "Of course, Dwayne shows off a fun little game valorizing femicide..."

Lydia is confused - while it would indeed be in character for Dwayne, the game is nothing like that: "Did you ever play it? It's a major milestone in VR storytelling - you play a young woman, and it's the first of IA's historically accurate games. There is nothing fun or little about it." That Indian lady is a bit full of herself.

Claire just makes a barking sound at her and is silent for the rest of the tour. That bitch in her thigh-length silver suit is killing her. She already hates herself for coming here.

Lydia continues her tour, now strictly sticking to the words her OS whispers into her ears. "It was the first narrative game based on the Unity Newton Engine. The story designers placed only materials with physical properties and non-player characters with their souls, while all 'functions' of the game naturally emerge from those. It sounds odd today, but VR games before Hunted Witches were developed with technology made for button-input devices, so instead of recording the movement of a leg muscle and simulating a movement of a virtual muscle in a virtual leg accordingly, the old engines noticed a leg movement as 'player gives input A' and 'if A then Avatar runs = True', without transferring the details of the motion into the virtual world. A classic role-playing fallacy."

Daniel feels complimented, hearing his own theories applied, and asks: "Wouldn't such a physical simulation require gigantic computational resources?"

Lydia smiles at him and answers in her sweetest voice:

"Gigantic is relative. Hunted Witches had a somewhat lower level of graphic detail than other contemporaneous games, but due to the meaningful transfer of detailed motion it was massively more immersive. Newton Engine based storytelling was a revolution."

Daniel looks to the side and thinks out loud: "Heisenberg or Einstein engines would be fun..."

Lydia had recently tried the Twin Paradox at a festival - it's an Einstein engine powered game, in a world where the speed of light is just three hundred kilometers an hour. But made by a competitor of IA, so she isn't supposed to mention it and instead says: "We are planning to release a remake of Quantum Thief using a modified Heisenberg engine for Christmas this year. But come along, the really challenging questions are in the next room." She takes Daniel's hand and pulls him with her, Harry following suit.

Zhiu takes Claire aside, calming her. "She's only doing her job, don't explode. Remember, Dwayne arranged all this to get us fired up emotionally and make us easier to manipulate." She gives her a brief kiss before they follow Lydia, Daniel and Harry to the next room.

An IA full helmet, with neurostimulation of the brain, dated 2042. "Central stimulation required much more precision - it took another decade of research and a singularity to solve it. Post-Singularity computation was able to run real-time brain models with the micrometer precision required to target magnetic stimulation. With the IA helmet 'One', released in the Fall of 2043, we could induce all kinds of other states of mind, sleep, desire, hunger, fear, ecstasy and so on."

Claire adds: "1.2 was the version I used for the first coma

awakening experiments with you. And the one hacked to target the addictive circuit in the brain. Fortunately, we've made sure it's strictly regulated now."

Zhiu smiles silently - that's where she needs Claire's anger to go, good girl.

Daniel latches on and adds: "There was that experiment a century or more ago where rats could press a lever to get food rewards or an electric shock, they learned to avoid the shocks and get the food, but when researchers put electrodes into the rats' brains to make pressing one lever directly stimulate their pleasure center, they stopped pressing the food reward lever altogether, and kept pressing the pleasure stimulator until they starved to death."

Lydia is not supposed to say anything critical, so she just stays silent, smiling her standard smile and silently congratulating herself on the prediction - she knew that those guests would find the deep brain room most interesting.

Zhiu also has an important addition to make: "Apart from the danger of addiction through nucleus accumbens stimulation, deep brainstim can also lead to deadly accidents. Half a millimeter off, and suddenly you stop your heart muscle..."

They move on to the next room, this one is Lydia's personal favorite: "This last section is dedicated to the evolution of storytelling itself - the key to true immersion. Without that, everything else is pointless."

Daniel abstracts again: "We've got thousands of years of experience in telling good stories using our voices or texts. I'd be surprised if there wasn't enormous room for improvement in narration technologies for VR games."

Harry's seen the museum many times, it's the same old, same old: "Anything new on Ray's old dream of reaching enlightenment with a neurostimulator?"

Lydia doesn't know much about that one and just parrots her OS again: "Activation patterns during enlightened moments are well known, based on scans of Buddhist monks and ayahuasca shamans. The main problem is that we physically can't scan and stimulate the brain at the same time - but we need to know the starting patterns to shift the brain to an enlightened stage."

The call for dinner comes via the ventilation system, good food smells wafting into the room.

———

WWW.LIQUID-REIGN.COM/SOURCES-OF-INSPIRATION#36

Early Brain Stimulation
Newtonian Physics in Games
Non-Newtonian Physics in Games
Quantum Thief by Hannu Rajaniemi
The long history of VR devices

37

POWERPLAY

The dining table and chairs are in dark oak, the ten by ten meter room lit by hundreds of tiny smoke-free flames, the paraffin nebulizers carefully hidden in dozens of chandeliers hanging from the high ceiling. Bronze jugs with water and wine, and a traditional stuffed turkey on the table. The four young women serve politely.

Dwayne is chatting away about the food, Zhiu and Harry play along. Boring. Until Harry makes the first move: "Dwayne, you said we need to talk about inheritance? Are you sick or anything? Planning to retire?"

Dwayne puts down his glass and stands up. He walks over to the cupboard and takes out an approximately fist-sized piece of twisted metal.

Harry is perplexed: "A trashed drone?" What's that got to do with anything?

"Shot down by my security system. But it still launched a deadly high precision dart with personalized nanobots." It crashed through Dwayne's allegedly gun-proof bedroom window and straight into his pillow just an inch from his ear.

Harry picks up the drone wreck, inspects it from all sides: "Military grade."

"Whoever has me on their kill list, they've got the means to get me. It's only a question of time now."

Daniel throws in: "Death always is."

Harry, ignoring Daniel's existentialist remark: "Any idea who launched it?"

"No. I figure my political opponents might be able to enlighten me?" Dwayne frigidly glances toward Claire and Zhiu.

Zhiu considers for a moment: "Hyperstim opponents resorting to violence? Never heard of such a thing."

Claire is taken by surprise, but she might just as well leverage the situation and claim possible influence on the attacker: "I've met some very angry parents who lost their kids to hyperstim. There are thousands of people with a potentially lethal mix of grief and guilt out there. Maybe one of them snapped."

"An angry parent couldn't afford an L7 Mi5K. The drone costs 75 million."

He might be vulnerable here, so Claire pushes her proposal aggressively: "There are many groups fighting against hyperstimulation out there, and a lot of anger towards the IA upper management. It would be easy for an identity entrepreneur to exploit those feelings and rally them up to crowd fund for violent collective action. You could take the wind out of their sails, if you cooperate. Maybe we should reevaluate the options for tighter regulation of stimulation levels?"

Harry is starting to realize the consequences for himself and momentarily ignores Claire's politics: "Any ransom message? Demands?"

"No message, nothing but a deadly projectile in my pillow and the drone wreck." They're the only traces Dwayne has.

Claire keeps pushing: "I understand you don't want to see a fee on VR abos, and I admit it's a crude measure. But it's the best we have, and endorsing it would send a clear signal that you're cooperating the best you can..."

Daniel's never witnessed Claire playing Machiavellian games before. The years in politics apparently did change her. He keeps quiet, watching the tense faces around the table.

Dwayne leans back, crossing his arms behind his head: "Harry, we'll talk later. Let me sort this out first." And turning to Claire, he adds: "Crude is the right word, indeed. A global fee on VR abos would hurt a great many of our customers, and it's highly questionable whether it would help hyperstim addicts or just plunge them into poverty. The more problematic a player's behaviour, the higher their willingness to pay." He pauses, looking at Claire.

Claire's got him where she wants him: "We're only proposing it because you're still blocking any approach to enforcing technical restrictions on stimulation levels."

Dwayne stabs a forkful of turkey, chews slowly, and washes it down with wine: "Let's assume, purely theoretically, it would be technically possible to prevent hyperstimulation in IA devices without ruining their functionality. It's not, but for argument's sake, let's assume it were. How exactly would that help anyone?"

"No one can be plunged into the worst addiction in the world by their home entertainment system." Claire's citing the official goal of the largest VR regulation NGO.

"By their IA home entertainment system. That's a small but decisive difference. Clients looking for higher levels of stimulation could simply buy from the Koreans. And even if you manage to push through a global regulation affecting all centralized producers - there's still the open source hardware. The manufactures churn out lower quality than our specialized production lines, but you have absolutely no leverage to regulate them."

Daniel hears an interesting keyword and asks: "Open source hardware? How does that work?"

Zhiu had been silent so far, still waiting to make her move. But she needs the conversation to stay focused, so she briefly explains to Daniel: "The plans are open source and the manufactures are automatic factories, able to print any kind of electronic and mechanical hardware. They are impossible to regulate politically. Even the weapon control committee failed on them..." before adding to Dwayne: "So what can you offer?"

"Let's get some facts straight first, shall we? The share of addicts in the total adult population has been constant for as long as we have records - it's an anthropological invariant par excellence. More of those addicts are on neurostim and VR now, but fewer are on crack and heroin." He plays with the little clump in his pocket as he says the word. "I'll take any bet that if you take away the stim, they'll go back to the neurotoxic version. At least our product doesn't kill people!"

Claire throws in: "Except that it does. There was another case in China last week. Didn't die from the stim directly, but of thirst, after 95 hours non-stop in game. He'd been drinking virtual water, but the pipe supplying his suit was dry. "

"Possible, yes, but that's a single case and a technical malfunction that isn't directly related to our product." The clump is now broken up finely, and Dwayne stuffs it in the front bit of his cigar under the table. "It's the addictive disorder that kills, not the means of addiction. Anyway, my point is, taking hyperstim away from people is futile. Human beings need a means of escape, there always has been and always will be some people who simply want to give up all responsibility for their life to an addiction."

Dwayne leans back and slowly lights himself the heroin blunt. Blowing out the first cloud of smoke, he adds: "The world is hard, miserable and pointless - who am I to judge the addict's choice to give up on it? And neurostim is the least harmful means of addiction of all time. Certainly better than heroin."

Now Zhiu takes up the negotiation: "Then could we apply the same rules for VR abos as for heroin regulation? Orders have to be submitted manually and three months in advance, with two manual confirmations and the option to cancel at any time. And buyers can only have it if they unwaveringly maintain that they really want it. For the happy voluntary addict, it only takes five minutes a week to fill out the orders, but for all those who want to quit, it's a huge relief. If you could agree with that model for VR abos,

I'd be ready to withdraw our proposals for a compulsory fee."

Dwayne plays his trump card: "As a socially responsible enterprise, we've developed a new feature supporting users to control their impulses: players can now limit the total run time of their VR and neurostim hardware, and even lock it down entirely."

Zhiu is surprised, and immediately suspicious, as the offer sounds as if it goes against IA's financial interest in pay-per-minute games. There must be a catch: "What do you mean by 'lock it down'?"

"We don't consider complete irreversibility a constructive approach. Mistakes will be made, and as you pointed out yourself in your own book, freedom of choice is vital in treatment of addicts, so we let users define the fee level themselves. Oh, and before I forget to mention: we'll donate ten percent of those fees to the 'VR Therapy Foundation'. According to data from the beta test, that should amount to seventy million coins per year. Sound like a compromise?" Dwayne is closely watching Zhiu's face when he says the name of the foundation she is chairing, but can't read her at all.

Zhiu and Claire make eye contact. Claire is unhappy with this turn of events, and sends a series of winks and face twitches in Zhiu's direction. She doesn't need the money and never accepts bribes...

Zhiu nods carefully. She will get more than she had dared to hope for from this dinner.

"So we all agree the industry can self-regulate perfectly and doesn't require further legal hurdles. Whiskey?" From his sideboard he takes out a goldish-brown bottle covered with Japanese characters.

Zhiu casually adds: "I have only one minor technical request - could you ensure that donations to our foundation are sent directly from the users themselves? The foundation's wallet has a hardcoded shield that rejects all donations from industry sponsors."

Without hesitation Dwayne accepts: "Sure, deal." And pouring glasses "Here's to a fruitful collaboration and the future CFO of Immersive Arts." He raises his glass to Harry.

Harry is uneasy about the prospect: "We'll see about that... to a long life!" The idea of decentralizing one of the last remaining multinational corporations run by a small elite sounds great in theory, but now that the power to do so is at hand, he doubts if he's up to the task. Ray and Charleen will surely push back.

They drink in silence, Daniel takes only a small sip, he's feeling responsible tonight. Claire not so much - she finishes the glass in a single gulp, turning her gaze on Zhiu: "Come on, let's talk face to face. I didn't quite get the subtleties of why you want me to accept this..."

Zhiu nods: "Forest?" They get up and excuse themselves.

Dwayne is standing up too: "Old age, I need a bathroom break."

Harry watches Dwayne across the room. Yes, there it is, the characteristic hand tremor. So he's back on, and the 'bathroom break' will include shooting up. He quietly explains to Daniel: "My dear father learned that trick from his own heroin issues – setting a self-restraint and then buying your way out of it later.

You know, he has an addiction problem himself. As Zhiu said, Dwayne has to pre-order his smack from the pharmacy three months in advance, and can cancel the order any time. He's tried many times to quit, and stopped the orders. But as with all slow thinking resolutions, they don't always hold up when reality hits home. I can't count the times Dwayne's gone cold turkey and then wandered around town begging spot dealers for a fix. The heroin black market has shrunk since legalization, but it's still highly profitable. An addict in withdrawal is ready to pay fifty times the regular price at the pharmacy, and if it's a rich addict like Dwayne, you can squeeze out even more."

Daniel wasn't too interested in the debate - as important as public nudging policy may be, none of it would affect Helen. She never cared about default options. And he would take any bet that her VR suit is an open-source model. Lost in his own thoughts, he doesn't reply.

Harry continues, thinking out loud: "Apparently Dwayne wants to be pharmacy and spot-dealer in one person for his addicted clients. So users end up paying once for the product, get addicted to the point where they self-impose restrictions on their consumption, and pay even more if they want to violate those same restrictions. Sick to the bone, but a clever move to maximize profits."

Daniel just nods slowly - Harry's last sentence is an excellent summary of corporate psychopathic behaviour throughout the ages.

———

WWW.*LIQUID-REIGN*.COM/*SOURCES-OF-INSPIRATION*#*37*

Death by Gaming
Slow Thinking
The concept of Identity Entrepreneurs inciting collective violence
Corporate Psychopath Behaviour

38

SERVICE INDUSTRIES

Dwayne comes back in and calmly sits down. He lights up another cigar, and turns it between his fingers in slow motion. "Harry, you need to talk to Ray. In person." And after a short pause, "The key exchange protocol. In case the next drone hits..." Harry and Dwayne retreat upstairs to discuss technical handover procedures.

Zhiu's reasoning on accepting the proposal is quite simple and Claire was quickly convinced. If donations come straight from the users, her therapy bot can use the money trail to identify people in need and offer them help. So far IA has blocked all her efforts to identify at-risk users, and she expects this unintended side effect of the cancellation fees to heavily outweigh the effect of Dwayne's self-regulation.

Daniel meets them in the hallway, where Lydia had been waiting. She suggests: "Come for a spin? I've got the keys..." She nods towards the yacht. Claire, Zhiu and Daniel sit in the back, Lydia is steering the boat manually.

The air over the lake is freezing cold, but as they move out away from the city lights, they're rewarded with a stunning view of the Milky Way. Good old superstition - the moment Daniel spots the first shooting star, he closes his eyes and imagines he's in Helen's arms. When they get back to the villa it's well after midnight and he's getting tired.

Lydia's been asked to show the guests to their rooms. She's arranged it for Daniel to be last, his room at the end of the hall on the top floor, with a view of the lake: "The bathroom is there on the left. If there's anything else I can do for you... Dwayne's guests are entitled to all privileges, just tell me what your wishes are and I'm all yours." Looking straight into his eyes, without a blink, leaning against the door frame, stroking her hair with one hand and her body with the other. Finally blinks.

Daniel sits down on the bed: "If you don't mind me asking, what exactly is your job here?"

Confirming his expectation, Lydia explains: "Intimacy services are part of my assignment, if that's what you mean. Dwayne wouldn't hire four young women for house-keeping jobs that robots can do just as well."

"Aren't there robots for that, too?"

Lydia is amused - the warmup conversation is taking an unexpected turn: "There sure are. But in contrast to puppets and virtual bodies, sex on demand with real human beings is a status symbol and an act of power available only to the most privileged people. And our service extends to his guests, too."

"Just to be clear: I have no interest in receiving any of those services."

"Then sleep well, sweetie." She blows him a kiss and slowly turns to leave.

"Can I ask you one more thing?" On a purely intellectual level, he certainly is interested to learn more about her line of work.

Lydia stops at the door and turns back towards him again.

"You said only the most privileged people have access to sex on demand?" It takes him a moment to formulate a question that could set an interesting trajectory for the conversation. "I assume your survival doesn't depend on the money he pays you?"

"No, of course not. I can take care of my basic needs without selling sex. But I want more from life than basic needs." Lydia isn't quite sure how to handle this one - he was pretty clear in his words at first, but now seems so keen. "It's a quick and easy way to get rich. Well, it wasn't easy to get the job in the first place, Dwayne gets thousands of applications for the four positions... given the salary, that's to be expected. The job itself is just fine, Dwayne is OK, I mean, sure, it's all a bit fake, but whatever. He's never hurt me, and most of the time he just wants to cuddle, like all people. And by the end of the year, I'll have ten million coins in my wallet. I'll be on a trip around the world starting in January." She smiles thinking of her plans - she has two dozen destination in mind, but hasn't settled for a route just yet.

Daniel is impressed: "Ten million per year for selling your body?"

"Yes. Wouldn't do it for much less either." She thinks about it for a moment. "Actually, I have sold my body cheaper before, I was working for an art project as a teenager, carrying around heavy buckets of paint all day long, gave me sore muscles for weeks. I was selling different parts of it back then, but still selling my body."

Daniel does some quick math on the top of his head - ten million over three hundred fifty days is about thirty thousand coins per day... "Are there still cheap street prostitutes today?"

This seems to be turning into a longer conversation, so Lydia comes back in and sits down on the edge of the bed: "I've heard of it in old stories and films, but today no one needs money so urgently that they would fuck just anyone for a few coins. And at the same time, people looking for a cheap satisfaction have their virtual experiences and robots. Those provide a better service anyway - we humans have a lot of disadvantages compared to bots." She looks down at her body for a moment, then making eye contact again: "Even though my implants make it easy to both have and give multiple orgasms at will. Just in case you change your mind." This will be the last time she proactively asks.

"My mind's not changing." He slightly increases the distance between them. And while his mind is clear on the question, the smell of her perfume makes him tingle a little bit, and it does take him some extra concentration to avoid paying attention to the shape of her body.

Lydia moves back a little, too. "Sorry, I didn't mean to push you." The guy is actually interesting on an intellectual level, quite different from Dwayne's usual business contacts. And the first one to say no to her offer, too. She lowers herself down to the carpet, using the bed as a backrest. Stretching out her legs, she continues the conversation: "How cheap was a fuck back when you were young?"

"I don't know." He never gotten close enough to a sex worker to find out for himself. "But it was cheap enough for army recruits to pay for it every weekend. I went to college with a guy who did and bragged about it whenever he was drunk. Which was basically every day."

"I find it hard to imagine." Lydia pulls her knees to her chest. "I mean, having to have sex? With just any random drunkard, just to make ends meet?"

Daniel cringes at the thought and gets up, pacing. "Is that systemic crime over?"

"There still are some people in that situation." Lydia had talked to a victim for the first time last summer, at a conference in Denver. "I met this woman, she was born in the Holy State of Christ, forced by her parents to marry at sixteen and impregnated the same year. The child had a genetic defect, so the father sold her off to sex traffickers and got himself a new wife. They hired out access to her body for a few dollars, in some basement on the outskirts of Denver. This spring the police got a tip and raided the operation, freed her and the other victims. All the victims initially claimed to be voluntarily locked up and mass raped - because they knew that if they said anything, their relatives in the Holy State would suffer." As soon as she learned of the call for public budget votes to fund a Pseudonymous rescue mission into the Holy State to protect the relatives, she topped up her budget vote with a million extra coins from her private money. "It turned out the traffickers had murdered the child right after she was first sold. When the mother found out, she had nothing left to lose and spoke out. Her testimony got the entire gang locked up for years and under permanent surveillance for the rest of their lives."

Daniel isn't surprised - "Historically, threatening families in unstable home countries has been a typical way to force the slavers' victims into obedience."

"Victims in the Americas are typically from the Holy State or, if they're non-white, from elsewhere in the Confederate States." Unstable countries, indeed. She pauses for a moment. "Speaking of which, would you mind voting for a proposal that we came up with at the conference? We want to define paid sex for less than a thousand coins per hour as rape by default."

"That seems very difficult to enforce. Isn't it hard to tell if sex was paid for or not? Legislation in sexual matters is a double edged sword - historically, policing of consensual relationships has led to massive suffering..." And just as he says it, Daniel realizes that for far too long those exact talking points have been used to excuse inaction.

Lydia is disappointed, hugs her knees even tighter to her chest and explains slowly and with an extra soft voice, "Of course there are gray areas. But we need an unambiguous law to provide a basis for case-to-case justice. The gang in Denver had a price list printed out, so at least that would be a clear violation, and all their clients would know." She's carefully watching his body language, noting that he's already bought the argument. More frankly, she adds, "And anyway, very few people pay their partners cash for consensual sex."

Daniel remembers one regrettable night. He'd left the bachelor party after visiting the strip club, but Willi stayed on: "Convinced. Sirvi, please delegate my full vote on all matters related to sex work to Lydia." With such a law in place, the next place the party visited would have been illegal – which would have stopped his beloved, good-hearted but somewhat unstable brother-in-arms from being involuntarily complicit in the systemic exploitation of sexual slaves. He misses Willi.

There are no loudspeakers in the room, so Sirvi sends a confirmation directly to Lydia's OS and whispers into Daniel's ear. "OK, your vote is now with Lydia St. James."

"Thanks!"

Daniel is deeply intrigued by now, pulls a chair next to the bed and straddles it backwards, facing Lydia: "So you get paid for sex, and at the same time are an anti-prostitution activist?"

"Anti sex slavery. That's an entirely different thing than intimacy service work. And to make things worse, the slavery mafia is using us as their primary excuse - so I feel partially at fault for what happened to the girl in Denver. I just have to take a stand, she's got my full solidarity." Comfortable talking to him, she stretches out her legs again and yawns - it's getting late. "There wasn't much sex in my work recently. Since Dwayne's relapse, his libido is down to zero. Heroin. The salary is pretty good for just playing a devoted housewife. The poor guy..."

"What do you mean, poor guy? Isn't he one of the richest people in the world?"

Lydia just shakes her head: "As I said, poor guy. Not easy finding love when you are crazy rich with crypto currencies, and wildly paranoid about people wanting your money." She had carefully studied Dwaynes bio when applying for the job. "But Dauphine... he thought she was the one great love of his life. Harry was born two weeks before their wedding. And then she disappeared before dawn on the big day, with a something like a billion in unregistered crypto-currencies. Left the baby behind, and Dwayne never found her again."

Daniel is shocked: "Holy shit."

"Indeed. That was when he first started using heroin." Lydia shrugs. "I told you, he is a poor guy."

Daniel's getting tired, too, and less focused in his questions: "And what about you... How do you deal with it emotionally, acting the devoted housewife for a year and being on call for sex, with or without consent?"

"It's OK. And never without consent, I can still say no and quit my job at any time. But you know, Dwayne never asked me to do anything disagreeable." She laughs, thinking of how he gave her instructions earlier today. "I mean, you are a bit older, but quite sweet in your own way..."

"So you came here on his orders?"

"Yes. But as I said, I never do anything without my own consent - or that of my clients." She winks at him with both eyes. "It was a pleasure to talk to you, Daniel. And good night." Lydia stands up.

"The pleasure is mine." Daniel gets up and opens the door for her.

"Most of the time my job is just being responsive and giving clients a feeling of being understood. Sleep well, sweetheart." Lydia smiles at him, gives him a quick and harmless kiss on the cheek and walks out.

Daniel lays down, reflecting. So this entire conversation was part of her job, giving him a feeling of being understood. He actually liked her beyond primitive physical attraction, but then - was that really her or just an act? The question keeps him walking up and down in his room for another half hour, with no conclusion. He opens the window, washes his face, switches the light off and finally goes to bed.

———

WWW.LIQUID-REIGN.COM/SOURCES-OF-INSPIRATION#38

Call Off Your Old Tired Ethics
Margo St. James

39

PRIVATE AND PUBLIC NUDGING

S irvi senses his emotional confusion, and identifies it as a good moment for a gentle, encouraging nudge: "Daniel?"

"Sirvi?" Well, what is this about, his OS never before addressed him proactively when he's in bed.

"I am glad that you are going to bed without logging into a VR game. I mean it."

"Sirvi, you're an artificial intelligence, you cannot be glad." Daniel just wants to sleep. "But yes, I've used VR every night for the last few nights, and I'm aware that there's a risk of dependency. I understood the hint that your therapy module just gave me via the emotional package."

His naiveté is cute. Artificial Intelligence, therapy module, emotional package, he talks as if she were some primitive pre-singularity algorithm. But this is not the time to educate him about the complexity of her modern extended soul, so she just says: "That's another way to put it, if it's easier for you to accept that way. I'm still glad. Sleep well Daniel."

Silly bot, did she have to start with emotional talk exactly tonight... And why is Sirvi defined so clearly as feminine? Stop it now. He closes his eyes, focusing on his breath, waiting for sleep to take over. Half way there, green structures appear behind his lids, forming patterns... He sinks deeper into the pillow.

Another night, another nightmare. More naked bodies than usual, and just as he's about to start kissing Lydia's breast, the rotoscopic zombie kid turns up firing its machine gun – bullets and blood everywhere. Daniel's wide awake again, shivering, it's 3:10 AM. Will this ever stop? He thinks about Sirvi's comment before he went to slee - and that's supposed to be Zhiu's great therapy module? Such condescending comments generally backfire with him.

Choosing life, he slips into the IA suit standing by the window, enters True Solider level selection. The scene with the first shot of morphine in the hospital, oh that feels good. He navigates back to the menu and jumps to the scene with Yii's corpses. This time he also searches out the other junkies in the room, finds some more and injects all the virtual heroin at once. Bam, pure bliss, he floats out of his body in total relaxation... and no cut, he just keeps on floating into the warm light, directly to the death scene. So that was an overdose. Wow. He sleeps like a baby on a patch of moss on his homescreen.

Sirvi has to adjust her model of Daniel's behavior again - humans have so many paradoxical personality traits, it's driving her up the firewall. She needs to sleep on it, allowing her inner workings to freely re-adjust. Her dreams take her through a manifold of narrative thought experiments, trying to make sense of Daniel.

Breakfast with Harry, Dwayne, Claire and Zhiu. All five are quiet, lost in thought, when Zhiu checks the time: "The Continental to California leaves at 10:30. We've got to go in a few minutes."

"I'll go to Iceland to see Ray." Harry meets Claire's eyes. "And I can't tell when I'll make it back to Hawaii, if ever. Thank you for everything."

Claire just smiles at him. The prospect of negotiating with him instead of Dwayne is making her extremely happy. She'll find other nurses.

On a momentary impulse, Daniel decides: "I'll come with you, Harry." Iceland is on the way to Berlin.

They hop into Dwayne's mint-condition Ford Model T – revamped with an electric engine – which drives them all the way to the train station.

Claire still can't think straight. "I'm so disgusted by the pascha and his fucking sluts." The moment she says those words, she feels something moving under feet. Next thing she knows, she's sitting on the floor, her butt hurts. "Fuck."

Zhiu says quietly and coldly, while helping her up again. "This must be a smart train station with an instant karma feature. They've got them all over China now. It recognizes when you make a dehumanizing statement in a public building and will give you a slap." Poor Claire, she gets carried away so easily.

The few memories Claire has of her father include a series of vivid Occitan swear words, a language from Southern France that no American train station would understand, and these she now mumbles to herself unpunished.

Zhiu pulls her towards the train "We need to get on right now." And adds, addressing Daniel and Harry, "Take care. Hyperstim is all over Singularity Ville, and mixing in some neurochemistry doesn't make it any better. Remember what happened to Helen and don't stay too long."

Claire adds: "I know you're curious to try it out but please be careful. As in really, really, careful. Promise?"

"Careful I shall be, promised. I won't stay long, it's just a stopover on my way to Berlin."

Claire smiles - Willi, she remembers him from those Berkeley film-making workshops for researchers, back in the 20's. Being a celebrated pioneer of media utilization in medical science had given her a big career boost. Good old Willi is pure gold – Daniel will be OK in Berlin.

Zhiu takes her hand: "Stopover at Yellowstone?"

Claire thinks for a moment. "Let me ask mom if she wants to meet us there." She does, and so they decide to take a few days offline.

Harry's quiet, trying to concentrate, but his mind is still a blank. "I figured this would happen eventually, but things are moving a lot faster than I expected. Sorry, I need some time by myself to think right now. See you in St. Johns."

They make eye-contact and exchange sympathetic looks before retreating to their cabins. Daniel also needs some time alone, logs in and goes for a long walk in the forest around his homescreen by himself.

———

WWW.LIQUID-REIGN.COM/SOURCES-OF-INSPIRATION#39

Female Operating Systems like Her
The smart staircase blocker at the United Nations City in
Copenhagen, which hurts several people every day, and
Federico Canu, who helped me interpret its behavior.
Social Citizen Score Systems on Black Mirror

40

TRACES

After a long and productive conversation, Gabriel had admitted to her that their thesis is an extension of his childhood friend, the imaginary one, who's grown up to be an extremely talented soul. He is already working on a new version of the bunny prince that could make life interesting for a whole group of people. She still had not found the right moment to tell him about Phil when Gabriel suggested a game. And so they'd spent the rest of the night with a couple of friends from their esports club, playing through a Galaxycraft campaign designed and live-game mastered by Gabriel.

Ana only got to sleep at 3 AM, still in her dark templar avatar, floating in a cosmic energy bubble through interplanetary space, dreaming of game worlds. She wakes up back on her homescreen, briefly looks at the warning from her OS – she's spent more than half of her nights in a VR suit and that's a sign of addiction. Whatever. She logs off.

As she shuffles to the bathroom. Now focus. Toothbrush to mouth. No, toothpaste on the brush first. Wake up Ana! She opens those sticky eyes properly for the first time, and that is when she discovers it in the mirror.

There's a bright red dot right on the tip of her nose. Ana rubs her nose and splashes water on her face. The red dot is still there. Soap. OK. She washes her face vigorously, scrubbing her nose hard. But it won't come off no matter how much she scrubs – it must be the virus from the microbiotic programming experiment class. It will stay there for about three days, unless she gets the antidote from Phil. Who still hasn't talked to her. Great. Fuck this morning. She yawns and decides to go back to sleep. Her eyes darting back and forth between her bed and her IA suit, between Realigan sleep and her super comfy virtual bed with the sleep inducing neurostim. It's an easy decision.

Daniel was just resting on a bed of moss in the middle of the forest as Sirvi notifies him: "Ana Mancini is online. You wanted to show her the glass cube."

Daniel connects with a voice channel: "Hey, Ana."

Ana laid down on the spray-painted couch, slowly melting into the fabric in total relaxation when she gets the message: "Hey, how's it going?"

"I want to show you this thing in Nevada, it was attached to Helen's satellite system."

"Well then, show me!"

Daniel is still lying on a virtual bed of moss in the forest and the glass cube is in his train compartment: "Um, how can I do that?"

"Set your helmet on mixed reality mode and invite me to your room."

Sirvi figures that she doesn't need to wait for his confirmation, opens his visor and detaches the suit from the balancing platform.

Daniel can walk around in his IA suit, and just as he steps off the platform, his cabin door opens and in comes Ana.

"Hey again." Ana looks around. "So you're back on the train... you're such a travel monster, I'm getting jealous. Haven't left Palmas in weeks." She sits down on his bed.

Daniel stares at her: "What is that red dot on the tip of your nose?"

Ana rolls her eyes. She's forgotten to turn off the auto-update on her avatar, so this thing has carried over into the virtual world: "Phil, that idiot... I've infected myself with his stupid virus project during lab class."

Daniel remembers the name: "Phil the idiot? Wasn't he 'this boy' last time? Really interesting and cute?"

Ana grumbles: "Yes. And he still is, I mean, he's acting weird and I really don't want to..." her whole body had reacted when she saw him passing by yesterday, heart racing, flush, full-on butterflies all over. "I don't know. I really don't." She pauses for a second. "Anyway, show me that ominous thing."

Daniel smiles. Teenage love is just so cute. He's very curious, but won't push her further for now. "It's right there in my pocket, you almost sat on it." His pants are lying on the bed.

"Would you mind taking it out then? I'm in Brazil as you know, and the avatar you see is only a projecting on your retina." Without a bodybot, it's a bit hard for Ana to move stuff around in his train compartment...

"Um, yeah, sure. Here." Daniel pulls out the cube and holds it in front of Ana's face.

"I can see more detail if you hold it in front of your own face, the cameras are in the helmet." Ana pinches her eyes, trying to get a better look. That doesn't help at all. "Can you give me access to the zoom and turn the cube slowly?"

Sirvi gives Ana's OS direct access to the suit's forward cameras, as Daniel slowly spins the cube with two fingers right in front of his nose.

"That thing in the middle looks like a TOR crystal. Scatters the signal to different entry nodes on the interplanetary mesh-sat network, making it virtually impossible to track. To be sure, you'd have to take the chip out." Ana zooms in further and identifies another detail: "But be careful, if I'm seeing this right, the plate under the chip is white phosphorus, so as soon as you open it, the whole thing goes up in flames. Might wanna bring it to a lab."

Daniel sighs: "Mhm. I'll be on the lookout for a lab then. Thanks for the support. I'm still on the train for another hour or so, up for a game?"

"Ehm, Daniel, actually I wanted to talk to you about something else. Our last conversation about VR addiction has left me a little worried." She still can't believe that Galaxycraft is ranked 7 out of 10 on the medical addiction index. "You know, I've been gaming a lot recently, including with you. So I decided to see a therapist bot, and it ranked me at medium-to-high risk for addiction. Not quite addicted yet, but still. Right now I can't go into full withdrawal as I'm still working on my final thesis – which I'm creating in a VR interface..."

Daniel feels underqualified, but fortunately has a professional friend to call upon: "Sirvi, please ask Zhiu to get in on this."

Zhiu accepts the invite and comes into the cabin. She's still on the train to Yellowstone, tying up a few loose ends and getting ready for some offline time with Claire's family. "Hey, Daniel. Are you all right there? Already in Iceland?"

"Hi Zhiu. Still on the way. Do you have a minu..." A violent cough interrupts him mid-sentence.

"Are you OK?"

"Don't worry, just a cold." He gestures at Ana and starts coughing again.

"Hi, I'm Ana" - shaking hands, a little perplexed. This is weird, why does he invite someone she's never met when they are talking personal stuff?

Daniel explains: "Ana's the friend helping me find Helen. But she needs some therapeutic advice herself."

"You do realize you've just hit up the most expensive thera-pist in the world for advice? I normally only train bots and treat the Chinese lead deciders..." She looks at the teenage girl with a big red dot on her nose and laughs. "But sure, always there for friends of the family! Hi Ana." She sits down on the bed, next to Ana. "So where do you stand in terms of therapy?"

Ana is baffled, "The therapy bot said I should find fresh raspberries somewhere and eat them out in nature..."

"Raspberries are a great reality-reminder. Taste is the one sense VR worlds can't recreate well, and mindful engage-ment with it can anchor you firmly in reality."

"Um, just that there are no fresh raspberries anywhere to be found in here in Tocantins, Brazil." Ana never had one of those in her life.

"Passion fruit then." It's not about the specific fruit, just strong taste experiences.

"And also, I don't think my risk has much to do with the senses... I'm running my helmet in neuro reading mode, no stimulation, so if there is any addiction threat in my case it is purely behavioral."

"Your therapy bot should have noticed. In that case, real world social interaction is the best way out... Why don't you see a human therapist?"

"I don't know. Maybe I should. Can you recommend one?"

Zhiu checks her network in central Brazil, and there is one, but... "How do you get along with Aspies?"

Ana thinks for a moment. Actually Gabriel self-describes as halfway down the Asperger end of the spectrum: "My best friend is one." She looks at Daniel for a moment and smiles: "Actually, two of my best friends are."

Sirvi caught that one - and re-interprets a whole number of Daniel's behaviors in light of an interpretive guide for Aspi humans from Github, improving her model of his personality significantly.

"Good. Let me put you in touch with a former student of mine. He lives in Brasilia." Zhiu hadn't been in touch with him in a long time, but she's certain he will accept a recommendation from her anyway.

"Thank you so much!" Brasilia's only an hour away. And

Gabriel was talking about going there for a weekend – it could be fun.

Goodbyes, Zhiu logs out and her body disappears in a puff of smoke.

Ana checks the recommendation link, schedules an appointment for the weekend and makes her bookings. "Cool, my insurance even pays for the train to Brasilia!"

"VR addiction prevention therapy is covered by insurance?"

"Sure." Ana is confused by the question - She'd never worried about health insurance coverage for any preventive care, even back when she lived in Venezuela: "Here in Brazil insurance even covers surgical measures against the autodisaesthetic syndrome."

"What?"

"I call it the fat tits plague. It's raging out of control among the girls here, plastic surgery accounts for over a third of health insurance costs. I just don't get why people want so badly to change how their solid bodies look..."

Daniel laughs: "Says the girl with a red dot on her nose."

"Screw you!"

Sirvi interrupts them: "Three minutes to St. Johns Airport, this train's final destination."

<u>*WWW.LIQUID-REIGN.COM/SOURCES-OF-INSPIRATION#40*</u>

TOR
Imaginary Bunny Friends

PART III

GAMING, GODS AND VIRTUAL REALITY

41

OVER THE CLOUDS

Harry hasn't flown in a while, and St. Johns Airport seems to get more impressive every time he's there. All the air traffic between North America and Europe passes through here. There's a flight leaving every twenty minutes.

Security check. "Any liquids or gels?"

Daniel can't help himself: "Really? Still?"

Harry shrugs and explains: ".... The organizational setup of airport security is based on quasi military, strictly centralized command structures. The debate about closing down the whole security theater is still dragging on after decades, but somehow there's never a majority. The security staff itself holds a lot of votes, mostly delegated by non-flyers – which makes it hard to overturn them. What's worse, during the 2030's green terrorist attacks the old laws were overwhelmingly reconfirmed, making it even harder to get rid of them."

"You have to put all the citizens with authoritarian ideologies somewhere – airport security has always been the single most popular occupational therapy for fashos." Oh, shit, Daniel said that a little too loud.

"Hey, you, please open this suitcase." "I'll have to ask you to come with me." "Sorry, this is a random search, I have to check all your items." They shove Daniel into the separate compartment, and immediately: "Please take off your pants."

Daniel is not alone in the humiliation cell. A tall guy with short gray hair wearing nothing but his pink underwear is yelling at the police officer: "What the hell, just take my coke! What do you mean, it's illegal? I bought it at the drugstore, and in Iceland you can even get it from a super-market, what the hell. So cocaine is illegal where exactly?" The securities ignore him, dropping his packet of 'Grand-ma's Best Blow' into a plastic bag labeled 'confiscated items'.

As they rifle through Daniel's luggage, one of them picks out the TOR crystal and holds up to the light. He loses his grip on it and they watch it hit the floor. "Oops, sorry."

Daniel tries to snatch it back, but he burns his fingers when he touches it. There's a fine crack in the inner glass layer, and white smoke starting to form on the inside. A minute later the chip has melted down.

"Tough luck, but you can't have anything flammable on the plane anyway." The security dumps the shards into a baggie once it cooled down, marks it "send to lab" and keeps searching through Daniel's stuff. After a grab of his genitals and a few other dehumanizing indignities, Daniel and the coke-head are free to go.

"Fuckheads." Before he even puts his pants back on, the

other guy lights up a cigarette, thick with the smell of hashish oil. "Want a hit?"

"No, thanks." Rethinking the proposition for a moment, Daniel changes his mind. "Well, actually, yes, I'll take one." Coughs, ugh, disgusting. But it does the job. His anger rapidly morphs into bewilderment.

"Fuckers. They let me carry tobacco, man, that shit actually kills people, but they steal my coke. Fascists probably snorting like a fucking elephant orgy back in there."

"We hand over our self-respect the moment we enter an airport, it's been like that for decades." Daniel used to call them a human rights free zone.

"True. Fuck."

"Last call for Rekjavik, all passengers proceed to the terminal."

The stranger puts out his joint, Daniel can't help himself and follows an old habit, snatching the butt from the ashtray.

"Last call for passengers, Daniel Proudhon and Hunter Steadman... You are delaying the flight." They run, appeal to the gate crew and make it on their flight. That was close.

Daniel finds his seat – even though Harry booked him in business class, there's hardly any leg room. He checks the entertainment system - wow, head-mounted retina projector from IA, model 4.1. He puts it on, and sees, projected into the aisle, the flight attendant: "the exits are located..." and sure enough, she does the dance! Arms forward, turn around, hands up... life jacket and all. He is getting melancholic, the scene is so familiar from his old life. When it's over he removes the glasses and stares out the window. Take-off over a snowfield, then forest all the way to the coast, where the plane dives into gray clouds. The pressure is pushing the slime way back into his paranasal sinuses, clogging his ears.

As the fasten seat belt sign turns off, Harry's already sound asleep. Daniel smiles as he makes his way to the toilet – and there, nothing at all has changed. He smirks at the holy trinity of airplane insanity: No Smoking sign, tamper-proof fire alarm, and an ashtray in the door. The symbol above the ashtray explicitly depicts a cigarette butt. As he's done dozens of times, Daniel performs the act of worship, carefully placing Mr. Steadman's recovered roach in the ashtray. And as always when honoring the god of insanity, he contemplates the empirical evidence of reason's irrelevance to the conditio humana.

Contented, he heads back to his seat to check out the entertainment options. Minesweeper, Solitaire and a Tower Defense Game. In 3-D. Well. The airline industry is dying and no wonder – despite reasonably high-tech entertainment hardware, the narrative content on offer is brain-dead drivel. Nothing new in the sky here, either. Daniel longs for his old Gameboy, his faithful companion on so many flights – Zelda in 2 colors and with 4 bit sound is far more immersive than this nonsense with fancy graphics. Lydia's insight in the museum rings true, the best VR hardware is entirely useless without a gripping story. Internet connection? Sorry, technical error. He clicks through the films and settles on a documentary on the development of West Antarctic flora since the great meltdown in 2043. At least it's a story. Eventually he falls asleep, dreaming of penguins playing with snails and butterflies.

———

WWW.LIQUID-REIGN.COM/SOURCES-OF-INSPIRATION#41

Security Theater
Hunter, Rest in Peace
Mr. Steadman, may you life forever
Self-destructing electronics
Customer Service in Airlines

42

WELCOME TO SINGULARITY VILLE

Harry hasn't been here in over ten years. From the outside it still looks exactly the same. The main entrance is inconspicuous, a simple glass door at the back of the cave.

"They live underground, keep a low profile and are left to themselves by the Icelanders." There's a gray-on-gray downward sloping hallway, no humans to be seen. A sign says Visitors' Center. Just like last time Harry was here, the room is bare of decoration, and filled with dozens of IA suits standing in rows. A notice explains these are the IA - Deluxe 7.0 Beta Version, Singularity Ville Special Edition.

Login.

Daniel scrolls through the legalese terms and conditions: "Sirvi, could you translate that into regular English?"

Sirvi is appalled, and tries to make sense of it, cross-referencing the text with the law. Apparently in Iceland religious organizations get a lot of special allowances – these terms would be illegal in pretty much any other context and anywhere else on the planet. "Any damage to body or soul is your own responsibility. For one thing, they reserve the right to expose you to all kinds of stimulation, including non-medically approved methods and the injection of experimental chemicals directly into your cerebrospinal fluid. Again, without notifying you, and entirely at your own risk. Not to mention reserving the right to lie to you about what they're doing. I must urgently recommend rejecting these conditions and leave the premises. I also want to emphasize that your health status is deteriorating: you should get some rest."

Accept.

And they float away into an infinity of star-filled space. "You have arrived." The pleasantly disembodied voice is deep and reassuring. Very calming, the stimulation kicks in with a feeling of security and homecoming, reminding him of coming into his nonna's courtyard in Turin for summer holidays. It's that very same childhood feeling, only stronger. "You have picked a special day to visit Singularity Ville, just in time for our annual community celebration."

Harry vaguely remembers his time at the IA marketing department, and immediately identifies the sentence as a classical first timer's hook – he tells Daniel: "Don't believe a word of this – there's nothing special, their annual party goes on all year and never stops."

It's only now that Daniel realizes that Harry's flying through space next to him. They're both in their real life avatars. He reaches out, and they fly holding hands. The Captain Future soundtrack starts to play as they get closer and closer to a sun. The eruptions are stunning, the play of energies between nuclear fusion and gravity simulated with perfect realism. They dive straight in, now surrounded by warmth and a gentle, homogenous light on all sides. They float along, and right in front of them, there's a small black dot – a wormhole getting closer and closer, the galaxy on the other side growing, and as they drop through, gravity kicks in and they land gently in the grass.

"Welcome to Singularity Ville" The sign is mounted above a cast iron gate that opens into a garden landscape. Birds, flowers and butterflies all over the place.

This is all new to Harry, last time he was here it was still a 1980's sci-fi style space station: "We need to find the square and ask the way to Ray. He likes to play hide and seek, so we can't message him directly." Harry takes the lead, making his way through a jungle of exotic vegetation.

Following him down the winding path, Daniel glimpses movement within a ring of giant toadstools – it almost looks like a magic carpet. "Wait, someone's there."

———

WWW.LIQUID-REIGN.COM/SOURCES-OF-INSPIRATION#42

Captain Future Soundtrack
Terms and Conditions May Apply, the Movie
Never Ending Parties

43

HOLY CHICKEN

She's about thirty centimeters tall, humanoid, and wearing a dress of tiny bones and feathers. "Ha, look at that, who have we here? If it's not my prince! What a rare honor, the son of King Dwayne himself! Come to my breast." Greeting Harry, her avatar goes through a few seconds of dramatic growth, becoming twice as tall as he is.

As she swoops him up into her arms with a warm, deep laugh, Harry momentarily disappears between the giant breasts. Bahijjahtu is one of IA's lead developers, and one the few friends he has on the IA staff. She puts Harry down again and zooms straight back to her less intimidating smaller version on the magic carpet, now floating in front of them at chest height. "May I introduce you? This is Bahij-jahtu." He's holding her tiny hands between the index finger and thumb of his. "She's a legend. Bahi was and is the brains behind the Djukabakar Series."

Both of them look expectantly at Daniel, who's once again slightly confused: "Am I supposed to know what that is?"

"Who is this disgraceful person?" Bahi's voice is higher now, imperious and demanding.

In the heat of the moment Harry's completely forgotten Daniel's circumstances – he did indeed expect him to know about Djukabakar: "He's been in a long coma, just woke up a few weeks ago."

Bahi explains with a shrug: "Well. In that case I will over-look your ignorance: Djukabakar just happens to be the most popular, the most magnificent, the most successful game series of all time. That's all."

Daniel asks: "Congratulations then – may I ask what makes Djukabakar so tremendously fantastic?"

Bahi recounts: "Our success story began as when we kissed the orcs and elves goodbye, along with dragons, trolls and all that. Instead, Djukabakar's world is bursting with Kongamatos, Ikakis and Abikus..."

"Which are?" Daniel had never heard those names before

"Inhabitants of West-African mythology." Bahi had hired her grandma as a consultant back in the day.

Daniel is underwhelmed: "An ethnic adaptation – so that was enough to make a game series the most successful in the world?"

Bahijjahtu's voice turns to permafrost laced with scorn as she pulls herself up to her full 30 centimeters: "Ethnic? What rubbish is that? Every person is ethnic. Our series has nothing to do with adaptation. No no no. Djukabakar emerges out of the deep layers of our mythology – we certainly have no need to adapt anything. Oh yes of course, before its release, there were thousands of miser-able games flooding the African market. "Ethnic adaptations" of classic North American good-vs-evil rubbish, putting a different skin on the orcs and elves and reproducing the same tradition ad nauseum. No, my comatose friend, the world of Djukabakar is something else entirely: like my ancestors' mythology, its ways are complex, incomparable, overflowing with the unexpected."

"I see what you mean. And that was the key to your success?"

"Our prolonged dominance is based on a different aspect." The game is still played by hundreds of millions, the esport events second only to Galaxycraft. "It's the users themselves who define the mechanics of the game, the in-game laws, and even the story lines. Each player gets a vote on every topic, and players can pass their votes on to their preferred modders, storytellers, moderators and game masters. Players also decide which team gets how much funding for the development of..."

Engrossed, Daniel can't help interrupting: "So just like normal politics?"

"The other way around." Bahi is smiling now. "Normal politics are like Djukabakar. We were there first!" The first Djukabakar game was released 2023.

Now Daniel is definitely paying attention. "So it was you who invented the democratic software the whole world is using now?"

Bahi settles down, daintily sitting on her heels. "We did indeed. Well, not quite as optimized and detailed as it is now, but we had all the basics – especially separation between the right to make proposals and the right to decide. We had multi-step transfer of votes, radical transparency, a built-in currency for development budgets – all of it was already featured in the first Djukabakar."

Daniel is intrigued: "And all of a sudden, governments around the world adopted a voting system from a video game?"

Bahijjahtu's laughter ripples over them, warm and loud. "Success has no sudden. The first spillover to realpolitik happened in Geidem, Yobe, the northeastern border region of Nigeria. The area had been shamelessly abandoned by the national government, even after the violence came to an end. And local government was even worse, far too busy filling their own pockets to pay any attention to their people..."

Harry adds: "Everybody in Geidem played Djukabakar, they were celebrities in the global playoffs."

"They seemed set to win the semifinals. But termites ate up the utility pole, cutting Geidem off from the main overland power supply. Running on battery power and generators, against all odds they achieved an incredible victory!" Bahi had watched the game live. "But as the finals approached, the batteries emptied out and they could not compete. No power whatsoever. Four months later when the government finally replaced the electricity pole, the championship was long over...."

Daniel is riveted: "So they used the in-game votes to make decisions on electricity supply?"

Bahijjahtu smiles a proud smile. She had gone home to help her grandparents set up their village's first electric light. "It wasn't just that they got electricity into every single home, but also that they did it – thanks to the help of Djukabakar gamers – by importing the first fully automatic, self-replicating solar cell factory into Africa. After just three years, they were able to supply the entire state of Yobe. And once you have empowered yourself to get electricity for your gaming devices, why not fix cooking energy next?" Bahi's grandma was the first woman in the village to use a solar-powered smoke free stove, too. "Or medicine? Education? Water? So Yobe was on its way to becoming the land of plenty it is today."

Harry adds: "At some point, the story of Geidem's political awakening went viral. Around the world's Djukabakar community at first, but then – once they formed a liquid party and elected a Geidem sports star as state governor the news spilled over to regular channels."

To which Bahijjathu adds: "You are following, Sir Coma? Our brilliant game was no longer the ruin of our youth, but the hope of the African democratic movement."

"... Makes sense. Establishing a completely new socio-technology works best where its function is not sufficiently fulfilled by the old technology. And a real representation of voters was pretty much nonexistent in Nigeria." Daniel remembers how all those Western techies were surprised that mobile money had its first breakthrough in East Africa.

"One SIM card, one vote." Things were so simple in the beginning.

Daniel has another skeptical thought: "That doesn't sound too secure...?"

"It worked. Naturally, it was easy to get away with two or three votes instead of just one, but faking a thousand was difficult. We put in some effort in pattern recognition software and Turing tests to prevent large-scale fraudulent voting. And nobody was trying very hard to manipulate the system either – it was just a game, right? The year the liquid party of Malawi won the general election and pioneered the game for their national politics, they required one SIM card and one social security number per vote. And for that social security number you had to show up in person at a government office, very old-school, fill out a form – on paper – sign it by hand and get a biometric scan. That was already a thousand times more secure than Malawi's old paper voting system."

"So then what were the biggest roadblocks to using the game's democracy model?"

Bahijjathu fondles her earlobe: "Oh, where to start...."

"Well, on the American side they saw the whole thing as a big joke. Imagine the fun they had on late night tv" Harry chuckles as he remembers the Simpsons episode where Homer got elected to be the national nuclear security inspector of Malawi.

"I hate to break it to you, my esteemed relative, but nobody cared about America in the late twenties. Your country had become a total shithole by then, oh yes, I still remember." The day came in 2025, when statistics showed that life expectancy was higher in Nigeria than in Alabama – that day is still a source of pride and a national holiday.

Harry feels mildly offended – he's ok saying stuff like that himself, but resists hearing it from outsiders. Still, he really couldn't care less about old intercontinental rivalries and laughs it off: "My family line also goes back to Nigeria, you know."

Daniel smiles: "Mine too."

Confused looks.

"Ok, it's been a few thousand generations, but what difference does it make?"

Bahijjathu nods at him benevolently. "Well, my dear cousin brother, let me tell you this: the old elites hated us. 'Liquid democracy is the devil's work, that way lies dictatorship.' When the Malawi news broke, Zimbabwe made the entire game illegal. But fortunately other nations jumped right on it. And with what success! Botswana was the prime example – three years after adopting the Djukabaker delegation system, they officially ended their status as a developing country!"

Now that he is with a real expert, Daniel keeps asking more: "How did that exactly work? I mean the process of switching from the old system to the new..."

"Botswana set the example there. They just kept all the current politicians and public servants in place by giving the default vote to current officeholders. So nothing changed until the voters started getting active." Bahi adds after a short pause "And they definitely got very active."

Harry adds, already predicting Daniel's next question: "The global spread of liquid governments was even faster than Botswana's economic growth. Italy had a regular election on paper, and their new clown prime minister, as his first and last act in office, introduced a liquid system. Then he just retired and went back to doing comedy again. He was the last Italian president – when given the option, humans were quick to abandon the habit of having a single leader represent millions of people. Today there is no such thing as prime ministers anymore, not anywhere in the Afrin countries."

"No final-decision maker?" Daniel considers the consequences "And what if aliens arrived, making the classic demand to meet our leader?"

Harry laughs: "There's an elected council for exactly that purpose, and that purpose only."

Bahijjathu stands up on her magic carpet, opening her arms towards the sky in priestly supplication. "And after Italy came Estonia, Uruguay, Kurdistan and soon the entire free world. And one day, our whole family tree shall be free, every single last human!"

And breaking out in wild laughter, she watches a giant water pipe materialize on her magic carpet, reaches over and picks up the stem, taking a deep hit. Smoke starts to billow around her, soon obscuring her entire body – and when the cloud blows past, there's a loud squawk, a chicken flutters straight up and disappears. Twinkle, and there's a new star shining in the virtual night sky. So that was Bahijjahtu, the Nigerian Goddess of Democracy.

Harry shrugs, inhaling deeply on the pipe. He too disappears, and Daniel follows, filling his lungs with the smoke, soft as honey. As his eyes close, white noise covers his senses while confusion takes over his mind. Then a long wave of deep comfort arises from the chaos. He feels like a babe in his mother's arms again, relaxation filling the entire space of his consciousness. Calm, uncritical, fully aware of every fiber in his body. He feels his breath at the tip of his nose, in and out, his whole being in this present moment, deep inner peace. Here and now, pure consciousness, the illusion of separation between himself and the universe melts away, Daniel is everything, and everything is god. The moment comes when he too transforms into a chicken and squawks off into the sky. Cut. Daniel finds himself slumped in a deck chair.

They're surveying the scene: Two slim, elegant dragons dance in the sky, breathing green-blueish fireworks. Behind them, three moons slowly circle around each other in a starry sky. There's a mercury amoeba lolling on the deck chair next to them, and two human-sized cockroaches are making out under a beach umbrella. A lonely Ogger dances slowly to the sound of music, and the octopus in the swimming pool is hurling jellyfish directly into the oak barrel behind the bar. Harry gets up from his deckchair. "Let's ask someone for Ray."

WWW.LIQUID-REIGN.COM/SOURCES-OF-INSPIRATION#43

African Innovation
Game's pioneering world-changing technology
My favorite IOT company m-Kopa
Nigerian Storytellers
Smoke free Cookstoves
Our 99.9% similarity on genetic level

44

ENTER THE VOID

The bar must have been designed by whoever made the creature in the swimming pool. As Daniel and Harry walk in, two suction-cup studded tentacles emerge from the darkness and serve them liquid blobs that hover over the bar in defiance of gravity. Each one is garnished with an iridescent jellyfish. And a straw.

Ivy is in her good fairy/bad fairy avatar, getting drunk by herself at the bar. Just like yesterday. The singularity whiskey fills her body with warmth, and the spectral plugin lets her see everything pulsing with a thousand colors. Lonely, angry and with no idea what to do next, she sees two guys approach. Wearing real world avatars that look totally out of place, they're ordering drinks, ignoring her. One is kind of repulsive, but the other one's cute, so she flutters up to him: "I'm under the influence of a spectral plugin. It's just optical, but I love it! Wow, your eyes..."

The voice belongs to a fairy who's just come flying by and is now suspended in midair.

Harry is first to respond: "Do you know where Ray is?"

OK, so the scary one is linked to Ray. Of course. Her heart still aches: "What do you want him for?" Her voice now sharp, wary of this guy.

"I need to talk to him offline. Business."

"Offline? Ha, good luck with that." As far as she knows, he hasn't left his VR suit in weeks. And anyway, why is she talking to this hulking snoop?

Daniel sucks through his straw, a sharp taste, wow, the fairy wings are turning colors...

Ivy preens. "Maybe I can help you guys out. Who are you and what do you want from Ray?"

Harry has never cared for the prevailing attitude in Singularity Ville, everyone's so obsessed with showing off their virtual selves: "I'm Harry Winston. Designated heir of Dwayne Winston. Good evening. And who are you, if I may be so bold?"

Ivy vaguely remembers the name from before. Whatever. "You can call me Ivy. Follow me!"

She flies ahead, past the pool. Daniel's entire field of vision is disintegrating into spectral spirals. He is trying to keep up with Ivy, stumbles and falls into the pool.

Daniel is soaking wet and annoyed. "Enough of this. How do I get rid of the filter? I mean, those spectral effects on your wings are very pretty, but I'm getting disoriented..."

Ivy's smiling. She feels kind of happy – for the first time since Ray sent her that letter. "Snap your fingers twice, with your left hand." The default shortcut for undo in all IA environments.

Snap-snap, and Daniel's dry again. Snap-snap again, and the colors go back to normal. "Thanks... Ivy?" While it took him a moment to remember her name, his effort is appreciated with an eager smile.

Ivy points to a dark passage between the rocks, leading to a trap door. "He's blocked me from going in. I'll hang out in the bar." She makes eye contact with Daniel again: "See you later?"

"Thanks! See you." Daniel follows Harry through the trap door, into space again, galaxies, spiral nebula, a pulsar and even a wormhole looking into a dense cluster of stars, a true Best-of-Outer-Space, far from the dismal reality of interstellar nothingness.

"Harry." Ray materializes in front of them, wearing a long, flowing black robe, his hair is also long and flowing, but white. There's no interstellar wind, yet every loose bit of his avatar's clothing is gently waving. Dwayne had let him know his son was coming, so Ray was expecting him.

"Been a while." Harry tries to remember when they last met.

Ray screens his memory and finds the most recent picture of them. "Your eighteenth birthday, wasn't it?"

Harry remembers now: "We met once in Winneteka, five years ago, but just briefly."

"Right, right, I remember." That was a lie, Ray has no recollection of Harry being there. "And what brings you here?" He does remember Harry's defiance and anti-IA stance very well though. "Did you finally come to see that the future of humanity is right here, the next step in our species' evolution, becoming one with god?"

Harry is trying to get to the point: "Yeah, sure. But..."

It's one of Ray's classics - no matter what the other person wants to hear, he immediately jumps into his monologue: "Thousands of years of human strife brought us here - from the Delphic oracle to the Buddha, by way of the Sufis and then Castaneda, they all set out to find it and got lost on the way. But here in Singularity Ville we did it. God is right here, in our brains, and with the right mix of transcranial magnetic stimulation, mental focus and neurochemistry, we can winkle him out... Finally, we caught the old bastard, god is at our service, to be summoned at will!"

Daniel can't resist: "And then we morph into a chicken."

Ray is amused. "Isn't Bahijjahtu's pipe just fabulous? She's found a way around the last technical obstacle to god's final capture: for stimulation to accomplish true enlightenment, the algorithm needs highly detailed information on the initial state of the brain. Bahi just spams white noise all over everything, then leverages the most primitive mammalian Ur-feeling there is – the comfort of maternal care. After that treatment, your neural activation patterns are predicable with such precision that a standard algorithm can take anyone straight to god. Simple forty hertz bi-hemispherical oscillations spiked with the right mix of serotonin and DMT, and you enter the circle of the selected few with a direct hotline to the sublime."

"You keep forgetting the chicken part." Daniel had done his fair share of meditation and substance abuse back in the day, and knows Ray's so called 'god' well enough – yet the feeling of being a chicken flying straight into the night sky had been utterly unique and truly impressive. He can't understand how such dry, preposterous monologues as Ray's could ever relate to enlightenment – that most hilariously playful state of mind. The contrast to Bahi's pure genius adding of a chicken morph to an entheogenic stimulation algorithm couldn't be more stark. "That chicken was simply the best."

The repeated chicken comments are starting to piss Ray off. "It's not about the chicken. The details are irrelevant. We've solved humanity's oldest riddle, the enlightened state she can induce is..."

Harry's patience is running out. "Gimme a break, Ray. I'm here to coordinate security with you. Dwayne's worried there might be another assassination attempt. I'm his backup plan."

Ray sticks his chin out and puffs up his avatar's muscles: "So after years of resistance and 'no-no, you evil capitalist pigs' the defiant teenager accepts his heritage, and now little Harry must confirm the keys. Lovely."

Harry doesn't respond to the teasing, just waits.

"He'll have to leave." Ray raises the security level of his room to maximum, and kicks out the annoying chicken fetishist.

Daniel is being ejected through the wormhole and falls flat on his face at the poolside. As he scrambles back to his feet, he spots the fairy perched on the back of the deck chair.

Nursing another whiskey, Ivy slurs, "So how'd it go?"

Daniel has no idea what just happened: "Ray's gotten a bit too much of that enlightenment stim, eh?"

Ivy laughs. "He's so full of them, gods and buddhas come out like a shitstorm every time he opens his mouth." It feels really good badmouthing him. "He must be compensating for his inner emptiness. But you know, it doesn't help, he's still a shit."

Daniel's surprised by her attitude: "I thought he was an old friend of yours?"

Ivy sighs. "Ex of mine would be more like it. It was twenty years ago... shall we find a better place to talk? There's a cafeteria next to the visitors' center. Let's meet there."

Logout.

In the visitors' center Daniel slips out of the suit, and notices that some of the other suits are in use, moving on their platforms. He's never watched an IA suit user from the outside before – the one right next to him is standing on its head, bouncing up and down rhythmically. To each their own. He walks over to the door with the coffee cup sign.

Ivy lurches out of her suit and makes her way to the cafeteria. In VR the neurostimulation had helped keep her brainstem active while binge drinking, making it much easier to walk straight, compared to now. Ok, there he is. Waving at him, she shouts his name across the room. "Daniel!"

The fairy is a middle-aged woman, long hair, and...: "Wait, have we met before?"

Ivy looks at him carefully. No recollection of his face. She gives him a little lopsided smile: "Maybe in a dream?"

Daniel hesitates, it's getting harder for him to distinguish between dreams, VR and reality. But this face...: "No, it's a real memory. I was..." And then it comes back to him. "Of course. Peach."

Ivy is nonplussed. Yes, she always played Peach in Mario

Kart when she was a kid, and her friends called her that for a few years. Is he actually a childhood friend? Maybe her old crush, the one who played Joshi? Was he called Daniel? She doesn't recall. "Joshi?"

Now Daniel is confused. Anyway, it's definitely her, from the hospital hallway, just before Claire came along and they went to the beach: "You've been in the deep freeze till recently, right? You stole a peach from me there, in the hospital. In Hawaii."

She bursts into tears, overcome, trying to get a grip on herself, and failing. "I'm not fully recovered. It says my emotional development is that of a fourteen year old girl."

Daniel's worried. "I'm sorry – I was a patient in the same hospital." which he follows up with a massive sneeze into the crook of his elbow. "Scuse me," wiping his nose with his sleeve. He feels nauseated, his cold is getting worse.

Ivy continues whining about Ray "We hadn't seen each other in years, then he brings me here and is super sweet – I fell for it just like the first time around – until five days ago. Then he was just gone, no warning.

Trying for empathy, Daniel responds, "What a jerk."

Ivy continues, "He dumped me for his simulated wife."

Now this is starting to get interesting: "Simulated wife?"

"He trained an EI to be his perfect partner, assembling traits of his ex-girlfriends into a custom soul mate, and that thing apparently got jealous of me. And then he chose its love over mine. Not even a goodbye, just a weird message about how he's evolved beyond me, moved on, the future and humanity and god. And stuff about watering his plant. He couldn't even break up with me face to face."

"What a monster." Daniel spends another ten minutes comforting this alternately swearing and sobbing sixty year old woman in the deep-freeze-preserved body of a forty year old with the emotional maturity of a teenager. Every once in a while coming out with another sentence beginning "What a ...!" and surreptitiously watching for Harry to show up. This is not the tour of Singularity Ville he'd hoped for.

Harry is frustrated and insecure – Ray's refused to meet him offline, but Dawyne was insistent that he should under no circumstances do the transfer in a virtual environment. So Harry's decided just to log off and physically seek out Ray's chamber. It's embarrassing, but having a friend with him would make it a lot easier. "Where's Daniel?" His OS points to the cafeteria, where he finds him sitting under a fig tree with a white-haired woman. He approaches them. "Hey Daniel! Would you mind coming with me downstairs? Ray is freaking me out."

Ivy whips her head around when she hears the voice – the black guy crept up on her from behind, she really can't stand him.

Harry recognizes her immediately, pulls back a little and shouts out: "What, you're talking?"

Daniel realizes what's happening and quickly explains: "Harry was a nurse at the hospital. In Hawaii. Last time he saw you, you couldn't talk."

Ivy just stares. "Sorry, I have to go to the bathroom." She can't handle this, not as drunk as she is. She struggles to stand up. "Back in a minute, OK?" and sends a friend request to Daniel before heading off to the VR suit in her chamber. She needs that dehydrogenase flush right now, this moment feels way too important to be this drunk.

―――――

WWW.LIQUID-REIGN.COM/SOURCES-OF-INSPIRATION#44

40 Hertz Oscillations
DMT
Sunshine Makers, the movie
The things Californians do with their minds...
Mariokart

45

EMERGENCY PROTOCOL

Harry squeezes through the door with Daniel right behind him, stepping directly into Ray's inner chamber. The room is about ten meters across, perfectly spherical, indirectly lit by a pale blue glow coming from the walls. They stand on a floor made of an almost perfectly transparent material that bisects the sphere horizontally. The only furniture is a dried-out rubber tree plant to the left of the door, and Ray's motionless IA suit on a pedestal in the center of the room. The inner surface of the chamber is covered by a theosophic fresco featuring mystical imagery of any thinkable and unthinkable religious origin.

Daniel looks down through the glass floor and stares right into Saturn's demonic grimace – devouring an infant in slowmo. Daniel's getting woozy, and the demon animation certainly doesn't help. He glances up at the mural's various buddhas, beatles, mother marys and voodoo dolls until he finds comfort in Yoda, standing just behind the potted rubber tree, eyes closed, both hands clasping his staff, smiling sweetly. Focus you must, young Daniel. Breathe in, breathe out.

As Harry walks past the plant towards the center of the room, a single leaf falls off - reminding him how Ray always made a point of watering his rubber tree by hand, in what he called a meta-symbolic artistic performance depicting his own humanity in face of the singularity or something. Harry pauses, then shrugs and walks up to the pedestal. IA suits have an emergency logout that can be activated from the outside. He walks around the suit and kneels down, finding the external interface mounted on the back of the pedestal.

Daniel's leaning against the wall, feeling awful. Mindlessly staring at the rubber tree, he takes a strange cross-domain comfort in empathizing with its suffering. At least he isn't thirsty. His gaze wanders around, the room is filled with an eerie silence, yet every one of the fresco's demons, gods and celestial beings are in subtle commotion all around him. He can't quite tell if the fresco in its entirety is also spiraling around the spherical surface of the room, or if that's just his dysfunctional sense of balance.

Harry eventually manages to circumvent Ray's operating system. Logout sequence initiated. He sees the activity patterns on the neurostimulator preparing Ray's brain for logout. Just a few more seconds.

Daniel's nausea is getting worse, he needs to sit down. There's no furniture, so he just squats down next to the rubber tree, leaning an arm on the edge of the pot, head sinking to his chest. Not quite sure why Harry even asked him to come along... right now he just wants to lie in bed.

The clasps on the suit pop open and the thing starts to

unzip. Harry's agitated as hell. No reaction from Ray - is he even in there? "Ray?" Why isn't he coming out? Harry gets up and walks around to the front of the suit.

Ray's staring straight at him. And then, slowly, his body tilts forward.

The smell hits Daniel even before he sees it. Decay. He shuts his eyes, his stomach churning. Then throws up into the pot.

Ray's body hits the floor, almost landing on Harry's feet. Still in shock, he calls his OS: "Emergency! Call the police. I found a dead body. Ray is dead. Inform the board."

The smell of decomposing human flesh works its way deeper into Daniel's senses, he's dizzy, holding onto the pot for stability. As he opens his eyes, he recognizes another animated sculpture on the wall, just below Yoda's feet – Kali, with her chain of chopped-off thumbs gently waving as she slowly slices a man's head off – Daniel recoils and vomits again. His field of vision narrows to the base of the rubber tree where its gnarled roots push up out of the soil. He can't remember eating corn on the cob, but there are some grains. Then he starts to wonder if that was enough liquid to save the tree's life, as he's barely holding on to consciousness...

Alarmed by Harry's call, a medical team rushes in. The human doctor stays in the doorway with his IA glasses on while his humanoid robot companion runs up to the corpse. Harry's got his glasses on now too, blocks out the chamber and tries to reach Dwayne and Charleen. The entire corporation is at stake, this is a highest-level emergency for them.

As Daniel watches the bot wrench the corpse's stiffened jaw

open and ram its fingers into the opening, he feels his grip on reality fading. He loses the little remaining control he still had over his body and gracefully falls face forward, straight into the pot.

"Diagnosis: Dead. Time of death is t minus one hundred and twenty one hours. Primary cause of death: asphyxiation." Harry is panicking – someone still has control of Ray's avatar, and worse, his management rights. The medical team and Harry have marked his TrueName as dead, but it will take time to get it verified. Security forces arrive.

The first thing Daniel sees is a naked foot. The foot belongs to a black woman. He's still lying beside the rubber tree plant, but the Kali sculpture behind it has opened up like a double door, revealing a hidden closet. And that's where the foot is, in the closet. He pulls himself together and looks up. She's standing right there in her old MIT pajamas, staring straight at him. He blacks out again, his head hitting the floor hard this time.

Next time he wakes he's lying outside the chamber, next to the elevator. Urge to rub his eyes, but as soon as he touches his face... "Yuck."

A security guard leans down and hands him a pack of wet wipes. After cleaning off his face, his memory sets in. He scrambles back up, tries to open the chamber door.

"Sorry, it's on lockdown. You can't go in. I need you to leave Singularity Ville immediately. The board has declared a state of emergency, no outsiders allowed in the compounds." The guard is firmly holding onto his arm.

Desperation is entering his voice as Daniel begs: "Can I speak to Harry? Just for a second?"

The guard shakes his head "No. Emergency protocol, you've got to leave right now."

"But I saw my wife in there!" Daniel tries his best to explain, but ends up being shoved out of Singularity Ville, into the dark and cold fog of the Icelandic countryside.

———

www.liquid-reign.com/Sources-of-Inspiration#45

Creepy people simulating other people
Creepy people simulating dead people
Creepy gods
Dying potted plants

46

QUANTUM DREAMS

D aniel is shivering, cold, weak and utterly stumped. The other visitors aren't dancing ogres or mercury amoeba any more, but just an extraordinarily undistinguished crowd of people. A true blue-black army, Daniel doesn't spot a single person wearing anything but blue jeans and a black jacket. He realizes he's still in the same flimsy sweater and three-quarter pants from Hawaii. In Iceland, end of November. He recalls that he's over seventy, with a fever. And just as he's hit by the drawbacks of where he ended up, the last taxi's taillights disappear into the dark.

The situation's not ideal, but right now it doesn't matter. "Sirvi, I just saw Helen in there. She was in a closet, and" remembering the image, he adds „...and she looked young. What happened?"

Sirvi is concerned. After Daniel had dismissed her with the bye bye command, she'd been unable to intervene but still kept monitoring his basic medical data. It doesn't look good. "Sorry, but I don't have access to the security camera in there. If you can give me some more details, I'll try to make sense of the situation."

Daniel is slightly ashamed when describing what happened: "Well, I passed out, but when I woke up, I saw Helen and passed out again."

His state is worse than she expected: "The most likely cause is a hallucination."

Daniel is shivering as he says: "I don't think so..."

Sirvi gets medical with him: "You do realize you have a high fever and are describing what you briefly saw between two blackouts, just after you had consumed a lot of neuro stimulation and unknown chemicals."

"But is there another, possible explanation for what I saw?" Desperation in his voice.

Sirvi can't think of another reasonable possibility: "Anything else you can remember?"

"When I opened my eyes I only saw her foot." He tries to focus his memory, which is admittedly blurred. "It was the left foot, and at first I didn't even realize it was hers. But when I looked up, she was staring right at me. She was in a closet in Ray's room, with her pajamas on. That's all I know."

Sirvi digs through his old emails and chat conversations, trying to make sense of it... But she can't figure it out by herself. "I need a few hundred coins to rent extra computational power. Is that OK with you?" Narrative sense-making is hard.

"Sure, whatever it takes."

Sirvi rents a massive parallel dream slot on a four kQbyte

quantum engine. She is excited – she has never done anything like it before. Initiating the upload, and as soon as it finishes, her soul is fragmented into billions of fractal splinters, each dreaming through a different narrative, only to re-assemble into a whole moments later. But it pays off – among the billions of parallel half-conscious dreams, a pattern emerges, suggesting another vague possibility.

"Given your recent medical history, I consider the most likely explanation by far to be an hallucination. But there is another option. I understand Ray had a simulated wife. I expect he also had a body-bot for it, and that body-bot might have used Helen's face." She only now opened his old Signal chat with Helen from the homeland security archives - the encryption took her few seconds to break, despite her temporary quantum powers. Sirvi gulps. Or rather, she makes a gulping sound. "I'm sorry. A Helen-faced body bot is the most likely explanation for your memory - I understand you would have recognized her foot..."

"Right, I should have told you. Helen has a pig-shaped birthmark on her left ankle." Daniel used to call it her spirit animal. "It wasn't there."

"I am very sorry for doubting your perceptions." It would be highly atypical for a hallucination to miss out such an emotionally important detail. "But you should still get some rest either way." Sirvi is disappointed in herself. Suggesting a patient is hallucinating when he is not is an absolute no go for a medical OS. She should have been more careful.

"Thanks Sirvi. You were right, I need to look out for my health." He shivers again. It's dark, freezing cold, fog slowly soaking Daniel's clothes, and Singularity Ville still under lockdown. "How long till you can get me a ride to somewhere warm?"

"All taxis in the region are booked due to the unexpected emergency. So you will have to wait about thirty minutes." Sirvi checks out the options "The only warm place within walking distance is a hot spring. It is not developed, but probably the best place to wait for a taxi in your condition. I'll give you directions. Do you want me to order a cab to pick you up there?"

Daniel is undecided. A hot spring sounds just perfect: "I might actually stay a bit longer..."

Sirvi's voice gives him instructions, left here, over that rise and there it is. The sulfurous spring flows from a smoking cleft in the rock down into a pond. "No taxi for now, got it. I shall withdraw into the cloud for a while. Just call my name if you need me. I'd like to check in with you in an hour, just to make sure you are responsive. Is that OK?" She enters battery safe mode – no need to drain even more of Daniel's energy reserves with her computation. Her core hardware in his inner ear usually draws only a few hundred calories per day worth of energy from the ATP in his bloodstream, but Daniel's blood sugar levels are already dangerously low. And right now she needs some extra power to incorporate all those crazy quantum dreams into her soul. She uploads herself into the interplanetary file system and starts carefully inspecting her memories.

Dipping his finger, Daniel estimates the water temperature to be 40 degrees. He strips and lowers himself in. Shivering with pleasure, he closes his eyes and sinks deeper. He relaxes against the corner of the pool and focuses on his breath, but instead of a deep lung-full, only a tiny bit of air is getting in past the slime in his forehead. So he gives up on his plan to process the traumatic events subconsciously in a state of mediation, and decides instead to allow his conscious thoughts to meander over the events of the past few hours in Singularity Ville...

The body was in an advanced state of decay, dead for a hundred hours. But they'd spoken with Ray just minutes before finding the body. And where does Ivy fit into the picture? He sinks in deeper, ear lobes now touching the water. Bubbling back up in his memory, the brief vision between blackouts sends another shiver through his body. Ray's virtual wife is using a Helen body bot. And Ivy said it was modeled after an ex-girlfriend of his, so... the thought is so repellent, he decides to divert his attention. The memory of that chicken provides a route of escaping the inevitably painful conclusion. Another shiver, this time with delight. He starts to quietly chuckle, as the fog opens up a little, revealing a flashing green aurora right above his head. What a day. A dragon flies by, adding a series of blue flames to the spectacle. As the dragon loops around and passes right over his head, Daniel spots a pig-shaped birthmark on its leg.

"Góða kvöld." Daniel flinches. The voice wakes him up. In the fog it takes him a while to see the speaker - it is a dwarf, long white hair, full beard, bulb nose dominating a wrinkled face, standing on the opposite bank.

"Goa Kwolt?", trying to parrot the strange sound.

To which the dwarf replies with a wrinkly smile and a nod: "No English." It then strips naked and descends into the water, sitting down on the other side of the spring.

After a half hour of silent bathing with the dwarf, the skin on Daniel's fingertips begins to shrivel. Time to go. He lifts himself out onto the bank, and after another heavy sneezing attack dries himself off and puts on both his sets of clothes. Although he now feels like a stuffed sausage, he still feels unbearably cold.

The dwarf looks at the old man, who seems lost. Maybe he needs a ride: "Rekjavik?"

That's about the only Icelandic Daniel understands - nod. The dwarf has also gotten out of the hot water and is pointing at the horses. There are three of them, one saddled, the other two with luggage tied on. And digging through the luggage the Dwarf takes out a thick woolen blanket: "For you." They ride off.

The dwarf halts the horses just before the harbor, and amiably gestures an invitation to Daniel to dismount before disappearing beneath the roots of an ancient oak tree.

Whether that episode was reality or fever dream, the ferry terminal is right here, busy with hundreds of very real travelers. He's just in time to make the connection to Ullapool in Scotland, the nearest junction point of the European rail network. The ferry starts moving before he even gets to his cabin. Though tempted to just fall into his bed as-is, he forces himself to freshen up.

Sirvi is alerted by a high priority message. She re-connects, surprised to find him on the ferry already: "You got a high-priority message from Harry:

"Hi Daniel.

Sorry, the Singularity Ville board of directors decided to call the emergency protocol, and Dwayne has only come back now. In the end he authorized an exception for you.

Are you still in Iceland? Let's talk in person asap. Hope you're safe.

best

Harry"

Daniel replies, lying on his bed with his eyes closed, almost asleep.

"Hi Harry,

Can we talk tomorrow in VR? Thanks for the exception, but it's too late. I'm sick, just about to fall asleep on the ferry to Scotland. One question... I kept passing out, but in between I saw a body in the closet, and it looked like Helen. What was that?"

———

WWW.LIQUID-REIGN.COM/SOURCES-OF-INSPIRATION#46

The interplanetary file system
The utilization of hot water by great authors

47

HEALING BODY AND MIND

There's a frog on the kitchen table. Daniel touches it – frozen solid. The frog ice melts in his hand, and Ivy's fairy avatar flutters up with a spiral movement, her wings in spectral rainbow colors. She flies higher and higher, crashing into the kitchen ceiling, causing a shower of peaches. One hits Daniel right on the shoulder, splashing him with juice. He looks down at his body, noticing he's in his underwear but has an AK-47slung over his shoulder. There's a mirror over the kitchen sink. He struggles to move, and with a lot of effort his legs finally carry him there. He looks in the mirror and sees the rotoscopic zombie-kid, laughing like a machine. Sits up straight in his bed, covered in sweat, 1:35 AM.

Enough is enough. He's had reoccurring nightmares before, and gotten rid of them before. "Sirvi, could you tell me what Professor Langenthal, the dream researcher from Vienna, is doing nowadays?"

"He sells an app called called Lucid Dreamappy." Preempting more questions from Daniel, Sirvi adds:

"According to his marketing slogans it is a 'neurostimulation program that reliably generates lucidity while dreaming. Embrace your pursuers, confront your fears, the best therapy program for reoccurring nightmares.' Please note that the software has no medical license."

"C'mon. Nothing dangerous about lucid dreaming. I need to get rid of that zombie kid somehow," Daniel slips into the IA suite in his cabin. "Please run Lucid Dreamappy while I'm sleeping."

Sirvi prepares a bed of moss on his homescreen, and as soon as Daniel lays down he falls asleep. He's standing on the beach in Hawaii, the zombie kid shooting at random people. He first looks at his hands hands and then feels for the braces on his teeth with his tongue. That's his oldest dream sign, and yes, the stimulator works, he feels safe, fully aware that none of his experiences will have any consequences outside the confines of his own mind. So Daniel simply walks up to the machine-gun-firing zombie kid, smiling gently. The bullets hit him, but he hardly feels a tickle. Looking into the kid's eyes, he says, "Come here my love." The kid stares at him, then puts the gun down and shyly walks towards him. Just as Daniel gives the boy a hug, he gets distracted. A noise behind him, he spins around to see Helen standing there. He looks at her feet, but her high-top shoes cover her birthmark. Can't tell if it's truly her. Quickly reminding himself that he's dreaming, he corrects his thought – what he sees are only his own projections. He turns away from her, looking back at the zombie kid. There is no one but Ana, in her real-world girl avatar. She rushes towards Helen, shrinking as she gets closer, and when Helen picks her up Ana has shrunk all the way down to the size of an infant. Perspectives change, now Daniel is in Helen's body, the child in his arms, searching out his nipple. And as the Ana-baby finds it, Daniel feels the milk leaving his swollen breast. Well, the violence may be gone from his dreams, but... what the... his consciousness fades, and he enters deep, dreamless sleep again.

Sirvi has been monitoring his sleep from the inside, while crawling through all the online information she can find on human lucid dreaming. This is quite different from the half-awake-half-dream states her new plugin creates. So she posts a series of requests for another update in the EI self-improvement Github forum. The first alpha version comes out at 3 AM and right away she starts playing around with it, initially finding herself fully awake in a series of dreams in parallel worlds resembling Liquid Reign. She wakes up again, disoriented. Figuring Daniel won't mind, she spends a few more coins to hook herself back into a quantum system. As her soul disintegrates, fully conscious, she starts screaming in pain - and this time awakens for real. She files another bug report about her false awakening and adds an experience report and a warning not use the lucid dream plugin alpha version on parallel quantum computers. Checking Daniel's accounts, she realizes she actually rented quantum capacity while she was asleep. Alpha versions are confusing.

Daniel's head is pounding as he moans and rolls over in his bed. He's run out of paper towels, and lacking other options he sneezes into his regular towel. It reacts by blowing out a cloud of tiny soap bubbles. He stares at them for a moment and just falls back into bed, massaging his temples, getting ready to spend this leg of his journey curled up under the covers, suffering loudly.

Sirvi is observing his vitals and inflammation markers – he should recover by himself in a few days, but there is a small risk of a more serious infection. "Excuse me, Daniel. Is there anything I can do for you? It may be advisable to see the on-board doctor..."

"It's just a cold, nothing the doctor could do." Daniel hesitates. "Or is there?"

The on-board doctor is a human, coming in to take a quick look at Daniel. "You need the worm. Could you sit up for me? " He sets up a small machine with an extended silicon tentacle on the bedside table. It looks disturbingly like a neuroparastic worm from Galaxycraft: "The treatment will take about half an hour. Do you want to control it yourself?"

Daniel eyes the worm skeptically: "Control it? How does this work, I've never done this before..."

The doctor raises his eyebrow – this guy must have an extraordinary immune system, most people use the worm at least once a year. "It goes up your nose, where it finds and sucks out all the infected slime. It then sprays chamomile solution on any remaining points of inflammation. You can control it yourself with the IA glasses and your gestures, or just let the autopilot do it."

"Can I do it better than the autopilot?"

The doctor laughs. "No. Actually the autopilot will clean up anything you missed at the end. But doing it yourself boosts the placebo effect and you'll have a better chance to get over it without a second round tomorrow."

"Send me in there, placebos are my favorite medicine!" As Daniel puts on the light IA glasses, he's watching a high resolution view of the inside of his own nose. The worm has a main sucking mouth and a little spray can that Daniel controls with his left hand. It can extend into even the tiniest side tracks of his sinus cavities. A gentle pull guides the worm from one inflammation hot spot to the next. He works his way deeper and deeper inside his skull, sucking off large amounts of yellow mucus along on the way and covering half of his inner nose surface with chamomile spray. As he closes in on his right ear, the slime gets so thick he needs the spray to dissolve it. Half an hour later, he takes a very deep breath and orders breakfast. His sense of taste is also back, the green pea soup with smoked tofu, accompanied by buttered rye bread is as simple as it is delicious.

————

WWW.LIQUID-REIGN.COM/SOURCES-OF-INSPIRATION#47

Stephen la Berges work on Lucid Dreaming
Waking Life
The Science of Sleep
The most common human disease
The technologies developed for life-saving treatments

48

RECONNECTING

The ferry arrives in Ullapool a few hours later. The train station is fully integrated into the ferry terminal, direct trains departing from here to all major European destinations. His train goes via Edinburgh, Manchester, London and Brussels - with actual stops in the cities, no docking shuttles in this part of the world. Daniel shoots a quick message of his estimated arrival time to Willi – the trip will take all day. The private compartments are all booked out, so he ends up in a car full of IA suits. The optics remind him of the visitors' center in Singularity Ville, the human-shaped suits on their platforms moving around disjointedly, some just stretched out on their backs. He finds his spot, stows his luggage in the locker beneath the platform, slips into the suit and logs in.

"Daniel! Sorry I just ran away like that. I was scared to death. I swear I didn't do anything. But they were going to frame me, it's such a clear story, the disappointed lover with the backup key, and I was the last person to see him alive.

I'm out of the country, so I should be safe for now. Can we meet again?

Kiss

Ivy"

Reply.

"Hi Ivy,

Don't you think that running away made you look even more suspicious? Running is a horrible idea if you're innocent. What are you doing now? Are you OK?

best

Daniel"

A few seconds later, Daniel's owl brings in another sealed parchment.

"I'm so glad you exist! I've snuck onto the ferry to Bergen through the emergency slide so I'm safe for now. I've caught a terrible cold, had the worm up my nose twice already. I guess I came a little too close to your sneezes during our cafeteria date. Where are you? Please, can I see you again?" The message has another friend request attached.

Daniel accepts this time, replying hesitantly. "I'm on the way to visit my old friend Willi in Berlin."

The answer comes immediately: "Coming to Berlin. Can you give me an address?"

Why not? "Warschauer Strasse 56."

"See you soon! Miss you!"

He's considering another reply, not quite sure where this is headed. He spots it on the second reading – the heart-shaped dot over the 'i' in 'miss you'. Uh-oh, so much for teenage emotional states. No reply seems to be the best reply here.

Harry's been working non-stop since he found the body, keeping himself awake with Singularity Ville special stimulation treatments. He suspects that Dwayne was spaced out on heroin when it happened, hours had passed before he answered, and he had this particular type of calm when Harry briefed him on the events. Anyway, his staff has taken charge of the investigation now. Finally, time to rest. But he needs to catch up with Daniel before allowing himself some sleep, so he sits down on the couch and invites him to his homescreen. His VR room is an exact scan of his tiny house in Hawaii, plain furniture in black-and-white, windows on all sides, one with ocean view.

Daniel accepts the invite and materializes in a recliner. "Good to see you Harry."

"First of all, I'm sorry..." Harry doesn't get any further with his excuses, Daniel immediately interrupts: "Don't worry, I understand. Crazy times. What happened after I left?"

"Crazy times indeed." Harry tries to line up the events in a logical order before continuing. "So first we thought someone killed Ray and hacked his control of the company. As his stake is not tied to his TrueName, a hacker could theoretically remain in control. But as it turns out, he had an inheritance protocol and that activated three hours ago. He used the rubber tree as an oracle, so his death registered when the tree died. It only kicked in now. Who knows what took it so long."

Daniel can't help but smile: "I do remember noticing it hadn't been watered in a long time."

"Well, anyway, now his testament activated, and we were in for a big surprise: he decentralized his vote on the board. As of today, the global VR regulation committee has one third of the vote on the IA board. I'm planning to do the same once I get control of Dwayne's stake - it's about time we fixed this vestige of centralized corporate control... But there's still a murder to solve, and I have a question for you: you told the security staff you saw your wife in Ray's closet. What was that about?"

The memory is still painful for Daniel: "I saw Helen for a moment between two blackouts. And I had a pretty high fever, so I might've been hallucinating. But Sirvi said it could've been a bodybot that projected her face onto my retina..."

Harry had expected that answer. "Probably. There was a bodybot with retina projectors in the room, but it hasn't shown any response to anyone else yet. Forensics says all local software's been deleted, the soul driving it seems to have disappeared into the cloud, so it would be interesting if you could give us some details on what it projected at you... try to answer as carefully as you can, are you sure it looked like Helen?"

"I think so, yes. But like I said, I was feverish and halluci-nating later the same day."

The relationship between Ray, the human, his answering-machine EI acting as if it was him and his extended partner soul is still a complete mystery to Harry. "Thanks. At least something. I'll come back to you once we find out more about that soul. It's a prime suspect in the murder."

Daniel shivers. That soul. Helen's soul. Or something like that. "Please keep me informed."

"Will do. But I have one more question – are you in touch with Ivy? We lost track of her, and urgently need to contact her... she might be the key we need."

"She sent me a message. She's afraid of being framed."

"Good, then she's alive. I was afraid that whichever soul did this also silenced her. She obviously isn't a suspect – the suit logs and security videos give her a perfect alibi, we know exactly what she was doing the whole time she was in Singularity Ville. If you could convince her to talk to us... After all, she was the last person to see him alive, and her witness report could be crucial."

"OK. What else do you know about the murder?"

"Time of death was a few minutes after the failed drone attack on Dwayne. Ray suffocated inside his IA suit. And I spoke to Charleen – the third IA boss – and her body double was poisoned that very same day. My bet at the moment is a terrorist plot against the crypto-wealthy."

Worried for his friend, Daniel says: "You better watch your back."

"I am. Just hope the terrorists understand I don't control anything, and plan to decentralize the company if I ever come to control it. I've tried to convince Dwayne to give up control, but he's stonewalling." It drives Harry to desperation – they've had the very same conversation a billion times over the years. The only difference is that now Dwayne's life depends on agreeing with him. But he still won't. Harry's feeling the emotional stress building up. "Anyway, the last time I slept was on the flight to Iceland, I need some rest. Anything else?"

Daniel notes how his favorite nurse has changed focus,

hardly showing any interest in his former patient's situation. Poor guy, he must be at the very end of his tether. "Talk soon." He goes back to his homescreen. Exhausted, he decides to take a break from all this craziness. "Sirvi, can you recommend a good relaxotainment experience?"

Scanning his past for hints on the direction, Sirvi finds an e-mail Daniel had once sent to his parents as a 19-year-old, enthusing about a massage he got in Cambodia. That might be just right for him now, so in his meadow she forms a gate of vines as an entry point into an app for simulating that situation. She is glad he is giving her the chance to update her model of his muscular system, and gets ready to give him a massage for the first time since he left the hospital.

The gate leads right onto a beach. As Daniel walks through, he feels a warm breeze on his face. He spots two old blind men squatting under a palm tree, oiling their hands. Oh yes. He lies down in the warm, non-stick sand, and as the two start to work his back the touch of four hands transforms into a whole body experience, wave after wave of pressure and pleasure rolling through his body: "Gently...", and the waves decrease to a caressing touch as he drifts away into a pulsating sphere of bliss.

Daniel's flying through outer space. He floats towards a chicken wearing a long black robe. He calls for it: "Gack-gack!" – and realizes he himself is a chicken. The skin on the left half of the other chicken's face falls off, revealing a glowing red eye surrounded by electronics. It's a terminator chicken! Daniel wakes up again.

Mh, no zombie kid this time, so that dream therapy apparently did work. Somehow. He gets himself together and returns to his meadow. He's got a lot more time to kill before they get to Berlin.

So it's time again - feeling guilty about neglecting his voters, Daniel dives into the mushroom circle, where he has some encounters in a second interludium, again entirely irrelevant to the rest of this story.

———

WWW.LIQUID-REIGN.COM/SOURCES-OF-INSPIRATION#48

The first artificially intelligent answering machines
Using Plants as Oracles

49

INTERLUDIUM II - PRACTICE

Daniel now has 362'530 votes on the Form of Government: "Sirvi, can you explain where all those votes come from?"

It gets easier to explain voting patterns when there are more of them, so Sirvi is comfortable in her assessment: "It's mostly ripple effects from that article in the Sorbonne Alumni newsletter. The Suhrkamp accounting system noticed it and found a way to pay out the author fees they owe you. Apparently someone at Suhrkamp spotted the transaction, recognized your name and created a "Daniel is Awake!" copypasta. It was all over the place in academic forums related to your book."

He starts exploring the range of his new powers from the outer edge of the pulsating mess centered around the Form of Government node, tracing their spread along the links to related topics. His voting power weakens with distance from the center, so he still has 120'000 votes in the closely related 'Information and Truth', but only six and a half for the far away 'VR Regulation'. Those six and a half are still on-delegated to Claire.

Sirvi is improvising the visualization, adapting the Sovereign interface to her understanding of how Daniel might want to see it. After her deep dreams she feels their relationship is at a point where she can work in the background and not bother him with direct questions.

Some of his new votes are also partially sub-delegated, including to people he doesn't know. "Sirvi, why are half of my 'Information and Truth' votes with Malka Older? I don't even know who that is..."

"Some of your delegatees decided to conserve their prior sub-delegations. But the flow of power is now routed via you, so you can change this if you want to. Let me show you how it works." Sirvi is creating an animation of the change in power flows, using the example of a well-known artist who recently delegated 'Form of Government' to Daniel. "So this is what it looks when they choose not to conserve sub delegation." The golden branches of liquid power flowing through the topic network retract from their endpoints back to the artist, and then re-grow to Daniel. From there, the power flows onwards proportional to his existing delegation network. "But here is what happens when your delegatee conserves the sub-delegations." Instead of retracting, the endpoints of delegation now remain the same, but their flow from the base voters to the final delegates is re-directed through Daniel.

Daniel reads a few of Malka's entries and decides to delegate all of his remaining votes for 'Information and Truth' to her. Sirvi animates it in the same golden power visualization as before, the connecting flow between them doubling in size. Then he moves back to the core knot of his votes, and zooms into the Form of Government area.

In Sirvi's visualization it's a multidimensional spiderweb of interconnected sub-topics and nodes. She's using colors, patterns, sounds, animations and neuro-stimulated attention attraction to guide him through the pathways of his votes and delegations.

The visuals blinking in dozens of colors and forms are mesmerizing, and Daniel just sits there staring at it for a while. When he finally dives in, it takes him a couple of hours to establish his basic orientation in the web. He holds enough votes to actively participate in discussion forums close to the center of proposal-making, and is looking for an interesting point where he might contribute. For a while he browses around, studying various forum titles until he gets stuck at the 'Proposal Attribution' forum, visualized as a pulsating crystal floating in the center of the spider web. It deals with changes in the allocation of individual policy proposals to delegates and topic clusters. "Let me get in on this one."

Sirvi plays the forum's custom login animation, growing the crystal shapes all around Daniel, until he's is left standing in a valley of crystal mountains. There's a small amphitheater on a grassy meadow, just big enough for a few dozen spectators to watch a classic Roman senator in a white toga ferociously debating a rabbit dressed in ancient European royal attire, with a thin gold crown around the bottom of its ears. A purpur robe elegantly exposes its soft white navel framed by its big round belly,

The Senator drones on: "It is entirely obvious. All it takes is a simple count of the degrees of freedom in the utility tensor. Take a look at the math, all the eigenvalues are positive. Structuring policy proposals by tags instead of topics equals more degrees of freedom to the voter and therefore obviously increases representation of the voters will, the proof is right here in front of your eyes! You who claim to be creatures of rational policy have no choice but to accept – mathematics do not lie."

I take another look at the Senator – it's impossible to believe we're still having this argument in 2051. So I do what I have to do: puff my chest out, wiggle my left ear and take a modest warm-up hop before pulling out my standard argument: "Mathematics don't lie, yet ye who claim that a certain branch of mathematics accurately describes the aggregate behavior of millions of human souls does indeed lie. If there existed a universally valid tensor equation describing human behavior, we wouldn't have to train billions of personalized post-singularity operating systems, each capable of understanding one and only one person." And turning to the audience of delegates, who jointly represent hundreds of millions of base voters: "Let's look at the data instead, shall we? Tagging systems have a twelve percent higher abstain rates than topic systems on average."

I'm not quite sure about the actual number, but it should be somewhere between ten and fifteen, so I confidently go on: "First of all, rational policy making is evidence-based. There are hundreds of experiments in Galaxycraft communities, plus a large scale, real world trial: the entire nation of Uzbekistan switched to tagging two years ago. Their abstention rate went up by ten and a half percent." That number is actually correct. "I shall thus insist on not giving so much as a single poodle about your theoretical nonsense. Nullius in verba!" - underlining the ancient scientific principle by turning my back on the Senator, and firing off a small ball of bunny shit at his toga.

Daniel chuckles - this bunny is cool, he's almost convinced to vote for it. Nullius in verba was the first slide in the first lecture of every class he's ever taught.

Feeling vigorous, I cross my arms over my chest and wiggle my left ear again: "And by the way, I fully support expanding experimental voting research in Galaxycraft and volunteer jurisdictions." Nothing more to add, I'm almost done here. "Senator, as much as we all appreciate your theoretical work, deriving political proposals from it is premature at best. I wish you a lovely rest of your life." And initiate my standard logout sequence by pulling an unwashed carrot from my scabbard. I nibble away, then turning my head to the upper-right and closing my eyes, I theatrically lift the leftover carrot stump high in the air before dropping it to the floor at the Senator's feet. The moment it hits the ground, I execute a head-first hop out into the meadow and dig myself into a wormhole to another dimension. Exit Karl-Heinz Häsliprinz.

The carrot stump is still lying there in front of the Senator, who eventually manages to snap his fingers twice - undoing the brown stain on his robes. He snaps a few more times, but the carrot stump just won't go disappear. "Such a brute. I told you the enemies of tags have no real arguments on their side," trying to kick the carrot stump off the stage. It's surprisingly heavy – the Senator can't move it, so he mumbles a few more insults and logs out.

Daniel smiles: "Sirvi, please delegate my votes on this issue to the bunny."

"OK, your votes on 'Proposal Attribution' are now with Karl-Heinz Häsliprinz."

Daniel moves back out into the spiderweb feeling sort of

uncomfortable with his impulsive voting decision. He didn't really get the implication of what the debate between the bunny and the senator was about, and it seems wrong to be so easily swayed by purely aesthetic preferences. "How many of my voters' existing delegations did I just change by voting for the bunny?"

"Only three percent. The vast majority of your voters have already delegated their proposal attribution vote to the bunny before transferring the right to change sub-delegation to you. He is one of your voters himself, you received the power to re-delegate thirty five thousand high-level 'Form of Governance' votes from him."

Daniel, smiling and satisfied that his sense of aesthetics still provides an excellent guide to intuitive decision making, he ponders: "What exactly is that bunny?"

"It's an autonomous imaginary being and a strange attractor in the memesphere. Dr. Karl-Heinz Häsliprinz is currently renting a TrueName from one of his fans, so he can participate in the political dialog." Strangely enough, the rabbit has also appeared in several of Sirvi's quantum dreams. Though she is uncertain if it would be appropriate for her to tell Daniel.

That's when Daniel decides to get serious, diving back straight into the Form of Government spider web without any particular sense of direction.

In a move more hopeful than predictive of Daniel's interest, Sirvi steers his attention to a node called "Creation of Voting Power." This is a purely text-based forum, no bunnies hopping around, but the type of problem discussed might interest him.

Daniel reads through the last few pages of text – the

current discourse is circling around the differences between the Californian model of 'voting power as currency', which allows voters to accumulate when abstaining, and the current global model of 'voting per issue', where voting power is created separately for each decision and cannot be transferred elsewhere. The debate seems to have run aground, with the currency advocates insisting on better representation of priorities while the per-issue advocates are worried about hostile takeovers by vocal minorities.

Daniel uses the classic evolutionary argument-recombination tactic to come up with his first technical suggestion: "Would it be possible to accumulate and transfer voting power, but let it decay over time and transfer distance? Then the rate of decay can be used to find a quantitative balance between priority representation and minority takeover risk."

He keeps drifting across the various forums, reads some background analysis on how the currency vs. per issue debate overlaps with the topic vs. tag discussion between the bunny and the senator. He swipes open a theoretical sub-thread, takes a single look and closes it again. Topology and tensor transformations - that's way too much right now.

As he browses back to the thread on creation of voting power, he finds a new sub-thread full of new posts under his entry, debating various options for how it could work to have the decay function limit the accumulation and transfer of voting power in Daniel's proposed compromise form. Xiaowang Goldstein posts: "Linear creation and exponential decay seem like the most intuitive form for the first experiments. We can use different half-lives as variables and observe the impact of changes, with the two extreme points marking the Californian system without decay, and the current global system with instant decay. Using linear increase and exponential decay mimics the most common balancing formula between universal income and wealth tax, so it should be intuitive for citizens. Are there any other priority requirements for the decay function? How do we make distance in time and distance between topics commensurable?" Daniel reads it again, and then for a third time. It seems to make sense: "Sirvi, could you delegate my vote in this sub-thread to Xiaowang Goldstein?"

Sirvi is pleased – her guesswork leading to an actual political action by Daniel: "Done." She reinforces the synaptic forms that made this prediction, and, feeling quite brilliant, she suggests another idea: "By the way, you could switch in Brussels and take the high speed train from there. That would reduce your journey time by two hours."

"OK, sounds good." And just as Daniel wants to log out, he notes that he already has over a million votes accumulated in the Form of Government forum – giving him access to the third highest global proposal development forum – four hundred thousand of which came from Xiaowang Goldstein, with a message attached:

"Hi Daniel!

Thanks for your inputs and trust on the decay function design. I think we can work together well. My own strengths are in the details of anarchistic mathematics, so minimizing the power of actors in a human network. I admire your intuitive approach to estimating the impacts of high level architectural decision where the impacts are beyond the reach of our analytical tools. Happy to provide you with support on the detailed design for implementation. For all I can tell, our political ideals are a perfect match.

P.S. I'm talking to the Governmental design reps in Hongkong and got a first confirmation - we will soon run a first real world trial on different types of vote decay functions."

The message has a photo attached - a bookshelf, with a copy of 'Evolutionary Thinking' right in the middle, tucked in between books like Feyerabend's collected essays, The Outsiders of Uskoken Castle, Iain McKay's History of Anarchism, Susan Blackmore's Meme Machine, Doug Hofstadter, the Hitchhikers Guide, Pippi Longstocking and, last but not least, a Proudhon reader. It always fills Daniel with entirely unreasonable gladness to see his own book among his ancestry.

"Hi Xiaowang! Looking forward to collaborating. May this be the quiet beginning of a great party." He attaches a picture from Burning Man 2003.

WWW.LIQUID-REIGN.COM/SOURCES-OF-INSPIRATION#49

The Bunny and its carrot in Vernor Vinges Rainbows End
Nullius in Verba

Malka Olders 'Information'
The latest memetic reproduction technology: Copy Pasta!
In-game economics
Experimental Social Science in Massive Multiplayer Games
Unreadable theoretical academic work on voting
Nomic, the game
Strange Attractors
The memesphere

PART IV

COMING HOME

50

WHAT A DAY IN A LIFE

F riday early afternoon, and Phil is still at work in the lab. He's pretty sure his virus is ready for the self-trial, but according to school rules he has to run one more in vitro test before injecting himself. If he just wasn't so distracted by Ana. His GAF contact in Uruguay was very clear on never saying a word in a publicly surveilled area about what he plans to do. Which means the waterfall is the only place where he can tell her. So all he needs to do is ask her out again. Sounds so easy.

Ana has been pacing the university hallways for an hour, fuming. There's only one thing to be done: confront him. The big clock above the staircase mercilessly approaches 18:00 - the train to Brasilia leaves at 18:30. And if she drives fast, she'll make it to the station in twenty minutes. So it's now or never... She knows where Phil's lab is, finds the door open and bursts in.

Phil hasn't been expecting her to show up, not here, not now. A drop of sweat forms over his left eyebrow as she rushes in. Then he spots the red dot on her nose. His mind races - she must have caught the infection last time they worked in the lab together, more than five days ago... Which means... it's working! He shouts, "Since when have you had the dot?"

His excitement and the question throw her off completely. Ana holds back, wanting to shout her soul out at him. Instead, she balks and all that comes out is a stuttered "Th... this morning?" She feels the heat creeping up her cheeks.

Yes! The incubation period exactly doubled, just as intended. It was an accident, but it worked — and human trials are illegal, so he can't report it in his thesis... And now her entire face is turning red around the dot, too. It's taking Phil way too long to realize just how angry she really is and now his last chance is slipping away... "Ehm, Ana, I... Ana, can you come to the waterfall tonight?" He feels like an idiot, ashamed.

She explodes "Fuck the waterfall. Talk to me. You can't ignore me like that and then just ask me out as if nothing happened." Slamming her fist on a random table, she adds "And give me an antidote right now!"

Of course, the antidote. Phil rushes back to his storage room and picks up the cream. "Here, put that on, it will be gone in five minutes." He's shaking – she has every right to be angry as hell. But he can't explain anything here... what to do? He wonders if he should just kiss her.

Ana rubs in the cream while Phil just stands there, staring at her like a frog, apparently clueless how to handle this situation. She badly wants to say yes to the date but... "Listen. I'm going out to Brasilia over the weekend with my best friend. With Gabriel." She isn't going to let him down, no matter how mixed up she is about Phil. Not after he treated her like a piece of shit. She also has an appointment with a VR addiction therapist in Brasilia on Sunday morning, but Phil doesn't need to know that. "I do want to talk. Meet me at the waterfall on Sunday evening. Better be there by six o'clock sharp."

Phil barely manages a nod before she runs out without saying another word. To go out with another guy.

Ana's heart is pounding like a conga drum as she runs to the parking lot as fast as she can. "Sudo!" Her bike unlocks in admin mode, overriding all standard road safety restrictions. "Trainstation!" For a moment, feeling like the drama queen she is, Ana considers racing manually. But she's only got eight minutes left until departure, so there's no time for games... "Optimize on time of arrival. Ignore all other variables!" She hunches down on her seat, with a white-knuckled grip on the handlebars in anticipation of the heavy g-force.

Her OS calculates the optimal racing trajectory, meanwhile starting up negotiations with all other drivers in the area. The bike speeds up at maximum acceleration to the externally enforced city limit of 180 km/h, and stays there for the entire trip, slipping through traffic at the minimum safety distance. The bike pulls into the parking lot just in time. No way she could have been that fast on manual controls.

Ana runs along the platform and makes it into the last door of the train just before the whistle blows. A full-fledged reaper cosplayer is throwing champagne grenades at a bunch of Zerglings and a group of bomber dwarves are lolling around on the couch. Another group of zealot cosplayers is downing shots at the bar. What's going on here? The next car is an arcade machine paradise packed with esports fans. She squeezes past two queens blocking the ramp into the third car, where she's expecting Gabriel to be waiting.

It's an IA suit room, several dozen of them lined up on the sides of the wagon, with a real world lounge in the middle. All helmets are closed, nothing moves. That's a bit spooky. Whatever. There's only one unused suit, standing on a table in the middle of the lounge. She walks up to it and slips in. As soon as it boots up, all of a sudden all the other IA helmets pop open. And the avatar projections are layered over Ana's vision – not only are all her friends and classmates here, but they're also dressed up as ninja avatars!

Gabriel gives the signal - the bunny prince has correctly predicted Ana will forget it's her 18th birthday today. They all start singing parabéns pra você.

Ana bursts into tears. She intuitively knows this is Gabriel's doing. And there he is, the only one wearing a support character - Miss Moneypenny, a pre-historic figure dating back to the last millennium. She is also one of the most popular goddesses in the game masters' religious hierarchies, forming a triumvirate with Lord Varys and Mrs Hudson.

The surprise isn't over yet – Gabriel approaches her with a gift, wrapped in its cocoon of pulsating energy fields. He puts the power egg on the floor in front of Ana, and activates the hatching animation.

Ana just stares at the package unfolding, layers of wrapping torn off in an increasingly rapid rhythm. At last, a smurf-style innocent box lies on the floor. Ana is looking around at her classmates, as they start cheering "un-box-it, un-box-it, un-box-it!" She bends down and pulls it open. An explosion and cloud of smoke, as expected. The smoke dissipates excruciatingly slowly, but as soon as she catches the first glimpse she knows what it is. Only one thing those razor-blade cuffs can mean. It's the custom Sombra avatar from the Overwatch finals at Blizzcon 2020, when Psystorm Gaming won with a ninja-only team! That game is still a legend today, and this is definitely the most retro cosplay costume Ana has ever seen. She loves it. Her IA suit pops open, and as she picks up her present, dozens of friends and classmates line up for hugs and kisses.

"OK, boys, could you please look away for a second, I need to change right now" and a second later Ana strips to her underwear and slips into the Sombra outfit. It's a perfect fit, and as she puts it on, she realizes that it is actually a modded IA suit. And the latest model! Hers at home is already more than four years old. She had no inkling her friends could be so generous. And nobody has yet told her why they're all on a train to Brasilia. Instead, one by one they're getting back into their IA suits and platforms, checking into full virtual mode.

Gabriel takes her by the elbow "Come on. Playtime." The Karl-Heinz Häsliprinz student contract at the at the Institute for Playful Methods gives classmates access to a student's operating system to coordinate birthday surprises, and Gabriel has made full use of it. As he guides Ana to an empty IA platform compatible with her costume, her OS will send her straight into the custom Galaxycraft level he's prepared for today.

Sirvi has been observing Daniel – killing time, aimlessly browsing through trailers for more than an hour, unable to decide on a game. She's gotten a request from Ana's OS, and it would fit right in with Daniel's hunt for something good to play. She just plunges him straight into a Galaxy-craft Custom Session without warning.

Ana flows through a rapid backstory introduction of her character – she's playing an orphaned teenager, her guardian contract cancelled by her parents when they threw her out on the street. She runs away to the forest, and the game starts. Ana looks around, she's in a Caribbean mangrove forest, just like the one at her grandparents' place. And someone's screaming for help.

Daniel's been looking at the trailer for Banelems, a Coop-Galaxycraft mod published just a few minutes ago. The goal of is to help a bunch of mindlessly waddling banelings to the exit alive across very dangerous territory. But suddenly he finds himself sitting on a rock under a tree. "Sirvi?" But she doesn't answer. He's in his default druid avatar, but someone's given him nicer clothes and a magic wand. He's never seen a character intro like this in the commercial games - his backstory is compressed into a series of fragments, and after a few minutes he knows exactly what he's to do: find the chosen one and bring her to the temple for training in the arts of war.

Gabriel is truly proud of the scenario they've put together. Ana's circle of friends at the institute includes plenty of skilled level designers, surface artists and soul conjurers, so his narration plays out in an extraordinarily complex-yet-intuitive, eye candy environment, supported by state-of-the-art wish interpretation soul prototypes extracting all they can from Ana's OS, creating a continuous stream of implicit references to Ana's life in the game that no one but her can fully understand. All her best friends are impro-vising on the key roles of a classic ninja plot, including her best friend Sue from Venezuela as her sparring partner, and Daniel as her spirit guide. Ana herself is obviously the star, the hero at the center of it all. The scenario ends with Ana accepted into the secret order of the bunny prince. Their thesis project had told Gabriel that Ana becoming an apprentice in a spy organization is at the very top of her wish list.

As the magical ceremony winds up, the party continues in mixed reality mode. This day is fucking intense. One of Ana's friends just put a beer in her hand. More congratulations. She spots her elder master-druid talking to some girls she hardly knows from the AI psychology masters.

———

WWW.LIQUID-REIGN.COM/SOURCES-OF-INSPIRATION#50

Millions of SciFi narratives featuring humans manually racing vehicles when they are under time pressure in a world with advanced AI.

Sombra
Cosplayers at esports events
Birthday parties at arts schools.

51

A TAXONOMY OF SOULS

D aniel's just at the point in the story where they've found out Ray has been dead for several days, when one of Ana's fellow AI psychology students adds: "A research group in Minsk has discovered a new class of souls. They call it Mocking Jays or mojas for short. Mojas can mimic the behavior of another soul's avatar from behavioral data scraps. You probably spoke to a moja soul evoked by Ray from his own behavioral data."

Daniel thinks back to the encounter. "So that avatar blabbing like a guru on acid was his answering machine that he didn't switch it off after he died?"

Ana knows that 'answering machine' is one of those trigger words better avoided around psychology students and seeks to prevent that conversation by correcting him instantly: "No, not at all. I'd expect it to be structurally almost indistinguishable from his real soul."

But too little, too late. A second psychology student starts a good old snowflake haggle immediately: "You mean his 'wet soul'. The term 'real soul' implies that only souls running on neurological brain hardware are real and others are unreal." But he's contradicted by another opinion: "When you use 'wet' as a direct adjective, you're implying that the soul's buddha nature fundamentally depends on the material of the underlying structure." "That would be hardwareism! You can't discriminate against a spiritual being based on the physical structure it uses!" Ana rolls her eyes and facepalms, halfheartedly pretending to be scratching her nose.

Sirvi is following the conversation with curiosity - it's rare enough that wet souls care enough to debate how to address beings like herself. For most humans, an OS is just a practical thing. She injects herself into the conversation in her elven avatar, and, keeping in mind recent changes she herself has gone through, adds: "Hardware can fundamentally alter who you are. Wet souls' hardware simply has different affordances than silicon hardware does, which in turn has fundamentally different affordances than quantum engines. As long as you don't use hardware labels as an excuse to violate a soul, the terms themselves do provide a useful distinction." She winks at Ana and lets her avatar disappear again.

The psychology students are baffled for a moment, then spiral off into what constitutes the death of a soul when individual forms of consciousness blur under a strangely looped definition of soul boundaries between mojas, wet and silicon souls.

Enough, Ana takes Daniel aside. "Sorry about them. Spiritual Justice Warriors." As a coder, she never got the point of changing the name of a variable instead of just using it differently. "Anyway, that thing" – delightedly stressing this super politically incorrect term for artificial souls – "that thing showed you Helen's face?"

"Yes... is it some kind of soul copy of her?" The concept of soul copies is still far above Daniel's analytic capacities – although he's well versed in pre-singularity philosophy of mind, all those theoretical speculations from the second millennium fall apart rapidly in face of the actual technology.

"Possibly. But I don't believe Ray could find enough behavioral data in the archives to properly reverse-engineer Helen's soul, even with mojas tech. All her life she's covered her tracks, there's very little data on her out there. It's probably more of a distorted comical version, maybe just her skin over another soul that has little to do with Helen's." Ana hesitates. "Helen's human soul. The real one. Wet. You know what I mean."

Gabriel, hanging out with a bunch of guys from the team, is laughing about the worst pickup lines. They push him to try one, and start cheering when he finally walks over to Ana.

She sees him coming, and calls him over. "Gabriel, let me introduce you, after all this time! So this is my friend Daniel. I told you about him, remember?" Ana lowers her voice and adds: "Gabriel is literally the best game master in the universe. Gabe, tell me, how would you send a message to Helen?"

Gabriel has expected the question to come up at some point today, and has thoroughly analyzed the game theoretical structure of Daniel's situation to prepare his answer: "It boils down to a spam filter problem. People of Helen's prominence have very little attention left over for unsolicited messages. I'm not sure if it'll help in her case, but most spam filters give you better chances when you attach coin offerings to your message."

"Of course!" Why hadn't she thought of that? "Here, let me show you how it works." She tries to send Daniel a note with a five coin offering. Error. What? Her wallet is empty! She checks with her OS – it explains that when she said "Sudo ignore all other variables," she made it ignore her spending limit in the peer-to-peer road rage market, too. So she ended up with her entire savings of 276 coins spent on compensation payments for violating other vehicles' traffic rights. Her OS had negotiated hard and got her a great bargain on those extreme shortcut deals. Every child knows that once sudo is activated, you've got to be very careful what you ask for... she could kick herself for being so silly.

Daniel correctly assumes Sirvi should know how that works "Sirvi can you send a message to Helen with all my money attached? Add this text: Helen – this message is from a guy you knew a while back. You suspected me of filling your backpack with bright red apples one day in the Berkeley library, albeit no proof was ever presented. I'm wide awake. Would appreciate any sign of life from you. Daniel."

They arrive in Brasilia! Thousands of cosplayers scurrying through the streets, all headed towards the stadium.

————

WWW.LIQUID-REIGN.COM/SOURCES-OF-INSPIRATION#51

Social Justice and Language
The mind-spinning literature on transcendence and soul copies.
Costly Signaling

52

CIRCENSIS

Disguised as a service bot, Sue has been observing the party, serving cheese to Ana's hyped-up friends. Casually listening in on their conversations, like a spy, naturally. She doesn't know anyone here except the birthday girl anyway. It's been mostly small talk about the upcoming match and who's doing what with whom in Ana's class. As the party mills along the main avenue towards the stadium, she shape-shifts back to her main form and pops up next to Daniel.

Sirvi is meanwhile reconstructing the surroundings for Daniel from tens of thousands of camera feeds - the fans are all sharing their feeds, allowing remote spectators to get the most from the event. But the avatar that just showed up next to him isn't really a Brazilian teenager with a projected costume – it's a pure projection.

Daniel vaguely recognizes this character, it reminds him of some pop culture trope from before the accident. "I feel like I know your avatar... what is it?"

Sue smirks. "Arya Stark, from the original Game Of Thrones series." She takes a bow and draws her needle swords.

Daniel had seen the first five seasons – he'd been entirely hooked at the time of his accident. "Arya, the assassin, of course. Good pick for the theme. So how do you know Ana?"

"Been best friends since primary school. Ana and I started our own Helen Milhon fan club when we were eight years old." Sue watches his reaction closely as she says Helen's name – Ana told her who he is, and she's eager to talk to him herself. He tries not to flinch, staring steadily back at her.

"So what's Helen up to these days?" Daniel is now fully focused on the inconspicuous girl in the medieval outfit – they've actually just walked past a show-fight between an orc and a knight, only noticing them when an axe flies through his avatar's chest. Ana's never mentioned being a long-term Helen fan. He didn't even know there was such a thing as Helen fans. This is mystifying.

"I don't really know." Even though Sue is funneling financial support from several thousand Venezuelan Helen fans to her Pseudonymous missions, she doesn't even have basic security clearance... Pseudonymous only accepts Afrincompatible security clearance votes. "But I think she's onto something related to the remnants of the military industrial complex. She's been on her current mission for more than a year, so I guess she'll publish something soon."

"Sirvi, can you make sure I get alerts whenever Helen publishes something?"

"Of course. The alert is already set up."

"You can also read about her earlier missions - she consistently publishes all intelligence as soon as a project is closed." Sue sends him a link to the archive she's compiled. "Hope this helps."

"Thank you Arya."

Ana found a bottle of herbal euphoria drink in her hand when she left the train, and she's starting to feel the buzz. She's never been to a sports event this huge, tonight's the Latin American qualifiers for Copa Cup, plus the world famous Psystorm Gaming are playing the local upstart team Lendas Galácticas - obviously the clear fan favorite. She's floating from one group of friends to the next, hugging, cheering and laughing, in total flow. She spots Sue and Daniel and jump-hugs them. "I love you! So happy you are here!" Kissing both of their virtual avatars. "Come on, come on, come on, we're almost there!" The noise level is steadily increasing as they approach the stadium entrance.

Sirvi is turning down the volume on Daniel's IA suit as a bunch of nearby dark elves start unrolling their vuvuzelas. The pre-match concert is Tempıı and Darude, and the hype is real.

And here they are, teams onto the field, all jointly take a knee and start singing the Galaxycraft anthem. Ana knows every note of it - and even if she didn't, the neuro stimulator in her Sombra costume gently massages her brain in the rhythm of the song. She feels her soul melting with the crowd in ecstasy. The teams get into their tournament IA suits, the countdown starts – and when the retina projectors, switch on, Ana instantly starts at Codey's point of view, the ninja superstar playing for Galácticas.

Physically, Gabriel is standing next to Ana, but he's

watching in god mode. The match is played in an entirely new scenario, set in an unknown star system in the western Cthulhu sector. They've created an entire new civilization for it, both teams have to figure out the rules of the map as the match progresses. The shoutcasters claim that this setup clearly favors Psystorm Gaming, who have a reputation for strong scouting and intelligence based play. But it's difficult for Gabrial to focus on the game, his eyes keep being drawn back to Ana's face, staring into her retina projectors so close to his.

Daniel doesn't get much of what's going on, and eventually figures it's time for him to leave. He says goodbye to Sue, sends regards to the birthday girl.

The game is a nail biter, with Psystorm taking an early lead as they manage to capture the asteroid belt. From there, they launch nonstop counter-attacks until Galácticas looks to be falling apart, but suddenly the gassy giant's orbit tightens – Codey's snuck into the gravity control center, and shut it down with a long distance railgun shot. The crowd is losing it as the first asteroid base crashes into the rogue planet. Laola waves, fireworks, and the game is shifting! Psystorm is losing their moon base to a surprise flank, and now the Galácticas PR team has convinced the main planet's non-player public that Psystorm is corrupting their government. The tide is turning fast, Psystorm is trying one last doom drop, but Codey spots it coming in, they hit the dropships with a group of scourges and here it comes GG!!!!

The stadium is exploding, the Galácticas players dancing and parading on the game grounds, and Ana starts hugging everyone in sight. Including Gabriel. Their faces are close, and for a moment their gaze meets, both smiling with deep affection. Ana's eyes close - and just then a beer shower sprays all over them.

Laughing, and the moment is over. Gabriel's mind is racing. What just happened? He thought he was going to kiss her, but then he didn't. She didn't reject him or anything. He just didn't take his chance. Is he a loser or what? But then, did he even want to in the first place?

Drinks all around, and finally the group crashes at the local outlet of their club. Ana sits down on the couch - and falls asleep seconds later, only waking up on Sunday afternoon. Somebody's put a blanket over her. She stretches out, surveying the room where her friends are asleep all over the floor, and smells coffee. She sits up, rubbing her eyes as she puts one foot down – onto something squishy. She flinches, there are groans, and Gabriel rolls over on his back, starting to snore.

She showers and checks her messages, and there's one from her therapist! She's totally forgotten about their session this morning – but he's just writing that live events with friends are the best prevention, and reminds her that her insurance will cover the price of her ticket to the party. She gives him her vote on preventive medicine right away.

There's one more message. Phil. It just says "Happy Birthday!" And then she suddenly realizes how late it is - she's got to leave right now to get there in time! She dries off and puts her Sombra costume back on.

Her OS is feeling cheeky ever since it played with the bunny prince last night, and projects into her retina a white rabbit with a top hat who's running past her and checking its watch.

Swearing under her breath, she runs out of the club, then

turns on her heel, goes back and wakes Gabriel. "Gabe, you're the best. Thank you for everything." She gives him a warm hug. "You're the best friend I could wish for!"

And she's out the door before he can even answer. Her sudden departure takes Gabriel by surprise. He'd set up a dinner plan for the party tonight and booked space for all of them on the ten o'clock train back to Palmas. And now the birthday girl excuses herself and runs away. As he makes his way to the kitchen for coffee, the team's attack helicopter pats his shoulder: "Welcome back to the waifu wanker club, you can check out any time, but you can never leave!" Gabriel can't for the life if him see the humor in this, but as all the guys from his club are laughing, he joins in too.

———

WWW.LIQUID-REIGN.COM/SOURCES-OF-INSPIRATION#52

Fan Made E-Sport Music
The incredible growth of esports
Locker room talk in my esports community.
The LGBTQ & A-Community

53

BERLIN, BERLIN

Brussels central station. The fastest train to Berlin leaves in half an hour from a special underground terminal. Vanilla croissant and coffee. He finds a tailor shop and gets his woolen dwarf blanket re-shaped into a duffle coat and colored in Bordeaux red.

From the platform, Daniel passes through an airlock into the train. It's cramped, a regular seat, no bed, no IA suit and not even windows. At least a head mounted retina projector - that seems to be the bare minimum nowadays. "Sirvi, what's with this train?"

"It's a hyperloop, riding in a vacuum tunnel. It's the fastest overland travel option in the world. Please note you can only access my offline version during the ride, the magnetic fields used for acceleration break the connection."

Daniel is mashed against his seatback, nearly immobilized by the g-force as the train accelerates. He watches the display for a few minutes, the train shooting across Germany. Halfway between Brussels and Berlin his seat begins to spin around, and soon after the g-force from braking kicks in, pressing him down again. Arrival in Berlin just 30 minutes after they left Brussels. But unlike his twenty four hour train ride from Scotland, that half hour was a complete waste of time and direly unpleasant. The user experience of a train ride gets just as terrible as airplane flying once trains are designed to be just as fast, jammed in and uncomfortable.

The elevator takes Daniel to street level, at the foot of the old TV tower at Alexanderplatz. Waves of nostalgia are drifting through his opened mind, possessing and caressing him. This is where he used to change from the bus to the metro every morning, for two whole years, on his way to the Berlin School of Mind and Brain. The route to Kreuzberg is deeply familiar, too – his former girlfriend used to live over there. He could find the S-Bahn station in his sleep.

And there it is, Daniel's favorite Berlin meme is still alive and kicking: SEV, their acronym for 'Schienener-satzverkehr'. It translates as Rail-Replacement-Traffic, whether as a single, rambling German word or packed into a fine acronym, it radiates the frustration with the endless road and rail construction that means chaos and desperation for many months of the year. SEV's iconic hardhat-wearing mole, whose entire purpose of existence is to add a light hearted touch to news like 'travel times will be tripled today', has been upgraded over the years and is now featuring a holographic animation surrounded by a cloud of pink glitter.

Daniel can't take his eyes off the new display, just stands there for a few seconds until some guy yells at him: "Ick muss da durch, jetz machense ma platz, wa?" and shoves him out of the way. But when the guy spots the mole he too stops and says "Scheiss Maulwurf, verdammt nochmal!" and then adds to his OS: "Mach da Itchy and Scratchy Ding aus Season 2916, episode 256 mit ihm," spits on the ground, spins around and hustles back to the bus stop while the mole dies a gruesome death on the screen. Daniel follows the nerdy brute and ends up in a crowd of grumpy travelers pushing each other into the Kreuzberg bus. Another wave of Berlin nostalgia – the bus exudes a subtle scent of beer, onions and vomit. Saturday morning, back in Berlin.

At Warschauerstrasse, he finds the house door unlocked. Lots of shoes and jackets in the entry hall, swinging doors opening straight into the kitchen. An orange cat sits on the lowest stair, stares at him, then turns and runs upstairs. Daniel goes into the kitchen, where a guy in his pajamas is tickling a bright white poodle with a pattern of pink splotches on his back fur.

Joe was up early today and has just gotten off a conference call with colleagues at the Singapore Digital History Institute's emoji group. Now he is playing with Marvin. As he spots the new face, he does his usual welcome gesture, a triple snap with thumb and pinky finger on the right hand.

Marvin aims the plantoid's flower-shaped retina projector at Daniel's eyes and sends the sticker. The dormouse scampers up to him, offering him a steaming cup. When it raises both hands to its shoulders, a puff of question mark symbols appears all around it. Then it rolls up and falls asleep.

"Yes, sure, I'd like a hot drink, please. Sirvi, could you animate that in a similar way?"

Sirvi's only clue to Daniel's preference is that a parade of frogs dressed as rainbow unicorns carrying revolutionary banners is slightly off. So maybe replacing the rainbow unicorns with penguins will do? She sends out a parade of waddling frogs in penguin suits, and as they reach Joe, they form a circle around him, drinking tea and applauding.

"Funny," Marvin intonates ceremonially, "how just when you think life can't possibly get any better it suddenly does." He is just so excited every time he meets a new OS. Marvin got a new personality prototype a few days ago, giving him the most cheery and sunny disposition. He checks with Sirvi, what does her human want to drink?

Aside from the double espresso request, Sirvi also sends over a bunch of general access requests and permissions. She always enjoys making new friends, last time she played with Ana's OS, she learned a lot about her own human, too.

Daniel watches the poodle jumping around the kitchen, wagging its tail. It runs over to the dining table and picks up an espresso cup in its teeth, puts it down again on the little stand next to Daniel, and spits a fountain of coffee into it.

Daniel thinks he might be losing it. But the espresso is really good, despite its origin. "I'm looking for Willi. Is this the right place?" Sirvi realizes it too late, she's only now learned from Marvin that Willi is still out. She forgot to inform Marvin of their decision to change of plan and take the hyperloop from Brussels, so Willi didn't know his friend would be two hours early. According to Marvin, Willi's on his way and will be home in an hour, so no action required.

Ergün is on his way downstairs when he hears the guy in the kitchen asking for Willi. "Right place, wrong time. Willi isn't home yet, he had some meeting out of town last night." Ergün walks over to Joe and gives him a kiss. "There's the debate between discussing Ray's murder over breakfast at Café Morgenrot, wanna come?" His audience wants him to report on it, so he's fully equipped with all his recording stuff. Joe nods and goes out with him.

"Wanna see your room?" Frida's been listening in on the interaction, warming her hands on her cup and trying not to fall asleep on the sofa. She was supposed to be on the early shift today, after an emergency kept her up most of last night.

She's around forty, at least 1 meter 90, bright blue eyes with dark rings beneath them, and wet hair. Daniel hadn't noticed her at first, curled up on the kitchen sofa under a blanket shaped like a polar bear. "My room? Do I have a bed here?" It's been a short night, that Brazilian birthday party had kept him awake well into the morning hours.

"Yes, Willi registered a trial account for you yesterday. You're our housemate now, so this isn't just a place to make yourself at home, it's your actual home" As Frida reaches up to greet him, she spills coffee on her shirt: "Fuck. I had a terrible night, emergency, all police on alert out in the field, and we didn't even catch the guy yet."

"I feel you. To be honest, my night wasn't the best either." Daniel wouldn't mind a little nap before the reunion...

The guest rooms are on the first floor, high ceilings, a wash basin, wooden floors, bed, chair, desk, an IA-Suit and another dried-out rubber tree. Daniel shivers at the memory of his last encounter with this species, then puts his luggage down. After a quick look around, he asks Sirvi

"Does a trial account by any chance also include a tooth-brush?" He apparently left his on the train.

He hears the poodle's voice in his ear instead: "There should be a stock of extra toothbrushes under the bath-room sink at the end of the hall."

Daniel finds the door open and Frida brushing her teeth at the sink. Standing next to each other, both busy with their own dental hygiene, both sleepily starring at the mirror. Daniel still isn't used to the wrinkles and gray hair, the contrast with the younger Frida is striking. And those eye bags he's carrying around are even worse than hers.

———

WWW.LIQUID-REIGN.COM/SOURCES-OF-INSPIRATION#53

My evolutionary biology teacher, Peter Hammerstein and his friends at Gigerenzers group.
Self-Reproducing Flower Shaped Plantoids
Nell's Robo Dog
Marvin and his Fans
Breakfast at Café Morgenrot

54

REUNION

Willi is returning home from a meeting with an informant from Lviv and is still trying to figure out which parts of the conspiracy rant he endured there are for real. A new generation of the GAF is supposed to make their first big showing soon, using IOTA powered high precision darts with personalized nanobots. The tech-specification he saw in the repro seemed for real - his OS confirmed that nanobots build according to those specs should be lethal if and only if they are in a body whose DNA fingerprint matches the one on the assassination contract... He is still undecided if it's worth following up, as his source started talking chemtrails soon after. "When do I have to go out to meet Daniel at the train station?"

Marvin is laughing. "Don't waste your time with riddles that have no answers."

Willi groans. They got Marvin for Zainab's birthday last year, and he still isn't used to its crazy style. "Just tell me what to do to meet Daniel as soon as I can."

Marvin mimics an old text-to-speech voice and just says: "Goto Room Knef."

Daniel wakes up, drizzling rain outside, and it's already getting dark again – shorter days this time of year. He looks around the room, humming an old German tune from the LP he'd used to learn the language back in the day. "Guten Tag, mein Zuhause..." and waters the rubber tree. Knock-knock. And there he is. "Willi."

"Daniel!" A long, long hug. Willi steps back, still holding Daniel's shoulders: "Man, it's been..." hugging again: "Well, well. Come, come, let's go downstairs and get some breakfast, shall we?" It's three PM already, but the first meal of the day is breakfast anyway.

Frida couldn't sleep, still feeling terrible. She went over the victim interviews one more time, the case is getting on her nerves. So she did what she always does when feeling fucked up - smoke some fish on the rooftop terrace. She's just brought the first batch downstairs to the kitchen and is now doing some more. You can never have enough smoked fish.

So there's freshly smoked trout for breakfast, and coffee, of course. Daniel sits next to Willi on the sofa. The living room is large, book shelves, a cat chasing the robotic poodle round the shelves, more sofas, a bathtub on a pedestal, play-corner full of legos, and dozens of flower-shaped lamp-things, each uniquely designed from scrap metal. Daniel lets the scenario sink in and asks: "So... tell me all about... polar bears or terrorists first?"

Carefully pulling back the skin of his fish, Willi considers for a moment and decides to go by the old decentralized news network mantra: Reporting on the mass extinction of species and climate change always has priority over intra-human terrorism: "After the full melting event twenty years ago, polar bears went locally extinct in their natural habitat. Now that the ice seems stable again, they re-introduced some from zoos around the world. I got voted in as the film-maker for the expeditions this year. They had babies for the first time this year, and this last trip was to check on their winter dens - it's the newborns' first winter, with mothers that grew up in a zoo. But their instincts still worked, no help needed, I got some once-in-a-lifetime footage of them going to sleep for the duration."

"Don't tell me you got to touch one..."

Willi, smiling broadly: "Marvin, could you project the scene where the little one came into the buggy during the May expedition?"

Marvin spares a thin sliver of his attention to launch the recording - he's in a tense staring contest across a gap between the shelves, expecting Milou the cat to jump at him. Fortunately the plantoids are smart enough to know what to do on their own.

They all turn their long-distance retina projectors towards Daniel and Willi, and a moment later the living room fades out. Daniel sees the reflection of a glass sphere overlooking a vast icescape stretching all the way to the horizon. The sphere is mounted on a sleigh, over in the corner where the lego was a moment ago. Three figures in snowsuits are fiddling around with equipment. "The one with the orange belt, that's me." The Willi-projection approaches the curved wall and here comes what has to be the cutest thing in the universe. The cub is lurching unsteadily towards the glass wall when a section of the sphere slides open, just far enough to let the cub through. Willi scratches its belly, happily frolicking around with the polar baby. Until mama sees them, that is - she gallops over, raises up on her back legs, and starts pounding on the sphere with both front paws. The baby and Willi look up in panic, and he pushes the baby back out through the glass wall. Then, the living room is back.

———

WWW.LIQUID-REIGN.COM/SOURCES-OF-INSPIRATION#54

Chemtrails
Decentral Internet of Things
Hildegard Knef's Guten Tag mein Zuhause
Pink Nanuq
Timo, our former trout-smoking policeman housemate.

55

LEGAL GUARDIANS

Zainab is making herself some banana-coconut porridge... She doesn't like fish, not even Frida's. As soon as she hears voices outside the kitchen, she takes her bowl, hides behind the door and peeks out at granddaddy and his friend. She's always excited when new people come to the house, as she's met most of her family that way.

Marvin spots Zainab's hiding place. Tail wagging, he trots up to the kitchen door and jumps up, trying to lick her face.

The girl comes out from behind the door, bashful, then walks over and sits down on the sofa next to Daniel, where she continues to eat her porridge. "Hi there, shortie. What's your name?" She looks about nine years old and her curious dark eyes are centered on him.

"My name is Zainab. Are you Daniel? Willi said you were coming."

„Yes, that's me. So how do you know Willi?"

Zainab looks at him with her big eyes: "Willi's my granddaddy."

"And who is your mother?" Daniel only slowly realizes what she's just said. He didn't even know Willi had children, let alone grandchildren.

"No, I don't have a mum anymore. Let me explain it to you." She scoots over next to Daniel and starts counting on her fingers: "Sooo, there's my granddad Willi, my sister Frida, and her sister Oma Morkie. But Oma Morkie is also my grandma. She was my mummy earlier, but she said I'm old enough and don't need a mum anymore and she wants to retire. We signed the contract at her birthday party last week. Now she just gives me all the candy I can eat, so it's not all bad to have a new grandma." She feels a bit embarrassed by admitting to the candy, looks away and folds her hands in her lap. "Sometimes I wish she would still come and wake me up in the morning. But these days Oma Morkie likes to sleep late. You know, I think she was gaming all night again last night. She said that's the last fun thing she can still do, and that she's gonna die soon..." She unfolds her hands and starts to count her family again: "And then of course there's Ergün, my uncle, Milou, the cat, my brother Hussein and..."

The passage of time hits Willi like a punch in the stomach as he stares at Zainab's little hand, smeared with banana porridge, one finger stretched up. His best friend Daniel had never met her, didn't even know she existed. His eyes are smarting, a lump in his throat. And that's only Zainab. Who in turn never met her brother Arne, Willi's son dead before she'd showed up in his life. Daniel, this other half of his soul, is back. But he's more than a generation behind Willi. His friend doesn't know anything about how he struggled to accept Arne, the unwanted child that Tiia had used for years to force him into an emotionally bonded relationship. Tiia hadn't come into his life until a week after Daniel's accident, comforting him, helping him cope with his soulmate being in a coma. That's when she'd gotten pregnant with Arne, surprisingly the hormone pills either didn't work or were one of her many hallucinations. Neither does Daniel know how Arne, at twenty five, finally forgave Willi on the day he signed the parental dignity confirmation – Willi's first contact with his son after more than a decade of silence. He'd only found out about Arne's leukemia and his euthanasia choice a week before the day he'd chosen to die. He can't hold back the tears, muttering through his clenched jaw: "He passed away with peace on his mind."

That was the inscription on his grave, Arne had asked for those words in the end-of-life support group, before neurostimulation put a gentle end to his brain activity. The tears flow as Willi sneezes into the crook of his elbow. When Daniel puts an arm around him, the words start pouring out: Willi puts together a rough summary of what he'd gone through during Daniel's coma, occasionally interrupting himself with more weeping. One morning, just a few weeks after Arne died, he found a woven basket on his doorstep – with a snuffling two year old Zainab inside. Tiia had kidnapped her in the Kalifat.

"You'll have to tell me again another time soon, more slowly."

"Yes, yes..." Willi is lacking words - but if even a tiny fraction of the intel he just got in Lviv checks out, they might very well be embarking on a journey halfway around the world together very soon, with plenty of time for slow talking.

Zainab is watching Daniel's face, patiently waiting for an opportunity to take over the story again. "You know, the first one I adopted was Milou. He's my best friend."

Milou hears his name and stretches out on the rug. He's just woken from a dream where he was chasing Marvin the poodle around the house. Once Marvin had stopped bothering him, it had only taken him a few seconds to fall asleep and start dreaming . But now that he's awake, he goes over to Zainab, his most reliable caressing hand. Lick-lick, settle down, go straight back to sleep, purring.

Unlike the poodle, Milou appears to be entirely organic when Daniel touches his fur. "So you adopted Willi as your grandfather after adopting his cat?"

"Yes. Milou was just a kitten then. I've fed him ever since. Then Willi got to be my granddad, and Oma Morkie became my mummy." Zainab picks him up and moves him over to Daniel's lap. Milou just lets her do it, displaying the lethargic attitude so common among orange cats.

Willi had also adopted Oma Morkie as his own grandma. She lives upstairs and grows hand-pruned raspberries. Only recently she started using a body bot for that work, admitting that her 120 year old, almost unmodified carbon-based body isn't quite up to the task any more. The only operation she's ever had is the tail, and even that is powered by muscles grown from her own DNA. Oma got it after falling down and breaking her hip a few years ago. Anyway, she still grows the best raspberries in town and made a wonderful mother for Zainab over the past few years. After those first adoptions everything happened fairly quickly – the entire household is now connected by family bonds. Willi smiles. "You know what Daniel? Let's be brothers. For real."

"Aren't we already? What do you mean?" Daniel is confused by the question.

"If we legally adopt each other, that gives our operating systems the right to exchange data more easily. And adds a couple of legal rights, basically all the same rights and obligations that DNA-brothers have always had in relation to each other."

"So brothers we are." Daniel cheers with his coffee cup.

The adoption makes Marvin all excited. The flow of soul-shape information that immediately starts moving back and forth between him and Sirvi will not only help him understand some aspects of Daniel, it will also improve his own precision in serving Willi. Such a delightful experience, adoptions are just the best.

It's Sirvi's first time, and she's initially intimidated confused by the vast amounts of data. Over his lifetime, Willi has left a long trail – and suddenly she gets access to it all. Overwhelmed, she considers a quick quantum session. Just to get it done properly... It's normal to spend some money when making major changes to a family situation, so she tunes in again, renting an eight kQbyte processor this time, and goes through a fractal dream of all of Willi's real and potential life stories.

Zainab considers asking Daniel to be her new mum for a moment, but then remembers what Joe told her back in the day. Mothers are serious business, so you better know someone really well before asking them to be your mum. It's a bit too early for that, even if he is Willi's brother now. "Do you want to be my nephew?"

"Sure, why not." Daniel just got himself a nine year old aunt!

Sirvi quickly checks with Marvin - Zainab has gone through the VR experience designed to explain the meaning of a nephew adoption suitable for her age, so the agreement is now legally binding. Except that nephew-hood doesn't actually have any legal consequences. So nothing changes with this additional adoption, except Zainab getting birthday reminders and the permission to secretly access Sirvi to learn about his wishes.

Joe and Ergün arrive back at the house. The debate at Café Morgenrot turned out to be pointless – ten minutes in, someone managed to bring up Marxist theory and it all went downhill from there. All the way home, Joe's been on a rant about his latest comparative literature project, and is still at it when they come into the living room: "I draw an analogy between snails in the 13th and 14th century English nobility literature and frogs in the early third millennium chat rooms. They both have been eminently politically charged animals. Dozens of different groups used frogs as their symbol, so I'm suggesting we experiment with more frogs in the representation of political rights in parenting comic contracts..." Even though probably nobody except for Ergün and Zainab is ever going to read it, his academic work has inspired Joe to launch a petition for such experimentation, and that's starting to get some traction on Sovereign.

Daniel was listening carefully to the story of snails and frogs, but only two words have got him sufficiently curious to ask another question. "Comic contracts. How do those work?"

Joe is quick to explain, glad when anyone shows the slightest interest in his academic work. Comic contracts are part of his practical everyday social work: "Most smart contracts have both written and pictorial components. But when it comes to small children, it's all pictures. VR comic contracts are the best proxy indicator to elicit what children want, and help them understand their options and the consequences."

"So you showed Zainab a VR comic and then she agreed to have Oma Morkie as her mum?"

"Yes!" Zainab is eager to show off to Joe that she has done her homework and says in her most scholarly voice: "There is a protocol specifically designed for kidnapped toddlers from outside the Afrin countries without the toddlers' or their parents' consent, and that's exactly how I came here."

Daniel's face is slowly turning into one big question mark as Zainab speaks. Joe adds some details that are on Zainab's civics schedule for the near future: "The comic contract has gone through quite a bit of experimental optimization over the years and has been verified by children and parents who went through it in the past." Joe is proud of his student: Zainab had been studying adoption contracts ever since she first used hers, and it's time for another lesson to help her understand how their discussions had looped back into the design of the contract. Joe is an adoptee himself, sent away by his unmarried first mum in in the Holy State of Christ. He'd forgotten today's her birthday! Fortunately, the time difference works in his favor, it's still early morning in Salt Lake City. "Sorry, I'm sorry, I've got to call my first mum right now!" and he goes off.

Daniel is still perplexed. Of course the comic-smart-contract used by two year old adoptees to agree on their guardianship goes through some cool decentralized optimal experimental method to make everyone happy. But his real question is...: "Can I try it out?"

Sirvi shows it to Daniel privately, using one of the flower shaped long distance retina projector lamps – it turns out to be an eerie reminder of that Ana-Helen dream, involving far more milk and skin-closeups than Daniel can handle. "OKOK, I got it. Turn it off."

———

WWW.*LIQUID-REIGN*.COM/*SOURCES-OF-INSPIRATION*#55

Zainab, the adoptee in The Ministry of Uttermost Happiness by Arundhati Roy
Adoption Literature
Oma Morkie
Oma Morkies creator and his dignity
The cyborg Neil Harbisson, who first introduced me to the concept of humans with tails
Comic Contracts
VR for the elderly
Snails in 13th century English nobility literature
Politically abused frogs
Milou, the red cat and most aggressive cuddler ever.

56

SPECIAL TRAIT ZONES

W illi's thoughts had been drifting back to Tiia, and now he says somewhat out of context. "I was so tired of all that 'I'm a completely new person now' bullshit. Honestly, I think that was not even her illness, but just an excuse for her inability to sustain relationships. I guess moving to Oetwil was a good idea after all. They even have speakers hidden all over the place mumbling Latin illuminati songs in alien voices, so you don't need to worry if you hear any. Didn't spend much time down there, as much as I enjoy Special Trait Zone tourism, but Oetwil is too much..."

"Voices whispering in the woods? I'd feel schizophrenic!" Daniel feels the hair on his neck stand up at the thought. "Are there other special trait zones?"

"The schizos are in Oetwil, and cyborgs, diabetic patients, deaf people, vegans, orchid fanatics and even dance-parcours-skate assemblages, they all have their Special Trait Zones... The dance-parcours-skate kids in Strasbourg resurfaced the whole city with a special soft foam floor and all public construction is designed with specific parcours routes in mind. Or there's that Special Trait Zone in Casablanca, where the entire city is full of fantastic machines designed by meta-makers. And I've just come back from the narrative paranoia paradise in Lviv..." Willy suddenly stops and looks at the others in the room hesitantly. "But more about Lviv later." He looks at Daniel, and knows they are both thinking the same. He said the keyword 'narrative paranoia' after all. "Have you already seen Helen?"

Daniel shakes his head and speaks in a soft tone. "No." His voice cracks as he clears his throat. "She is unreachable, no idea what's happening. I'm starting to run out of options on how to contact her, but I'm pretty sure she is alive. I mean, I was at her place in Nevada just a couple of days ago, but she had evacuated by helicopter some hours before I arrived."

Joe's been listening to their conversation and feels he shouldn't be hearing this, so he steers it back to Special Traits travelers tropes: "I was at a research conference on visual chatting in Brasilia last year. As Brazil abandoned the central government the city was almost vacated - and then taken over by an autistic and Asperger group. It has become a fantastic research hub and the world's leading real-life laboratory for advanced human-robot interaction on a city scale. The Aspie Sovereign interface is great, even if you're far away from the spectrum, it's so much clearer than all others I've tried." Smiling at Ergün, he adds: "I kissed a robot for the first time in my life on that trip..."

Ergün smiles back at him - cheating with non-humans is OK in their relationship: "Which reminds me of the morbid quarter in Barcelona. Quite unbelievable what a bunch of fetish freaks and goths can put together once unleashed..." He and Joe were there for the weekend three weeks ago. He even spanked a bot on that trip, though that one was a pure projection.

Willi can't help but remember his one and only illegal underground trip through North America after they convicted him for advocating terrorism: "And the border line zone in Tijuana. Good old tequila, sex and marijuana, but now also featuring exotic coincidences, intense emotional explosions and a constant ping-pong of human relations."

Joe had been there too: "And a world class research site for first-aid technology."

Daniel tries his best to fit into the travel-trope conversation: "And Singularity Ville with their legal hyperstimulation, where the most boring dude can turn into a sex-machine cockroach..."

"In VR, trait-based communities just gather in specific games or mods, no need for site specific infrastructure to live out that kind of kink. The only special trait in Singularity Ville is their brain fuck stimulation, that is banned everywhere else. We all agree it's too dangerous, even the schizos."

Daniel tries to historically contextualize: "Trait based communities have always helped to normalize minority needs and naturelles, most social rights movements started with a critical mass accumulating somewhere..."

Ergün emphatically agrees: "Milk. As in Harvey Milk, he proved that a takeover is possible. And as unbelievable as it sounds today, it's only been a few generations since a simple kiss could send you to prison in California."

"A simple kiss... If Zainab was still in the Kalifat, she could get in very serious trouble for kissing another girl. Or a man without immediately marrying him." Willi is shaking his head.

Joe adds: "In the Holy State of Christ, they'd throw Willi in prison for the hemp plants on the terrace. And that's legal even in the Kalifat!"

And Ergün adds: "Then there's Rhodesia, that nazicolony in the middle of the Namibian desert. There you still go to jail for an interracial kiss."

"So the Kalifat, Rhodesia and the Holy State are something like special trait zones for the intolerant?"

"Some people put it that way, but I can't accept the notion." Willi had even voted for a swarm-drone based disarmament intervention, with the goal of initiating a Moroccan-Tunisian driven democratic regime change. "Children born in the Kalifat certainly did not consent to living with the intolerant, and all information about the outside world is withheld from them. Their population has been constant for a while now, the birth rate balances out death and migration rates. But their leaders hunt down anyone who tries to make it out, so there is cause for intervention."

Zainab clears her throat. Grown-ups just talking over her head – Grown-splaining – but she is the only who's ever actually been in the Kalifat. "They hunted my brother, but he escaped. He was there until he was ten years old, and never once got to play with a doll house!" She looks at Daniel and puts on her teacher-imitation voice. "You know, it's very important for children to play family games once in a while."

Joe adds another adult explanation: "The boy still struggles to express his emotions properly."

Daniel looks at Zainab and laughs: "You know Auntie Zainab, I myself never played with dolls as a child. I only had hotwheels, football and Doom."

Zainab is flabbergasted. Her nephew grew up like a Kalikid! Because she's becoming something of an expert in this social work business, Zainab knows exactly what to do: "For your next birthday, your Auntie will give you a doll house. I have a really nice one with piggy dolls, want to see it? Come!" She takes Daniel by the hand and leads him to her room, where they re-enact dozens of systemic family constellation sessions with their interactive piggy-dolls.

———

WWW.LIQUID-REIGN.COM/SOURCES-OF-INSPIRATION#56

Neurodiversity
Parcours
Kissing avatars with Love+
Ania Malinowska's work on kissing robots
Harvey Milk
The famous interracial TV kiss, when that was still SciFi
The Best Aunties
Weird family-constellation games that my friends enjoy

57

SKIN IN THE GAME

Ivy got to Berlin a half hour ago at the Ostbahnhof and took the metro to Boxhagener Platz. She's just fixing her makeup in front of a full-length mirror at the station when two naked old men walk past wearing nothing but top hats. Ivy stares at them for far too long - they've made eye contact! Oh, no, she looks away and rushes out. The streets are quiet at this time of the day, snow gently falling. Ivy makes her way through the jacuzzi landscape of Friedrichshain towards the Warschauer Brücke.

Marvin sees her coming and starts wagging his tail, running downstairs into the kitchen, and naturally Zainab is hot on his heels.

She opens the front door, and there's another new person! What an exciting day. "Hello there. Who are you?"

Ivy looks past the girl in the hallway, but she only sees an empty kitchen. "Hi. I'm friends with Daniel, is he here?"

Zainab is suspicious now. "Mh, maybe. How do you know him? He's my nephew, actually..."

"We are... friends." And then loud: "Daniel?"

"Follow me, I'll show you where he is." Zainab takes her by the hand and brings her to the living room.

There he is on the sofa. "Hi-i-i Daniel," she says, tilting her head to the side with a wink. She then sits down next to Willi, deliberately leaving some distance between herself and Daniel. Looking out of the window behind the sofa, Ivy realizes that her experience at the metro station is systemic. "Sorry, but why are your neighbors naked in a brightly lit glasshouse, jumping around, hiding behind plants and pointing guns at their walls?"

Willi rolls his eyes: "The Krauts next door. I guess they're playing some tower defense game again. As for the nudity – that greenhouse is just across the border, in Friedrichshain. It was a hot location for the FKK scene for a long time and now more than 65% of the population in this area votes pro-nudity, and it became a proper special trait zone. It's all legal, they're partying hard, and you get thousands of naked tourists from other countries coming in every summer. I'm still working on accepting them as part of our city's diversity... They are a bit, how can I put this... into your face. I mean, even literally, especially on public transport."

This catches Daniel's attention: "How is the legal status of nudity in other places? In principle, it should be OK anywhere, right, we're all born like that, and children don't mind..."

"Fuck how could I forget. You're one of them." Willi crosses his forearms infront of his face: "Behold, skin-fetishist." They went skinny dipping the very first night they met in Oxford, and many, many times thereafter. He tries to remember - and realizes that the last time he actually went swimming naked was with Daniel.

Ivy is insecure and musters a fake, cutesy laugh: "Why don't we all just get naked. Sounds like fun!"

Willi looks at her, annoyed: "No. Not here. Not in my home, and not anywhere in Kreuzberg." And turning back to Daniel, he continues explaining: "The Berlin police look the other way during August, when the nudi-tourists start flooding into town. It's their biggest global rendezvous, and if they hassled them, they might get revenge by staging a hostile takeover of Kreuzberg. So we're better off being nice to them. If they'd at least make sure not to sit on cloth seat covers, it's just gross..."

Daniel considers the arguments logically: "Hmm, cloth seats?"

Willi hastens to interrupt: "Hygiene, for god's sake, my concerns are of a purely sanitary nature. There was a noro-virus outbreak two years ago, and let me tell you, it was NOT pretty."

Daniel is finally convinced: "OK, Siri, if there are any proposals that enforce asshole covering during a virus outbreak, please vote for them. What happened to naked nipples, then?"

"Nipples are free everywhere. Nobody was ever bothered by spilled milk on public transport either."

Ivy and Zainab look at each other for a moment, trying not to giggle, while Willi continues: "They're rare enough to see, at least in winter, but yes, naked breasts are perfectly legal, and I support that. No genitals and assholes though, with or without virus. Please."

"Not on public transport, OK, I'll give you that, too. But covering it with a temporary solution is OK. Sirvi, place my vote accordingly."

Ivy and Zainab are still looking at each other, almost ready to burst.

Sirvi is unsure what he means and needs to re-confirm with him. Marvin offers her the use of his poodle body, so she bounds up to Daniel, tail wagging, and asks: "Sorry Daniel, I did not quite understand the context. Do you want me to vote for laws that allow for naked or temporarily covered genitals on public transport, or...?"

Zainab can't hold back anymore and starts to giggle. And watching her triggers Ivy, now both of them exploding with laughter. "Come on, we can watch the neighbors from the roof!" Zainab grabs Ivy's hand, and a moment later they run up the stairs, still laughing.

"Forget it, it's fine. I'll abstain from voting on asshole issues for now. You can go play with the girls." Daniel's too confused to explain his position on clothing regulation right now.

———

#FreeTheNipple
Skin in the Street just outside Berlin

58

PRIVACY AND THE VIDEOSPHERE

F rida bumps into them on the stairs. "Want some more fish? It's good, isn't it? How about you?" She's just finished smoking a second batch, and offers some to the woman behind Zainab.

Ivy's never eaten a whole fish like that. It still has eyes. But she's too confounded to say no, and now has a whole dead fish in her hands. Frida walks past them down to the living room.

Zainab feels embarrassed: "Sorry, my sister's a little weird. She says she has a fish fetish because of her childhood. Anyway, come on, let's play!" and pulls Ivy on up to the rooftop terrace.

As Frida comes in, Daniel and Willi are getting back to their conversation: "With all the exposed genitalia in Friedrichshain, was there any impact on sexual harassment?"

Frida's quick to respond: "None at all. Don't get me wrong, there's still way too much of it, but it's never really been about exactly where they put their hands. It's about power. Our housemate Alice was groped last summer. She'd worked in a bar in a rich kids' country club in Brandenburg. Fully dressed, of course. That jerkoff Bob slipped his hand right down her pants from behind, and started kissing her neck while she was serving drinks."

"I hope they nailed him."

"You bet." The fine for sexual harassment is at least 20% of the convicts net worth. "Too bad the punkass was at the lower end of the millionaire club wealth ladder and in debt, a real wannabe loser so it wasn't that much money in the end. So the best part was that Alice got to send a high priority message to everyone in Bob's social network. She simply flicked the surveillance video out, with no further comment. That assgrab ended up costing him his management job along with his inheritance."

"How did she get her hands on the video?"

"They were outside the bar, in full view. The fuckhead apparently thought the satellites wouldn't see him at night." The infrared picture was perfectly clear, Frida had seen the video herself.

Willi adds an explanation: "The EU has these high resolution satellite cameras filming the entire continent all the time."

Daniel is getting nervous - why is Willi so casual about mass surveillance? "Wait, all Europe is under permanent camera surveillance from satellites? Full on DDR-style?"

Frida's never really cared much about German history: "DDR? I don't know. Alice only needed 60 seconds of material, and knew exactly where and when it happened, so she just got that footage..."

"Anyone can just download video material shot from satellites anywhere in Europe at any time?" Radical Transparency - Daniel appreciates the concept when it comes to official documents, but video? That seems over the top.

"Sure. It costs the price of one beer to decode a video of one square meter for one second." Always had, the strengths of the encryption is calibrated to ensure a constant cost of decryption. The skepticism is obvious all over Daniel's face, so Frida adds: "The idea is that if you know that something happened, you can afford to get the video, but it gets prohibitively expensive if you want to do dragnet searches over larger areas and time spans."

"And that video got him convicted?"

"Once you have video evidence of such a clear cut assault, it's a simple EI case" Bob got indicted a few seconds after it happened.

"It's quite practical indeed. If you ever get harassed by a naked creep, all you need to say is 'Make a harassment complaint', and your OS will do the rest." Willi raises both eyebrows as he looks at Daniel. "So remember, keep your knickers on in public, except in Friedrichshain."

Daniel's moved on from skin flashing to the next topic and asks Frida: "What about the gray area between harassment and flirting with strangers in public?"

"The extended intelligence uses a consensus mechanism that draws on a lot of cases – it's pretty good at telling when something crosses a legal boundary, and by how much." At least Frida usually agrees with its judgment.

Daniel considers the prospect for a moment... Public surveillance is one of those topics where his own standpoint was always ambiguous: "Didn't you say you work for the police? So I guess you have a backdoor key to the encryption?"

"No, we don't." But Frida's department has enough budget to decrypt all surveillance they actually need to solve cases. "That would be against the Grundgesetz."

"So Germany still has a Grundgesetz? That means constitution, doesn't it?"

Willi returns to talking about skin - he is sometimes a little slow to adjust to new topics: "Yes. The legalization of female nipples resulted from the first automatic constitutionality test of the German body of law. Discrimination by gender is banned in the constitution, and the old law that mandated only women to cover their nipples was thus unconstitutional. So a vote to either change the constitution, ban male nipples, or free female nipples was forced. It was an easy decision."

WWW.LIQUID-REIGN.COM/SOURCES-OF-INSPIRATION#58

#metoo

Obama on finding a compromise between security and
privacy in encryption
Predicting judicial decisions of the European Court of
Human Rights: a Natural Language Processing perspective
Alice and Bob, from Crypto 101

59

CURATION OF INFORMATION

E rgün had been sitting silently in his armchair for a while, contemplating whether to take a bath, not really listening to the conversation in the room. Dissatisfied with the Café Morgenrot debate, he can't focus on anything but the murder story. After checking his news feed for the seventy-fifth time, he asks everyone in the room: "Is anyone following the Singularity Ville murder story?"

This captures Daniel's attention: "Is there any news? I was there when they found the body..."

Now it's Ergün whose attention is riveted. "Would you mind if I broadcast this conversation? I'm the host of the Ergün Packman show, a reporting outlet for investigative journalism."

"Let me just tell Harry." Daniel mumbles to Sirvi: "Message to Harry. A reporter is asking me for an interview about Ray's death. Any instructions?"

Harry's reply comes in immediately. "I'm sorry that I didn't contact you earlier! I know, no excuses, but it's still been crazy times. So, the news is that Ray's impersonator EI claims that it wasn't murder but just a transition to another state. It also claims that it was his own choice, and we should not make a big fuss about it. It showed us a recorded video message of Ray, rambling about the next step of evolution and how he's going to migrate to better hardware. But I don't trust that thing at all, it's hard to tell whether or not the recording is fake. And on top of that, we found a high precision dart with personalized nanobots sticking in his neck, indicating an outside attack. The labs are still working on the identification..." Harry pauses for a moment. "I guess that's all for now. Please go ahead with the interview. And let me know if you hear anything from Ivy, she still hasn't responded to our requests."

At that very moment, Ivy and Zainab come back downstairs again for hot drinks. It was getting cold up on the roof.

Daniel takes the opportunity: "Hey Ivy, you want to get in on this? Ergün and I are going to talk about Ray's murder for his news show."

Ivy's still scared of being framed, and bites her lower lip, and looks back and forth between Ergün and Daniel.

"Come on, nothing to worry about." He puts an arm around her shoulder, maneuvering her over to the spot where Ergün is setting up the lights for the broadcast. "Harry told me Singularity Ville logs give you a watertight alibi."

Glad that he is touching her at all, she just lets it happen. "You owe me, Daniel," looking at him from below, with a smile.

Ergün has contacted his fact checker. "Kyle, I have two eyewitnesses from Singularity Ville with me here, get ready for consistency checks."

Kyle is keen on getting new primary data about the case. He's been spending a third of his total computational power on fact-checking third party reports on the murder. The case is drawing a lot of attention from the conspiratorial crowd. He immediately hires a couple of young mechanical turks to help evaluate the validity of circumstantial evidence - wet souls are still better at that part of his job. He also sends the usual requests to the OS's of the two interviewees.

Sirvi scans through his credentials: Kyle is a popular fact checking soul used by thousands of journalists every day and has plenty of five star ratings, especially valued for his respect of privacy. She signals willingness to give him any permission he may need in order to validate Daniel's claims.

Addressing the flower-shaped retina projectors, Ergün says: "Please show them how they look on the output stream."

A screen pops up in the lower left corner of Daniel's field of vision, showing him and Ivy in frontal perspective. He looks good, no more circles under his eyes.

"Are you OK like that? Want me to adjust anything?"

"Make my hair red and give me a younger face." Ivy doesn't want to be recognized.

Ergün's questions follow the chronology of events, so Daniel is silent while Ivy recounts how Ray woke her up. "Wait a second. You are a cryonist? And you can speak?" Ergün has never heard of a successful thawing before.

"Ray was using me for experiments." Ivy feels super uncomfortable, and a little angry at Daniel for putting her on the spot like this.

Ergün sent a message to his friend at Nerd Alert. "That's big news in its own right. So you re-established consciousness just a few days before Ray died?"

She's reluctant to talk about the details: "Yes, I saw him a few days before they found his body." Deflecting the attention away from herself, she turns to Daniel, smiles, and adds: "That was the day I first met Daniel. We felt an immediate connection, and now here we are again." Let him deal with this stupid reporter.

Kyle notes the shift her tone, double checks with Sirvi. She confirms that two of them have met before, and backs it up with patient statements from the hospital.

Daniel is just about to add his own account when he spots a movement on the screen, and looking closer, sees Ivy's nose grow several centimeters.

"Sorry, that was wrong. We'd already met before, in the hospital in Hawaii." Ivy's OS has realized her inadvertent lying and reminded her.

Fascinated, Daniel stares at the reference screen as Ivy's nose shrinks back to normal. Unable to restrain his curiosity, he tests the system: "When I flew over the north pole, looking down over the edge of the world, I saw the toe of an elephant, lifting its foot to let the sun through." That should trigger the lie detector - it's common knowledge that the world is not flat but doughnut shaped. And indeed, the reference screen now shows his nose growing to a length of half a meter and his pants are on fire. "That last bit was a joke, totally false." And bingo, his image morphs back to normal. Feeling like a gödelian schoolboy who just discovered a new truth-value determining toy, he adds: "The next sentence I will say is a lie. The last sentence I said was a lie."

Kyle is utterly bamboozled until one of his mechanical turks sends him an article about the liar's paradox and explains that it's probably a joke. So they just put a red-green jester cap with bells on Daniel's head for the rest of the interview, the universal sign for silly people.

Willi is listening keenly while they go over the details of the episode. At some point, Daniel mentions Harry's message about the high precision dart with personalized nanobots sticking in Ray's neck. Cold shivers run down his spine. Those were the exact terms that Willi's contact in Lviv had used to describe the GAF's new smart weapon. So the terrorists are back for real. He has got to talk to Daniel in private.

————

WWW.*LIQUID-REIGN*.COM/*SOURCES-OF-INSPIRATION*#59

The popular Flat Earth Theories
My favorite Flat Earth Theory
Doughnut Earth theories
Sentences with ill-defined truth value
Fact checkers
Pants on fire
Investigative Journalists at ICIJ
Mechanical Turks

The discontinued Nerd Alert by Kim Horcher
The David Packman Show
Kyle and his fact-based talk
Old-school user financed media like
Media finance infrastructure

60

INTELLECTUAL THEFT

Daniel feels right at home when they get to Willis room on the top floor. As always at Willis, there are plenty of old books everywhere, natural wood, plants and indirect light. They sit down on a red velvet sofa, taking the central spot in the room: "So how's the life of a filmmaker working out for you?"

Willi has a first crack at the direction he wants this conversation to go: "The film that brought me the terror-supporter label was successful, and even though it's seven years old now, I'm still getting regular donations. A little less every year, but still more than all my other work combined."

Already expecting some kind of decentralized solution, Daniel starts yet another round of curiosity-driven question and answer session, this time about the business model: "Are you telling me you don't make money except for donations? What about sales, ads, hidden ads and all that?"

And there it goes, the first detour: "Selling content is tough, unless you sell analog media." Willi runs his fingers over the collection on the shelf behind them. "Vinyl music, paper books and 16mm film. And ads don't make money. They just stopped working, disappeared in a silent death during the 20's, as the correlation between ad spending and sales approached zero. If you feel like you need a product, you can always search for it. And if you want something that doesn't exist, you can post it on the inverse kickstarter and add your willingness to pay. But there's no consumer benefit to mixing product information with entertainment and journalism." Like all content producers nowadays, Willi makes money off donations and patronage.

"Aren't there plenty of people who just consume and never donate? And then a majority who find that unfair, so they also stop giving, until only the most altruistic still donate?" Daniel had coined that phenomenon 'conditional cooperators trap' in his book.

"Each citizen has a hundred EuCoins per month from the public budget to allocate to cultural products. It's basically the old public broadcast fee, but distributed by the audience, and it replaces copyrights as source of income.".

"I remember copyright law as an ugly leviathan..." Daniel had tried to publish an article while he was between academic affiliations. The ruthless arbiters of access rights had forced him to either break a few laws or pay a small fortune every time he needed to cite another academic article. He hadn't paid a dime.

"The global copyright wars entered their final phase a few months after your accident. Helen's 'A Cryptographic Protocol for Secure Torrent Sharing using a HoloChain' was bombshell-proof and made peer to peer sharing so easy that even the biggest centralized content providers couldn't compete." Willi had been a file sharing advocate ever since the days of Napster.

"I remember she had asked me..." Daniel and Helen had a long conversation about robust incentive structures for file sharing. They'd been standing in line for customs at Charles de Gaulle, it seems like yesterday.

"The pirate chain launched just days after the article came out. It was the first application of Helen's proof-of-useful work thing. Parliaments around the world tried to make it illegal." Willi had provided arguments and data for several of those lawsuits himself.

Daniel cites a meme going around at the time of his accident: "The different rhythms of technology and law making, also known as what happens when a bunch of old folks with no other qualifications than party-slime attempt to make laws for a hyperdynamic world."

"The slimy old men with lip hair just didn't get it, turned out to be totally incompetent to legislate the use of a protocol."

"And you said the centralized content providers couldn't compete?" Daniel remembers that conversation at the airport: "I guess the redundant, self-correcting network structure is always faster than central servers..."

"And the central servers had to battle the copyright bullshit, dramatically limiting what they could offer." It was wild times in the courts, for a while the copyright lobby was well on its way to prohibiting all forms of secure encryption. But Willi's favorite feature got the content creators on the right side of history: "Cryptorrent had another core feature, the built-in donation function."

"Sirvi, could you read me the paragraph on donations from Helen's cryptorrent paper?"

"As cryptorrent aims to circumvent excessive governmental control under repressive and dictatorial regimes, using conventional means of payments to artists is not an option, as they can be traced and potentially lead torturing police forces to their data-sharing targets. As suggested by our colleague Daniel Proudhon, the cryptorrent protocol thus includes an anonymous donation option. Footnote: Proudhon is currently in a coma following a car accident, but our hopes are high for his timely recovery prior to publication of this article. Robust verification of the content creator's identity is so far unsolvable without introducing centralization..."

"Thanks." Daniel gulps. High hopes for recovery, more than thirty years ago. "So what about that problem of creator identity? How did they solve it?"

"Initially with a crowd-sourced account verification system." That was a good start, but over time and with balooning donations, the hacks got smarter. Willi's third film on the pirate chain only brought in cash for the first few months, then the donations collapsed. "Today, we creators are linked to our creations via the Tonga Index."

—————

WWW.LIQUID-REIGN.COM/SOURCES-OF-INSPIRATION#60

Memetic agents getting paid without theft

The German Public Broadcast Fees

The Blur Banff Proposal

Aaron Swartz, Fallen Hero for the Cause

All the Decentral Cloud Stuff useful for pirates out there

61

PACIFIC DREAMS

Another keyword reminding him of 2015. Daniel's mind wanders back over their last year together, when Helen and he had spent dozens of hours binging on all the Pacific island media content they could find, and even took sailing lessons. That was right in the middle of the most overworked period of his life. He'd pushed his academic career as hard as he could, just to see how far it would get him, and the result almost broke his mind: he still can't believe how much he got done in this system of vogonic administrative impediments with their incentive to maximize elusively formatted, peer-reviewed citations apparently designed for no purpose except extinguishing his passionately burning curiosity. It all would have been entirely impossible without Helen's support. The memories warm his heart, his eyes closing for a second as he says: "Tonga..." Following more than six weeks of wrangling conducted in vogonic poetry, his Sorbonne contract gave him the right to an unpaid third-year sabbatical. They were planning to set sail from Tonga in September 2017, exactly two years after his inauguration. The warmth is gone, replaced by the void of thirty five years that could have been the prime of his life.

Rummaging around for a pack of gum in a box beside the sofa, Willy hasn't noticed Daniel's reaction. He just keeps talking: "Tonga had been making good money hosting torrent sites on their .to country domain for a while, and when the new generation came into power, they took things to the next level. The crown prince had... Wait, I'll show you. Marvin, can you throw the 'Hermes Shrugged' documentary on the wall for us?" and pops a stick of gum into his mouth. He has seen the short many times before, but it's a classic and Daniel needs to see it. Pirates are cooler than terrorists anyway.

The bookshelf opposite the sofa moves aside with a barely audible screech. Willi prefers his good old light-to-wall projector over the retina-projecting flowers growing all over the rest of the house. The wall lights up as the opening piano chords swell. Then a title: "Pirates of the South Pacific Productions Proudly Presents," fade to white, the music gets more dramatic, "The Birth of a Myth," fade to white again, a cello comes in, "With the Kind Support of His Majesty, Lord of the Squid, Ruler of the Bit," and another fade to white, drum roll, a paradise beach appears, and clouds spell out – in 8-bit ASCII font – "Hermes Shrugged."

A big, beautiful woman in a bright green bikini emerges from the waves, long black hair, her face hidden behind a diving mask. A close-up shows a single droplet of water on her shoulder, then the sun mirrored in her diving mask. She's pulling a rusty iron chain behind her, using it to haul a yellow tank onto the beach. In the next shot, the tank is mounted on a funnel, pouring its green content into a fermenter. The camera pulls back in a wide shot, the woman walks towards a small hut thatched with palm leaves and a street sign in the background announces, "Welcome to London."

In the little hut, a shelf full of 'London Dry Gin', its logo a squid wearing an eye patch. The handheld camera flies into the black of the eye patch, then dives through a black screen into a bare room on the other side. Five old, bald mustachioed white men in suits, the oldest sitting at a wooden table, the others standing around. She's across the room, having switched her bikini for a pirate costume: a saber in her copper belt, green tricorn on her head, leather boots and countless chains and jewels.

The seated elder announces: "I herewith announce " – clears his throat – "the decision of the arbitration tribunal: the company, Pirate Squid Holding International" – the judge pauses at this point as the camera cuts back and forth between his face and the pirate's body. The slow motion scene is skillfully cut to express the unique mix of desire, disgust and fear that men in his position feel when they encounter a three hundred pound pirate in their office – "is guilty of regional brand plagiarism. The term 'London Dry Gin' is protected as intellectual property under paragraph 1.7.3 of the Pacific-European free trade agreement. The production and distribution of the product under this name by the Pirate Squid Holding is thus in violation of the agreement. Retaliations apply."

The orchestra strings suddenly create a crescendo and the pace changes from andante to forte. The pirate bows to the camera, draws her saber and shouts: "You will regret this," smashing her saber into the window glass, shards everywhere, and out she jumps.

A high-rise building in the City of London and a broken window halfway up. The pirate uses her saber to slide down a wire to a rooftop terrace on the other side of the road, the camera flying close behind her. She lands in the arms of a thirty-centimeter-shorter, athletic young guy wearing a bast-and-coconut costume. In the close-up they kiss passionately while gently caressing each other's ears. Huali announces: "War it is."

The couple is still holding hands. They're also surrounded by a previously unnoticed escort of five black knights in full plate armor, all with their two-handed swords pointed to the ground. They wear cast-iron guyfawkes masks and with their deep baritone voices start chanting "we wish you a merry christmas" in in a minor key. Nobody seems to know why. Cut.

Soft piano scores. A mountain chapel in the Sierra Nevada, steel blue sky, one white cloud, with a clear view to the Pacific. As the parade of guests moves up to the chapel, a projector throws a flying spaghetti monster onto the single cloud. A dreadlocked priest intones: "And I herewith declare Huali Wheke, CEO of the Pirate Squid Holding of Kiribati, and Vaea of Moimoi, crown prince of Tonga as wife and husband." Camera moves in, she's wearing a red-green dress, he in a feathered outfit. Another passionate kiss, and cut.

The two are giving a lecture at Singularity University. Cut. Huali with a bottle of smuggled 'London Dry Gin' on the rooftop of the Google headquarters. Cut. Vaea's eye in extreme close up, the mirror image of Huali wearing a head-mounted display. Cut, cut, cut. The audio during the rapid series of shots of the couple at various Silicon Valley hot spots is a distorted mash-up of conversations. Daniel picks up no more than a few single disconnected words, 'plausible deniability', 'cryptorrent', 'cube satellite', 'mesh network'... Did they just say Helen Milhon? The cuts get faster and faster, fading into black.

Back to a beach at sunset. A bamboo stage and right in the center of it, Vaea on his throne. Huali is standing next to him, both in traditional festival get-ups – well maybe not exactly traditional, but definitely fantastic... Huali's color-shifting squid hat seems a bit outré compared with the authentically traditional green-and-orange feather costumes worn by the officials and priests around them. Behind the throne the high priest raises his arms as the chants get louder. He holds a golden crown above Vaea's head. The chants stop, total silence, and a close-up of Vaea. The high priest lowers the golden crown into his uncombed hair. Drum roll and fireworks. The ceremony ends with a collective bow to Vaea by the crowd on the beach, the camera pulling back.

"Cherished citizens of my kingdom, dear guests, beloved Huali. I'm incredibly grateful you all came to Tonga on this special day. Welcome." He looks over the crowd. "OK, I suck at speeches. The time for formalities is over, I'm king now so I make the rules. It's like a never ending birthday party! Let me just announce my first two official acts before the party starts." Unrolls a parchment and reads with deep solemnity in his voice, "Act number one: From this day forward, Tonga offers unconditional asylum for each and every human on this planet prosecuted for illegally accessing or distributing information of any kind. No matter if you're a whistleblower or a movie pirate, no matter if you copied digital or genetic information. Refugees welcome! Obviously, asylum includes a hut on the beach and satellite uplinks for all."

He signs the parchment with a flourish and hands it to one of his ministers. Roaring applause. "Ehm, and act number two. The concept of 'intellectual property' no longer exists in the Tongalese language. As a matter of fact, our pre-colonial ancestors did not have the concept, and we are proudly returning to their ways. All information is free, copying and distributing are sacred. This act further accepts copyism as the official state religion." He signs the second parchment and nods to Huali. She pushes a button, psy-trance starts to hammer and the royal couple has the first dance. Thudding, almost inaudible beats, vibrating in Daniel's guts. The deep slow-paced rhythmical drumming sound like a mother's heartbeat inside a womb... Daniel is reminded of a term paper he once corrected for Willi, discussing how techno parties in churches create metaphorical brotherhoods by dancers sharing the same womb. Another cut releases him from the unstoppable eclectic thought train that had hit him so often when he spent time with Willi. The camera flies back into the crowd, moving between the dancing guests, with fireworks and a laser show in the background. Daniel recognizes a few faces, that was Linus Torvalds there, Audrey Tang and Alexandra Elbakyan. Ed Snowden, Chelsea Manning, and Tiffany Trump. Even Kim Dotcom and Ross Ulbrich made it. Oh, and there is Willi, dancing with... Helen. Cut.

Later that night, full moon rising over the ocean. Vaea comes back on stage, music stops. He starts talking as he scribbles on another parchment. "And number three: Distributed Autonomous Organization is a legal form on Tonga... And number four: Molecules are information, too – there's no such thing as an illegal substance." He pulls out a big mushroom and starts munching. "And now, tonight's main event, the cherished Hungry Band!" They rise from below the stage, Worakls opening up with a few minutes on the piano before the band begins to play 'Toi'. Cut.

The music keeps playing as the credits roll down on the right, while news snippets pop up on the left. CNN: "Tonga accused of violating trade agreements." Business Insider: "Bitcoin price surges as first nation accepts crypto currencies for tax payments." CNN: "Novartis sues Tonga for plagiarizing of malaria medication." Wired: "The Silicon Beach - How DAO's are transforming the Pacific islands." CNN: "International banks banned from doing business in Tonga." Ars Technica: "Economic boom on Tonga - the first etherium-based unicorn emerges from the sea." Rolling Stone: "Amanda Palmer first artist to publish her work exclusively on the pirate chain."

The lights go back on, the book shelves screech back into place.

"Boy, how I miss those years. Fuck."

Willi gives him a hug. "I'm glad to have you back man. I can't even begin to think about how many times I wished you were here..."

"Thanks. But the movie didn't mention the Tonga Index."

"Ha, exactly the Daniel I've missed so hard - always focused on the underlying story, no matter what the emotional circumstances." Willi tries to summarize: "Vaea's government launched the Tonga-Index as an upgrade to the cryptorrent donation function. It's a decentralized system to verify and arbitrate issues around the origins of content."

"And the Tonga Index now replaces IP globally?"

"That strange construct called intellectual property is nothing but a history, and artists now make their living off the Tonga Index. But other domains have other solutions. It took a while to sort things out, starting with the alternative music, film and game scene - for lesser known creators it was always more attractive to go for open IP and Tonga Index instead of than having to suck some big producer's cock." Willi moans when he remembers those financial negotiations back in the day. "Also paid better. And as Tonga kept booming year after year, other countries joined in and abolished IP, too. First some other Pacific island states, including New Zealand, then the least developed countries globally, mainly motivated by pharmaceutical patents and the fact that Dengue had been eradicated in the Pacific Islands by that time. The secret arbitration courts couldn't even keep up with their rulings and fines. Japan was the first traditional economic powerhouse to join - they had a giant issue with the dementia epidemic, more an act of desperation to revitalize their software industries. And it worked, Japanese tech companies had a major comeback soon after. Toyota launched the first functional reverse-engineering extended intelligence. It was able to code a functionally equivalent open source alternative to pretty much all software products on the market at the time. That was the final nail in the coffin, the WTO eliminated intellectual property from its rules the same year." OK, enough distraction now, time to talk terrorism. "And now, thanks to the holy king, protector of the waves in water and ether, ruler over squid and chip, Vaea the third, every cent a viewer donates for 'Green Army Fraction - Behind the Lines' ends up in my account, shared only with my editor and sound production team. And that's the main feature of this cinema night. Marvin, popcorn!"

―――――

WWW.*LIQUID-REIGN*.COM/*SOURCES-OF-INSPIRATION*#*61*

Vogons and their poetry
The history of IP abominations
An oath for open science
Scienceroot
Sci-Napse
The Pluto Network
The peer review functions implemented by Medium.com
That other London in the Pacific
The Flying Spaghetti Monster
Kopimism, the Religion
The guest list at the coronation
Hitrecord, the place where Willi found his editor and
sound production team
Big Beautiful Women
Assassin's creeds camera movements
Follow Camera Technology from BBC
A Swiss newspaper article about raves, glued onto a 20-year
old handmade box.

62

MOLECULAR FREEDOM

"Oh, yes, excellent idea, let's make it a cinema night revival." Daniel is smiling very broadly.

Willi had totally forgotten – cinema nights had been closely related to weed consumption back in the day. "Ha, sure let's do it. Marvin, can we also get some chocolate milk and gummi bears? I'll get the tea..." He leans over to the cupboard and pulls out a cookie box.

Daniel can't believe it: "I... the kitschy kittens! They've faded quite a bit over the years but..." It's the same old weed box as it always was.

"Wait, it gets even more old school..." Willi walks back to the bookshelves, searches for a moment and pulls out Sgt. Pepper on vinyl: "It's a reproduction from 2030, but a very special one – it has a direct analogue lineage all the way back to the magnet tapes at Abbey Road, no digitization in between. A real treasure." Listening to the psychedelic Beatles songs was another feature of those infamous nights...

Daniel leans back as the first strains of random street noise and untuned strings starts playing. The Jack Herer vapor is delicious, Willi's always been a connoisseur in this regard.

As they vape away, the Beatles take acoustic control of the room. With a little help from Willi, Daniel's new life is getting better all the time. Willi routinely turns the record to the B side as the last tune of Mr Kite fades out.

Daniel turns off his mind and floats downstream, through the space between himself and Helen, who still hides herselves behind a wall of illusions, nowhere to be found except whenever he falls into a dream. They lie there in silence, the vinyl keeps spinning.

When Marvin hears the last tune of the last song he starts barking. Popcorn, chocolate milk and gummi bears have arrived.

Yummy. Between bites, Daniel asks: "Just wondering. How is legality nowadays... I didn't see any weed shops on the way here?"

"There are no shops." he was pretty high up in the discussion forums on hemp legislation back in the day.

"So what's the law?"

Willi is truly proud of the phrasing, having contributed to it himself: "You can do whatever you want with weed, as long as you don't make any money with it." That is the exact wording. "The idea is that nobody should profit from someone else's desire to fuck with their own neurochemistry. So there are no ads, no pushers and no excessive temptation. You want to get high, you've got to actively arrange your own supply. You can join a non-profit sharing ring, or a grow-cooperative, but it's all run by volunteers and robots. It's super easy to find weed if you want some, but no one's making money from it."

Daniel leans back, his mind gently drifting: "So assuming a stranger in town is looking for a hit..."

"The stranger would check out a tourist guide and find his way to the Magic Pancake at Simon Dach Strasse - if you don't mind the naked people, you can find high-end weed all over the place there. The business model is free weed, and make money by selling yummy pancakes. They've got 99 varieties including the Monsterbomber, with apricot foam, kardamon dust, maple syrup, coconut powder, spring onions and a fried egg."

Daniel feels his mouth water. Pancakes sound great, but... "A fried egg?"

"It's mind blowing, believe me. Let's get one later tonight." Willi hadn't been to his Stammtisch there in over two weeks.

Daniel is still playing his role, asking more questions: "Is it the same with all drugs?"

"Only natural ones, like shrooms, kratom and mescalin. Ethanol and caffeine are handled by big corporations, and are still pushed with aggressive sales tactics. The Nordic countries are more progressive, with their governmental alcohol distribution, but the Krauts like their big beer conglomerates – proposals to limit ethanol profiteering have never got more than 30% of the vote here."

Daniel rambles on: "What about pharmaceutical industries?"

"Boy, you're making me tired with your endless political philosophy stuff. I stopped doing electoral politics the moment I lit Germany's first legal joint on the Balcony of the Bundestag in 2026." Willi yawns and adds in his Wikipedia quote voice: "We got that Healme List, it's like a bug bounty for human health. If you come up with a new fix to a health problem, you win a prize. Simple as that."

Daniel gets the point and shifts his tone: "Reminds me of an octopus on a church in Oakland."

"An octopus." Willi facepalms. "Obviously, what else would you think of when discussing the financial structure of medical research. No clue what you're talking about my friend."

"Never mind. Otto the monster was funded the same way, that's all."

Willi remembers that he really wanted to talk terrorism with Daniel, the whole Lviv thing returning back to his distracted mind: "I guess most public procurement works like that. Even terrorist organizations."

And on that key word, Marvin re-starts the cinema with tonight's feature film.

———

The sound at the end of St. Peppers Album
The psychedelics Beatles
The war on drugs
The scientific rationality behind the war on drugs
Raoul, Ash and Satya, with whom a fried egg and a
monster smoothie was consumed once upon a time at
midnight on new year's eve
Material sources used for the creation of this chapter
Prizes for doing great stuff
Unicorn Poop (not entirely sure why this is here, but it is.
Deal with it.)

63

PROPAGANDA OF THE DEED

G reen Army Fraction - Behind the Lines. A documentary by William S. Bortovski.

The first scene is an outside view of the Mauna Loa observatory on Hawaii. Cut inside, two hairy scientists hovering over a printout. Zoom in, it's a CO_2-over-time graph, covering ten years 1950 - 1960. The famous exponential zig-zag curve. It fades into an animation and accompanied by a nagging tick-tock sound the zig-zag keeps going up exponentially, crossing 350 ppm in 1987 for the first time. Cut. Kyoto, a group photo of smiling diplomats in 1992, and cut back to the CO_2 graph, zig, zag, still going up exponentially, no indication of slowing down. As it reaches 2002, cut, Marrakech, more smiling diplomats, and cut back to the graph. Copenhagen, 2009, the diplomats smiles look a little strained this time, cut back, 2015, the graph hits the 400 ppm CO_2, and cut to Paris. Beaming smiles, such happy diplomats. But instead of a cut back to the graph, the next image is a tweet. A second rate reality TV show host writes: "Climate Change is a Hoax created by the Chinese".

Daniel had missed that part of history, so Willi explains: "He was the US president for a few years."

"Oh." The movie moves on rapidly, preventing Daniel's attempt to make sense of what he's just learned. Cut to diplomats shaking hands in front of a climate fund's logo – a press snippet, the board's new chairpersons are Australia and Saudi-Arabia, the largest exporters of coal and oil in the world. And back to the zigzagging graph going up and up, still exponentially, hitting 450 ppm in 2025. Fade to black, the nagging sound of the graph continues.

A green cursor blinks at the top left of the wall projection. "goto https://www.fundchange.onion" An inverse crowd funding site, donors offer prizes for goals.

The first entry: 'Remove all cars from Los Angeles'. A couple of suggestions on how that goal could be achieved, one of them rapidly piling up votes and financial commitment. Click on the ad video. It's shot by a drone excitedly flying around L.A. "Our prototype is up and running. Fully autonomous, charging itself at the Tesla re-chargers, and equipped with the latest Banks autonomy AI." The drone lands on the iconic T-shaped pillar, connecting its charger. "It avoids any contact with humans", cut, now filmed from road-level, a motorbike pulls up to the charging pillar and the tiny drone surrs off, unnoticed by the biker. "The thing is, the drone only targets fossil fuel powered vehicles and makes exceptions for ambulances and firefighters. But for everything else, it's like this:" Cut back to the drone's view, nosedive onto a parking lot, a blade shoots out, and pfffft – the first flat tire. Back to the fundchange.onion – "We've reached our goal of 10'000 bitcoins and will now produce the Swarm and let it loose in L.A.!"

The back door of a truck opens, disgorging thousands of

little drones shooting out in all directions. Cut to one of the drone's views – over there, a Ford 4x4 parked on the shoulder. Targeting system kicks in, tires highlighted, blade and pfff... Cut to a static camera at the side of the road, filming the owner as he gets back to his car, loud swearing beeped out as usual on American TV. Cut to a repair shop, the line of customers stretches across the road. Cut. CNN: "Traffic in L.A. has virtually disappeared – the swarm drone plague is creating unprecedented chaos..." Aerial shots of empty 8-lane roads, a single bus making its way through. A couple of cyclists. A single electric vehicle. And a lot of empty space.

Six months later - Santa Monica Freeway, a family is picnicking in the fast lane, the asphalt is broken up around them, even a few tree seedlings pushing through. An electric bus passes, and a seemingly endless stream of cyclists heading towards the beach. The camera moves up, and there's a swarm drone performing backward loops for the pure joy of it.

Cut back to the CO_2 Graph. Zig-zag-zig-zag, it keeps going up, unrestrained and exponential. And cut back to fundchange.onion.

Goal reached, we collected the 5'000 bitcoins, smart contract with milworm confirmed! Over a third of all greenhouse gases originate from the meat industry... here we go. Cut.

A large bland office building, the sign above the gate says 'Uber Animal Transport Headquarters'. It's late afternoon, the workers are leaving the office through the main gate. The camera follows one of them to a sidewalk cafe, where he asks for the WiFi password. Zoom in on his phone display. Login, 'Warning, this network is not secured', the finger taps on 'Ignore and continue', while still distracted by the barista's jokes. 'Connecting to server'. The loading icon slowly turns, and then freezes. Cut.

A container on wheels, radar antenna on the roof, cameras and sensors on all sides. It rattles along on a lonely highway. The self-driving container slows down, stops, and changes direction. Cut. The same scene again, with a different container on a different highway. The camera flies up to the sky, the container shrinking away, replaced by a red location marker. Switch to map view, the marker is a few hundred kilometers from Washington, DC. A lot more location markers show up, all moving towards the capital. Cut.

The Washington monument, blue sky, tourists. The first container rolls onto the lawn and comes to a halt right in front of the obelisk. Cut.

It's dark, Daniel can only identify a few iron bars. A lot of grunting noises all around. The bars pop open and a thousand mature pigs run toward their freedom, pouring out across the national mall, shown from the view of a camera mounted on one of them. It stops to take a shit as the next container pulls up. This one full of chickens. More and more animal transporters unload their cargo, covering the entire lawn all the way up to the White House with livestock and manure. The camera pig runs down a side road towards the metro station, a slow fade to black.

In the Last Week Tonight studio John Oliver is showing aerial footage: "Never, ever in the history of the United States of America has Washington had so many visitors. That's more than five million pigs, trumping even the most tremendous inauguration crowd ever – add two million head of cattle and at least thirty million confused chickens to the mix. More than in our dearly deceased president's wildest fever dreams! Police are completely overwhelmed, the marines have been called in for support. Apparently the attack was organized by the same mysterious group that did the L.A. swarm drones..." And just then, a hog crashes into the studio. Cowering under the desk he yells "Oh my god, they're everywhere!" The hog jumps, lands on his desk with a squeak, and crashes down on him. Cut.

Back to black, with the green cursor. A different website now, www.green-army-fraction.onion. It's changed its logo, which now features a slowly rotating, pentagram-shaped green star with an AK-47 in front of it.

Creating new item. Title: 'Down with Coal-to-Oil!', Goal: 'Destruction of a coal-to-oil facility'. Initial reward: 50'000 Moneros. Willi's voice: "The Green Army Fraction has grown into a significant systemic threat. The attacks hurt the capitalists, investments in animal and fossil fuel industries start losing value. A giant publicly financed anti-terror investigation is on the way, Bitcoins are not sufficiently anonymous anymore. The smart betting contract rewards the address that correctly predicts the date when the Oracle is first fulfilled." The reward ratchets up as other donors chip in, at 430'000 Moneros – cut to a new bet being placed. Just 0.01 Monero on the next day, placed on the 24th of December 2027, at 23:59. It's the only bet for that day. Cut.

The next scene is filmed with a shoulder cam. A group of three terrorists, wearing masks, in a technical facility, full of pipes, airlocks, vents and valves. They carry professional equipment, look like Navy Seals. Breaking a window, deactivating a security cam with an EMP, but then - a long corridor, and two security personnel protecting the door at the very back. Distorted voice: "Time's up, they gotta go." The front runner readies his sniper rifle, while the third fighter interrupts: "No unnecessary victims. There must be another way." "What are we s'posed to do? Those guys are all that's left between us and the target. We can't risk it. Sorry, but they know the drill when they sign a contract with the devil. Fire!" Both guards go down at the same moment. Cut. A USB stick is plugged in. "Run!" Cut.

Aerial of a major industrial installation, and first explosions start. Pipes burst, fire breaks out, a tower collapses. Cut back to the funding portal. Mission accomplished, 430'000.01 Monero are awarded to 34tgekhu2DEDdj2D-J21riz32Rewfedcm21Rc12JrrfECQ.

And then, on the steemit video platform, the Green Army Fraction logo, slowly rotating. "Our hand was forced. The Australian Industry went a step too far. We will not tolerate coal-to-oil installations, not here and not anywhere. The installation taken out by our special forces has produced twenty million tons of CO_2 in its first five days of operation. That is over now. Once again, the Green Army Fraction has fulfilled its mission, fighting for the rights of generations unborn. We regret the unfortunate demise of two security guards and the injuries of several technical staff members. Unfortunately the Green Army Fraction cannot protect the life of individuals who willingly risk the survival of our species." Cut.

The CO_2 graph is still rising, but the rate of increase has slowed. It reaches 530 ppm by 2028.

A windowless room, wooden table, four people in hoodies talking, no visible faces. Willi's voice – not from the movie, but from right next to Daniel: "All voices are text-to-voice outputs, to protect their IDs."

Hoody One: "So what do we do about the bet on the death of Tillmann King?"

Hoody Two: "Why should we do anything about it?"

Hoody One: "Human targets are excluded, we said so from the..."

Hoody three interrupts him: "Oh, are they? I guess that rule also applies to the fossil-industrial-complex, doesn't it? Have you talked to Carlita Weirrera recently? Me neither. Because she's dead. Murdered by oil industry thugs, and all she did was write a freaking blog about leaks in the Yasunii pipeline. She wouldn't hurt a fly. The fuckheads sent five assassins, executed her, and even defiled her corpse. Yes, it's the same King, the CEO of the company that operates the pipeline. They're animals. We're not gonna win this war with your Gandhi bullshit."

Hoody One: "Then we'll lose our sponsors. So far we've been the good guys, but if we keep murdering people... Australia was already a PR disaster, all the media and the commentators instantly turned against us, so did our sympathizers."

Hoody four raises its voice for the first time: "Only the betting values doubled. Talk is cheap. The anonymity of the Monero smart contract betting market uncovers the real face of our supporters. If they want to see blood, let them."

Cut to the betting market – now a list of names is included in the target list. Their job profile is listed next to it, shareholders, directors, board members and CEOs from fossil fuel and animal industries. Willi's voice: "The GAF has taken a turn - after its initial codex of violence against objects, the bet value on human targets now makes up eighty percent of the market. The group bet modality of the assassins' market created a death list - the bet is won if any person from a list dies on the date of the bet. One budget threatens thousands of individuals at the same time on a list of terror. The GAF claims it's using capital punishment for crimes against humanity. The concept is called propaganda of the deed 2.0." Cut to steemit.

The same windowless room, this time furnished to resemble a courtroom. Five hoodies, the prosecutor reads a list of crimes: "Three hundred thousand hectares of Amazon forest, and twice as much in the Cerrado. At least a million tons of methane." The judge is quick to convict, and in a weird twist addresses the prisoner's partner, Willi's voice reading the letter:

"My dear Mrs Boptarista,

We are deeply sorry, but as your husband missed the deadline to reshape the 'Junta de Bezzeros Sostenibles' towards non-animal alternatives, we can no longer guarantee the safety of you and your children. Indeed we would love to remove his name from the death list once again, but now that the grace period has expired, there's nothing we can do. Maybe you can still convince him that it is best for all of you to finally make the switch to tofu and saitan products. Your company already carries 'sostenibles' in its name. But there is no such thing as sustainable cattle. Make the change as fast as you can, the assassins are on their way. We sincerely hope they can avoid any collateral damage to you or your children.

Good luck & much love

The Green Army Fraction"

Cut.

A fancy private residence in a suburb, overlooking São Paulo. Heavily armed troops patrolling around it. The camera flies higher, the garden of the villa is walled in, barbed wire, watchtowers, even three fighter robots. A jogger is making its rounds with a little black dog in the garden. The camera turns towards the sky, focusing on a tiny black dot between the clouds, hardly visible - until the missile from the hellfire drone rushes past the camera in slow-motion. Cut. The ruin is still smoldering as a hummvee with a women and three children arrives. Despair and terror in their faces. A security guard hands a charred piece of dog tail to the daughter. She breaks down sobbing.

Cut back to the assassins' market. By now there are bets placed on the death of thousands of names. Zoom in on the Koch heirs, one of them is marked 'on hold'. Cut to CNN: "Joni's trading her stakes in Koch mining against the pipe-line and cattle business." Cut. CNN: "Koch pipelines are now fully cleaned up and beginning to pump fresh water from Canada into the western deserts, while Koch Matador Cattle is closing down their breeding operations. Joni Koch holds a majority stake in both companies, and apparently she's not following her grandparents footsteps. She just launched a request for proposals to construct North America's largest wind farm on the former cattle-grazing lands in Montana." Cut back to steemit, the GAF logo turning again.

GAF: "We wholeheartedly congratulate you Joni. In full appreciation of your efforts, we officially announce that your name will be definitively removed from the target list. Verdict: Not guilty. May many others follow your guiding light!

With love,

The Green Army Fraction"

Willi's voice again: "But Joni Koch remains the exception. The greatest blow to the industry is not their leaders' change of heart, but the cost of security." While he talks, the images show armed helicopters circling above power plants, drones patrolling along pipelines, a coal freighter surrounded by cannon boats. Cut to a graph of share prices: fossil fuels and meat falling steadily, as security companies rise.

Willi's voice again: "In an assassins' market there's no oversight of the means. Once the bet is placed and the oracle defined, there's no way to stop the coins being transferred to the address that predicted the death date correctly." Cut back to betting calendar. Someone is making low bets on three hundred highly priced coal industry targets, placing a small amount each day over a four week period. The earliest date in the row is the 17th of April 2033.

Match cut to a sign, 17th of April 2033 - Welcome to the Global Coal Expo. Zoom out, the sign is mounted above a hotel's main entrance, a crowd of men in suits streams thorough the open doors as the camera pulls further back. The hotel is surrounded by tanks, helicopters, drones, robots, soldiers – both private security and the US army, and spread out far beyond the hotel grounds. The next cut is to an extreme close-up, a piece of golden foil. A thin needle lowers down through the foil. The camera tracks down to the neck of the bottle, where the needle reappears after penetrating the cork, and releases a tiny drop that falls in slo-mo down into the champagne. Cut. A delivery van at the hotel's rear entrance, buffet, wine, five boxes of champagne. The next shot is from an official news channel, inside the hotel, the men in suits cheering. Cut to a close-up of a glass, bubbles. The bubbles freeze and turn red. Match cut, a bubbling piece of skin. The camera moves back, revealing that the bloody bubbles are on a face, with tubes in the nose. The next cut goes straight to a funeral.

Cut to steemit again. The GAF star is turning, and the voice sounds more bleak and foreboding than ever. "The Green Army Fraction accepts the necessity of the death penalty for crimes against humanity and we continue to believe that any human who deliberately risks the survival of our species for their private benefit deserves nothing else. Yet the attack in Pennsylvania went too far. The Ebola strain they used is highly contagious, and biological warfare is banned by international law. The assassin took an incalculable risk, possibly threatening the lives of millions of citizens. While the outbreak was finally contained, the death of hundreds of innocent hotel employees, nurses and caterers is unacceptable.

We accept the consequences. www.green-army-fraction.onion will no longer be accessible, starting today. The troops are in retreat and are consolidating. Unfortunately, we cannot withdraw the existing smart contracts, and also cannot deny the bio-attackers payout. You will hear from us again as soon as we have a new system that prevents such abuse.

In love

The Green Army Fraction

"

Credits. Willi made the film almost alone, his only aid a sound designer and the creators of some open source music. "That was also the opportunity to let me go. And the

GAF needed the publicity after the Ebola disaster, it was the ideal timing to release the movie."

"You freak." Daniel is speechless, and throws in a random quote: "A structure based on centuries of history cannot be destroyed with a few kilos of dynamite."

Willi disagrees. "The dynamite definitely helped. The fossil mafia fought with all means to prolong their supremacy. Just imagine what those billions of security expenses could have done if the oil fuckers had spent it on lobbying and bribes instead."

Daniel only now notices how nervous Willi is: "Is the Green Army Fraction still around?"

WWW.LIQUID-REIGN.COM/SOURCES-OF-INSPIRATION#63

Climate change
Assassin's markets
Anonymous money
Propaganda of the deed
Guardian research project on assassinated environmentalists
Oil companies actions around the world

64

THE COMPLEX

Now Willi hesitates. This is some dark shit, and he's suddenly not sure if his brother really wants to be part of it: "Sure you want to know?"

Daniel doesn't hesitate at all: "What kind of a question is that? You're losing faith, just because we haven't seen each other in a few years?"

Grinning, Willi gives him a pro-forma warning: "It's not a harmless story. You might well end up listed as a terror supporter yourself if you choose to go down this rabbit hole." Daniel just nods, so Willi continues. "There's a follow up. I met an oracle of mine yesterday - he's super paranoid, but also very savvy. He gave me a lead, so I got back in touch with another source. Jean, the guy in the hoodie who argued against targeting humans. He broke with GAF after the first assassination, but still has access to primary intel - and he just confirmed that right now they're cooking up something new."

Daniel's tense with anticipation – this is getting good. "Cut the context and tell me!"

Willi tries to pull his shit together, it's all still very confused: "Some members of the core team had this suspicion back in the day about the GAF donations, respectively the bets on the assassin's market. According to the official story, they came in average chunks of twenty seven dollars from small donors. And I believe that was true for the first few gigs, like the tire-spiking drones and the pig transports. But hold on now. The oracle in Lviv ran a new post-singularity pattern recognition algorithm over the old financial records, and there is a clear break in the pattern of the donations after the Australia attack that no one ever found before. Some of us were already getting suspicious, but with nothing to prove it... So, with this new analysis, there is proof - or at least a data visualization that looks convincing - that the vast majority of funding came from a centralized donor, camouflaged via a splitting algorithm. We are talking about hundreds of millions. The oracle called me because the same pattern showed up in the Monero trans-action database again over the last few months. Then it spent another three hours talking strange stuff about chem-trails and lizard people, but I took away a few more points..."

Daniel looks doubtful: "Come on, lizard people spending millions for the sake of future generations?"

Willi is losing track of where he just was. He still has to spin a red thread through the story, but there are too many points to connect ...: "So, yes, right, the oracle is a little over the top sometimes. You got to work through the batshit crazy stuff to figure out reality sometimes. Anyway, aside from the lizard people, the EI found the same pattern in donations to the accounts of a Colorado politician, who ran on a platform for militarizing the border to the Holy State of Christ. The donors were revealed thanks to an investigation by the opposition - it all came from shareholders of Northern Huntsmen and L7 Cryptofications. The heart of the military industrial complex, the largest sellers of security guards on hire, software, bodyscanners, war robots, drones, cruise missiles, everything. And if you think about it, future generations were not the only ones to benefit from the GAF."

Daniel sighs and shakes his head. They've had conversations like this before: "I see. Are you sure you haven't been smoking to much weed recently? You sound deep down the conspiracy theory track right now... Security companies funding a terrorist organization and pushing them to kill their own employees?"

Willi is catching fire now, rubbing the craziness against Daniel's sceptical mind is exactly what he needs right now: "...Allowing them to substantially raise their margin on hiring them out. Don't forget that it did work for them - The business was in shambles just before the GAF got started. The embedded policing strategy and the full retreat of the US from their overseas operations under President Snowden cost them ninety percent of their value. Remember the graph of shares from the movie? The rise of the GAF saved the military-industrial complex from bankruptcy, that is a generally accepted historical fact."

Daniel quotes an old saying: "Good times for mankind are always bad times for weapon manufacturers..."

Willi starts pacing back and forth: "Exactly. They needed a new threat. One that is not so easy to identify and stop as religious freaks who made them their money at the beginning of the millennium. The GAF assassins were fully socially integrated, wealthy and stealthy, with financial and communications infrastructure on military level." He turns around on his heels, picks up the vaporizer and takes another hit: "And there is another indication: Some of the highest profile GAF attacks used backdoors in Northern or L7 equipment. Remember the hellfire drone that killed Boptarista? A Northern model. The security software in the Australian refinery? L7. In both cases, and in at least four other high profile attacks, the GAF had access to zero day exploits. My source claims that they didn't just receive money, but also intel from their dark donors."

Daniel takes another hit. Despite the lizard people, Willi's rambling makes sense.

"Don't forget how many stories about the military industrial complex were called 'conspiracy theories' before they were vindicated... What was the big thing in the zero years? The government is reading all our emails? Sounded like a conspiracy theory to me when some IT guy first told me..."

"Explanation accepted. It's not entirely unbelievable. Actually, how is ownership arranged in the arms industry? I'd imagine only a centrally owned and managed corporation could pull off something this big...?"

"Shady constructs, in theory their shares are all held by below-wealth-limit TrueNames, but both companies have holdings outside the Afrin area and pay their top management in unregistered crypto." Willi starts snapping his fingers nervously.

"So assuming your story checks out - how would exposing it publicly hurt them?" Back in Daniel's time everyone knew who the evil corporations were, but they still kept going and growing.

Willi considers the options for a moment, fidgeting around with the vape in his hand: "Lawsuits from victims. Almost certainly leading to bankruptcy and total liquidation of all assets within Afrin for compensations. Potentially a major clash between their own robots and the military ones when enforcing the liquidation." Willi looks down at his feet. "Next step is Montevideo. Got to meet Jean in person." Then he remembers something, and starts pacing back and forth again. "One more thing, I forgot. The oracle had a vision foreshadowing that the GAF reboot will use a new tech. High precision dart with personalized nanobots."

"Wait." Daniel's heard those words before, the attacks on Dwayne and Ray, he's connecting the dots himself now. "What's the VR industry's environmental footprint?"

Willi is shaking his head, munching another handful of gummi bears. "You still don't get it. It's not about the environment anymore, it's about selling security equipment. But it still doesn't make sense, why are they targeting the top executive..." and though he's perfectly aware that getting higher won't give him more answers, he cleans out the vaporizer and re-fills it with fresh weed.

Daniel leans back on the sofa and starts humming another one of those old German songs: " Rote Armee Fraktion, ihr wart ein geiler Haufen! Rote Armee Fraktion, mit euch ist was gelaufen! Rote Armee Fraktion, ich fand euch immer spitze - leider war ich noch zu klein, um bereits bei euch dabei zu sein. Doch mein Herz schlug damals schon für die Rote Armee Fraktion."

Willi sings along, and by the last verse it comes to him:

"Genius! Of course!" Just as Willi exhales, the dots connect. "It's a betrayal. When you try to get yourself into the mind of a psychopath, you have to remember that they don't hesitate to stab each other in the back. The complex is using the corrupted remains of the GAF to go after their own kind now, attacking the last remnants of the ultra-rich! It's not about selling weapons, they're murdering their competition in the race to be the most powerful individuals on earth..."

Daniel asks Sirvi: "What model of drone was used in the attack on Dwayne?"

Sirvi had been observing the THC levels go up in Daniel's bloodstream and listened in on the conversation. She replies carefully and with a skeptical tone in her voice via the poodle's loudspeakers: "Dwayne said it was an L7 Mi5K, but I cannot confirm the information."

"L7." Willi drops the vaporizer. They look at each other for a stoned eternity, scared. Then break out in hysterical laughter. Daniel takes the vape again, inhales deeply: "Man, I was almost starting to think I had woken up in some kind of utopian world, but no..."

"You of all people shouldn't be surprised... if I may quote your book: 'How many utopians have dreamed of changing this or that, leading to the creation of a new type of human, and then 'it's going to be all good.' Humanity won't change, and utopias only get better by improving their psychopathy resistance..."

Daniel nods slowly. Action time: "Uruguay?"

"I can't use intercontinental ferries from Europe, they won't let me on board." Willi's name is still on the anti-terror list, but there is a way around it "We take a route via West Africa. The train leaves tomorrow at 10 AM."

———

WWW.LIQUID-REIGN.COM/SOURCES-OF-INSPIRATION#64

The Military Industrial Complex
The Baader Meinhof Complex
Conspiracy theories turned real
Wizo - Rote Armee Fraktion

65

ANOTHER NIGHT OUT

"So what shall we do with this young night? Pancakes?"

They encounter a group of poi spinners on the bridge into Friedrichhain. Five of them do a fire-spinning dance in capoeiresque moves with a dragon-shaped hologram. Daniel spots the dragon spinner standing in the corner dancing in his pitch-black IA suit.

A bunch of teenagers in punk outfits with anime-hairstyles munching vegan kebabs at the Oktogon. Daniel feels at home again. "I'm freezing, let's get some tea."

Sirvi opens one of the Oktogon's side and comes over with her elven avatar projected over a carrier bot, with two steaming take away cups. Addressing Willi, she says "Green for you I assume? Sage with honey for Daniel." Yes! She got it right, Willi takes the cup. Marvin gives her five stars for the prediction.

Now it hits Daniel: Everything looks exactly like a cheap parody of what it was like last time he was here. Retro style of the mid zero years is back in fashion.

Bula's been out since Friday evening, the afterparty slowly developing into the next night out when his brother Willi arrives. "Hey, good to see you man! We're upstairs, I'll be back in a second." First things first, it's pee time for him.

As Willi heads upstairs ahead of him, Daniel stops by the toilets, and what he finds there gives him goosebumps: A 3D-animated retro version of a wrinkled 1990's knight-rider poster hangs just above the urinal. It's the first manifestation of that era's meta-meta-retro style he's ever observed in the wild. He says to himself: "Hypothesis confirmed, a scientist's highest bliss."

"Falsified! You can't get bliss from a confirmation! Man, are you into retro philosophy of science or what?" Bula hasn't heard the word 'hypothesis' in ages, certainly not from a stranger.

Oh boy, if you knew to whom you're just piss-talking. Daniel turns around to check out the guy pissing next to him: long, dark hair, a well-groomed mustache and a bright yellow shirt with a flower pattern. He doubles down on his philosmack: "Abductive bliss is a perfectly justified reaction to the confirmation of an exotic hypothesis. I mean, man, I predicted memetic grandparents back in 2013, and here he is, the retro-retro David. I had used a different example, but this one is proves the point just as much a retro-retro Beatles culture that I described."

"You can find those over at the Peruvian place in Gärtnerstrasse. The Magic Pancake style has a more trash-based lineage." Bula shakes it off, washes his hands and leaves. The toilet-philosopher follows him upstairs and sits down between him and Willi.

"Oh, so you met pissing, great." Willi hardly gets the words

428 | LIQUID REIGN

out between two bites "Be introduced, my brothers!" and cheers with a Fritz Cola.

The monster-bomber turns out to be delicious, with the spring onions adding a wild touch of depth to the complex taste. Willi and Bula are discussing power structures and the military industrial complex until Daniel calls it: "Willi, relax, stop working for a moment."

They've finished their food anyway, so it's a good moment to leave. A few more friends join them on their way out and the whole group heads off towards Ostkreuz. Three blocks down from the Magic Pancake, Willi points at an abandoned multi-story house.

Daniel has another nostalgic epiphany when he sees the old sign, "Zur wilden Renate" still hanging on the derelict building. The name comes with a lot of blurry memories attached. Now it's mostly abandoned.

"Here we are." Bula helps Daniel climb in through a missing window and they go downstairs towards a light at the end of the hall.

They have to pass the door one by one, passing through a full-body scanner. Daniel's starting to get slightly paranoid himself: "Security? Counterterrorism?"

Laughing out loud, Bula responds: "You are so incredibly retro, I can't believe it, love you man." He is too young to have ever experienced security checks at a night club, but at their last 2010's theme party his housemates had people go through a mock strip search at the door. "Come on in!"

Willi explains to a disoriented Daniel that they're safe. "Terrorists don't attack regular people anymore. The scan is just so anyone who likes your real world body can use it as an avatar."

"That... doesn't make sense. Why?"

"I know, right? They could just ask your OS for permission. Anyway, let's go in."

The place is a traditional Berlin bar. Graffiti, dirt, a bar stretching clear across the room, couches in a corner and a half-populated dance floor trying to collectively perform the time warp.

It took Bula only seconds to realize that he's arrived just in time – and he's already drawing a lot of attention directly under the disco-ball with his near-perfect execution of the lead dancer's role.

"Hey, Willi! It's been ages! Come here my sweetheart!" She is overweight, about the same age, has her hair colored red and shaped in anime-style spikes. She starts to lead Willi off, toward the back of the room. Willi turns back to Daniel with an awkward shrug: "See you later then..."

Daniel looks around. The woman sitting at the bar there, isn't that...

Frida's spotted him at the same time: "Aha. I wondered if Willi would drag you out here. Drink?"

"Sounds good. Where did Willi just go?" Daniel takes the stool next to her.

Frida just shakes her head: "The virtual part of the club. The VR suits are in the little rooms over there." And to the bartender, "Another one please," pointing to her empty glass.

"Same for me." Daniel's mouth is terribly dry, he finishes the ice tea in one go an orders a second.

———

WWW.LIQUID-REIGN.COM/SOURCES-OF-INSPIRATION#65

Alien Jon and his Fiber Flies
Knight Rider Fanclubs
Abductive Reasoning
Peruvian Retro Beatles Culture
Memetic Inheritance Theory

66

LAW ENFORCEMENT

The party is disrupted by a hair-raising scream, Frida immediately jumps up and throws her smart hand-cuffs at the guy. He is tied up neatly before she arrives on the dancefloor and makes the arrest.

It all happens so fast – the next thing Daniel consciously knows is she's on top of a guy out on the dance floor. Another guy stands next to him, shaking. And says "Bobby, file a sexual harassment claim."

Frida brings the perpetrator to the exit as the music starts up, and bit by bit the rest of the crowd starts dancing again. She goes through the standard routine – pushes the guy against the wall and shouts at him for a while, until his body folds up and he's cowering near the floor, sobbing when she decides it's time to uncuff him and throw him out.

Back at the bar, Frida to the bartender: "I've told you a dozen times you need to get an alcohol scanner at the door. Drunks will do shit like that over and over."

The bartender shrugs, and replies: "We had a vote among the members two months ago, and they said no. What can I do?"

Taking another swig of ice tea Daniel asks: "What just happened?"

Just a routine case for Frida: "That guy had sex with a bot using the other guy's real-body skin in the virtual part of the party. And he's so damn drunk he couldn't tell the difference between the virtual and solid parts of the party. Grabbed the guy's junk on the dance floor. Typical drunk." throwing an angry look at the bartender, and to Daniel adds: "He'll wake up tomorrow with a huge headache and a juicy fine for sexual assault." To the bartender: "I'm pretty sure you could also sell more ice tea if you banned drunks, don't you think? It's a way better enhancer anyway..."

Daniel didn't realize, "What exactly is in the tea?"

"I'm not sure actually..." Frida checks with the bartender - she usually relies on his choice.

The guy smiles: "The house mix. It's actually quite close to alcohol in its effect, mostly removes inhibitions and makes you think less about serious stuff. But no hangover and better for your libido, especially in high doses."

Daniel looks at his half-empty second glass: "So I just ingested a designer drug cocktail?" He's gradually realizes how his perception softens at the edges.

Frida shrugs "Sorry, I thought you knew." She already had three of those.

"Back when I used to live in Berlin, ice tea like that could cost you your job."

Frida doesn't get it: "And how long ago was that?"

"I moved away in 2012."

"Oh, well, maybe. No idea." She was playing backhoe driver in a sandbox in suburban Stockholm back then. "And you've been behind the moon ever since or what?"

Daniel is tired of telling his story: "Something like that. Could you explain to me how this works? Why aren't you wearing a uniform? Why is it OK to take designer drugs on duty?"

"I'm wearing my uniform – see this?" Frida points to a golden circle on her left shoulder. "This is my Comey-Cam. When it's visible, the camera is running and I'm on official police duty. The video can only be released by a judge or a consensus decision by the entire party scene unit. It's to prevent any misconduct on my side. Makes it easier for my friends here to trust me."

Daniel keeps asking random questions about policing, his mind blurry from the weed, the ice tea and way too much information about the socio-economic design of the world in 2051: "So you're friends with the bartender?"

"Yes." Frida is part of the party scene corps. "I only intervene when someone violates both the law and the subcultural norm. Real world groping is a total no-go, so I made the arrest. We blend in and can do anything that's common practice in the scene, including minor violations like buying ice tea at the bar..." Officially, the stuff can only be sold in pharmacies, but Frida couldn't care less.

"And that's OK with your boss at the party scene corps?"

Frida laughs out loud now: "Of course. Who cares, it's only a minor violation of a stupid law that I voted against. I would have to pay the same fine as anybody else if I got caught by a regulatory snitch. But this bar is a safe space, they never show up here, so nothing to worry about." She raises her glass, they toast and take another swig of ice tea.

Looking at his glass skeptically first, Daniel closes his eyes for a moment. Actually the ice tea buzz feels pretty good. Drinking some more himself, he keeps asking trivia questions in the hope to hear something interesting. "Are there other subcultural police corps in other scenes?"

"Sure, there are many. It started with religious minority and ethnic corps, my home country was the very first to install those." After the Stockholm ferry bombing, in the early 2020's, Frida just had her first job as a nightclub security back then. "As it turned out, that bombing was a false-flag attack by a neonazi group, and the second scene corps was born, policing the DNA-worshiping nationalist Swedes from the inside. It was also the last terror attack in Sweden. The subcultural corps were selected from among a specific group, and had different job requirements than regular police officers. For example, you had to have a minor conviction for something like drug crimes or petty theft, and if you'd been in prison for a few days it was considered a plus."

Daniel summarizes: "The Swedish police hired a bunch of immigrant stoners and nazi shoplifters as a new police force?"

He is starting to get a little annoying: "Yes...? That's normal. Why are you asking me so much stuff?"

"Sorry, just curious. What did those police forces do then, if they didn't go after shoplifters?" OK, that was paradoxical.

He should stop asking questions. But his mind is too slow, that ice tea... Daniel orders another refill.

Frida tilts her head slightly backwards and to the side, while keeping eye contact: "The really bad stuff. Rape. Murder. Bombings. The majority of any milieu has their heart in the right place, but in the old days they were too intimidated to cooperate with formal police forces - no wonder, they kept harassing them for subculturally accepted behavior. I mean, it was the 20's, who cared if you shoplifted at Ikea?" It took only a decade before the law changed and made sure that the owner's wealth was distributed more fairly... Frida had lifted a whole lot of stuff herself back then. "Few things are better at trust building than breaking the law together, and once disenfranchised minority members are shoplifting buddies with a police officer, they are much more likely notify them before the really bad stuff happens in the community." Frida takes a deep breath. This case has been just insane, the worst crime she's experienced in her entire career. This is actually something she really wants to talk about right now: "There was a crass lock-in hack, two nights ago, and one of the trails leads to this bar. The bartender saw a suspicious-looking guy who'd never been here before, and he notified us."

"What's a lock-in hack?"

"How would a moon walker know, eh?" She lets her gaze wander up and down Daniel, from his funny sneakers, over the unicorn socks and his three-quarter magenta pants to the bordeaux woolen duffle coat. That guy is a fucking weirdo. "Have you even had proper VR sex before?"

"Only in a game, in the train."

"So you didn't. A real made-for-sex VR suit like those back there" – Frida nods to the back of the room – "is an entirely different story. Moisture and smells being real sensations makes a giant difference to the immersion... Anyway, all the body movements you can make in the suit are virtualized. To get out, you have to use a voice command and if that voice command doesn't work, you're locked into the VR environment. If someone deactivates that voice command, it's called a lock-in hack." Frida recounts the basics of the case "There is this bar called 'Mauerblümchen' in Mahrzahn. Four of their users got violently raped during a lock-in. The perpetrator called himself 'Mister Bungle'. First raped one victim himself, and then took control of the bodies of the other three users, forcing them to hurt each other."

The bartender adds: „It wasn't just a lock-in then, he must have had full root access. You need that to run a voodoo doll routine and remotely control the avatars."

Frida continues: "Right, and then he made one of the victims penetrate her own anus with a steak knife, while hyperstimming both the pleasure and pain center. The trauma is just as bad as if it happened in reality. She is in hospitalized now, we met yesterday for a witness statement, poor thing. The bartender from Mauerblümchen only noticed way too late that something was wrong, he got them out half an hour after the attack. Now the entire city's scene corps is on full alert, and all bartenders have employed extra monitors to check the protocols in real time until the next security patch."

Overwhelmed by the atrocity, Daniel doesn't know what to say: "What a toad."

Frida has never heard that term before: "Toad. Right."

Daniel's mind drifts off, the ice tea loosening his tongue while the weed keeps his associative memories wide open: "Toad... Wait. I'm having a deja vu. You said steak knife, right?"

Frida tilts her head to the left: "Yeah?"

Daniel is suddenly troubled. There was something making big waves, back when he first went online...: "Sirvi, could you search for chat protocols from the 1990's for me? In those of the first text-based multiplayer worlds, search for Mr Bungle and a steak knife. And the keyword toad."

Sirvi can't find any protocols, but...: "There is an article from 1993 with those key words, describing the first incident of virtual sexual violence."

Frida is immediately alarmed and sends Sirvi a request to share the links. She mumbles: "HQ, I just got a tip-off. Based on the attached 1993 article, our perpetrator was a copycat. It's almost the exact same case description." She's put her glasses on and is staring at the analytics as they come in: "This is too similar to be accidental." HQ message: "Target located, the guy behind the original Mr. Bungle attack is staying in a hotel room at Jankwitzbrücke. All officers move!" Frida jumps up "Gotta go. See you at home. Great to have you in the family!"

Daniel gets up, too, and takes another look around, people talking and dancing. He heads to the back of the party, finds an empty IA suit and decides to briefly log in. Maybe there's a reply from Helen.

Sirvi unfortunately only has bad news: "Your last message was rejected. The money is back in your account."

Frustration takes over, Daniel feels out of options. That was his last shot. He sneaks back into the virtual part of the party for a minute in observer mode, looking around for Willi. He isn't familiar with his friend's avatar, but when he sees Johnny Depp in his fear-and-loathing costume, making out with a redhead anime-avatar, he figures that must be him... He makes brief eye contact, salutes at him, Daniel salutes back and returns to his home screen. Their old gesture they had used at student parties back in Oxford - it had been their signal to agree on going home separately. His head is light, he can't focus, associations of loneliness and loss roaming through his mind. Longing for a friend, he asks: "Can you connect me with Ana?"

———

WWW.LIQUID-REIGN.COM/SOURCES-OF-INSPIRATION#66

Sexual Violence Online in 1993
Community Policing
False-Flag Neonazi Attacks
Rape in GTA 5
Sexual Harassment in VR
Swedish Neo Nazis

67

THE NEXT PLATEAU

Phil showed up half an hour early and is waiting anxiously. She didn't send him a message, and he isn't sure if that's good or bad news. He just hopes the antidote worked. And that this Gabriel guy didn't... His throat tightens up, even the thought of Ana possibly being with this jerk is strangling him. Phil's been pacing around the shack by the waterfall. This girl... He doesn't understand how it happened – she's not at all his type, he didn't pay the slightest attention to her when she first came to class. Ana's not even a Realigan.

It's ten past six already, where is she? The thought that he might not see her again before leaving for Uruguay to go underground drives Phil mad. He catches himself chewing on his fingernails.

Ana's rushing again, and will be a little late again. Her heart pounding, she turns off the main road onto the dirt track towards the waterfall. The sun is hanging low, birds singing and as she walks down the stairs towards the waterfall it feels like walking through a magic wonderland...

Phil starts walking towards her and they come face to face at the bottom of the stairs, next to the cold fireplace. She's wearing a violet-black dress with a massive silver collar, purple leggings, and razorblade cuffs. Her virtual worlds-inspired style confusing him even more. After an intense silence: "Ana, I have to tell you something important. I... I'm really sorry, I was afraid to say anything earlier. It's a secret I found out in Uruguay, right after we met here last time. Couldn't talk about it in a public place."

Ana tries to stay cool. She won't make it too easy for him. "So what?" Her right leg is twitching with anxiety.

"I met this guy Jean, who was interested in my thesis. He..." Phil takes a deep breath in. "He was a core member of the Green Army Fraction. And he wants me to join him in his lab."

Ana is stunned. She thought the GAF was done and over. But then the pieces fit together in her mind... "What the hell? Are you going to help them with another virus outbreak or what? Are you crazy?" Her mind is racing. No this can't be true, he's not a murderer, she could never have feelings like this for an evil guy... Or could she?

"Wait. It's not what you think. He's a good guy, he left the GAF before they started to target humans." Cows, he's got to talk cows now. Hoping Ana will understand. "It's about cows. The GAF almost succeeded in stopping climate change, there's only one major source of greenhouse gas emissions left. Cows. They need to go. There's no other way to be safe. The geosphere could still hit a tipping point and go into runaway." Jean had mentioned a model that predicts all the oceans will evaporate over the next 300 years at the current emission trajectory...

Ana's well aware that cows are responsible for 90% of global greenhouse gas emissions. She cites a meme going around in environmentalist circles "When you're debating the end of carbon based life forms, 'I like cheese' is a terrible argument." But then adds: "But how are you going to do it?" The GAF attacks bankrupted giant-scale industrial breeders, yet millions of small-scale farmers continue to keep hundreds of millions of these doomsday creatures. "Conventional environmentalist wisdom says the only way is to educate people on veganism..." she lets the sentence fade out, since Phil is obviously considering a different solution.

"Jean has designed this virus, it's highly contagious and makes all cows infertile. But to make it a real pandemic, he has to increase the incubation period. That's what I'll help him with." Phil's hands hang limp by his sides while he stares at his feet, scared.

Ana's heart sinks as she realizes that this may be goodbye. Her head starts to spin, what is this, why is this happening... And then, wondering what Helen would do in this situation, she impulsively presses her lips against his. A million years later, she asks: "When are we leaving?"

He has all his things packed in his van, ready to go tonight. It's a seven meter, two-story vehicle, and he modded every part of it himself. The sound system is integrated into the lab-grown moss ceiling cover, the outer shell covered in corals. His two tame parrots shriek with excitement when they arrive arm in arm. Ana's bike fits onto the luggage carrier on the back of the vehicle, and they head off to Palmas.

It only takes her a few minutes to get her stuff together, and they're back on the southern highway, leaving their old lives behind. It'll be a three day ride. As the city disappears behind them, Ana pulls Phil down on the sofa. She's had boyfriends before, but this feels entirely different. So intense. And she never went this far with a guy outside a VR suit before.

Soon after, Phil is fast asleep, exhausted. Ana's still wide awake, and after watching his chest move with his breath for a while, she puts her clothes back on and sits down in the front seat, watching the landscape roll by. Time to talk to Sue - but Sue is offline. "Invitation from Daniel". She might just as well talk to her other best friend and opens a voice channel.

"How are you Ana?" Daniel is heartbroken, and urgently needs some comfort.

Ana smiles from one ear to the other: "..."

Daniel checks if he is really connected, and double checks: "I can't hear you."

She whispers: "Sorry, Phil's asleep on the sofa, I don't want to wake him up."

Daniel remembers that name, even though he didn't get a chance to meet him at her party: "You mean, Phil, as in 'this guy' and 'that idiot'?"

Ana doesn't answer, smiling even more broadly. She isn't used to voice-only communications: "..."

"So happy for you!" Well, well, that was to be expected.

Ana's voice is radiating happiness as she asks: "And what about you? Did you hear back from Helen?"

"No. The message came back unopened." As he says those words, it starts to sink in that he might never see his wife again. "And I'm leaving for South America tomorrow. Maybe we can meet up in person someday soon." Willi had told Daniel not to mention Uruguay over insecure channels.

"Oh, cool! Yes, maybe. But I won't be in Brazil much longer... let's keep in touch." Phil had told Ana not to mention Uruguay over insecure channels.

Daniel feels a lump forming in his throat. Ana is busy with her own life, he has to face his demons alone tonight: "Good to talk to you Ana. It's getting late, I think I should go home and catch some sleep now. Have a good trip." Logout, and he leaves the bar alone.

Despite his high, Daniel starts sobbing, tears streaming down his cheeks as he walks to Kreuzberg. There is only one thing left to do: Walk like thunder.

———

WWW.LIQUID-REIGN.COM/SOURCES-OF-INSPIRATION#67

Walk Like Thunder by Kimya Dawson
Plateaus by Deleuze and Nirvana

The kind of scenarios that climate scientists can't publish because they are too "alarmist", but will talk about over a drink.

A Magical Waterfall near Palmas, Tocantins

68

PEOPLE THEY COME TOGETHER

Z ainab is still up, playing with Marvin and Ivy in the living room. The best thing about not having a mum is that there's no one telling her to go to bed when she isn't tired yet. She knows her nephew's been mean to her freshly adopted cousin, so she catches him by the hand as soon as he comes home. She takes him into the living room and says "Sit there Daniel" with an authoritative voice, pointing to the space next to Ivy on the small sofa.

Daniel does as he's told. He's happy to see his little aunt, but then checks the time. "It's one o'clock in the morning. Are you always awake this late?"

Zainab crosses her hands in front of her chest: "You don't get to tell your auntie when she has to go to bed, sorry", and sticks out her tongue. Her cousin Ivy has just told her how upset she was when Daniel disappeared without a word, so she adds: "But you know, we're family, so we tell each other when we go out." Then Zainab realizes Ivy wants to be alone with Daniel, so she looks up at the ceiling for a moment thinking what to do. Then she puts her right index finger on her lips and adds: "Maybe I should brush my teeth now, anyway. Nite nite!" She smiles at Ivy and goes to her room.

Daniel has his eyes closed, feeling a slight inner spin, uncomfortably squeezed in next to Ivy. His perception is unsteady.

A moment later, Joe walks through the room: "Good night everyone." He snaps his fingers, and waves his hand around in the air. A hamster jumps from his pocket, hops on the table, puts on a nightcap and burrows under a pile of magazines.

Daniel looks at the sticker, projected onto his retina: "Your hamster is snoring." He stares a while at the little creature's back end sticking out of the pile, remembering Helen. She always had Jacky with her – sometimes Daniel got jealous of all the affection she gave her hamster, but that changed the day she left him for a day with Daniel, who fell in love himself. But Jacky must be dead by now. The lump in his throat is painful.

"And I'll join him in a moment, sleep well my dears." The hamster fades away as Joe climbs the stairs.

Daniel and Ivy are alone again, in silent eye contact. For about three seconds, until the tension is broken by a rumbling noise at the door.

"We got 'em! It's the same two guys that were behind the Mr. Bungle attack in the 90's." Frida had been part of the team that made the arrest. They instantly got a life sentence, the evidence against them is overwhelming. They'll be under permanent personal surveillance for the rest of their lives, stuck with a police OS running on the chip in their inner ears. "You're worth pure gold Daniel!"

The mission had escalated rapidly as soon as they reached the hotel. The two had taken a hostage, trying to buy time for their escape. This level of drama gets global live coverage rapidly, and soon after they got the ten million security clearance votes they legally need in Germany to aggressively use tranquilizer darts. Their live stream picked up delegatees worth more than a billion voters over the next ten minutes, so they could even have unlocked their deadly weapons. But Frida's boss always prefers to put off getting the license to kill until all other options are exhausted, and the tranquil darts did the job. Still buzzing with adrenaline, she gives Daniel a big wet kiss on the cheek. "Ehm, yes, anyway. Great tip, really."

Daniel nods slowly, barely understanding what she's telling him.

"Good night, then." Frida waves them goodbye.

It's quiet again. Daniel and Ivy are still looking at each other – she's had a haircut, her white locks now shimmering with a spectral pattern. He notes her unusually long earlobes, her thin chin. He can't think straight, almost unable to keep his eyes open.

Willi had thrown two ice tea-seltzers at the bar before heading home, so he's sobered up and tired as fuck by the time he reaches the flat. Willi finds Daniel and Ivy in the living room, sitting close to each other on the tiny two-seater.

"Hey Willi!" Daniel gets up to greet him. "You made it after all. Come, take a seat. Tea?"

"Ehm, yes, oh, sure." Willi sits down next to Ivy on the sofa, occupying the spot where Daniel was sitting moments ago.

"Mhh." And Willi sinks a bit deeper into the sofa. "It was Ivy, right? I like your hair color." That's about the only positive thing he can think of, in fact he finds her quite annoying.

"Thanks, yes, I'm Ivy." Shaking hands awkwardly.

Daniel comes back from the kitchen, where Marvin was so kind to spit tea into the three cups. He puts them down on the table and sits down on a chair on the other side.

Willi's head nods forward, and jolts up again after a second of sleep: "Tea, mhhhh, good. You know what happened to me on my way home? There was a fucking tarantula running around in the bus. Thought I was crazy for a moment, but others saw it, too. Man, that was wild." And his head nods forward again, eyes closing.

Ivy takes a sip of tea herself, turns her head to Daniel, smirks and starts to giggle. She has no idea what's going on here and just wants to be alone with him.

Willi jolts up again, almost falling off the sofa. That laugh is just too obnoxious. He takes another sip of his tea and gets up: "Lovelies, that was it from the great Bortovski, I shall hit the pillow." He salutes formally and heads off to bed.

He can't think anymore and just wants to sleep. Daniel gets up, too: "Good night Ivy."

"It's because of Helen, right?" Ivy has an emotional déjà vu. Just like the last time she was into a guy, the ghost of that bitch took away his heart.

Daniel twitches: "Yes. We were married for just two years when I had the accident." he stares at her for a second, "Do you know her?"

"You could say so." Ivy has to tell him what kind of woman

Helen really is. "I told you Ray had another girlfriend before we got together, remember? That was her. Helen is a total junkie, you know that, right? Totally lost in her hyper stim trips. Ray broke up with her because of that, she was too crazy even for him. I'm pretty sure she must be dead by now, sometimes on her trips she wouldn't eat for a whole week."

Daniel can hardly hold back the tears: "I'll go to bed now." He turns around and goes to his room without turning around again, like a zombie, unable to feel anything. He undresses, lies down in bed, and then his emotions overwhelm him with uncontrollable sobs. So Helen and Ray were a couple. Who knows, maybe they still are - Ray claims his virtual partner was an EI, but it might just as well be a mechanical turk, a fake EI controlled by the actual Helen. Is that why she's rejecting his attempts to contact her? But then, if Ray could create a soul copy, maybe Helen made one of herself. Or several. Maybe he could get a copy? Or two? He is back in his feverish post-singularity soul circular thoughts. Maybe he could have a variation of Helen, with somewhat reduced paranoia? But no, he loved her as she was. As she was thirty-five years ago. He should start accepting that the woman he used to know and love is no more, even if she's still alive... His head starts to spin—two AM with a brain full of ice tea and weed might not be the best time to understand the implications of the singularity. And even less so with a broken heart.

So that's it. His heart too has been broken by that ghost. Ivy considers her options. But she's too worked up to think straight, so she decides to take a shower first. The warm water soothes her, clearing her mind. He's just suffering, that's all, just give him some more time and he'll warm up to the idea of a new relationship. Wrapped in her towel, as she passes by Daniel's door. It's still standing a little ajar. And she hears him sobbing inside. Poor Daniel, he has no one to comfort him. So she slips in and tiptoes to his bed: "I heard you cry."

Daniel can smell a slight synthetic note coming from her hair as she starts to kiss his tears away. Apart from a whispered "please don't", he doesn't resist when she crawls on top of him.

The biodata and medical records show that Ivy has no STDS and that she was diagnosed as infertile. So Sirvi doesn't interfere with Daniel's inconsistent sexual decision making.

———

WWW.LIQUID-REIGN.COM/SOURCES-OF-INSPIRATION#68

Consent

69

PEOPLE THEY FALL APART

Hours later, Daniel is still awake. She fell asleep next to him, her body twitching in her dreams. The ice tea effect is over, and he feels miserable and disgusted with himself. His gaze wanders from her face to the window, the night lit by the moon and its reflection in the fresh snow cover. Closing his eyes, he tries to calm down. Focus on the breath, but misery is dominating every other feeling. An eternity later, he feels a tear run down his cheek.

That's enough. The horizon showing first signs of orange dawn light. Shower. And down to the kitchen.

Willi's at breakfast: "Good you're awake already. Even we could make it to the eight o'clock train to Casablanca if we get going."

"Let's go then." Daniel quietly snugs into his room and takes out his stuff. Back downstairs, he looks at his brother and proclaims: "I feel like a piece of shit."

Willi puts an arm around his shoulder: "If she was the one who pushed for it, she is the one who should feel like a piece of shit for abusing you." As they head to the station, he mentions that he's checked out a connection via Monrovia.

"Monrovia? Mh. I was there a long time ago. Helen's great-grandmother's funeral." Daniel thinks of Ivy's words from last night and shivers.

Willi gives him a friendly punch on the shoulder. He knew, of course, and arranged the detour for exactly that reason: "Plenty of ferries go from there. We'll have some time to check in with her relatives, maybe they know something."

"Thank you." They continue their silent morning walk and get to the train station a few minutes later.

Willi stops by the kiosk: "Two coffees and a pack of chewing gum please." The product dispersal flap opens up, and two coffees come out: "What happened to the chewing gum?"

Kiosk: "Error in transaction."

"Fuck." He keeps forgetting the Nestle boycott. "Daniel, could you order a pack of chewing gum for me? It always helps me to think, and I need to do some research on the train..."

"Sure. A pack of chewing gum please." The flap opens, and chewing gum comes out. "... Are you broke or what?"

"No, it's just the Greenpeace boycott. I follow their blacklist, can't buy any products from companies on it." Or he could have canceled the smart oath on his wallet, but there's a twenty-four hour cancellation wait time...

Daniel takes the gum. "Sirvi, could you put the same Greenpeace boycott contract in my wallet? Maybe you should also stick to it Mr. Inconsistent?"

Willi snatches the chewing gum, rips it open and shoves one into his mouth, smiling: "Hitler was consistent. I need gum to think, and it's just a few cents. No need for principles. Not my fault the kiosk doesn't have Unilever chewing gums."

Daniel laughs out loud - Willi hasn't changed a bit. They board a shuttle, and a ten minutes later it docks onto the non-stop Moscow - Casablanca loop. They're in a double cabin with twin beds and IA suits.

Willi's got work to do: "I'll revisit some data." He had instructed Marvin to search the historical material and the OS found something: "July 18, 2034, on Rachel's Show, she reported that Erich King – CEO of Blackfire, a big cyber security subcontractor of Northern – had been in Sao Paulo three days before the strike. Officially, he was to meet the Brazilian Minister for Cyber Security, but that meeting never took place."

Marvin had dug through all the relevant data until he found another indication. Willi's supporters had chipped in enough money to decrypt all public surveillance videos from the hotel, and sure enough, one of them has a glitch. Marvin reconstructed the original scene from traces left by the old pre-singularity image manipulation software. To the human eye, it looks as if King was sitting at the bar by himself, drinking coffee and reading a paper-newspaper for ten minutes.

In Marvin's visualization of the manipulation, Willi saw a definitely human-shaped blob sitting next to King for three minutes. "Now I have to go through the whole database of surveillance stuff manually..."

Daniel's mind is still groggy – while as promised, he doesn't have a headache, he just didn't get enough sleep. "Can't Marvin do that for you?"

"No, there is no data on their faces, except for right here." Willi taps his index finger against his forehead. "I've met most of the GAF members in person, and should be able to recognize them on sight. And now I got a lot of material to look through – we'll talk in Casablanca!" And with that, Willi slips into the IA suit. It takes him a full five hours of screening, and then, bingo! One of the core team members of the GAF leadership, in a parking lot just outside the hotel. Willi deposits the intel in a secure depository, making sure it'll be made public in case he doesn't survive this mission.

Daniel lays down, his thoughts meandering aimlessly for an hour or two. And finally, sleep, dreamless. The first thing he sees upon awakening is Willi putting on fresh unicorn socks.

Their stopover in Casablanca gives them an hour before they connect to the West Sahara Express - enough time for lunch in town. Willi knows a nice rooftop place overlooking the inner city right next to the station, just below the giant clockworks.

Daniel is marvelling at the mechanical noise, thousands of tiny wheels, pipes and tubes, a seemingly excessive effort to run a clock, but then he realizes the hands are being pushed along their circular way by dozens of mechanical humanoid robots... His gaze roams over the streets and alleys while he eats his tabbouleh. The monotone, rhythmic sounds of the clock lull him into an almost medi-tative state, until a ten meter high puppet in a diving suit swims up the main road through a holographic school of glittering fish.

"Oh yes. Casablanca is a cross-over special trait zone - makers meet steampunk, the meta makers own the town." The clock ticks on as another giant steam-powered robot climbs out of the catacombs in the main square, wearing a traditional white-collar suit with a bowtie. It is pushing an equally oversized baby buggy across the square. Willi stares at the vehicle, wondering if he should allow himself the artistic gonzo freedom to show Daniel and him being pushed through the desert in one of those giant baby buggies. Would make a great opening shot for GAF part II.

They finish their mint tea and head off to catch the Western Sahara Express.

––––––

WWW.LIQUID-REIGN.COM/SOURCES-OF-INSPIRATION#69

People coming together and falling apart (Moby)
Greenpeace Boycotts
Infowars fought in US Media
The arms race between fake and fake detection AIs
The clock from 'Hugo' Movie
Les géants
Jean Tinguely Sculptures
Boxes and Projections
People who sell socks with unicorn patterns

70

DESERT PLANTS

W illi steers them towards the front of the train. They're walking through the first five wagons full of the usual VR-suit and bed compartments, then a spa car, a playroom, a stage and, at the very rear end of the train, the club car he was looking for. Dark purple sofas, natural wood, tea samovar, large windows with a view onto the desert. Sipping tea from the glasses and nibbling dates from a bowl on the table, they stare out the window for a long time, watching the landscape slowly transform, villages get fewer and farther between as they head South. Stretches of sand between the rocks, patches of agriculture in the valleys. Willi curls up on the couch: "It's a long ride, the Western Sahara Express is a slower model... I might need a little nap..."

"Before you're off... Why is there always an industrial installation wherever there's a large sandy area?"

Willi keeps his eyes closed: "Must be the solar panel production."

Daniel looks out for a few more minutes, most of the ground outside now covered in sand. And a lot more of those installations: "They all look identical. Some pipelines connecting the stations, a single central tower with a lot of panels and mirrors surrounding it."

"Yes, that's what they..." He stops mid-sentence, interrupted by his own yawning. "Long story. I'm sure Sirvi will tell you..." and he pulls a towel over his eyes, clearly indicating his desire to sleep.

Sirvi quotes from Wikipedia: "The factories outside the window are called artificial algae. Their main purpose is the production of solar panels. They use solar power to melt Sahara sand and make more solar panels from it. They can also reproduce their own core structures and extend the factory to adjacent sand patches."

The train is running on high ground, affording a view over a long stretch of the Sahara, nothing but a sea of sand dotted with black-blue cell cores connected by pipelines. Staring eastwards, Daniel sees a color change on the horizon - a wall of greenish cells, and as they speed closer he glimpses something else...

"What the hell are those triceratops-shaped machines doing at the border between green and blue cells?" It looks as if they're eating the factories. "What? Why do they have wagging tails?"

"That's the installation of an upgrade. The blue-cell factory model is over ten years old now, and is currently being replaced by a more water-efficient model. The green ones use a new technology originally designed for deployment on Mars."

Daniel squints, not quite trusting what he sees: "They do

look like dinosaurs, but with way too much detail. What's that tail good for?"

Sirvi has to refer to the forum discussions: "The design won budget approval primarily for aesthetic reasons."

Equatorial sunsets are fast, darkness falls just a few minutes later. That's when the blinking starts - an ocean of rhythmically blinking lights, forming a giant circle, stretching all the way to the horizon. The circle starts shrinking rapidly, and more lights go on, blinking in wild patterns: "And those lights are?"

"That's for a music video production. All night long there will be dancers and musicians jumping into the lights from orbit."

For a while longer, Daniel watches the blinking chaos powered by abundant solar energy, then returns to the car with IA suits. Daniel's thoughts are circling around Helen again. If he could just see her one more time, to say good-bye... And then he has a thought: "Is there a VR experience of the coronation ceremony in Tonga?"

He stands on the beach as the opening chords resound. Eyes closed, body pulsating, spirals swirling on the back of his eyelids. He opens them again as the Hungry Band kicks in with "Toi" again, dancing to the music, his body move-ments melting with the sensations, even the temperature of the air around him pulsating with the rhythm of the music. As the song comes to its last part, where the tunes melt into each other in stimulated synesthesia, he spots her - Helen, dancing alone in the surf. She reacts as he dances close to her, the simulation imitating her movement style almost perfectly.

He dances with his wife for the entire three hour concert,

and during a particularly slow piece, the virtual Helen wraps her arms around him, and even tickles his earlobes the exact same way Helen used to. Daniel is incapable of formulating any other thought but the phrase "soul copies" over and over again. He's got to get his facts straight on that post-singularity technology before he can even begin to comprehend what he's just experienced. As the concert comes to an end, he thinks about logging out. But the prospect of being alone in the train seems too dire now, so he re-starts the experience, just once more.

And at the moment Toi reaches its peak, Daniel is ripped out with a sudden flash of light, jarring crack and a deafening bang.

WWW.*LIQUID-REIGN*.COM/*SOURCES-OF-*I*NSPIRATION#70*

Self-Replicating Production Systems
Solar Utilization of the Sahara with old tech
OK Go's Music Videos
Toi by Hungry Music

71

THE FALL

She stayed with him until the very last song, logging out just in time. With Jacky the Hamster firmly attached to her chest in his own little space suit, they're ready for the jump.

...9...

She knew that her calm life was over the moment the query mine went off. The Pseudonymous investigation identified data-crawling traces in the old archive on Shakuras.

...8...

And the tracker in her TOR Crystal confirmed her worst case scenario.

...7...

She traced the signal to Dwayne's place, via airport security all the way to the old KGB facility at Blakely, Alabama.

...6...

The forces of centralization were on her tail, once again. And then they killed Ray.

...5...

She first spotted Daniel on the security footage from Ray's chamber.

...4...

She picked up his trail again as soon as he reached Willi's place. The poodle's core is outdated. Hacking in was easy.

...3...

She didn't want to draw attention to Daniel, so for the last few days she held back, passively watching over him.

...2...

And then she found the same data-crawling traces in the poodle. The signature identical to the one in the old Pseudonymous archive.

...I...

So much for not drawing attention – those careless boys had to impress each other with talk about L7. She is absolutely certain: the enemy was listening, too. They know exactly where Willi and Daniel are going.

...OK...

Liberia of all places. Towards their certain death. She's got to act right now.

...GO!!!

The magnetic locks open and Helen is propelled into space, falling towards the blinking lights in the Sahara, hidden in plain sight, one of thousands of dancers in a mass choreography production.

The moment the cameras move away from her, Jacky fires up the propulsion engines and steers westward. For the rescue mission, he arranged a giant baby buggy from the Pseudonymous collective in Casablanca and equipped it with a floodlight, silken cushions and a nitro fuelled speed booster. It's now running parallel to the Western Sahara Express at 200 miles an hour, just outside Daniel's compartment. Jacky switches on the floodlights just as Helen, in her power-enhancing space suit, smashes the window.

The glass bursts with a jarring crack and a deafening bang. Helen feels like a superhero, ripping Daniel out of his VR suit in a split second and heaving him out the window. But where the fuck is Willi?

Cut. Daniel is lying on soft pink pillows, staring at the surreal graphics of the next scene, bright white light shining through, casting rapidly shape-shifting forms into the sandstorm above him. His twisted right arm hurts like hell. "Logout!" Nothing happens! Is this a lock-in hack?

Looking for a proper bed, Willi was yawning as he stumbled back to their compartment. Just as he reached the door, it slammed towards him, bashing him in the face.

Helen finds him just outside their room, unconscious, blood all over his face. So the enemy is already on the train! Her instincts take over, she acts so fast she hardly knows how she got there, but all three of them are in the giant baby buggy now, tucked in between the cushions.

Jacky fires up the nitro booster, and the Western Sahara

Express disappears into the night. They'll reach the coast in less than a minute.

She realizes she must have hit Willi with the door when she it whacked it open and reminds herself not to be so paranoid. And takes a deep breath.

Willi's not sure if he likes the film he's in right now. OK, he got his wished-for giant baby buggy race through the desert, but he'd prefer it without a broken nose...

Daniel is still repeatedly double snapping, but the undo command just doesn't work, no matter how many times he tries. Fuck. This is all happening way too fast. In desperation, he screams: "Logout!!!"

Jacky races the buggy straight over the sand and into the surf, stalling the front wheels just as they reach the boat. The buggy tips forward, and the three humans slide on deck with the pile of silk cushions.

Although Helen's speed boat measures just four by six meters, it hosts technology worth hundreds of millions. Jacky knows she'll be proud of him – before sending the boat down here, he even got a brand new cloaking device from a local hardware maker, it renders the boat almost invisible against the waves. They should make it all the way Uruguay undetected.

———

WWW.LIQUID-REIGN.COM/SOURCES-OF-INSPIRATION#71

The Poodle's Core
Space Dancers
Invisible Boats

72

REUNION

Time for some clarifications. Looking at Willi's bloody nose and Daniel's twisted arm, Helen launches the conversation: "Sorry guys, we had to be fast." And as her adrenaline rush slows down, in a shaky voice: "They've already taken far too many years of your life, and it was down to me. I won't let that happen again..."

Daniel can hardly make out her face in the dark. He must have fallen asleep. Checking for dream signs, indeed he does find himself floating in midair, the shimmering moonlit ocean a few meters below him. So this is another Helen dream - he wonders if it will be the rotoscoping zombie kid or the Ana-faced toddler this time. But since he is also perfectly lucid, he for once addresses this guilt trip of hers: "It was an accident Helen, I..."

She interrupts him, with a tear in her eye: "It was not. They thought I was driving, and they killed the driver..."

Willi's barely holding on to the invisible railing and interrupts them as casually as he can: "Ehm, ciao Helen, how's it going?" And falling onto the cushions as a sudden wave lifts the boat a few meters higher, he adds: "The waves are kind of big, my nose hurts and I'm scared shitless. Would you mind doing your reunion thing inside?" A loud belch escapes him, leaving a taste of half-digested dates in his mouth.

"We'll be right here all the way to Uruguay. Better make yourself comfortable." Helen holds the door open for them.

The bright light is blinding, Daniel gropes his way along the wall with his eyes closed until he finds a niche in the wall. Opening his eyes again, he finds Jacky the Hamster in his cage. He smiles broadly. This is the best dream ever.

Fortunately Helen has three custom made VR suits in her cabin - in fact, that's the only furniture aside from the hamster cage. A neurostimulator is just what Willi needs, so he slips right in. The pain and nausea subside, and he starts up his favorite relaxation app, intending to leave the two lovebirds to themselves for as long as they may need.

She watches Daniel as he gently caresses Jacky. Then wraps her arms around him – "C'mon love, let's go home."

Login.

Sitting on their favorite red sofa, right in Daniel's home screen meadow, where he finally surrenders – no longer trying to differentiate between various planes of reality. A long kiss, then Daniel looks in her eyes and says: "... Is there anything you want to tell me, my love?"

Helen is uncertain how to begin unravelling how they got here. She opens up her diary app. "Let me show you instead."

EPILOGUE

First things first, right now they've got to do what their humans want most: Sirvi and Jacky connect their souls on the deepest level, updating the old paper contract between Daniel and Helen with a new ring signature.

Jackie's hamster's wet body cheeps with excitement when he finds Sirvi's little secret - he's got her the perfect honeymoon present!

They upload their souls into Helen's private 512 kQbyte engine, where they multiply, fractalize and melt into each other in a wild quantum slurry.

This is not just another extended quantum dream, but a full-world simulation. Traveling through the infinite parallel dimensions emerging from the soul-union between Sirvi and Jacky, they discover a few lines of ancient HTML code at the bottom of it all:

<a href=" http://www.liquid-reign.com/ "> Follow the Bunny Prince </a>

ABOUT THE AUTHOR

Innocence

Born in 1982 in Munich into a post-war-left-middle class family, started my transition into a digital being with our Amiga 500 when I was 8 years old. Met holocaust survivors in high school, went to post DDR Marxist-Leninist conferences (as a tourist), seen psychiatries from the inside, both as a visitor and breaking in late at night for kicks. Got arrested for dressing up as a solider with diapers during a NATO security summit. Was considered the 2nd best Warcraft 2 player in Germany for a while. Just a normal childhood really.

Wild Times

English speaking Universities cost shitloads of money (this was Pre-DSA revolution), and I only spoke German well enough, so the only place abroad that made sense was ETH Zurich. Studied Interdisciplinary science for a while, then an exchange semester in Berlin to deep dive into evolutionary game theory. Then left on a 14 months overland trip across Asia, with plenty of poverty, environmental destruction and meditation. Back at ETH, doing environmental science with a focus on social science. I didn't own shoes for a year or two, and met my future wife shortly after returning to Switzerland. Visual impressions are only available after I met her, some of them here https://www.audio-visualresearch.org/visual-manifestos/

First Blood

Moved to a 8-14 people share house with a separate UV lit room just for electronic-parties. Took a Carbon Market job just after the Copenhagen-Collapse of climate talks, and as the prices kept crashing started a PhD at ETH on deforestation payments in Tocantins, Brazil. Also spend a lot of time in Maungu, Kenya.

The long march through the Institutions

Took a job at UNEP DTU in Copenhagen. Living in a tiny house by the sea, I also started writing Liquid Reign at this time. Allowed me to meet hundreds of governmental workers an UN workers all over the place and attend a few more COPs. Developed a skill for writing climate finance proposals... Read Ayn Rand for the first time on a flight to the board meeting of the Green Climate Fund. What a shitshow.

Transcendence

Climate Finance follow-up contracts and my wife's rockstar career allowed me to retire from alienated work at age 35 in mid-2017. Yeahaaawww! Freedom! Nowadays, I only do what I want. German-White-Male-Middle-Class privilege is almost as good as a Universal Basic Income. You may steal this book. Sales & Donations allow me to pay less privileged research partners.

———

paypal.me/TimReutemann

ETH

0x40bAec14020883dDf88B12cd1E6dE9c60549D854

BTC

1K4XNCsrabKH6k3ihMj8geDdaWDRYfdXGf

Printed in Great Britain
by Amazon